BROKEN WORLD

Printed in the United States of America

First printing, 2024

ISBN 978-1-945747-07-6

Dapper Press

For Maple and Ivy.

I started this book when we were hoping for you, and I finished it when you were both real people--loving, beautiful, silly, and perfect. Without even trying, you remade this series into something personal, and heartbreaking, and new, for me.

I love you to the end of the world.

Ben's not even in this one.

BROKEN WORLD

CLAYTON SMITH

1.

Patrick set the empty pudding container down on the ledge and reached into his back pocket, working hard to ignore the pain from the sword wound in his stomach as he shifted his weight. He pulled out the letter and unfolded it, gingerly and for the last time. Tears stung his eyes as he moved his fingers over the familiar scrawl. The letters were sharp and uneven, the careful scribble of a child.

My summer vacation, it said across the top. *Isabella Deen, age 6.* Patrick wiped a tear from his cheek and blinked hard as he read the words he knew so well.

This summer I will go to Disney World. I am iksited. Daddy says I can be a princess like Cinderella. Mommy likes Mulan becus she is a good rore model, but I like Cinderella. Mommy says magic things happen at Disney World. It is our first vacayshun. Daddy never went to Disney World and I never went too. Daddy says our first time will be together and that makes it speshul. I am so happy to be going to Disney World.

Patrick folded the letter and held it to his lips. He breathed in the musty smell of the worn paper, remembering the scent of baby powder and Annie's lavender lotion.

He looked down and saw the last of the Red Caps disappearing into the castle. He thought he could hear the rattle of their footfalls on the metal staircase. He clutched the letter tightly in his hand and turned to face the rising sun. A gust of wind blustered up from the east and pushed the yellow fog swirling away. The wan yellow disc appeared on the horizon, bathing the park in its glow. Cinderella's Castle sparkled in the light.

"We made it, Izzy," he sighed with a smile. "I am so happy to be at Disney World with you."

Then he closed his eyes and waited for the end of the world.

"*Wait!*" a squeaky voice shrieked from the other end of the chamber. A bundle of Red Caps burst through the door, all trying to squeeze through the opening at once. Three of them got stuck in the doorframe, smashing their limbs together and grunting and swearing as they each tried to push the others loose. "Wait," one of them said again, the one in the middle getting smooshed by bigger, broader men on either side. This time, his voice wasn't as shrieky, or as urgent. It was a whimper that limped into a heaving gasp for air as he finally slipped out from between his companions and hit the floor on his hands and knees, wheezing and coughing.

A fourth Red Cap barreled in from the hall, plowing over the two oafs in the doorway, and all three of them went tumbling forward, crashing onto the smaller man.

Something inside him went *CRACK*.

Patrick raised an eyebrow, watching the circus unfold across the chamber. Two more Red Caps came barging through the door; they, too, tripped over the pile of sweaty, squirming bodies and went sprawling across the hard wood.

"This is the saddest thing I've ever seen," Patrick decided with a sigh. Then he remembered the letter in his hand, and he looked down at it with a frown. A bit of blood from the wound in his stomach had smeared across the page. "Well," he said quietly. "One of the saddest."

"Wait!" the crushed Red Cap wheezed again, reaching out with one hand, his fingers scrabbling in Patrick's general direction. His face was darkening through a few dozen shades of purple, until, with an admirably Herculean effort for such a small and injured man, he wrenched himself out of the dogpile and flopped forward on the floor like a bloated fish. "Don't jump," he rasped.

The other Red Caps nodded enthusiastically. "Don't jump!" they agreed as they awkwardly disentangled themselves.

Patrick screwed up his face in confusion. "You think I'm going to jump?"

The short Red Cap frowned. "Aren't you?" he asked.

Patrick shrugged. "To be honest, I hadn't really thought about it," he said. "But it wouldn't be very on-brand. I am astonishingly afraid of heights." He craned his neck and looked out the window, down through the swirling green mist at the theme park spread out before him. "It's weird that I'm sitting here," he decided. He pressed his hand to the wound in his belly, and his palm came away wet and red with blood. "Do we think blood loss has made me fearless? Oh my God, did I just solve phobias?"

An airy lightness spun through his head, and he swayed on the windowsill. Small black dots speckled in over his vision as the whole castle seemed to spin. He tilted backward out the open window, his head and shoulders falling out into empty air. The Red Caps rushed forward as Patrick threw out his hands, pushed his palms against the wall on either side of the opening, and pulled himself back into the room.

"What a breakthrough…I'm a genius," he said happily, finishing his thought as if he hadn't almost fallen one hundred feet to his death.

The short Red Cap and one of his friends inched forward cautiously, reaching out and taking Patrick gently by either elbow. "Maybe let's come all the way inside," said the small one uneasily, pulling Patrick off the windowsill. "Come on. My name's Gary, this is Frank."

"You know I want to be called Turbo," Frank hissed

Gary gave him a look. "Not the time," he hissed back.

Patrick let himself be pulled up to his feet, but as they tried to lead him over toward the bed, he suddenly jerked free of their grasp and stumbled back against the window ledge. "Wait!" he cried, his limbs flailing wildly with a combination of indignation and blood loss. "You tried to kill me seventy-eight times, and *don't think I didn't count!*" he shrieked, sticking a bloody finger into the air. This threw him off balance further. He tripped over his own foot, his shoulder slamming against the wall. "Why don't you want me to jump? You want to kill me with your own hands?"

He closed his eyes. It felt *so good* to close his eyes.

"You killed Bloom," Gary said.

"I did not kill Bloom," Patrick sighed, his eyes still closed. "Ben killed Bloom. With a…" His mind searched for the right word, but it came up blank. He swung his arm through the air, miming a machete. "With a… you know…a hammer."

Frank raised an eyebrow and looked at Gary. *A hammer?* he mouthed.

Gary waved him off. "Whichever one of you killed Bloom," he said, "listen: We owe you."

Patrick opened one eye. The world was swimming, and there were even more Red Caps in the room now, eight or nine of them in all, most of them lingering uneasily by the door. "You owe me?" he said.

"Bloom was a…he was a bad guy. He was cruel, but he had a plan, and Horace was a nice guy, but weak as hell, and…well…we didn't know what to do."

The other Red Caps nodded slowly, looking down in shame.

Patrick sighed. His legs felt rubbery as he eased himself back down onto the windowsill once more. "You did terrible things," he said quietly. He looked down at the blood-soaked letter in his hands. "To innocent people."

"We ain't bad," Frank insisted. "We're just...self-survivalers."

"That's not a word," Patrick pointed out. He began to hear buzzing in his ears. It started out softly, but the volume was increasing rapidly. He closed his eyes again, trying to shut out the sound. "You're not good people."

"We've done bad things," Gary said cautiously. "I know it. But we thought we were doing them for the right reason."

Patrick shook his head. It felt like trying to turn a hot air balloon with a rope, his bulbous skull rocking awkwardly from side to side and bouncing hard on his neck. He opened his mouth to speak, but another dizzy spell took him, and he swooned. His head fell back through the window, and his arms wheeled in a panic. The foil Snack Pack lid and Izzy's letter slipped through his fingers and went fluttering out the window, into the air above Disney World.

Frank, sensing a chance to prove that he was, in fact, good, lurched forward and snatched at the letter as the wind caught it and lifted it beyond the window opening. But he overextended his reach and threw himself off-balance just as he slipped in the pool of Patrick's blood. He screamed as he went toppling out the window.

The other Red Caps gasped in horror. Their faces turned sour as they heard the soft *splat* of Frank hitting the pavement below.

The blood had drained from Patrick's face, and his skin was white and chalky. He stood up, but swayed uneasily on his feet as he looked over his shoulder at the mess of Frank down on the blacktop. "Ben's gonna be so mad at me," he whispered to no one in particular.

Then he closed his eyes and fell into darkness.

2.

Patrick's head hit the ground with a sickening *crack*. His eyes flew open, and red fireworks exploded across his vision.

"Ow!" he cried.

"Careful, dang it—careful!" a voice above him said.

"But he's heavy," a second voice whined.

"He's fifty pounds soaking wet!" insisted the first.

"He was for the first twenty miles," a third voice wheezed. "He's put on a few thousand pounds since then."

The fireworks dissolved, and Patrick squinted against the harsh glare of the sun blazing through shifting layers of yellow-green mist. Six silhouettes stood over him, inspecting him closely. They encircled his vision like numbers on a clock.

"He's still alive," said the man at position III, sounding surprised.

"Are you sure?" asked the man at VII. "He looks kinda dead."

XI reached down and snapped his fingers above Patrick's nose. Patrick blinked furiously, trying to squirm away, but his head burst with dull, heavy pain. His neck felt as stiff as iron, and he couldn't really feel most of the parts of his body. "Stop snapping," he fussed.

"He's alive!" XI confirmed, reaching down with his other hand and snapping with those fingers, too. "Look, he hates this."

"I hate it," Patrick confirmed, his voice thick with sleep and confusion. "Stop it."

"Yeah, he's alive," said XI.

"All right, that's enough," said II, and Patrick recognized the voice as Gary's. "Let's break for camp. Rest your arms. We've got to stop dropping him on his head."

The rest of the Red Caps shrugged and wandered off, but Gary stayed behind and crouched down at Patrick's side. His stiff red hat blocked out the glare of the sun, and Patrick could see his face pretty clearly, beyond the flashing lights of pain shooting across his eyes. He had a dark beard that was cut rough, as if he trimmed it with a hunting knife sometimes, and his eyes were dark, with deep wells beneath them. "How you feeling?" Gary asked.

"Like I fell under a dump truck." Patrick coughed out a ball of phlegm that had formed in his throat, and it almost killed him. His throat felt as hot and dry as brimstone; pieces of it seemed to flake off with every breath. His skin was warm, and clammy with sweat, but cold chills rippled through his bones every few seconds. "Death sucks," he decided.

Gary snorted. "You're not lucky enough to be dead," he said. "You're mostly alive."

Patrick frowned. "Which parts?" he asked, honestly confused. He struggled to sit up, and his body revolted. But Gary put a hand under his arm and helped him rise up to an awkward half-reclining lie-down. "Where are we? How long was I unconscious? What happened to me?"

"You got stabbed in the gut."

Patrick nodded miserably. "Yeah, but like…*after* that."

"It caught up with you," Gary said. "You bled more blood than I thought a body had in it."

"I am a walking Tarantino movie," Patrick confirmed glumly. "Or, I guess, a not-walking one."

"You passed out in the castle. I thought you were dead. But Jimmy there…" Gary nodded toward the Red Cap who had snapped his fingers at Patrick's face. "He used to be an EMT, before M-Day, he said you were just *mostly* dead."

"To blave," Patrick whispered. He closed his eyes and chuckled. This brought a shot of pain through his belly, and he winced sharply.

Gary screwed up his face, confused. "Sure," he said dismissively. "So Jimmy, he got in there and did his thing. Stopped the bleeding, cleaned the wound, stitched you up, hoped for the best. Took a few weeks—shit, I don't know about time anymore, but honestly, I think it's been over a month. Seemed like forever. But here you are."

"A month…?" Patrick struggled onto one elbow and pulled up the hem of his ratty t-shirt. He frowned as he looked down at the sword wound and the uneven scar to the left of his belly button. "What did he sew me up with?" he demanded, gingerly touching the raised welts where, from the looks of it, a surprisingly thick cord had been used as a suture.

"Only thing he could find," Gary said with a frown. "His shoelace."

Patrick blenched. "I don't suppose it was a new one," he said quietly, trying to swallow down against the vomit that was threatening to rise in his throat. "Fresh out of the package from a Disney gift shop?"

"Fresh off his eight-year-old boot," Gary corrected him. "But he washed it first."

"With soap?"

"With rotgut."

Patrick pulled down his shirt and let himself collapse back onto the ground. "How am I still alive?" he grumbled.

"No sepsis yet," Gary shrugged.

"Lucky me," Patrick grunted. He closed his eyes to hide them from the high sun's harsh glare. "Where are we now?"

"North Carolina."

This bit of information tried to penetrate the fog of confusion that surrounded Patrick's understanding of his current predicament. It failed. He did not understand. "North Carolina?"

"We passed Myrtle Beach about a week ago, so I don't know…somewhere on the Crystal Coast?"

"Talk to me like my parents didn't wear sweaters tied around their necks."

"Halfway through North Carolina, maybe. On the water." Gary waved out toward the space to his left, and Patrick turned his head. Through the challenging light, he saw a distant ridge of sand, and beyond that, a gray-blue streak. "There's the Atlantic."

Patrick's head swam. He tried to form words from the complex cloud of injustices that swelled in his mind and in his heart at the thought of being dragged north along the East Coast against his will and without his knowledge. "Gary," he finally managed to say, "my blood sugar is at zero, and this news is making my head spin, and I have to close my eyes for a while." He laid back and exhaled, giving up the fight against exhaustion. "But I want to be clear that when I wake up, I am going to be very, *very* angry about being in North Carolina."

He fell asleep and started snoring softly. Gary sighed. He called for a few of the others, and together they lifted Patrick and carried him up the beach.

3.

"You hate the beach," Ben said.

"I do not hate the beach, and I've never said that," Patrick insisted.

"Literally last week, I asked if you wanted to go to the beach, and you said, 'No way, never, I hate the beach.'"

"Oh." Patrick blinked. "Well, that was last week. This week, I think the beach is fine."

He and Ben were sitting at the rooftop bar at the LondonHouse hotel. The skyscrapers of downtown Chicago rippled out around them, proud and gleaming in the summer sunshine. Far below, speed boats puttered along the Chicago River, heading toward the lake, crammed full of tanned bodies in swimsuits.

"Why is it when *I* want to go to the beach, you hate it, but when *you* want to go to the beach, it's fine?" Ben asked grumpily.

"Because why would I want to go to the beach when I don't want to go to the beach?" Patrick countered. "Do you even hear yourself? You're not making any sense."

"Sometimes I'm not clear on why we're friends." Ben drank his $12 beer. It tasted like watery orange peel. "This beer sucks, and it cost my month's rent. Why did we come up here?"

"I thought you wanted to."

"I thought *you* wanted to!"

"I'm pretty sure it was you," Patrick insisted.

"Why would I want to come up here? I hate being around people."

"Hm. That's true," Patrick nodded, tapping his chin. "But why would *I* want to be up here? I can't stand heights."

"Well, Jesus, Pat, let's get the hell out of here," Ben grumbled. He choked down the rest of his beer and slammed the empty glass on the table. He stood up and tossed a few bills down.

Patrick followed suit, drinking his beer in smaller sips. "It's so hard to keep making it go down my throat," he said miserably. He abandoned the last couple inches of beer, stuck his own money under the glass, and trotted to catch up to Ben, who had already boarded the elevator. "Slow down! My stomach's all sloshy!"

Ben jammed his finger against the button to take them to the lobby. "Do you want to go to the beach or not?"

"Yes, when I said, 'Let's go to the beach' a few minutes ago, I meant that we should go to the beach."

"In jeans and t-shirts and tennis shoes."

"Yessir. I want to stand on the beach, but I don't want to get all sandy and stuff."

"I don't think you understand the concept of beach," Ben pointed out.

The elevator opened, and they scooted through the lobby and out onto Wacker Drive. Traffic was light, but the tourists were plenty, so they hopped down into the road to avoid the congested sidewalks. A taxi blared its horn at them, and Ben flipped the driver off. "Fuck off, I live here!" he yelled.

They ran across Michigan Avenue against the light and nearly got creamed by a tour bus. "You know, I don't think we can actually get to the beach this way," Patrick realized, looking around.

"This is going great," Ben sighed.

"So hard to think with stomach so sloshy," Patrick frowned. He looked south along Michigan. "Ah, who cares, let's just go down to Millennium Park and go over to the waterfront. Who wants sand anyway?"

"So you *don't* want a beach."

"I always want a beach," Patrick corrected him. "But sometimes, just the edge of land will do."

"You are so weird sometimes."

They hustled along Michigan, then cut through the park, avoiding vacationers on Segway tours and families taking selfies by the Bean. They crossed the bridge over the train tracks and came out into a sprawling lawn on the east side of the park. "Actually, let's just stop here," Patrick said.

"But the water's like three blocks away."

"That's okay. I don't need the water."

"Then what are we doing this for?!" Ben exploded.

Patrick flopped down onto the grass, rolling over onto his back and drinking in the sunshine. "I just had to get out of the buildings," he said happily.

Ben frowned. Then he shrugged. "Yeah...fine," he decided. He sat down next to Patrick and breathed in the smell of the fresh-cut grass. "Sometimes the buildings are the worst part of the city."

"Raze them to the ground, I always say."

They lay like that for over an hour, chatting away in the fresh air and sunshine until Patrick fell asleep, sprawled out across the grass.

4.

Patrick awoke, stiff and cranky, as he'd promised, with something bumpy and uncomfortable pressing up against his shoulder blades.

"Are we on a beach?" he asked, annoyed. "It's cold, are we on a beach? I hate a cold beach." He heaved over onto his side, biting back the pain in his stomach. He checked the wound again; the raised bumps from the shoelaces were red and angry-looking, and now they were leaking with some sort of yellowish fluid. The scar from the sword was fine. It was the filthy sutures that were going to kill him

But for now, he had a different pain to deal with.

"What is under me? Something hurts under me. I can't turn to look… it hurts. Someone come in here and tell me what's under me!"

Gary threw open the flap to Patrick's tent. "What's wrong?" he asked, rubbing the sleep from his eyes.

"I slept on something hard and now I'm cranky!" Patrick exclaimed, struggling over onto his side. "I am a *patient*, I am *sickly*, and I need absolute perfect rest to allow my glorious corporeal body to heal!"

Gary frowned down at the sand. "Your 'glorious body' slept on a dead crab." He nudged the fossilized crab carcass with his toe and flipped it across the tent.

"I was keeping it warm," Patrick insisted grumpily. He let himself collapse back onto the sand. "This is exactly why I need a tent with a floor. Richie has a tent with a floor. I should have a tent with a floor."

"Richie has contact dermatitis," Gary reminded him.

"I have contact belly-split-open," Patrick countered, narrowing his eyes.

"And since you're being like this about it, I guess you're feeling better?"

"I'm not having fever dreams about demon-preachers chasing me on buffalo-back to put bombs through my hands anymore, if that's what you're asking," Patrick sighed.

"You were having those?"

"Often," Patrick nodded. His muscles had experienced some level of atrophy since the showdown at Disney World, and his entire body felt like a jumble of slack wires. His head trembled with the strain of moving it up and down. "But they've stopped now, so that's a good sign. I am still of the very strong opinion that a bootlace belongs on the outside of a person's skin, and my surgical wound seems to agree with me. The stitches that saved me are going to kill me. I'll have to cut off half of my midsection and bounce around on my waist like a Slinky Dog."

"You do paint a picture," Gary sighed. "Does that mean we can start expecting you to walk on your own now?"

"I am fully capable of transporting my own weight by means of my own feet," Patrick grumped.

"Good. We'll go a lot faster if you could walk a full day," Gary said.

"Oh. Right. I've been meaning to talk to you about that progress," Patrick groaned, struggling up to his feet. Gary reached out and pulled him up by the forearm. Patrick nodded his thanks and patted Gary on the shoulder. "Where is it we're progressing to?" His brow wrinkled. "Where is it to where we're progressing? To where are we progressing to? Boy, that question is a syntax nightmare."

"We're going northeast," Gary said, pulling back the tent flap and cinching it open, letting in a stream of watery-green light.

Patrick closed his eyes against the soft glare and waited for his pupils to adjust. "But why? Are we coastal elites now?"

Gary frowned. "I know it hasn't been ideal, keeping you on the move. You'd have healed faster if we could have stayed put. But Bloom put us in a bad spot." His face darkened a few shades, and he lowered his eyes to the sand. "Not just Bloom; the way we were with Bloom. It *all* put us in a bad spot." Patrick noticed the worn lines around Gary's eyes and at the corners of his frown. Beneath his stiff red hat, he'd had gone prematurely gray. Though he wasn't far from Patrick in age, standing there now, in the misty morning light, he looked old.

"What kind of spot?"

Gary raised his eyes. He looked at Patrick as if he'd forgotten he was there. He blinked a few times and cleared away the clouds. "The shit we did…it was bad. You don't know the half of it. We broke a whole lot of people. We broke just about every part of the world we touched. We couldn't stay in Florida…people were looking for us. Angry people. All along the Lincoln Service and the Texas Eagle, too. Chicago to San Antonio. Then when we were hunting you guys down, we cut that same kind of path through the South, too. Lots of people looking for us there now. Looking for vengeance. We had to get out of Florida, and we were running out of places to go.

"After you passed out in the castle, we dragged you to the Palmetto Line. We didn't know the conductor, or any of the crew, which I guess was lucky. Our uniforms were enough to get us on the train, and we rode you up as far as Charleston. The plan was to go all the way north to New York, then jump a Maple Leaf into Canada. Rumor is, M-Day wasn't so bad up there, in some parts, at least. Things might be better, with more civilization. That was our plan. But when we got to Charleston, the train swapped crews, and some of the old boys who came on board, they *did* know us— two of them, for sure. So we hopped out and ran. We've been running northeast ever since. We're a pretty safe distance from the tracks now."

Patrick swallowed, his own spit hot and insufficient in his dry, dusty throat. "What'd you do to the other Red Caps, the ones who recognized you? And what did they recognize?"

Gary exhaled. "This older man, Buck, we crossed his path in Joliet once. He used to have a partner. Someone from the old days, someone he'd trained on the Southwest Chief before M-Day. The guy stood between Bloom and a nice-looking widow on a Joliet run. Bloom did him like he did you," Gary nodded down at Patrick's belly, "but better. Buck was there to see it."

Patrick nodded slowly. "And the other one?"

"The other kid…Steve or Stu…he was on our crew for a few months, back toward the beginning. Now the kid's got a scar running down the side of his face, forehead to chin. Nearly got his eye cut out," Gary said. "The man who did that is sleeping next door, in a tent with a floor."

Patrick glowered and shook his head. "Contact dermatitis is letting him off too easy."

"Maybe," Gary said. "We've all been let off easy. You're not keeping good company here. We were scared. Scared of Bloom, scared to holy shit of Calico. We were cowards, and we turned mean to hide it."

Patrick rubbed his forehead. His skull was throbbing; his skin felt the warm flush of a receding fever. He thought back on the things he'd done since M-Day, things he wouldn't have done in his previous life. Things he never would have even dreamed he was capable of doing.

The end of the world had changed them all.

"What's your plan to make it right?" he finally asked.

Gary frowned. "The plan is to follow a new direction. A better direction." He raised an eyebrow. "The plan is to follow *your* direction."

Patrick started. "Me? No. People don't follow me. People get tricked into doing stupid things *by* me. You don't want to follow me."

"We saw how you stood up to Bloom. How you stood up for what was right. We need that. We need you to show us."

"Go watch an after-school special."

"Look. We all work as a crew, and we work well together," Gary said. "But we're not conductors."

"*I'm* not a conductor!" Patrick cried.

"You're someone we can rally around," Gary insisted.

"The last person who rallied around me took off someone's head with a machete and got sent out alone into the goddamn apocalyptic wasteland," Patrick snapped.

"And the fact that you feel bad about that means you might be the last good person in the apocalypse."

But Patrick shook his head. "I'm not a good person," he said. "I'm just…a person."

"Good enough to get behind," Gary said, his eyes level and serious. "You're right, we should know how to make this work on our own. But turns out, we don't. None of us was that good to begin with. The end of the world sure as shit didn't make us better. But we saw what you did. We're with you. Whatever you need."

Patrick sighed. He limped over to the opening of the tent and pushed past the canvas, stepping out into the gloomy green morning. He inhaled deeply, his lungs spasming with the Monkey Dust whipped up by the ocean wind. He hacked and spat a yellow-green glob onto the sand. "Pretend I didn't do that," he wheezed, doubled over and breathing hard. "I was trying to strike a look."

"Want to come back in? Take it from the top?" Gary snorted.

Patrick waved him off. "No, but thank you for indulging me. It's a feature I greatly admire." He straightened up and took a few resettling breaths. He stared out over the waves, and he opened his mouth to speak… but then he closed it again, and turned back to Gary. "Actually, wait. Yes. Let's do that. Give me your line again."

"Which line?"

"The 'whatever I need' thing. Can you do that again?"

"I don't remember exactly what I said…" Gary frowned.

"Just do your best," Patrick insisted. "Let it be natural."

"Um…whatever you need, we can do," Gary tried.

Patrick shook his head and frowned. "No, it wasn't that…" he said, tapping his lips as he trailed off.

"We can do whatever you need? Just say the word?" Gary tried again.

"No, that's not it. It was like, something about me being really good, and then you're with me…"

"Oh. We're with you, whatever you need?"

"Was that–?" Patrick wondered, squinting thoughtfully. "No…it was more like…"

"Man, I didn't think I'd have to remember it. It wasn't rehearsed or anything."

"No, no, I know," Patrick assured him, waving both his hands frantically. "It was just so…" He sighed with frustration. "It's okay. Just say what you were just saying. 'We're with you, whatever you need.'"

Gary nodded. "We *are* with you. Whatever you need."

Patrick turned and gazed out toward the ocean, stiffening his spine and squaring his jaw as he squinted against the shifting mists and light. He spoke again, this time in a gravelly, guttural tone: "I hope that's true," he rasped. "Because what I need…is to go back."

Gary blinked. "Back?" he said.

"Back," Patrick confirmed with a nod. "We have to go back."

"Back where?" Gary asked. "To Disney World?"

"We have to go back!" Patrick shouted, lifting his eyes to the sky and wailing dramatically.

Gary took a step back. "What are you doing?" he asked.

"We have to go back, Kate," Patrick said, his eyes misting over. "*We have to go back.*"

Gary looked around uncertainly. "What's happening right now?"

Patrick frowned. "Come on, Gary. *Lost*? 'We have to go back'? No? Nothing?"

Gary shook his head. "I didn't watch *Lost*," he shrugged.

Patrick's shoulders slumped. "Oh, Gary. You are such a disappointment."

"Are you just quoting a show now, or do you actually want to go back somewhere?" Gary asked.

"Both. I actually want to go back somewhere," Patrick confirmed. "Much like Jack, I have to go back to a place I have already been. And in this scenario, you're Kate. And this green fog is a very dramatic rainfall, and I guess Spiver would be the smoke monster? Introduced, important for a few episodes, then completely ignored and never revisited again."

Gary furrowed his brow. "Who's Spiver?" he asked.

"Exactly," Patrick said, tapping the side of his nose knowingly.

Gary sighed. "So you *do* want us to go back to Disney World," he said.
But Patrick shook his head. "Not Disney World," he replied. "Mobile."
Gary cocked an eyebrow. "Mobile, Alabama?"

"That's the one."

Gary rubbed his cheek and tried to place Mobile in the timeline of semi-recent events. Bloom had taken them through Alabama, though not through Mobile. The Red Caps had looped north in order to make the intercept at Disney World. Gary had never been to Mobile, but he knew that Patrick had, and that he had been there for a decent length of time. The Red Caps had camped out near the Magic Kingdom for weeks, maybe months, waiting for Patrick to arrive. "What's in Mobile?"

Patrick crossed his arms. "Ben is in Mobile," he said. "Ben went back to Fort Doom. And I need to get back to Ben."

5.

"Okay, gather 'round," Patrick said, waving everyone in close.

The Red Caps eyed each other. They were already gathered pretty tightly around.

"I don't know any of your names," Patrick admitted, slapping the sand with a stick he'd found among a pile of driftwood down the beach. "You've probably all said them out loud lots of times in the last few weeks, but I've been delirious with death and I basically didn't register any of them. Except Gary," he said, nodding Gary's way. "And truth be told, I'm terrible with names. It's going to take me about a year to get them right. But that's not a *you* thing; that's a *me* thing. That's my struggle, and my personal journey. I'll be stronger for taking it. Now," he said, pointing the stick at one of the Red Caps across the circle, "I want to know your first name, last name, where you're from, and one interesting thing about you."

The Red Cap on the business end of the stick shifted uncomfortably. It had been years since he'd done an ice breaker. "Okay, well–" he began.

"Wait!" Patrick cried, shaking his head and waving his hands, nearly taking Gary's eye out with the stick. "I should go first. Right?" He leaned conspiratorially toward the Red Cap on his right and whispered, "I'm not very good at being in charge." Then he straightened up and addressed the whole group. "I'm Patrick Deen. I'm from Chicago, sort of, but I grew up in St. Louis. My religion is the Cardinals, mostly. One interesting fact about me is that I once had a psychopathic preacher drive a railroad spike through my palm. See?" He held up his right hand, showcasing the raised, purplish scar in the center of his palm. He swung his hand in an arc so everybody could get a good look. Then he took the stick and pointed once again at the man across from him. "*Now.* Your turn."

The Red Cap shifted again. He waved awkwardly at his colleagues around the circle. "I'm Ted. Ted Purdy. I'm from Iowa."

"Where in Iowa?" Patrick interrupted.

"Iowa City. Thereabouts."

"How far from the Mississippi?" Patrick inquired, leaning forward with interest.

"About...maybe an hour?" Ted guessed.

"Congratulations on winning the dead-body ash water lottery," Patrick beamed.

Ted pulled back from the circle and looked nervously at the rest of his group. "I–what?"

"Nothing, nothing," Patrick said, waving away Ted's concerns. "Please continue. One interesting fact?"

Ted swallowed. "Umm...I guess...one time I was on a talent show?"

"A talent show!" Patrick gasped. "Which talent show? 'American Idol'?"

Ted's cheeks burned red. "Oh. No. Nothing that big. It was small. A public access thing, I think? Called 'Impressive Iowans'."

"Weird, but great! What's your talent?"

The tips of Ted's ears darkened. "This was like ten years ago..." he explained sheepishly.

Patrick waved off his embarrassment. "The talents of all ages are equal in the eyes of the great Jamaican bomb-lords," he said. His head swam with a sudden rush of dizziness, and he threw out a hand to balance himself on the sand. He blinked hard, clearing his head as the world came back into focus. "Sorry," he muttered, his voice suddenly muted. "That... keeps happening. He cleared his throat and beckoned Ted onward. "Keep going. Sorry."

Ted looked around the circle uncertainly, but Gary nodded, so he continued. "I sang 'Vesti la Giubba' from 'Pagliacci'."

Patrick cocked an eyebrow. "The opera 'Pagliacci'?" Ted nodded. "You sing *opera*?"

"I *sang* opera," Ted corrected him quietly. "I studied it, and I was good—pretty good, before..." Tears welled up in the man's eyes and he pushed himself up from the beach and ran into the trees on the far side of the dunes, weeping quietly.

Patrick watched, stunned. "I love 'Pagliacci'," he said, watching Ted run away in awe. "I mean, I've never *seen* it, but there was a really good issue of Batman, the whole Hush storyline, where Joker was the clown in 'Pagliacci', and *boy*...goosebumps."

The Red Caps eyed each other uncomfortably. One of them coughed.

The man sitting to what had previously been Ted's left raised his hand. "Should…I go?" he asked.

"Please," Patrick nodded. "Name, where you're from, and fun fact."

"I'm Richie," the young man offered, taking off his hat and mussing his shaggy blond hair. "Richie Frye. I'm from Mellwood, Arkansas, originally. One interesting thing about me, I guess, is that I got contact dermatitis."

The other Red Caps groaned. But it was Patrick who put a voice to their frustrations.

"You're the one with the *tent*," he said, his eyes narrowing. "The tent with the *floor*."

"I got contact dermatitis!" Richie whined. He scratched his elbow, just to prove how intensely he suffered.

"I slept on a dead crab," Patrick whispered harshly. The pain in his back suddenly returned, a small, digging knob, like a six-sided die pressing against his spine. He turned and struggled with his t-shirt, pulling it up over his shoulder blades. "Look at the bruise!"

The Red Caps frowned at Patrick's back. There was no bruise.

"That is a *crab bruise!*" Patrick shouted, throwing his shirttail back down and turning to glare at Richie. "Dead crab is the hardest kind of crab, it's scientifically petrified, and I may never walk again."

"You walked to this fire," Richie pointed out.

"Only by dint of my miraculous fortitude!" Patrick cried.

"Maybe we should get this moving," Gary interrupted, noting with some concern the thin sheen of sweat that covered Patrick's clammy skin. "I grew up in Hannibal." He nodded around the circle, ticking off each of the remaining Red Caps by name: "That's Lawrence, he's good in a scrape. He used to be a bouncer, from Memphis. That's Brett over there, from some shithole in Illinois; he used to be a plumber. And this is Jimmy. He's the one who stitched you up."

"Don't tell me," Patrick said, narrowing his eyes and running his fingers over the scar in his side and the large, raised welts from the bootlace. "He used to be a cobbler."

Jimmy frowned. "No—an EMT," he said.

Patrick rolled his eyes and threw up his hands dramatically. "Well, I *hope* so. It was a *joke*, Johnny."

"Jimmy," Jimmy corrected him.

"Don't you remember jokes?" Patrick demanded, steamrolling right past the correction. Sharp pain shot through Patrick's torso, and he winced, sucking air in sharply through his teeth. The pain had a clarifying effect, cutting through the fog of fever and mania that threatened to take control of his head. He closed his eyes and took a few deep breaths, letting the cool ocean wind bring relief to his burning forehead. "Thank you all for your help," he said, his tone calmer and measured. "Thank you for saving my life, Johnny."

"Jimmy."

"I think the suture wounds are pretty infected, and if I die of sepsis, I take back my gratitude."

"Oh." Jimmy frowned. "I'll take a look at that tonight."

"That would be great," Patrick nodded. "And thank you…all of you. For keeping me alive and getting me out of Florida."

The men exchanged glances. "You're welcome," they said.

Patrick nodded. "Having said all that," he continued, "I need to go back."

"Back?" Brett said, swatting at a sand flea that had found its breakfast on the back of his hand. "Back to Florida?"

"Back to Mobile. Alabama."

"And we're going with him," Gary added.

A grumble rose around the fire as the other Red Caps shifted in their seats; arms were crossed, heads were shaken, and heels were dug down into the sand. It was Lawrence, the former bouncer, who strung together the first full sentence of angry dissent. "We just spent the last *month* getting *out* of the South. At pretty serious risk to ourselves. And you want us to turn around and go *back?*"

"I don't want anyone to do anything," Patrick said, shaking his head. "*I'm* going back. Anyone who wants to tag along is welcome."

"Tag along?," Brett snorted. "Be serious. If you wanted to stay, you should have said something before we lugged your broken ass halfway across the country."

"I never asked you to drag my broken ass halfway across the country," Patrick reminded him. "I was just a little too completely unconscious to protest. If anything, you kidnapped me, and you should be ashamed."

"Kidnapped?!" Brett cried. He looked like he was one wrong word away from charging across the fire and choking the re-emerging life right out of Patrick's throat. "We *saved* you!"

"And I told you, I'm grateful for it!" Patrick shot back. His cheeks flamed red with sickness and frustration. "But now, I'm going back to Mobile. You can stay. In fact," he added quickly, "it's probably best that you do."

"We're going," Gary cut in again, sending a hard look around the fire.

"What the hell, Gary?" Brett demanded. "We risked our lives to get him out, now we're gonna risk 'em again to put him back?"

"We got *ourselves* out," Gary replied. "We brought him along. But don't kid yourself, Brett; don't *any* of you kid yourselves. We got ourselves out of the mess we put ourselves in. That's on us. But this is a chance to do something good. Help him get back to his friend. That's a noble thing. Hell of a lot better than—than all that shit we used to do," he finished hurriedly.

"They want our heads in the south," Lawrence said. "I mean, there's plenty of folks who literally want our heads. That's a suicide mission for us—into a lion's den."

"What makes you think we'll do any better going north?" Gary asked. "Look. It's shitty to say it. But we're no good on our own. All of us, we nearly fuckin' died in this place, before Bloom found us and gave us a life. It took me a long time to realize it, but shit, I don't have the first clue about surviving on my own. And neither do any of you, because if you did, you never would have joined up with Bloom, like I did, and none of us would be malnourished and vulnerable like we are now. So if you don't want to head back south, don't. You can keep going on. But I'm going wherever Patrick goes, because this man," he said, throwing a strong and level finger in Patrick's direction, "this man knows something that not a single one of us does: He knows how to live in the apocalypse."

Patrick frowned. He wondered if he should point out that he was actually pretty bad at apocalypse life, and that at least some part of his desire to get back to Mobile was so that he could reunite with Ben, who had some decidedly blunt ideas about how life in the apocalypse could be successfully lived.

But before he could open his mouth, Lawrence spoke, his words heavy with concern. "I get what you're saying—both of you," he began, indicating Patrick and Gary with a sweep of his hand. "And you're right, Gary, we're not good at this. And we did come up here for *us*, not for him…when it comes down to it, we've got a whole lot of bad shit between us that we need to make up for. I'm not opposed to the idea of getting the gimp back to his people."

"Gimp?" Patrick frowned.

"But," Lawrence continued, "there's a lot of land between here and there. And that land is covered with a whole lot of tracks, and those tracks are full of people who want to see us hang."

"That's exactly why we won't go by land," Patrick offered, pushing himself up from his seat and standing proudly over the fire. "I'm not going to ask you to retrace your steps, especially when those steps take you through a lethal firewall of super-righteous anger."

Lawrence tilted his head. "But…you want to go back to Alabama. What other choice do we have?"

"I'm glad you asked," Patrick beamed. "This is the good part of the plan." He walked dramatically to the edge of the fire, standing between the Red Caps and the crashing ocean to the east. "We're going to take to the water," he said proudly, spreading his arms toward the sea. "Gird your loins and man your sails, boys!" he cried, his eyes glinting with glee. "We're about to become extremely fearsome pirates."

6.

The plan was simple, and nobody liked it.

"So just to make sure I'm clear," Gary said after the pregnant silence that followed Patrick's breathless explanation of the scheme, "you want us to steal a boat—*that* boat," he added, pointing to a small yacht anchored about half a mile offshore. "You want us to steal that boat and sail it all the way to the Gulf of Mexico?"

Patrick bobbed his head from side to side. "That's sort of accurate," he decided. "A few points of clarification. I'm not comfortable with the word 'steal.' You can't steal something that belongs to the ocean. You can only borrow it. And also, we're not sailing. It's not a sailboat. We're driving it. But other than that, yes, you've got the gist."

"Do you know how to drive a boat?" Ted asked.

"Nope!" Patrick said. "But I don't know how to sail a boat either, so we're no worse off."

The Red Caps exchanged worried looks.

"Hey, listen, don't get too wound up in the details," Patrick encouraged. "Do I know how to drive a boat? No. Do I think there will be usable gas in the fuel tank? No. Do I have any idea how we're actually going to use the boat to move ourselves from here to there? I do not. But we'll figure it out." He placed his hand on Jimmy's shoulder. "Together."

Jimmy shuffled sideways, out of reach. Patrick's hand dropped.

Gary was trying to stay positive. "I guess if we can't figure it out, we're no worse off than we are now," he said.

"Exactly! And I'm confident we'll be able to figure it out. I've got an ace in the hole, here."

"Oh yeah?" Brett asked, crossing his arms. "What's that?"

Patrick crossed his arms, too, and he smiled confidently. "I am an engineer." The Red Caps groaned. Patrick's face fell. "What?"

"I thought you were going to say something useful," Richie frowned. "Like, 'I'm a survivalist.'"

"An engineer is *like* a survivalist! Of the mind." Patrick tapped his temple. Everyone groaned again. "Oh, come on, stop doing that."

"But, I mean, how do we even get out there?" Richie asked. "We can't swim that far! It's like a mile!"

"It's not a mile," Patrick corrected him, "and anyway, you don't have to swim. It's easy. Look out there. Look at all the boats." He swept his hand out toward the water, and indeed, there were about a dozen boats bobbing on the waves, at various distances from the shore, and in various stages of disrepair and neglect. "We swim to one of *those* boats, then we row that boat to the *big* boat, and then we figure out how to take the big boat down the seaboard and into the Gulf." He crossed his arms, very satisfied with himself. "It's almost too simple. And that simplicity is what an engineer brings to the table."

The Red Caps huddled together and conferred. Some of them shook their heads violently. Others just sort of shrugged their shoulders. Their whispers were heated, and it was clear that no one was happy. But in the end, they turned back to Patrick, and Gary said, "Okay. We're going to try your plan."

"Excellent," Patrick smiled. "We will definitely not regret this."

7.

Patrick frowned. He was starting to regret this.

No one was doing what he asked. Being in charge of half a dozen people was nowhere near as efficient as being in charge of just himself and Ben.

"Why aren't you getting the boat," he called down to Ted and Jimmy, who were standing uncertainly at the water's edge. Patrick raised his hand and pointed at the well-worn dinghy that was bobbing on the uneven surface of the ocean, held down by an anchor that someone had inexplicably dropped fifty feet away from the shore. "Go get the boat."

The two men turned back to Patrick and frowned. "The water looks cold," Ted complained.

Patrick rolled his eyes. "Of *course* it looks cold!" he said. "But it only *looks* cold because it *is* cold! It's the Atlantic Ocean, not a hot tub at the Hilton Royale!"

"What's the Hilton Royale?" Jimmy asked, blinking.

"I didn't want to ask, but I am also confused about that," Ted quietly confided to his colleague. "Was that even part of their portfolio?"

"Look—it is *right there*," Patrick said, stabbing his finger in the sad, badly weathered boat's general direction. "I could pick up one of you and hit it with you."

Ted and Jimmy exchanged worried glances.

"Maybe this is something…you could do?" Jimmy asked nervously.

"As our new and undisputed leader?" Ted threw in quickly. Jimmy gave him an affirming nod.

Patrick narrowed his eyes. "First of all, I don't like having the feeling that maybe what you're saying is actually a patronizing insult, and I *defi-*

nitely don't like not being able to tell if it is or not," he said, crossing his arms. "And second of all, I can't wade into neck-deep apocalyptic Monkey Dust-water…*I might get sepsis*." He directed this last comment directly at Jimmy, his eyes shooting daggers.

Jimmy frowned and turned to Ted. "He's actually right," he admitted. "He could get sepsis."

"I told you not to sew him up with a bootlace!" Ted hissed.

"You are not a medical professional!" Jimmy cried, thrusting a finger into the air and taking extraordinary umbrage.

Ted rolled his eyes. "You rode in the back of an ambulance. You're not exactly Dr. Quinn," he said.

"You mean the fictional character, Dr. Quinn, Medicine Woman?"

"She was a frontier *treasure*," Ted replied, planting his hands on his hips. "She saved the lives of every single person in Colorado Springs, and she learned how to use a broom, even though she grew up with servants!"

"*She is fictional!*" Jimmy shrieked.

"So are your medical skills!" Ted shouted back.

"Hey! Downstairs people!" Patrick said, snapping his fingers to bring them back to attention. "Can we please focus on the important things, which are getting that stupid dinghy over here so we can load it up and row it out to that yacht, which we will then sail to the Gulf of Mexico?!" He nodded out toward the Sea Ray 58 that was bobbing on the water about 500 yards from the shore.

Ted and Jimmy both stopped and turned to face Patrick. "We're not taking the dinghy?" they said in unison.

Patrick dropped his head into his hand. "Of *course* we're not taking the dinghy," he sighed. "You can't take a dinghy from North Carolina to the Gulf of Mexico."

Ted's face screwed up in confusion, and asked, "Are you sure?"

"I am more than willing to let you try it," Patrick sighed. "But first, we need that Sea Ray."

Ted frowned at the ocean. "It's just…the water's *so* cold," he repeated

"It's *really* cold," Jimmy agreed again.

Patrick shook his head and pinched the bridge of his nose. "Would you prefer to wait until nuclear summer appears and melts us all in sweet, sweet release?" he murmured.

Ted looked at Jimmy. Jimmy shrugged at Ted. "That doesn't sound so bad," they both agreed.

Patrick gritted his teeth and stomped toward the ocean. "Fine," he said, rolling up the cuffs of his jeans. "I'll do it myself. But if I get sepsis, I'm going to chop your legs off with the dullest machete I can find."

Jimmy sighed. "No—wait." He made his way down the shore and met Patrick at the water's edge. "I'll do it. I can't let you take the risk; I took an oath."

Ted snorted. "I'll keep saying it, you were an EMT. You weren't a doctor."

"EMTs are like doctors!" Jimmy insisted.

"EMTs are the Jonah Hills of the medical world," Brett snickered from up the beach.

"I love Jonah Hill, so *thank you*," Ted retorted, crossing his arms.

"Jonah Hill is dead, and so is your lame-ass profession."

"EMTs take an oath!" Jimmy shrieked.

"To do what?" Ted demanded.

"'To consider for the benefit of patients and abstain from whatever is deleterious and mischievous!'" he recited.

Ted narrowed his eyes. "You made those words up."

"I didn't. And sepsis is *extremely* deleterious."

"I happen to agree," Patrick piped up. "And I, for one, salute our medical heroes." He grabbed Jimmy's hand and shook it vigorously. "Thank you for your service, Johnny. Now which one of us is going after that dinghy?"

Jimmy nodded resolutely. "I am," he said, his voice firm. Then he turned to Ted. "Are you coming with me?"

Ted pressed his teeth together, giving Jimmy a guilty look. "I'm not an EMT," he said.

Jimmy shook his head in disappointment. Then he turned to the ocean, rubbed his hands together, took a deep breath, and dove into the ice-cold water.

•

"He shouldn't have dived," Ted said, concerned.

"No," Patrick agreed, hiding his eyes behind his fingers. "What was he thinking?"

"It sounded like his neck cracked," Ted blenched.

"I think Johnny might be dead," Patrick agreed grimly.

Then the surface of the water broke, and Jimmy flailed into the air, wheeling his arms and sending cold water spattering in every direction. "*It's cold! It's cold! It's cold!*" he shrieked.

"Oh, you're alive!" Patrick cried happily. He gave Jimmy a round of applause. "Excellent work! Go get the boat."

They watched as Jimmy bobbed awkwardly through the yellow-crusted water, cursing and shivering and making extremely slow progress. "I can't feel my legs!" he cried out over his shoulder. "My legs have gone numb!"

"Well, you're our only medical professional. What do *you* think you should do about that?" Patrick called out.

"I think I should get out of this fucking water," Jimmy grumbled.

He splashed his way toward the dingy and was only a few yards away when he suddenly stopped. His body went stiff, and the water around him calmed.

"What's wrong?" Ted shouted.

Jimmy turned his head slowly, his mouth was open wide and his skin blue-white from cold and from fear. "There's something out here," he whispered.

"You mean besides the boat?" Ted asked.

"I mean in the water. There's something *in the water*!" Jimmy hissed. He turned his attention back to the ocean and swiveled his head, looking for signs of movement beneath the surface. "It touched me. Something *touched* me! It swam into my legs!"

"I thought you said your legs were numb," Patrick said suspiciously, crossing his arms.

"It's probably just a fish," Ted said, but his breath was short and sharp. He clearly did not actually think that it was probably just a fish.

"It feels big," Jimmy said, spinning around frantically in the water and somehow finding a way to turn even paler. His skin looked like it had been run through a rinse cycle with bleach.

Then, a few yards to Jimmy's left, the water splashed.

It was a big splash.

Patrick's spine tightened. The corners of his mouth drew down. "Get to the boat," he said. His voice was hoarse from the lack of speaking authoritatively, so he cleared his throat and said it again louder. "Get to the boat!"

"It might be a shark," Ted said, going pale as the blood drained from his face. He had seen the splash too.

"I know it might be a shark!" Patrick hissed, swatting Ted's shoulder. "That's why we have to get him into the dinghy!" He turned back toward the ocean, and toward Jimmy, cupping his hands around his mouth as he shouted, "Jimmy! Get to the boat!"

"I'm *trying* to get to the boat!" Jimmy shrieked. He lurched forward, his arms and wheeling as he struggled against the cold, crusty ocean and made desperate dive at the anchored, bobbing dingy. His fingers scrabbled over the edge of the wood, trying to pull himself up. But then he plunged back into the water as if his feet had suddenly taken on a fifty-pound weight. "*Oh God!*" he screamed as his shoulders disappeared beneath the waves. "It bit me!"

"It *bit* you?!" Ted cried.

"*It bit me!*" Jimmy screamed, thrashing in the ocean. Streams of yellowish water flung out in every direction. "Oh, fucking God, *it bit me!*"

"Jimmy!" Patrick screamed, rushing to the shore, stopping short as the water lapped at his shoes. "Get in the fucking boat!"

"I'm *trying* to get in the fucking boat!" Jimmy screeched. "But it *bit* me! It *bit* me! Oh, God!" He lunged for the boat, his hands slipping off the edge. The dinghy rocked on the waves, threatening to tip as Jimmy screamed and scrambled, splashing the ocean into a yellow-green froth. He yanked the edge of the boat down to the water and launched himself into the wet belly of the dinghy, hollering with pain as the boat righted itself.

The slippery top ridge of a mysterious creature surfaced, as if it had followed Jimmy, spurred on by a taste for human flesh. Its spikes were visible for only an instant. Then it slipped back beneath the water, disappearing into the green-tipped foam.

"Did you see that?" Patrick whispered, his face turning pale.

Ted swallowed hard. "Yeah," he whispered back. "I saw it."

Jimmy scrambled to the far end of the boat and set to work examining his leg. He couldn't remember if his worn-out Dickey pants had already been that shredded, or if the ocean monster had ripped new strips apart with its ghastly fangs. His fingers scrambled over the skin, searching for the warm rush of blood, but he felt nothing but cold water and goosebumps. Jimmy breathed a sigh of relief. He had not been bitten. He was safe. He was fine.

He had survived his first sea monster attack.

He situated himself in the dinghy, his heart slipping with each shake of the boat. He raised himself up to his shaky knees, balancing his weight as best he could. He leaned out and peered over the side. The monster seemed to have retreated.

"It's okay!" he shouted back toward the shore. He laughed, a high-pitched sound that was strange to his own ears. "I'm okay, it's–"

He didn't get a chance to finish.

The slick, spiny back of the monster resurfaced.

It was headed for Patrick and Ted on the shore.

"It's not okay! It is *not* okay!" Jimmy shrieked. "Look!"

Back on the beach, Patrick's eyes had grown to three times their normal size. The monster's hump was knifing through the crusty ocean, headed directly for them.

Patrick and Ted watched with alarm as the creature slid closer and closer. They stumbled backward up the sand. "It won't come out of the water, right?" Ted cried, his lips tight curled back in fear.

"Definitely not," Patrick tried to assure him, his hands clenched into airtight anxiety balls. "If there's one thing I know about fish, it's that they don't come out of the sea *oh God, it's coming out of the sea!*" he shrieked.

The creature barreled through the surf and emerged onto the sand in a frenzy of yellow foam. It writhed on the beach, hissing and spitting and gasping for air.

Ted drew his mouth open in a grimace. "What...*is* it?" he asked sourly.

Patrick furrowed his brow. "That," he said, "is a demon-spawn."

The fish looked like the result of a horrific science experiment, as if King Triton's mad scientist had successfully bonded a moray eel with a lizard, screwed a fish's head onto the grotesque body, then enrolled the thing in Barry's Boot Camp for six months. It was big and broad, about ten inches from shoulder to shoulder—which was, Patrick noted, a strange way to measure a fish, since he didn't remember them ever *having* shoulders. But this one did, two wide, knobby shoulders, each one attached to a floppy, fin-like arm that bent around an elbow in the middle. The creature's eel-like body stretched out behind its almost three feet. Its grimy, black-green tail thrashed against the ground, spraying sand in every direction. And the monster's head...it was huge and swollen, like a grotesque, bumpy-scaled fish suffering from an allergic reaction to a bee sting. Its eyes were wide-set and gaping, with tiny yellow veins shot through an off-grey white bulge. Long spindles thrust out from the sides of its head like needles; one had a dead minnow skewered on the end of it. It had been impaled so long ago, the tiny body was half-lost to rot.

The monster's mouth opened and closed as the angry thing gasped for air; they could see the yellow-gray flash of thin, flat teeth every time the mouth opened. And every time the mouth closed, they could hear those teeth go *clop, clop, clop.*

"Gary!" Patrick hollered, yelling up the beach without taking his eyes from the squirming monster. "Bring the machete!"

"What do we do?" Ted whispered without moving his lips. He was petrified with fear. His whole body was rigid, as if the eel-lizard-fish monster had already ripped his guts from his belly and left him dead and stiffening on the cold ocean border.

"We wait for the machete." Patrick narrowed his eyes. "Then we make ceviche."

The two men eyed the creature carefully, neither daring to blink as it wriggled its leg-fins against the sand, getting used to the feel of the shifting earth beneath its weight. Its slick, slimy appendages spun before the monster adjusted, snarling and spitting and with eyes that raged. Then the flimsy arms made purchase. The fish lurched forward on the beach, pushed along by its clumsy arms.

Patrick and Ted leapt back, screaming.

"Kill it!" Patrick cried.

"*You* kill it!" Ted squeaked back.

"No—*you*! It's a goddamn catfish, it'll be easy!" Patrick screeched, darting behind Ted.

"It's *not* a catfish…catfish don't walk!" Ted screamed, stumbling backward, tripping over Patrick and sprawling sideways onto the cold sand.

"Walking catfish do," Gary said, out of breath as he hurried down the beach. He slid to a stop next to Patrick and handed him a weapon.

"This is a bat," Patrick frowned, staring down at the bat.

"I couldn't find the machete."

"Rule number 82, Gary!"

"I know, I know: always know where the machete is."

"*Always* know where the machete is!" Patrick repeated, incredulous. "What even is the point of making new rules if no one's going to *oh, fuck!*"

The monster launched itself into the air, snarling and snapping its wide, flat teeth. Patrick moved on instinct, swinging the bat clumsily. He connected with the broad side of the fish and sent it sailing at a new angle, one that delivered the creature teeth-first into Ted's leg.

"*Ahhhhhhhh!*" Ted screeched, dancing on his non-fished leg and kicking with the other, trying to unseat the water demon. "*It's fucking eating me!*"

"Hold still!" Patrick cried. He gripped the bat and held it up on his shoulder, rushing over to the besieged Red Cap. Ted flailed in a manic dance, slapping at the mutant catfish with an open palm. Luckily, the monster's teeth weren't sharp, so they hadn't gotten deep into his flesh. But its jaw was powerful and clamped down like a vice, holding Ted's leg in its mouth and slowly crushing the structure beneath the skin. "Hold *still!*" Patrick repeated.

"*The fish! The fucking fish!*" Ted shrieked. "*Get it!*"

"I'm trying!" Patrick wagged the bat, the tip of his tongue poking out of the corner of his mouth. He concentrated on the creature, dangling from Ted's leg like a marionette on speed. "Hold still!"

"*Kill it!*" Ted yelled. "*Kill it, kill it, kill it!*"

Patrick saw his chance. He dropped his shoulder and swung the bat as hard as he could, aiming for the monster's head. At the same time, ted spun in his mad pirouette and brought the fish directly into the arc of the bat. The wood connected against the monster's side with a loud *CRACK*.

The bat splintered into pieces that went skittering across the sand.

"Huh," Patrick said, holding up the jagged remains of the handle. He scratched his head. "This feels familiar."

"Fuck me," Gary murmured in awe.

"*It is* killing *me!*" Ted screamed, snapping them out of their stunned thoughts. The monster was still firmly clamped onto the Red Cap's leg; the possessed catfish's jaws were tightening so much that Patrick could see the shape of Ted's leg changing, collapsing beneath the monster's bite. "*Help!*"

Bright lights shot through Patrick's vision. The beach faded in the glare of memory, and he saw a slow-motion tableau of the recent past: there he was, beneath a marquee in Mobile, and the short jester, Spiver, was swinging a bat at Ben's head. He saw the bat connect hard with Ben's temple. He saw Ben spin in a lifeless twist as blood misted in the cold, heavy air.

Patrick felt something inside of him crack and splinter, like the leg of a bridge that was hit by a wrecking ball. A piece of him broke into a sideways place, not enough to take down his whole structure, but enough to unsteady him and make him, in that one instant, question the sort of support he'd had, and the sort of support he'd been.

It was a glimpse into the consequence of a life he'd taken for granted—not his own…but his best friend's.

Yeah. Keep making jokes. You're pretty fucking good at that, Ben had spat, blood crusting at his temple, tears of frustration running down his cheeks. *You're not very fucking good at keeping your best friend safe, you're not very fucking good at keeping anybody safe, with your stupid ass decisions, but, hey, you can deliver a punch line. Congratu-fucking-lations.*

The vision of Ben faded as Patrick blinked away the past. He looked at the struggle in front of his eyes again, at the mutant catfish that was crushing Red's leg.

His hands tightened on the handle of the shattered bat. He stepped forward, toward the ferocious fish with its teeth buried deep in Ted's flesh. He flipped the wood in his hands like a dagger, with the smooth, knobby end faced the sky, and the sharp, splintered end pointed down toward the sand. Then he gave a warrior's scream as he raised the bat above his head, lurched forward, and drove the sharp wood down into the sea creature's eye.

Shards of planed oak sheared away on impact, shattering against the fish's hardened sclera and exploding outward in a halo of splinters. A shank split down from the center of the stake found purchase in the soft part of the monster's eye, and the spear drove in. The eyeball popped like a grape, a thick, gummy wetness exploding up in a geyser. Then, Patrick drove the bat down through the fish's orbital socket until it punctured its brain.

The monster convulsed, waving away from Ted's leg like a wind sock before it went slack, held half-rigid by the strength of its reinforced bones and hardened veins.

Patrick pulled the bat handle out of the creature's eye socket. The wooden spike dripped with thick, yellow mucous. Then jammed the stick into the opening between the monster's mouth and Ted's flesh, and with a quick jerk, he popped the Red Cap's leg free.

"Oh my God!" Ted cried, falling onto the sand and grabbing at his injured calf. Blood oozed out through his fingers. "What if it gave me *rabies*?!"

"Can fish even get rabies?" Gary asked uncertainly. He looked at Patrick.

Patrick shrugged.

"Fish-rabies!" Ted insisted with a wail. He grabbed ahold of the hole that the fish had ripped in his pants and pulled, tearing off a long strip of dirty, bloody fabric. He wound it around his leg and cinched it tight.

"Make sure you clean it," Patrick advised.

"Oh, with what—apocalypse soap?!" Ted sniped.

Patrick rubbed his chin. "I bet Old Spice made something called 'Apocalypse Soap,'" he decided. "Cleanliness is next to world-endliness." *I can make jokes* and *save my friends, thank you very much, Memory Ben.* "What about the moonshine you cleaned my stitches with?"

"We used the last of it on you," Gary replied.

Patrick turned back to Ted. "Okay, well...I used the last of disinfectant, but it was for good reason, because if I had died, no one would have saved you from the creature from the black spittoon over there. So, call me crazy, but I'm gonna say we're even."

Ted mumbled something angry under his breath. He struggled to his feet and leaned on Gary for support. "Help me down to the water, I'll flush it out."

"I'd use clean water," Patrick said. "Like some of the drinking water. Not *my* drinking water," he added quickly. "In fact, I recommend Richie's drinking water." Patrick gritted his teeth with envy at the thought of Richie's tent, with its thin, nylon floor. "Fucking Richie..." he muttered.

"Hey! Are you guys all right?" Jimmy called out from the boat. He was bobbing helplessly on the yellow-foam bay, holding one oar in front of him like a spear.

"We're fucking roses," Ted snarled. He and Gary began making their way up toward the camp.

"What *was* that thing?" Jimmy asked.

Patrick frowned down at the dead creature. He nudged it with the toe of his shoe. The corpse made a *thunk* when he tapped it. "Something we should have seen coming," Patrick said, sizing up the creature.

"What's that supposed to mean?" Jimmy asked.

Patrick frowned. "Swimmers are also runners now."

8.

"Wait. You're saying that the *fish* are—?" Gary asked uncertainly.

"*Not* zombies," Patrick said quickly. "They're the…you know. The drugged-out, metal-skull, hungry people who act like zombies, but who are definitely *not* zombies."

"We call them zombies," Richie offered.

Patrick motioned to Richie. "Can I murder him?" he asked Gary seriously.

Gary considered this. "It's your crew," he finally decided.

"You're marked for death," Patrick said, pointing at Richie. "Don't let me forget."

Gary, Patrick, Lawrence, and Richie had all piled into the dinghy that Johnny had paddled back to the shore, and now they were slowly making their way across the water, heading toward the yacht. Being the only one with any sort of formal medical training, Johnny had stayed behind with Ted on the beach, tending to his mangled leg. Brett loomed behind them, providing cover from any post-apocalyptic eventualities that might arise while the mending proceeded.

Gary gripped the edge of the boat and peered down into the water. "You think there are more of them down there? The fish monsters?"

Patrick nodded. "As best I can tell, people turn into runners when they ingest concentrated amounts of Monkey Dust—snorting it, shooting it, whatever. Look how thickly it's settled on the water." He waved with one hand as the other men gazed out over the surface of the ocean. The greenish-yellow foam was so thick that it had formed a crust in some places. "This dust has been in the water for years now. It makes sense that fish have taken it into their gills like crazy. At their size, the transformation is bound to happen a whole lot faster than it does in humans." Patrick crossed his arms, fighting off a sudden chill. "My guess is, half the fish in the ocean are probably dusters by now."

The men all drew themselves back from the edges of the boat.

"Great," Richie muttered. "Now we have to be scared of *fish*, too."

"I've always been scared of fish," Lawrence said.

The others turned to look at him. They blinked.

"What?" Lawrence asked.

"You've...*always* been scared of fish?" Gary asked.

"I thought you were the 'good in a scrape' guy," Patrick said.

Lawrence shrugged. "Not good in a fish attack." He nodded back toward the beach. "Say what you want. Looks like I was ahead of the curve."

"I think it's worth noting, it's probably not *just* fish," Patrick added. "There are a lot of animals with a lot of access to a lot of Monkey Dust around here."

It was an uncomfortable thought to process.

Richie pulled on the oar and they glided through the water. The mist whipped and swirled like autumn leaves in a storm, blocking out the sunlight and casting the ship before them in a shadowy gloom. The Sea Ray 58 had once been a sleek, sparkling craft, with a handsome navy-blue hull and a gleaming white body. It had once been smooth, and new, and impressive. But that was years ago, before M-Day.

The boat hadn't fared well in the apocalypse.

The hull was covered with thick, slimy sea gunk and frosted with hard, yellow-green flecks. The fiberglass was stained with grime and blood, in dark, lumpy smears that coated the boat from stem to stern. The windows around the captain's cabin had been smashed; jagged points stabbed out from the frame like the teeth of a small shark. Many of them were stained with blood. *Most* of them were stained with blood, in fact.

The metal railing around the deck had exploded outward, the steel twisted to oblivion, as if the Kool-Aid Man had blown right through it. One of the bent bars dipped loosely down into the water, tapping against the hull as the boat rocked on the waves. The deep sound was muffled by the water. It was the only sound they could hear, bobbing on the ocean, surrounded by the mist.

"What's the plan?" Gary whispered. His eyes were wide and restless with anxiety.

"We board the boat," Patrick said. Though he made his voice sound confident, it took effort. There was something undeniably spooky about the abandoned Sea Ray.

"Think it still runs?" Richie asked at full volume.

"Shh!" Patrick and Gary hissed at the same time, though neither of them could have said why they felt the need for quiet.

Richie lifted his hands in confusion. "What?" he asked.

"It probably doesn't run," Patrick said. "Even if the engine is still good, any gas in the tank is bound to be useless by now."

Lawrence frowned. "Then what do we do? he asked. "Sail it to the Gulf?"

"If you're into semantics, we're not going to sail it," Patrick replied, eyeing the boat carefully. "We're going to drive it. The only thing I know how to sail is a heart-shaped Jacuzzi, and I'll tell you, I'm shocked I was able to manage that."

"Okay. So…how?" Lawrence needled. He glanced around uncomfortably, looking for fish monsters in the water. "I didn't come out here for nothing."

"No. You came out here to bond with your favorite post-apocalyptic mechanical engineer," Patrick snapped. "If the engine's in good-enough shape, I should be able to modify it to use a different kind of fuel. We'll need some tools and supplies, but nothing we shouldn't be able to find lying—"

Patrick was interrupted by a loud creaking sound from within the belly of the boat. The Red Caps exchanged uneasy glances.

"Probably just the bones of the craft," Patrick said doubtfully. "Just… settling. Like houses do."

Lawrence scooted forward in the dinghy and cracked his knuckles. Now that they were about to dock at a mini-yacht that held any number of unknown dangers, they were officially in his wheelhouse. And also, he desperately wanted out of the dinghy. If he was going to be floating above an ocean full of mutant fish, he wanted to do it in the biggest boat he could find. "Get me closer. I'll go first."

Richie rowed them up against the side of the Sea Ray. Lawrence jumped out and grabbed the side of the bigger boat with both hands. In one smooth, easy motion, he pulled himself over the edge and disappeared onto the deck of the yacht.

"I should have gone first," Patrick frowned, clamoring along in the dinghy and bumbling toward the Sea Ray. "Now I'm going to look ridiculous by comparison." He motioned at Richie, who dropped his oar and carefully sidled up alongside Patrick, trying not to rock the boat. "Give me a boost," he said grumpily.

Richie laced his fingers together and held them near Patrick's foot. Patrick put one hand on Richie's shoulder and the other on the side of the Sea Ray. Then he lifted his right foot and placed it squarely in Richie's finger net. "If you drop me, I'm aiming for your head on my way back down," he warned.

Richie nodded. He struggled under Patrick's weight as he worked to heft him toward the boat. "I thought you'd be lighter," he admitted. Beads of sweat were already squeezing out of the pores of his forehead.

"My head weighs fifty pounds!" Patrick cried, shifting crazily on the uneven foundation of Richie's hands. "Hold still!"

"My hands are delicate!" Richie whined.

Gary hurried over, moving unsteadily in the rocking boat as he lifted Patrick's left foot with his hands. He looked at Richie and nodded. "Ready? One…two…"

"Wait—be gentle!" Patrick said, but they had already reached three.

Together, Richie and Gary shoved him clumsily over the side of the yacht. Patrick pitched forward, his hands flailing, and he crashed onto the deck of the boat.

"You okay?" Gary asked.

"Fine," Patrick mumbled, picking himself up. "My nose broke my fall."

He brushed himself off and scanned the deck of the boat. Through the fog, he peered down toward the rear and saw the silhouette of Lawrence disappear around the corner. The Red Cap was headed swiftly into the depths of the boat.

Patrick followed cautiously, unnerved by the silence as he glanced through the shifting clouds. He reached down and pulled out the hammer he'd slipped into his belt loop. He twirled it in his hand, letting the weight of it settle into his grip. "This is fine," he said to himself, his voice quiet even to his own ears as the mist muffled it. "This is almost definitely fine."

Hammer raised, he stepped toward the back of the boat and the staircase that descended into darkness.

9.

Patrick tightened his grip on the hammer as he peered into the cabin. It was empty.

He breathed a sigh of relief and turned the corner, slipping through the entryway that had lost its door somewhere in the flux of the apocalypse. He crept through the shadows, feeling his way along the broken cabinets and ripped-up bench seats until he reached the staircase, a rectangular void in the floor that disappeared into absolute darkness below.

"Lawrence?" he called quietly, trying to quiet his heart as it hammered against his chest. "You down there?"

His ears tingled as they reached for a response, the fine hairs within bristling with anticipation. His sweaty palm slipped against the worn handle of the hammer, so he tightened his grip. The scar on his belly prickled and burned.

Patrick's throat was so dry, he could barely hear his next utterance as it scratched through his own mouth: "Lawrence?"

"What?"

Patrick jumped, nearly cracking himself in the forehead with his hammer. He closed his eyes and swore quietly under his breath.

"*What?*" Lawrence repeated from the darkness below.

"Nothing," Patrick said, wiping his hands on his jeans. "Just making sure you weren't eaten by a boat monster." He carefully descended the stairs, checking for each new step with his toe before stepping down. "I never appreciated electric lights enough," he decided aloud, feeling his way into the room with his free hand. "You ever think about that? About how we should have appreciated lights?"

"I'd appreciate some light right now," Lawrence grumbled from the far end of the room. Patrick's eyes were adjusting to the darkness. He could make out Lawrence's shape as he crept across the near-black space. "Feel around, see if you can find a flashlight or something."

"A flashlight!" Patrick grimaced. "Why didn't we bring a flashlight?! What in the absolute world is going on with my brain?"

The boat creaked as Gary took a few steps down into the hull of the boat. "Good thing you've got me," he said. He flipped on the solar-powered emergency flashlight he'd rummaged out of his tent. Though the beam was weak, it seemed bright as the sun in that darkness.

Patrick shielded his eyes and squinted hard against the glare. "Very helpful," he said. "Maybe too bright, but very helpful." He turned away and blinked hard, waiting for his eyes to readjust to the new illumination. As the red halo faded from his vision, the interior of the Sea Ray came into focus. He felt his whole body relax. They were alone. He and Gary were at one end; Lawrence was at the other. He looked annoyed by the sudden shift of light. There was nothing but a couple dozen feet of empty air between them.

Patrick breathed a sigh of relief. "If there's one thing I've learned," he said, stepping forward through the cabin, "it's that a dark room that you hoped would be empty is always better when it actually *is* empt–*oh fuck!*"

"What?" Lawrence turned just in time to see the thing that had been lurking silently in the corner leap across the room and slash his throat wide open.

Patrick stared in horror as Gary's light caught Lawrence's body in its beam…his eyes turning confused, his muscles going slack, his body collapsing on itself as a bright red spray exploded from the gash in his neck. Lawrence fell to his knees, then onto his side. His body fluttered on the floor, blood spraying out of his neck in short bursts and pumping out his life into the darkness of the boat in slower and slower pulses.

The thing that had slashed his neck landed in a crouch in the corner, the sharp blade in its hand held up against the flashlight. The creature was framed in the dim glare, and Patrick gasped in horror; it was a young woman, with oily, tangled hair falling in front of her eyes. Her clothes hung ragged on her emaciated body, her teeth bared between her lips as she snarled. Her eyes were wild, and they burned with anger.

For interminable seconds, she held Patrick's eyes, her cold fury striking like flint against his horror. Then she broke the connection, turning her head toward the twitching heap of meat that used to be Lawrence. She leapt across his body like a panther, then sank her teeth into the oozing flesh of his throat.

"Jesus Christ!" Patrick screamed. He stumbled backward, his arms flailing. He crashed into Gary, who was pale as a statue and rooted to the floor in fear. "Move!" Patrick shrieked, turning and shoving Gary toward the staircase. "Fucking *move!*"

But just as Gary found his feet, another woman dropped through the hole above, with an identical blade glinting between her fingers. She swiped at Gary's throat. Patrick grabbed the Red Cap by the shirt and yanked him backward, the blade missing his neck by centimeters.

Patrick pulled Gary into the darkness of the hull, stumbling blindly backward. He smashed into a chair and fell, dragging Gary with him. The woman who had killed Lawrence remained hunched over his body, tearing at his skin with her sharp fingers, yanking off pieces of his flesh and stuffing them into her mouth. Lawrence's blood made her cheeks shine.

The second woman launched forward, swinging her knife in wide arcs. Patrick pushed Gary toward the front of the boat as he rolled to his left. Gary slammed into a bed frame, crying out as he fell onto the mattress. The box spring squeaked like a rusty swing set as the woman turned and slashed blindly in the darkness.

Patrick got his feet beneath him and pushed forward, ramming his shoulder into the small of her back. It was like tackling a pillowcase full of sticks. As skinny as Patrick was, he nearly doubled her weight. When he drove his shoulder into her, he heard her spine crack.

The woman didn't scream. She only made a frustrated, whimpering grunt. But her body went slack, and she hit the ground hard, landing on her outstretched hand The bones in her wrist cracked then too, and she dropped the blade held in her free hand. It clattered to the floor at Patrick's feet.

"Go!" Patrick commanded. He dove forward and snatched the knife as Gary, still too shocked to speak, pushed up from the mattress and ran toward the watery light of the stairwell. He clamored up the steps as Patrick pushed him from behind, urging him to move.

They burst through the floor of the cabin so quickly that Gary didn't notice the third woman until the edge of her machete had hacked into the meat of his shoulder. She stood just behind the stairwell opening, straddling the open door that allowed access to the hull. The machete in her hands was dull and didn't cut very deep. Still, it hurt like hell. Gary yelled as he tried to wrestle himself free of the blade.

Patrick burst up through the doorway wielding his hammer. He swung it in a tight arc, connecting just beneath the woman's ribs. The air rushed out of her lungs, and she fell backward. She kept a firm grip on the handle of the machete, the metal twisting as she yanked it out of Gary's skin.

The wound widened a bit, a stream of blood beginning to flow down his shirtsleeve.

Patrick pushed Gary forward again, shoving him toward the door. Gary moved slowly clutching his injured shoulder, his eyes glassy and strange. "Move!" Patrick screamed. He heard a scraping sound over his right shoulder and turned to see the woman limping forward. He rammed Gary through the doorway, then turned and swung the hammer at the machete as the woman slashed it at his head. The two weapons met with a dull *clonk*, a cloud of rust shattering from the machete blade. A rusty cloud fell into Patrick's eyes and he blinked furiously, tears welling up and masking his vision. He dropped the hammer, rubbing at his eyes as his free hand pulled the knife from his belt. He swung it blindly in the woman's direction, which was enough to keep her back until his vision cleared. When it did, he saw was her charging at him with the machete raised above her head, her sharp teeth bared and her tangled hair flying out behind her.

Patrick didn't think or hesitate. He pulled back his arm, turned his shoulder, and drove his fist straight into the bridge of the woman's nose. The *CRACK* of breaking bone echoed through the cabin. The woman's head jerked back, but her legs kept moving forward, forcing her into a backward somersault in the air as she crashed head-first to the floor.

"What the *fuck?*" she shrieked. Her nose gushed with blood. She looked up at Patrick, her eyes angry...and hungry. "*Fuck you*—you punched me in the *face!*"

Patrick heaved as he caught his breath. "Oh my God—I'm sorry. I shouldn't have done that. That didn't feel right. I'm sorry. You were just... boy, I don't know; you're a woman. I don't think I should have done that." Then he realized that she had been trying to kill him just a second before, and below deck, this woman's friend was literally ripping the flesh from Lawrence's bones. "Wait—Fuck *you!* Your friend is literally *eating* my friend! I'm *glad* I punched you in the face!"

He picked up the hammer, flipping the door to the bottom deck closed with his foot. It fell hard, sealing the two women below in total darkness. Near the handle, Patrick saw a catch that sat flush with a metal loop set into the floor. He didn't find a padlock nearby, but he had a hammer... He bludgeoned the metal catch as hard as he could, twisting it over the loop and smashing them both into a lumpy metal tangle. It wouldn't be impossible for the woman with the broken nose to pry it open, but it would take time. With any luck, Patrick hoped, the things below would eventually turn and eat each other to death.

But that was unlikely. Lawrence was enough meat to keep them satisfied for a while.

He stared at the woman whose nose he'd smashed, cowering in the corner yet glaring up at him with rage. "This world is fucking broken," he said bitterly.

Then he left the cabin, joined the others in the boat, and sat quietly as Richie rowed them back to shore.

10.

"What happened?" Ben asked.

Patrick plopped down on the couch and covered his face with a pillow. "Nothing," he mumbled into the fabric.

"Your leg's half gone," Ben pointed out.

"It's not half gone."

"It's partially gone."

"It's not any gone. It's just bleeding."

"It's bleeding a lot," Ben pointed out. "All over my couch."

Patrick pulled the pillow off his face. "I thought this was my couch." He looked around, confused. "Is this—? Whose apartment are we in?"

"You're in my apartment. Where I live. On a couch I used to like to sit on."

"I thought this was my couch," Patrick repeated. He placed the pillow back over his face.

"Your couch is two miles away from here. Patrick, how much blood have you lost?"

Patrick waved lazily at the floor. "Such much."

Ben pulled his phone from his pocket and tapped the screen. "Should I call Annie or an ambulance?"

"Better make it Annie."

"Boy, she's going to hate this," Ben sighed, opening up his contacts. He tapped on her name and walked into the bathroom while the number rang. He returned a minute later with a first aid kit. "Voicemail," he said.

"Lucky."

Ben sat down and rolled Patrick's pant leg up over his calf. "Jesus, Pat! What did you do?"

"I was walking to the train, but the sidewalk was closed 'cause they were tearing up the road."

"And you didn't go around?"

"I hate to backtrack." Patrick winced as Ben dribbled hydrogen peroxide over the hole in his ankle. "It wasn't very wide. I was like, 'I can clear that.'"

"And let me guess: You didn't clear it."

"Benny Boy, I did not clear it. I landed on rebar."

"Shit, Pat."

Patrick held up his hand, pinching his thumb and forefinger close together. "It was a small rebar."

"I hope you're up on your tetanus shots."

"Tetanus? I barely know us."

"Oh no...all your funny leaked out," Ben frowned.

"We'll look back on it and laugh later," Patrick decided.

Ben sighed. He squeezed a blob of Neosporin onto the wound, then he wrapped it carefully in bandages. "Do you think you'll make good decisions someday?"

"I hope so."

"Me too. You're gonna be a dad, in like two weeks."

"Three months," Patrick corrected him. "Plenty of time."

Ben's phone buzzed. "Great. It's Annie."

"Tell her I'm fine."

"I'm telling her she owes me a couch."

Ben wandered off to explain things to Annie as Patrick dropped the pillow and gazed up at the ceiling. "It's your funeral," he said.

The white popcorn finish began to spin, and then it was sucked up into the sky, and the room went with it, and the couch did too. A different kind of world was revealed behind it, like a curtain was rising. He was on the beach, splayed out on the sand, shivering, damp, and exhausted.

"You okay?"

Patrick turned his head and saw Gary sitting close by, pressing a dirty towel to the wound on his shoulder. "Yeah. I guess. I don't know."

Gary grunted. "Okay. It just seemed like you were somewhere else."

"I've had a couple of these...memories. Dream-like." Patrick sat up and brushed the sand off his arms. "But not actual dreams. Just weird memories. Out of nowhere. That feel real."

"Huh." Gary lifted the towel and checked his shoulder. He grimaced at what he saw. "Well. We all have memories," he said.

"That is universally true," Patrick sighed.

"The way things are now," Gary proposed, "they might as well be dreams."

That was true as well.

•

Patrick and the Red Caps held a memorial of sorts for Lawrence on the beach. Jimmy drew the short stick, winning the unpleasant task of sorting the dead man's belongings into two piles; one pile was for things they could use, and one pile was for things that had only meant something to Lawrence. They kept his clothes, his knife, and his compass, and a few other items they thought might be worth something. Everything else was piled on the sand. It was a strange mix: a well-used handkerchief, a Don Mattingly baseball card, a medallion of St. Michael, a pen that didn't work, a 1998 Nashville Predators schedule, an unopened packet of hot sauce, a ring with two keys, a pet I.D. tag for a dog named Highball, and Lawrence's old wallet, with his driver's license, his credit cards, his medical insurance, and a 2012 pass to the Children's Museum of Memphis.

"He must have had a kid," Jimmy said, surprised. He ran his finger over the museum pass. "I didn't know that."

"He told me once," Gary said gruffly. "He was drunk on rotgut, somewhere on the rail. He had a boy—Aaron. Or Adam. Six, I think. He lost him on M-Day."

Jimmy closed his hands around the card. "Why didn't he ever talk about him?" he wondered.

"It's…" Patrick started. He cleared his throat. Then, he rubbed his eyes. "It's not the kind of thing that just comes up."

Gary squeezed Patrick's shoulder as Jimmy slipped the card back into Lawrence's wallet and laid it on top of the pile. They covered the pile in sticks and dry seaweed and lit it on fire with one precious match. They looked out past the fire as it grew, at the Sea Ray, with its devils and bones. The heat sent waves through the air that distorted the yacht and made it look like a hallucination. Then the fire went out, before anything had really burned away. So they dug a hole in the sand and pushed the things in instead, covering it all without another word.

Later that evening, Ted sat rigidly on the beach, his arms folded, chewing his lip and staring out at the Sea Ray. It bobbed quietly in the water, looking innocent and harmless. "I can't stay here," he said. "I can't keep seeing that thing. Knowing what's in there."

Richie nodded vigorously. "What if they're still hungry? Or pissed off that you hit them or stabbed them or whatever? They could come for us."

"I don't think I'll be able to sleep," Jimmy said.

"Not too keen on it myself," Gary admitted.

"*And* there's the whole mutant fish-monster thing," Ted added.

Brett spat into the sand. "Too fuckin' quiet here, anyway," he said, wiping his lips.

The Red Caps all turned and looked at Patrick, their newly-appointed leader, waiting for word of what they should do next.

Their collective gaze finally drew his attention.

"What?" he asked, raising his hands.

"You tell us," Gary said.

Patrick stood and brushed the sand from his pants. "Well, I've been ready to leave since we got here."

11.

"We've got about two hours 'til sunset," Gary guessed. "If we're gonna move, it should be soon."

The crew had packed up their camp and moved up the beach, to a spot over the grassy dunes. They could still hear the splash of the waves on the shore, but sitting low in the hills put the boat out of their line of sight. It didn't make any of them feel better, necessarily. But at least the Sea Ray was further away.

"I've been thinking about it," Patrick said, "and I have a plan,"

"Is it as bad as your last one?" Richie said bitterly.

Patrick scowled. But Richie wasn't wrong to ask.

He was just an asshole.

"I don't know—maybe. You're welcome to join me and you're just as welcome to stay behind. Once more, for the record: I'm grateful for the help, but I did not ask to be part of this group."

"We're with you," Gary assured him as he shot Richie a look.

"You want a safety guarantee?" Brett asked. "You're in the wrong apocalypse." He hocked a wad of phlegm near Richie's shoes, and that was the end of that.

"So what's the plan?" Gary asked.

Patrick pulled out a thick knob of paper and unfolded it on the grass. It was a map of the United States, heavily creased and covered in pencil marks.

"Is that Lawrence's map?" Ted frowned.

"It was," Gary answered. He nodded for Patrick to continue.

"Okay," Patrick began, "it's safe to assume we all agree that traveling by sea is out—yes?" The Red Caps nodded. None of them were particularly interested in taking their chances on the open ocean. Not anymore. "Since your collective reputation as absolute savages precedes you, traveling by rail is out, too. And heading back the way we came is a no-go, for the same reason. We need a new path." He pointed to a spot near the middle of the map. "And I think it's here."

The Red Caps furrowed their brows. "Kentucky?" Richie said.

Brett snorted. "Tennessee, genius."

Patrick nodded. "Asheville, Tennessee, specifically."

Gary held up two fingers. "Sorry. I thought you wanted to go back to Mobile."

"Yes. Alabama is the goal, but Asheville is the key. Look." Patrick tapped the map, indicating their current location. "We're here; we can avoid the trains by going southwest, but then we're cutting a long path right through the Smokies."

"I'm not sure my leg could handle mountains," Ted said sadly. He pointed at his bandage to remind everyone how injured he was.

"True. And it would take a long time to go over that range. But…if we cut west," and Patrick traced his finger along the map to trace his imagined route, "we can get to Asheville regardless. Still some mountains to cover, but not nearly as many."

"But…that's *north* and west," Jimmy pointed out. "Wrong direction."

"It's a *little* north, yes—thank you, Johnny," Patrick sniped. "But it's the kind of wrong direction that'll save us a lot of time."

"I still don't follow," Gary said shortly, starting to get annoyed. "How does Asheville help us get to Mobile?"

Patrick wagged a thoughtful finger in the air. "At Asheville, we can swipe a boat and coast down a series of rivers. The highways of the Midwest. Look at the map. All these rivers connect. We can make it to the Mississippi, and that'll take us all the way to the Gulf."

The Red Caps tilted their heads and stared at the map. Most of them found it inscrutable.

"It works," Brett decided. "It's faster. Potentially a lot faster."

"We're back to finding a boat," Gary soured.

"But a *river* boat," Patrick clarified, "not an ocean boat. It doesn't have to be a *good* boat. Hell, it doesn't have to be a boat at all. You can float down the Mississippi on a raft made by a kid. There's a whole book about it."

Brett shrugged. "It checks out," he said.

"Are you serious? He just got Lawrence *killed* on a boat! Now we're going to follow him to a new boat? No way," Richie said, crossing his arms. "I hate it."

"I actually kind of like it," Jimmy decided. "It's a pretty good solution. I think I'm in."

"Me too," said Ted.

"Guess it's unanimous," said Gary.

"It's not," whined Richie.

Patrick folded up the map and stuffed it into his bag. "I appreciate your trust. Really. What happened to Lawrence was…" The words left him, carried away on empty breath. "You know. It was…"

"Horrible," Brett said.

"Scarring," Jimmy agreed.

"The stuff of nightmares," Ted added, shivering.

"And not your fault," Gary said finally. "It rips my guts out. Lawrence is the one who found me, out there wandering. He's the one who brought me to the train. Changed my life. Gave me something. You know? He saved my life. But, shit. This isn't new. We've all lost people, and I'm sure we'll lose more. It's this place. It wasn't you."

"But it was *my* decision," Patrick said softly. He squirmed against the too-familiar gnaw of guilt in his stomach.

"And if it's ever your *fault*, we'll tell you," Ted said, trying to be helpful.

Patrick sighed. "Please do."

"And then we'll put your head on a stick," Brett added.

Patrick gulped. "Good to know." He glanced up at the sky. The light was starting to fade in the west. "If we want to be out of enemy territory by nightfall, we'd better get moving."

"More walking," Ted groaned. Most of the others grunted their dismal agreement as they picked up their packs.

Jimmy brightened up as he raised a finger. "Actually, I went exploring the boardwalk earlier. I think I found something that could make the trip easier!"

"It had better be either tequila or women," Brett said.

"Both would be great," Richie hoped.

"Even better," Jimmy beamed. "I found a beach bike rental hut, and some of the bikes still work!"

Brett threw a rock at Jimmy's head, and everyone agreed it was the right thing to do. Rental bikes were nowhere near as good as tequila.

12.

Brett smiled and closed his eyes as he sailed through the warm breeze, his hair blowing in the wind. The bike's rainbow streamers tickled against his wrists. The sweet, floral fragrance of wild yellow jessamine filled his nose as he pumped his legs powerfully, smoothly, relishing the movement of gliding along the interstate. He slipped through the mist on his cotton candy pink bike, feeling free and fast, alone and remarkable. He lifted his hands from the handlebars and sailed along the pavement with his chest lifted to the setting sun.

Then he hit a deep pothole, skidded out of control, ricocheted off a tractor trailer, and flew off the bike, smashing head-first into the rusty metal guardrail.

"Fuck this shit," he spat, pressing his hand against the lump forming on his head.

"Toe pick, *bitch!*" Richie screeched as he sped past, howling with laughter. His laughter abruptly changed into an, "Oh, shit!" as he clipped a Prius and went flying over the handlebars and sailing over the car. He skidded to a rough stop on the asphalt.

"Have these guys ever ridden bikes before?" Patrick asked, navigating cars and potholes and hardened piles of M-Day victims he was actively forcing his brain to ignore.

Gary just shrugged. He was too focused on trying not to wreck himself.

In crash-along fashion, they inched their way along Highway 74. They hadn't made much progress by the time the sun had set, but they were on the road, with a maze-barrier of cars between them and the ocean. They stopped and made camp beneath an overpass somewhere in the overgrown wild of North Carolina, trying not to think too much about the coyotes that howled in the distance.

It had been a hell of a day. No one ate much. No one said much. No one cared much. They set up their bedrolls, they closed their eyes, and they left the ocean behind.

•

Patrick awoke to a tiny finger tapping on his head.

"Snzzh-*stop!*" he snorted awake, swatting at the hand.

"He ain't dead!" a small voice gasped.

Patrick opened his eyes. Through the mid-morning gloom of his tent, he could just make out two small shapes standing near the open flap. He blinked away his fitful sleep as the shapes resolved into the scared forms of two children, a girl and a boy, holding hands and shaking.

"What's going on?" Patrick asked, his brain fumbling awake. "Are you okay?"

"Our mama's stuck," the girl said, her thick Southern accent hushed with fear.

The boy nodded. "She's gonna get eaten up."

Patrick blinked. He blinked again. "I should probably go wake up the guys."

No one in the camp had slept well that night. It took a few minutes for the whole crew to break through the morning fog. But eventually, they fell into motion. Ted and Richie stayed behind with the kids, while Patrick led the rest of the Red Caps up the embankment and across an old cow pasture, heading in the direction the little girl had pointed.

"What the hell did they mean, she's stuck?" Gary grumbled, kicking through the cold tangle of dead grass that pulled at their feet.

"I'm a little more concerned about the 'eaten up' part," Jimmy frowned.

"You don't think the fish-monster followed us, do you?" Patrick asked.

No one thought it was funny.

They jumped over a small creek and carefully worked their way through the lines of a barbed wire fence that bordered a property line which used to mean something to someone. This far into the apocalypse, the fence was rusty, the barbs flaking orange dust when disturbed. Patrick heard Ben's voice echo in his head again. *Hope you're up on your tetanus.*

He sighed.

The Red Caps had climbed up the ravine they found on the other side when Brett stopped them. He crouched down in the grass, motioning for everyone else to do the same.

"What is it?" Patrick whispered.

Brett pointed ahead at two dark shapes near the far end of the field. No one couldn't quite make out the details; they saw only figures bobbing like leaves on water.

"Not sure," Brett said. "Just be careful."

"And here I thought we'd just charge in screaming," Gary snorted.

They crept further across the field, staying low to the ground. The tall, dry grass crunched underfoot as they made their way along the fence line. After a few dozen yards, the dark silhouettes began to take shape.

"Oh," Patrick frowned. "Well, that's not good."

One of the figures was the carcass of a coyote that had gotten tangled in the barbed wire. By the looks of it, the cause of death was a slow bleed. A few feet away was the body of a woman. "Is this…" Brett asked.

"Their mother," Patrick finished. She'd met the same fate as the coyote. Her limbs hung down from the wire like a tortured scarecrow.

Gary spat into the field. "Must've got caught up while running from the wolf."

"It's not a wolf," Jimmy said.

"Whatever it is."

Patrick stepped wide around the dead coyote and knelt down next to the woman. He cleared the grass away from her dangling torso. "Hey, Jimmy. You're a doctor."

"Sort of."

Patrick watched her chest rise. "Do dead people usually breathe like this?"

"Oh shit." Jimmy hurried over and gently pressed two fingers against her neck. "She's alive," he confirmed.

The woman lifted her head and gasped as Jimmy screamed. "Help me," she said, her voice wet. She coughed up a chunk of blood-twinged mucous and spat it into the grass. "Please…"

The others ran over and set about the careful work of untangling her body from the twisted metal wire. The woman grimaced and grunted whenever they put pressure on the wrong places. Patrick fumbled apologies as he pulled a loop of wire open so they could slide her leg out of it. The shifting caused the wire around her wrist to tighten, a new line of blood leaking from the wound that opened on the back of her hand.

After long minutes of painstaking and painful work, the woman slipped free from the fence and collapsed onto the ground. "Thank you," she whispered, breathing heavily.

Patrick and Brett supported her on either side as they slowly walked back to the highway. The children ran to her with a mix of fear and relief. The woman's color flushed back to her face when she saw them. Her energy surged as she pulled them in close, crying and kissing their heads and ignoring her own wounds.

The family stayed with the Red Caps that night. The woman was soft and buoyant with the children, but her bones turned to steel when she spoke to the men, and she made no secret of the fact that she wore a hunting knife high in her boot. She allowed Jimmy to dress her wounds, but she watched him with eyes of fire and hardly blinked the whole time. She gave her name as Sarah, though judging by the confused looks on the children's faces, that was probably a lie. The Red Caps carried the conversation around the fire that night, telling stories and telling jokes and apologizing when they got too blue for children's ears, which was every few minutes or so. When they made their introductions, Brett cut in on Patrick and said, "But he likes to be called the apocalypticon."

Patrick's head jerked back. "How did you know that?" he demanded.

Brett snorted. "You kept talking about it in your sleep, all through your fever. *I am the apocalypticon…so sayeth the apocalypticon.*"

"The whole train ride up the coast," Ted confirmed.

"Like, constantly," Richie nodded.

Patrick frowned. "Well, that is embarrassing."

"What's an ahca-lypticon?" the young girl asked, her face pinched with confusion.

"The apocalyptic icon," Brett said, rolling his eyes. "The end of the world's most perfect survivor."

"So far, still alive," Patrick pointed out.

"Somehow," Brett reluctantly agreed.

"And you're the one in charge?" Sarah asked, her voice thick with doubt.

"They just keep following me," Patrick explained.

Sarah looked at him, unblinking. "I probably would have died on the fence if you hadn't come."

Patrick nodded. "Well," he said. "Happy to help."

The day passed. They stayed close to camp, trying to make Sarah and her children comfortable, while wondering if they should let themselves be comfortable with Sarah and her children. Night fell. They ate their dinner, and then they turned in. They gave the small family the good tent, the one with the floor, and Richie sulked off to sleep in the field. The next morning, they woke to find Sarah and the children gone. She had stolen some of their food, though not much. The crew didn't mind. They'd have given her more, if she had told them they were leaving. The family also took three bikes, which caused a few grumbles. In the end, though, the Red Caps agreed that the kids were better off riding than grown men. They eventually stopped complaining and packed their things and set off down the road on foot.

Behind one of the tents they found a note, scribbled onto the highway with the chalk-white edge of a rock:

THANK YOU APOCALYPTICON.

13.

They pushed on toward Asheville, where they'd catch the river that would be their salvation. The highway had been a hell of a lot more popular on M-Day than it was now. They had walked all day and hadn't seen a single other person…but the road itself was littered with hundreds of dead cars and dead remains that they had to weave their ways around as they trekked across North Carolina. "Boy, there sure are a lot of dead-chunks on this road," Richie frowned.

"Dead chunks?" Jimmy asked.

"Yeah, you know. The chunky shit all the people turned into. Dead-chunks." Richie scuffed his boot through a hardened black lump. "It's all over the highway!"

"You shouldn't do that," Ted said, giving Richie a nudge. "That's a person."

Richie grimaced down at the dead-goop lump. "That is not a person."

"You know what I mean."

"Show some respect," Gary said. "Jesus, Richie."

"Who cares?" Richie rolled his eyes. He pointed to the city limit sign. "It's just Charlotte."

Patrick pressed on in front of the pack, pretending not to hear them. Fighting tooth and claw inside his own brain to box out the mental image of Izzy—of her *after*. Of what had become of his whole heart, the perfect piece of him that had been embodied in a small human frame that loved hot dogs and Telly Monster and Pteranodons and zerberts. The piece that was so fragile, in the end.

"Hey. You okay?"

Patrick looked up. Ben's eyebrows were arched in the weird, off-kilter way they got whenever he was genuinely and hopelessly concerned.

"Not really," Patrick admitted.

Ben squirmed. "Well. I don't like that."

"You don't like what?"

"Emotions," Ben frowned. "And how they make people feel."

Patrick nodded. "Okay."

Ben sighed. "No...I don't mean it like that. Shit. Okay, come on." He beckoned Patrick with his hands. "Hit me."

Patrick slid his half-empty glass across the bar, from one hand to the other and back again. "I mean, I'm okay," he affirmed. "I mean, I'm great, actually. Izzy started crawling last week. Which doesn't sound like a major feat when you've been able to walk for, like, thirty-five years. But it's pretty awesome to watch her go."

Ben nodded. "Okay. She does bare-minimum human stuff now. That's cool."

"And on Monday, she said 'dog'!"

"Really?"

"Well, she didn't say 'dog' exactly, but I'm pretty sure she said, 'oggo,' which is short for doggo, which she probably thinks is how you say dog. It's wild. She's already talking."

"She's not," Ben said flatly, taking a sip of his beer. "But it's cool that you think she is. So, again, tell me: What's the problem?"

"There's no problem," Patrick insisted.

"Yet when you say those words, your voice sounds like someone's about to hit your penis with a hammer."

Patrick frowned. "There's a lot about that sentence I do not like."

"Don't make me find a hammer."

"It's a dumb thing," Patrick sighed.

"Yes, I assumed."

Patrick stared into the amber liquid in his glass. The beer was getting warm. "It's just—well, it's starting to dawn on me exactly how many ways there are to really screw up your child for life."

"Childhood is a real smorgasbord of trauma," Ben agreed.

"Herdee-verdee-traumer!"

Ben blinked. "Did you just Swedish Chef your trauma?"

"Yes. But to be fair, the Swedish Chef trauma-ed me first."

"It's the hands, isn't it?"

"It's the fucking hands!" Patrick cried. "Why are they human?!"

"Rare misstep by Jim Henson. Now, in what way do you think are you screwing up your kid?"

"I don't know! That's the whole thing—I don't know! I do everything I think I'm supposed to do, and it all seems to be working so far, she's not a blossoming serial killer or anything, as far as I can tell. But what about all the things I have no clue about? The human brain really logs some small stuff that later become big, beautiful trauma trees when you get older. The other day, Annie and I were arguing about the best way to clean Izzy's Bear-Bear—damp cloth or full washing machine—and it wasn't a huge argument or anything. But I got so frustrated because I haven't slept in six months, so I slammed Bear-Bear down on the coffee table, and Izzy saw it, and she just started bawling. So now I'm the dad who physically abuses her best—and at this moment in her life, her only friend!"

The bartender placed another beer in front of Patrick. "I didn't ask for this," he said.

"I know," she replied. She looked so concerned. "It's on me."

"Ugh." Patrick fell forward and banged his forehead on the bar. "Every single second is another moment in which I might accidentally, completely scar my daughter for life."

Ben shook his head, slowly and sadly. "What the fuck is a Bear-Bear?" he asked.

Patrick laughed. "It's weird to hear these words coming out of my own mouth, but I think you're actually going to be a great dad someday."

"Me?" Ben said, alarmed. "Oh, no. No thank you. Not for me."

"Someday you'll find the right gal, and all you'll want is to grow the substantial love that will surely exist between you, by creating a new human." Patrick tousled Ben's hair.

"Thanks, no," Ben grumbled, swatting Patrick's hand away. "Not in this life."

Patrick chuckled. "Well. Anyway." He picked up his new beer and took a sip. It was ice-cold and made him feel…new. A little, at least. "Here's to parents, huh?" He raised his glass. Ben picked up his and knocked it against his friend's.

"Cheers," he said.

"Cheers."

They sat quietly for the next few minutes, enjoying the day-drink and letting the happy sound of the lunchtime crowd wash over them. Patrick hadn't had a day-drink in months. It felt good to be out again, breaking a norm.

"You're doing great," Ben eventually said, breaking the white noise of the bar. "Izzy's going to be fine. If in doubt, teach her how to ride a bike. That's like 70% of parenting."

"It's not."

"Tell that to my dad Bill."

"Your dad's name was Phil."

"What he lacked in familiarity, he made up for in bike lessons."

"You're not making me feel better," Patrick frowned.

"You want to feel better, go to a therapist," Ben said, signaling the bartender for another round.

"Is that—?" Patrick looked around the bar, confused. "Is that not what this is?"

"Is what not what *what* is?" Gary said.

The bar evaporated, and Patrick was standing on the Carolinian interstate, surrounded by dead, dusty cars and yellow-green fog.

Patrick turned, confused. "Oh…" he said, his eyes adjusting to the midday glare, "Nothing."

"You okay?" Jimmy asked. He leaned in and inspecting Patrick's pupils. "You're all pale."

Patrick blinked. "I've always been pale."

"I mean, like, see-through pale. Translucent, at least."

"I'm fine, Johnny," Patrick said, waving Jimmy away. "I was having a normal, everyday full-mind-and-body hallucination, it's fine."

Jimmy frowned. "Let me know if they keep happening, will you?"

"I will not."

"Look alive, fellas," Brett called back from the front. He pointed up the highway. There was a single silhouette looming near the next overpass,. The person was waving them in.

"It's just one guy," Richie said. He pulled out the hatchet he carried in the side of his knapsack and gave it a few swings. "Shouldn't be a problem."

"You don't know it's a guy, and you don't know it's just one," Gary growled. "They could have a whole crew hiding behind the overpass."

"Yeah…if your brain worked as well as your bitch-baby cry-box, you might finally start reading at an eighth-grade level," Brett snorted at Ritchie.

"I don't even know what that means!" Richie screamed.

"Hey!" Gary hissed. "Can you idiots focus up and try not to get us killed? Spread out. Brett and Jimmy, take the embankment. Richie, get your ass up the hill and make sure the overpass is clear. Ted, you and me cut up the middle. Patrick, go talk to the person who appears to be one guy all by himself. And try to make sure he doesn't kill you."

"Wow, Take-Charge Gary is a real take-charge kind of guy," Patrick said, impressed.

Gary turned and stalked up the center of the highway, his iron pipe dangling from his hand and dragging behind him. "I just get so annoyed with them," he mumbled.

They moved up in formation, Patrick holding back while the others filtered into their spots. It didn't seem like the sharpest strategic move, since the person waving them in could very clearly see how they were dispersing. But he decided to let Gary have this moment.

When Patrick finally moved forward, he did so with his hands out to his sides, so the person could see that he wasn't a threat. As he got closer, the figure took color and form; he saw that it was indeed a man, an older man, with a wavy white beard and tufts of gray-white hair bursting out from beneath his fisherman cap. He held his hands up to show they were empty. He appeared to be wearing a poncho, which could have been hiding any manner of vile weaponry, but his cheeks were rosy, his eyes were kind and his smile twinkled. He had a whole Santa Claus vibe that Patrick couldn't help but trust. *If childhood whimsy gets me killed today, then adulthood was never really worth reaching,* he thought decisively.

"Hello there," Patrick called out when he was a few dozen yards away. "What are you doing?"

"Oh!" The man started hopping from one foot to the other, clearly very excited and very happy. "I'm so sorry to bother you! And your friends! They…spread out really well," he said, struggling to find a compliment. "I'm sorry to impose, but I…I need some help. Please don't threaten to stab me like the last guy did." He took a few quick steps, and frowning at the memory. "I can't give anything in return, so I guess I'm actually *begging* for your help."

"Help with what?" Patrick asked. He moved in closer.

The old man nodded and lowered his hands, smoothing out his poncho and trying to make himself presentable. "I was heading north, following that highway up there," he said, pointing to the overpass. "Got here yesterday and this band of angry young people surrounded me. They said a lot of words I didn't understand, to be honest with you. Slang, I guess. About poppin' off? And wildebeests?"

"If you're looking for a youth interpreter," Patrick said, "I should warn you: I was born in 1981."

"No, sorry. I just mean, it went badly. They shoved me around, and they took my pack. All my supplies. All my stuff." The old man shook his head. "What's gone is gone. But the worst thing they did…" He looked toward the heavens, pointing his finger at a streetlight overhead.

Patrick squinted up. "What am I looking for?" he asked. But as soon as the words had passed his lips, he saw it: a thin, gray ribbon swinging in the breeze, caught on the neck of the streetlight, near the spot where it widened into a bulb.

"It's a locket," the old man explained. "A cheap one. Dime-store links that I can't believe didn't turn her neck green. But it was my Edith's. Fifty-two years together, I almost never saw her take it off. Now it's up there," he said, nodding up at the lamppost. "And I can't bear it."

Patrick's shoulders relaxed. His body took on the heaviness of recognition. "You lost her," he said.

"On M-Day," the old man replied. "Spent more of my life with her than I ever did without her, even now. She's got our wedding photo in there. These kids, they…they made it a game. Took turns throwing it up there 'til one of them got it stuck." He pulled at his fingers and looked down at the highway, ashamed to show his tears. "I'd have given them everything I had just to get that locket back. But they took everything anyway. The only thing I need is up there, hanging over me."

Patrick squinted back up at the streetlight. "That's got to be eighty feet tall," he said.

The old man nodded sadly. "It's a tall one. Had to work for both this highway and the overpass, I reckon."

"I didn't even know they made them that tall."

"The arms of the youth possess so much strength," the old man said regrettably.

Patrick frowned. "I don't know how to climb poles."

"There's footholds every so often," the old man said, pointing up at the light post. "It's made for climbing."

"I'm terrified of heights."

"So was Edith," the old man wailed.

Patrick squirmed. "I *want* to help. It's just that I once lived on the fourth floor of an apartment building and I put a bike lock on my balcony doors so even guests couldn't go out there, just so I wouldn't have to see them standing out there. I'm not just afraid of heights, I am AFRAID of heights. And the first rung is, like, ten feet in the air. You'd need a ladder…I can't even get up there."

"I'll boost you." Brett had just strolled down the embankment, having found no other threat, and he sidled up next to Patrick. "I'll get you up there."

The old man beamed with joy, but Patrick swatted Brett's hand away. "Why don't *you* climb up there?" he demanded.

"Too powerful. Too big." Brett rubbed his arm. "My contours are all off. Guy like me can't get balance up there. It's a suicide mission. You gotta be lean and light to climb those poles. Gotta have a Juliette Lewis build."

He took a step back and eyed Patrick up and down. "Honestly, you were made for this role."

"Tell Richie to do it—he's lean and light!" Patrick pleaded.

"I can't touch metal," Richie called down from the hill. "It gets my dermatitis going."

"Gets his dermatitis going," Brett repeated.

"Please," the old man begged. Tears filled his eyes. He wore desperation like sweat on his collar. "No one will help me. *Please.*"

Patrick squinted at the old man. He squinted at Brett. He squinted at the pole. He squinted back at Brett. "Well, fuck it," he said angrily. "Let's get this over with."

Brett slapped Patrick on the back. "That's how you know you've met the apocalypticon," he said happily.

"Will you stop saying that?" Patrick hissed.

The old man frowned. "What's that?" he asked.

"I'll tell you while he's getting the necklace."

"No, you won't!" Patrick demanded.

Brett winked at the old man. "I will," he promised.

"Just boost me!"

Brett threaded his fingers together, and Patrick planted the toe of his shoe in the net. "Now, be steady, this is a precision—" Patrick started, and then Brett launched him into the air.

Patrick went flying toward the sky.

He screamed as he rocketed up into the air. His arms flailed until an elbow hooked over the lowest climbing rung, and he dangled there by one arm, screaming and wheezing and kicking his legs and screaming a whole lot more. "You should have let me die at Disney World!" he shrieked.

"You're doing great," the old man lied.

"No you're not!" Richie corrected him.

"Shut up, Richie!" Patrick scrambled to hug the pole, then shot his free hand up into the air and caught hold of the next rung. Like an especially awkward new-born bonobo, he swung out and slapped his free hand up toward the rung until he caught it firmly, which took five or six tries. His legs were now dangling below him. He tried to loop them over the lower rung, but his body was having trouble responding to his brain. So he just hung there like a comma, his ankles wrapped around the light post.

"I hate it here," he muttered under his breath.

He kicked out his left foot until it pushed against the bottom rung. He pulled himself into it and used the weight of his head to lever himself forward, pulling his right leg up behind him. He looked more like a desktop drinking bird than an icon of the apocalypse, but he finally managed to ease himself up to a standing position on the rung. There was a smattering of applause from the highway below, which he found incredibly patronizing. He would have glared at them if he'd trusted himself to look down without letting go and falling to his death. Instead, he climbed higher one rung at a time, inching up the street light as he drew closer and closer to the top.

Before long, he was at eye level with the overpass, a realization that sent his stomach into a lurch. But he kept going, even though his hands were sweaty and his feet were wet in his socks. He kept going up, up, up until he reached the top of the pole.

Holy hell, he thought. *I did it!*

The locket was hanging from the lamp itself, so Patrick had to stretch out over the highway to grab it. His fingers struggled, but the locket was just out of reach. With a deep and terrified breath, he lifted his left sneaker off its rung and leaned even further out, over the open air. His fingertips brushed against the fine metal chain, then grabbed it completely. In one powerful and desperate motion, he flung the necklace off the lamp. It went sailing out over the interstate. The crowd below cheered louder. This time, Patrick did feel a little pride.

Annoyed and scared out of his goddamn mind. But proudly.

Then the cheers from below faded into a dull ringing in his brain as it dawned on him that now he had to find a way to get down.

"If I drop, will you catch me?" he screamed at no one in particular. The question was met by silence. "I'm very mad at you," he informed them, loudly.

With no other option, he began easing himself down the rungs, moving slowly, searching for each next step down with the toe of his sneaker. His palms were so slick with sweat now that they slid horizontally across every rung. If the metal prongs hadn't angled 90 degrees at each end, he would have slipped right off the pole. The physics of the situation made his stomach lurch. He thought he might throw up.

He looked down to get his bearings. If he did hurl, he wanted to make sure it was onto Richie's head, if possible.

Perspiration dripped into his eyes, stinging his vision and sending the world into a blur. A breeze kicked up, rippling his t-shirt. It was a light gust, but in his heightened anxiety, he felt like a sail on a ship, catching the wind and billowing out over the highway, his lines straining and threatening to come undone.

"Screw this," he muttered angrily. He wouldn't make it all the way to the ground. And he wasn't far from the overpass; an easy six-foot jump down would set him on the bridge. He didn't give himself a chance to think. He simply planted his feet and pushed, launching himself backward into the air. But his left foot slipped as it left the pole, making his knee buckle before he could get the force he needed.

And Patrick screamed as he fell through the air.

He slammed shoulder-first into the outside of the guardrail, bouncing off the side and dropped through the air. He came to a violent stop on top of an old UPS delivery truck. The wind burst out of his lungs. He rolled over onto his side off the edge of the roof, crashing to the asphalt in a heap.

Jimmy was the first to reach the crumpled pile of Patrick. He stabilized Pat's head and peeled open one eyelid with his thumb. "Patrick? Are you with me?"

"Patrick will return after a brief hiatus," he mumbled. Then he went unconscious.

"Your friend is a hero," the old man told the Red Caps, wiping tears of gratitude from his cheeks. He stroked his fingers lovingly over the photo of his wife, his Edith. "He brought my world back to me." Then he looked sorrowfully at Patrick. "Will he be okay?"

"Yeah, he'll live," Brett assured him. "Dude can't die. That's the whole point of being the apocalypticon."

14.

The apocalypticon..

In the end times, a man will come, Dylan had said. *A man built to stand the test. He is good, and strong, a leader of men. He is the icon of the apocalypse. The apocalypticon.*

"That's me, all right," Patrick muttered to himself, rubbing the back of his head. "The icon of the apocalypse. Nailed it. No notes."

"You sure you don't want to rest?" Jimmy asked, frowning at Patrick.

"No. I just fell off a lamp, and I'd like to put as much distance between me and my humiliation as possible," he insisted grumpily.

"Everyone passes out sometimes," Jimmy offered.

"And everyone hits a bridge on a diagonal from above at least once," Richie laughed. Gary slugged him in the arm. "Ow!"

"You really made a difference for that guy, Patrick," Gary said. "When you said you were afraid of heights, I thought you were being a pansy."

"Pansies are actually pretty hardy flowers," Ted pointed out.

Gary ignored him and pressed on. "You were up in that Cinderella window like it was no big ideal. But that shit scared you, didn't it? You were scared as hell up on that pole. You must have been scared in the castle, too. But you climbed them both anyway." His brow furrowed as he lowered his head, chewing his bottom lip as if trying to work out some internal calculus. Finally, he just asked, "Why would you do that if it scares you so much?"

"I climbed the swamp castle because name one better way to see the swamp. I'll wait."

"Swamp boat," Gary said.

"Huh." Patrick scratched his cheek. "Well, you've got me there."

"Disney World also hasn't been a swamp for a long time."

"Depends on who you ask."

Gary glowered. Patrick sighed. He shook his head. "Look. Here's the thing. You're thinking about this all wrong. The question isn't why would I do things that scare me to help other people; the question is, why won't you do things that scare you to help those people?"

The question slowed Gary's steps, until he came to a stop on the quiet highway. His face was pained; his eyes were confused. He blinked. "What if you're scared for good reason and you do that shit for someone you've never met. What if you die trying to do it?"

"Boy, that's a great question," Patrick admitted. "And why do I do that shit to get strangers out of trouble when I also spent a whole lot of time doing shit that got my best friend *into* trouble? I'll be honest—I do not know." He bit his bottom lip. He turned away. He stood quietly like that for a while.

Gary fumbled for a way to respond. He came up empty, so he decided to let his feet wander, pulling him away from Patrick the group. He set off on his own trajectory along the shoulder of the highway, thinking his thoughts and working his brow and struggling with some unnamed internal frustration. Everyone in the pack followed suit, falling silent as they traveled.

After a few miles of walking in silence, they came across a man who was tied to a tree.

That was enough to bring everyone out of their heads.

"Hey, are you okay?" Ted asked. He was the first one to reach the young man, who couldn't have been out of his twenties.

The man rolled his head up on his shoulders, and he stared dully at Ted. "Am I okay? I'm a black man who was tied to a tree by a bunch of white assholes with southern accents. Do *you* think I'm okay?"

"Sorry—stupid question," Ted said, chiding himself. "No one who's tied to a tree is doing okay."

The man grimaced. "No shit."

Patrick hurried over and pulled his machete from his bag. "Watch your limbs…I'm not great with this." He started hacking at the rope, but the blade was pretty dull. It took a while, but eventually the nylon bindings fell away and the young man was freed.

He stretched his arms and curled his finger as he inspected the Red Caps. "Thank you," he said. "They'll likely be back any second, so you'd better fucking run." Before they could ask him to clarify, he was off like a shot, sprinting away from the highway and toward the rolling wooded mountains in the north.

The Red Caps were confused as they watched him go. "That was weird...right?" Jimmy asked.

No one got the chance to answer. The sound of horse hooves beating the ground rose as a line of riders appeared in the distance, cresting the Appalachian foothill to the west. They rode with fury and purpose into the interstate valley, deep within the Carolina nowhere.

There were seventeen riders in all, each one a stout, white male, all clad in dirty gray uniforms and forage caps. They carried front-loader rifles slung over their shoulders, with gunpowder horns and old-fashioned canteens hanging off their saddles. The man who rode in front also had a saber strapped to his waist; he wore a hat with a brim that encircled his head, with one side pinned flat against the crown. He also had a ridiculous mustache and pork-chop sideburns.

Patrick frowned. "Well, this can't be good."

The riders formed a circle and surrounded the Red Caps. The leader made a grand show of ogling the tree, with the chopped rope still wound loosely around the roots. He pulled his sword and leveled it at Patrick. "What pools of treason have you devils swam in today?"

The Red Caps looked at each other, confused.

"Normal ones," Patrick finally decided. "Normal pools of treason."

"Where's the boy who was tied up there?" demanded a soldier in the back.

"You can't call him 'boy'—that's very racist," Patrick frowned. The other Red Caps murmured their agreement.

"And he was like thirty, at least," Richie said.

The lead rider climbed down off his horse and pointed the saber at Patrick's chest. "Y'all cut him loose?" he asked.

Patrick nodded. "He was a human person who was tied to a tree. So yeah, *Cold Mountain* cosplay, we cut him loose."

The man with the sword gritted his teeth. "Y'all've done sinful treason here today." He looked back at his men and twirled a finger in the air. "Tie 'em up. They're coming with us."

Several of the riders pulled lengths of rope from their saddle bags and dismounted their horses. Richie held up his hands, giving in immediately. "What the fuck, Richie?" Ted grumbled. He clenched his fists and tried to make himself look like he was ready to fight. Brett just crossed his arms at the men, snorted and said, "Yeah. Good fucking luck."

The leader frowned. "Someone shoot him," he ordered.

One of the men on horseback immediately shouldered his rifle, drew his bead, and pulled the trigger. The gun exploded with smoke and noise.

Brett screamed. He fell to the ground, clutching his leg. Blood spilled out through his fingers, soaking the green grass red.

"Any other objections?" the leader asked. "No? All right. Drop your bags. Let's get this done." He made the twirling motion with his finger again and the soldiers resumed their approach.

"They got Brett!" Jimmy shouted breathlessly. "Holy shit."

He was the strongest among them, and every one of them knew it. Richie dropped down to his knees first, and it wasn't long before the others were forced to follow suit. The Red Caps were red-faced with anger and indignation, but if the soldiers could shoot a man like Brett so easily, what sort of havoc could they wreak to the rest of the crew?

"Brett! Get up!" Gary struggled as the attackers bound his wrists with coarse rope, but the man tying him up cuffed him on the back of the head hard enough to shut him up. Ted and Jimmy didn't fight, but just knelt there, bewildered, as their hands were tied.

Patrick was the only one who managed to work his legs. He ducked the man who approached him and dropped to his knees next to Brett. He nodded furiously as he looked at the wound. "It just grazed you. You're okay, you hear me? *You're okay.*"

"I know I'm okay!" Brett yelled. "I'm just fucking furious!" He hobbled up on his good leg and charged the leader of the group. Another rider stepped up and smashed him in the face with the butt of a rifle. Brett hit the ground like a sack of bricks.

Several of the riders pointed their rifles at Patrick, and he put his hands in the air. He offered no resistance as a man pulled his knapsack off his shoulders, then looped a rope around his wrists and pulled the knot taut. But his eyes burned with an anger that seemed more and more accessible since the night he'd made it to Disney World.

The leader of the gray suits slipped his sword back into its scabbard and climbed back onto his horse. He clicked his tongue, and the horse trotted forward, crossing the highway and heading toward the hills to the south. "Hope you wore your walking shoes, Yankees," the man called out over his shoulder. "Y'all may need to help your friend. Seems he's got himself shot, and we've got a little ways to go."

15.

They stumbled along, surrounded by riders, until the sun touched the western horizon. By Patrick's estimation, they'd probably gone eight or ten miles when they came upon an old 19th-century homestead. It was set off from the end of a rock-dust road by a split-rail fence running in both directions as far as the eye could see. A bonfire burned in the yard beyond the fence; behind that loomed a large two-story log cabin, smoke puffing out of all three of its chimneys. There was a sun-faded pole barn off to the right, and over to the left, a low stone cottage that had could have once served as servants' quarters, but was now fitted with thick iron bars in the windows and doorway. As the riders and the prisoners approached, and elderly man appeared from the barn, hurrying over to the stone house. He hissed through the bars, making an unheard threat to some unseen person. Then he unlocked the gate and held the door open to welcome the new batch of prisoners.

Brett had been hobbling badly the last few miles. By the time they reached the compound, his bleeding leg was shaking and wouldn't bear any weight. Patrick and Gary helped him into the stone house with the other Red Caps following, being shoved by the barrels of rifles loaded with live ammunition. Brett collapsed on a pile of straw beneath the window. They held out their hands to have their ropes cut free, but the men in the gray outfits just laughed. Then they slammed the door, locked it tight, and went to the fire in the middle of the courtyard. A half-dozen women in bell-bustle dresses emerged from the main house and led their horses to the stable.

"What in the absolute fuck is going on?" Patrick whispered, watching through the bars.

"Man, you don't even want to know."

They all turned around, surprised by a voice that came from the far corner of the shed. Sitting in the shadows was a young man in his mid-twenties or so, with tattered clothes and bare feet. His hair was long and knotted, stabbed through with straw and grass. His dark brown skin was covered in blisters, his bones pressed through every other inch of his flesh. "Y'all have landed in some real shit," he said. "I'll tell you that."

"What is this place?" Gary asked. He nodded toward the door. "Who are they?"

"First things first. You want out of those ropes? They keep a rusty-ass blade in here. I got it up on the window sill. I think they put it in here like some sort of game—see how long I can go before I cut my own wrists. But I ain't going out like that. Help yourself, though. I won't judge."

Gary crossed over to the window and found the rusty razor blade sitting on the ledge. His hands were tied in front, which made him able to pick up the blade and saw through Patrick's ropes. Once he was free, Patrick took the blade and returned the favor. Soon, the Red Caps were all free of their bonds and rubbing their wrists. Now Jimmy could attend to Brett's leg. Supplies were limited, but he made a paste of mud and straw and smeared it on the wound. "It doesn't look too bad," Jimmy said thankfully.

They all made introductions, learning the man's name was Maurice, and that he'd been locked in the stone house prison for over two years now. "Jesus," Ted exhaled. "This isn't just a blip."

Maurice snorted. "Nah. It's not a blip. This is a long-term type of deal."

The mood shifted down into deep-shadow darkness. All at once, each one of the Red Caps had the same revelation: They'd known things were bad, and they clearly knew things could get worse. But they hadn't experienced the worse side of apocalyptic-bad, and now it had come for them, with all its darkness and despair. The weight of it was sudden and suffocating.

"This is bullshit," Brett grumbled.

"We have to get out of here," Richie said, his voice tight.

"Great idea," Maurice scoffed. "If you find a way, you take me with you."

"Who are they?" Patrick asked, sitting down in the corner next to Maurice. "What do they want?"

"Those motherfuckers?" Maurice asked, pointing out toward the bonfire in the yard. "What they want is to punish people. Mostly people who

70

look like me. But seems like y'all will do, too. I don't know what you did, but y'all are the first white men I've seen in here since they got me."

"What the hell?" Ted asked, joining them in the growing dark. "Why?"

Maurice shook his head. "Because of the 'who' they are. Every single one of those motherfuckers around the fire is a war reenactor who is taking the game *way* too seriously."

"So they're Southern racist assholes," Brett muttered from his straw bed.

Maurice snorted. "I mean, yeah, but…literally: *they are Civil War reenactors*. That was their whole deal before the bombs. Those white assholes are Sons of the South, did their whole pageantry shit every weekend for kicks. Then the bombs hit and they must've gone absolutely bug-fuck, because they are so deep in their own fiction, I have not once seen them come out of it. You saw their outfits—the Confederate grays? Not sure if you caught the flag they fly on that house, but it's the Stars and Bars, alright. You know how they shot your friend when every other motherfucker north of Texas ran out of ammo two years ago? It's because they use those old guns… they make their own ball shot, in a forge behind the house. They ransack the countryside for metal, then they melt it down to make gunshot. Got cows and pigs out back, too. This is rural Charlotte, guys. These people are fully self-sustained. I think they truly believe they are fighting a war against the Union that took place 150 years ago. And I'll tell you this, you get thrown in here, you are fucked. Just like me, just like every other poor son of a bitch I've seen come through here in my time. We're all fucked in this together."

"But others have come through?" Richie squeaked. "So…some people get out."

Maurice's eyes blazed. "Yeah, they got out," he said. "Out on a stretcher, and thrown in the ground."

"I'm sorry…this can't be real," Jimmy said, frowning and tugging at his own fingers. "You're saying we're here because those men out there *actually think* they're in the Civil War, and they're taken us as, what—prisoners of war?"

"Sounds like you got it just right," Maurice said.

"Impossible," Jimmy frowned.

Patrick scratched his jaw. "Hold on," he said. He walked over to the iron bar door and shouted out at the men around the fire, "Hey! Who's the president right now?"

"Jefferson Davis!" they all shouted in unison.

Patrick returned to the group. "I think Maurice might be onto something," he admitted.

Maurice nodded. He leaned his head back against the rough stone wall. "Make yourself at home, fellas. You're gonna be here a while."

16.

The gravity of their situation began to sink in over the next week. The soldiers barely paid them any attention, except to toss food scraps into the stone house a couple times a day. It was usually dried strips of salted pork and a few pale turnips; once, there was a single hardboiled egg for all of them to split. The soldiers gave them two rusty buckets: One was filled with rainwater from the barrel, and the other was empty, meant for their own waste. Every two days, they let Maurice out of the stone house to empty the bucket in the creek at the edge of the property, but always and only under the watchful eyes of five men with rifles drawn. The Red Caps tried to get the soldiers to talk or even to listen to reason, but they wouldn't bite. The longest conversation they had was on the third day, when Ted put his head to the bars and shouted, "Talk to us, you racist, slave-owning assholes!"

The soldiers around the fire all gasped. "This war isn't about *slavery!*" one of the soldiers shouted back. "It is about *states' rights!*"

They lost interest in talking to the soldiers after that.

The Red Caps also couldn't really tell what the racist lunatics were actually *doing*. Every day after breakfast, they rode out on their horses, dressed in full Johnny Reb gear, and every afternoon, they rode back before sundown, and almost never arrived home with anything gained or lost. If there was some demented Union analog out there, their battles were bloodless; the gray uniforms weren't clean, by any means, but they never showed any red stains. More and more, the men seemed to be part of a sick social club that cosplayed as Confederates and sometimes rounded up black men and perceived Abolitionists and threw them into the stone house. Maurice assured the Red Caps that the soldiers were dangerous;

he'd seen more than one prisoner get dragged out of the stone house when the soldiers had had too much to drinks and hauled up on a branch of the big oak by the barn with a blood-stained rope they called Justice. Sure enough, somewhere around week three or four, when Brett spat in the face of the man delivering their food, they did hear the leader of the group tell Maurice, "You better keep those Union sympathizers in line, boy, or Justice goin' come for you—*and* them."

The seasons didn't behave quite the same, now that the lower atmosphere was clogged with yellow-green dust, but temperatures tended to move along their old curves. Soon, the crisp air of fall gave way to colder winter temperatures. There had been almost no snow since M-Day, at least not in the upper Midwest, but the winds were still bitterly cold. That proved to be the case in the Appalachians, too. Winter moved in, and the crew woke up to sixty-three straight days of frost on the grass, according to the tally marks Jimmy scratched into the wall. Brett somehow managed to avoid getting gangrene in his leg, and the gunshot wound healed well, if slower than he would have liked. But he felt fine by the time the leaves had fallen from the trees, though something about the cold air made that leg stiff and sore, when it had never been an issue before. And though during slaughters the soldiers did up their rations to include more pork, and every once in a while they got a pail of milk, everyone in the group was shedding weight.

Shaving was always a challenging bit of hygiene in the apocalypse, but it became impossible in the prison. They all grew beards, haggard and wild, whether they wanted to or not. Patrick's was patchy, as was Jimmy's, but once they got long enough, no one could really tell. Brett and Gary looked right at home on the mountain with their full salt-and-pepper beards; Ted surprised them all by growing thick, shining bristles that grew naturally into a beautiful cone shape. Richie's beard only grew on his cheeks, not on his chin. It looked weird as hell. He often complained that his dermatitis was to blame, but Patrick suspected it was just his body's evolutionary attempt to not attract a mate so that Richie would never have the chance to spread his seed.

He shared this theory with Richie once. It was not graciously received.

The soldiers stayed close to home much more often during those winter months, and tending the bonfire became a round-the-clock endeavor. Smoke puffed out from the log cabin chimneys nonstop, and its windows reflected a rosy glow. That was the worst thing about winter for the prisoners…they could see signs of such warmth, day in and day out, but they were never granted the benefit of it. Eventually, the soldiers handed some horses blankets in through the bars, and they smelled moldy and gamey, but they were warm, so the prisoners made do.

But eventually, the frozen ground gave way to a thaw in the warming creep of spring. The soldiers started venturing out again, back to the Quixotic endeavors that seemed to provide them with so much life. Soon it was warm enough for them to leave their coats behind, and the springtime temperatures seemed to heat their blood; though they had spent the whole winter drinking to build walls for themselves against the freezing air and the early darkness, now they drank for enjoyment. They told stories and swapped jokes, laughing uproariously around the fire and shoving each other playfully into the flames. They dared each other to games of five-finger fillet; they stripped down to their bare chests and boxing each other with cold and hungry fists.

They never saw the women much. They mostly kept inside.

One warm night, when the moon was full and the whole camp was deep in its cups, the soldiers came for Maurice.

It happened fast. One minute, the soldiers were kicking flaming logs at each other's feet, and the next, they'd gone to fetch Justice. One of them had come up to the bars, tapping his hunting knife against the metal and slurring, "Time's come, boy." He beckoned for Maurice to step forward; when Maurice didn't obey, the soldier became flushed with anger. "Don't make me come in there for you," he said. It became clear that this was exactly what he was going to have to do. He threw the hunting knife off to the side, unholstered a pistol from his hip and fumbled with the key to the door. It took him almost a full twenty seconds to fit the lock, but finally he did it. He pulled open the door, waving his gun as he commanded the Red Caps, "Up against the wall!"

Patrick stepped forward and planted his feet squarely against the soldier's. Brett fell in behind him, and Gary, too, and then Jimmy shuffled over, and Ted followed, and finally, Richie too. The Red Caps formed a wall between the soldier and Maurice, and Patrick said, "If you're going to take him, you'd better be ready to take us all."

The soldier hesitated. He waggled the pistol from one man to the next. "Give him over," he said, his tongue thick in his mouth, "and there'll be no trouble for the rest of you."

"We've been in here for months," Gary growled, flexing his fingers. "We're aching for some trouble."

"The only reason we don't rush you right now is you've got a couple dozen drunk assholes with live weapons waiting to see who comes out this door; you, or one of us," Patrick said. "It's going to be you. But it's going to be *only* you. If you want to use that front-loader, you can take out one of us. But that's all the ammo you've got. The rest of us will tear you apart and use your pieces as meat shields when we run out that door. If I were you, I'd turn around and forget you ever came in here."

"*Hell* yeah," Jimmy piped up. "What he said."

The drunk soldier swayed on his feet. He slid his shaking eyes over the Red Caps, and he found nothing but resolve. A bead of sweat dribbled down his brow. "You all are fucked," he growled. Then he scampered out the door, his pistol still waving at the prisoners. When he slammed and locked the iron gate, Patrick met him at the bars.

"Hey. One more thing: Maurice is off-limits." Patrick reached through the gate, grabbed the soldier by his shirt, and pulled him hard. The soldier's forehead smashed against the bars and he fell backward, unconscious. The other Confederates seemed to have lost interest, and they'd returned to the fire to keep drinking whatever rotgut they kept in their bottles, and no one noticed their comrade lying face-up in the mud. Patrick frowned down at him. "Well, we should have done that *weeks* ago," he decided.

The next morning, the whole yard was filled with haggard soldiers with incredible hangovers dragging themselves on the ground. The one who'd spent his night knocked out next to the gate woke up after sunrise with no memory of how he'd come to be at the stone house, or why he had a knot the size of a tennis ball on his forehead. None of the soldiers could recall a thing from the night before. They gave the prisoners an uneasy distance that lasted a few days.

But they never came for Maurice again.

17.

Marking time became something of an obsession for Jimmy. He'd started with the first frost, but he kept on making notches in the wall well into the spring thaw. Even when the days were getting stiflingly hot, he still cut a hash in the stone first thing every morning. He was angry with himself for not starting on their first day. If he'd known they would be locked in the stone house for so long, he would have started tracking the days immediately. But as it was, he'd missed at least six weeks, maybe more. Because of that block of lost time, he could only estimate that they had been locked away in that Confederate lunatic fever dream hell hole for 255 days when they finally experienced death.

More than eight months. Almost nine.

That was how much time had passed when dusters swarmed the camp.

There were only three of them—not actually a "swarm"—but they were fast and hungry, and they cut through the soldiers like a hundred-member horde.

The Confederates had been sitting around their morning campfire, percolating their coffee and prepping for their bullshit day, when they heard what sounded like an animal growling up the hill. Wolves were common and bears weren't impossible, so they all grabbed their guns and waited for movement in the trees.

But they weren't expecting dusters.

It was after only a few moments that the trees began to shake. But before the soldiers could bring their rifles to their shoulders, the three dusters were on them, snarling and starving and full of fury. They leapt at the soldiers like crazed velociraptors, all four limbs out, mouths savage and teeth snapping. They each took down a soldier, tearing into them with huge, hungry bites. Instantly, the dusters were covered in blood, with slimy threads of flesh hanging from their teeth.

The other Confederates were in shock. One of them managed to fire his rifle, but even at point blank range, the little metal ball just ricocheted off the duster's hardened skull. The fight was over before it even began. The dusters leapt from one man to the next, in a gruesome hailstorm of teeth and hands that left the entire Confederate unit splayed on the ground, their internal organs exposed in various states of display.

The Red Caps watched in horror as the scene unfolded, all within seconds. One moment, the soldiers were laughing around the fire; the next, they were dead—all of them, dead, with their entrails spread across the grass and their faces chewed to pieces.

"Oh my God," Richie said.

One of the dusters perked up when she heard it. She turned her head and saw the men peering from the stone house.

She licked her lips.

"Goddammit, Richie," Gary snapped in a rough whisper.

The duster launched herself across the yard. She slammed into the iron bars like a crazed beast. The gate groaned under the impact, and the bars bent inward. The force of the collision knocked the duster back. Dazed, she shook her head but found her ground, ramming the gate again and bending the bars further inward. Again and again, she slammed her shoulder into the iron. Richie screamed, Ted dove behind Gary, and even Brett stumbled backward a few steps. But miraculously, the lock held, even as jumped into the door and threw her weight into the upper corner. But the bars there kept bending further inward, until there was enough of a gap between the bars and the doorframe for the duster to scramble through. She clawed her way across the metal as the Red Caps shrank back, pressing into the far corner, not ready to die. Not like this. Not here. Not now.

Somewhere behind the cabin, a cow lowed.

The duster lifted her head, turning her ear toward the sound. Then air was silent, and the duster went still. The other dusters in the yard stopped. They froze.

They waited.

The cow lowed again.

The duster on the gate sprang back into the yard. She turned and sprinted around the cabin in search of easier prey. The other dusters followed, and suddenly, the yard was clear...except for the bodies of the dead Confederates, and the mangled prison door bent inward, with a gap big enough to clear.

The prisoners looked at each other.

Then they bolted for the opening and dove out toward freedom.

Without a word, they broke north, away from the compound and away from the dusters. They ran as hard as they could up the road, and they didn't stop to look back until their legs were rubber and their lungs were on fire and they were deep in a forest, far out of sight of the prison.

They stood in a circle, the Red Caps and Maurice, their hands on their knees, sucking wind, not knowing if they should be excited or terrified. "We have to keep going," Patrick wheezed. "The dusters may be on our trail."

"Sounds like water that way," Gary panted, pointing west. "We can hide our scent."

"I'm *this* way," Maurice said, pointing east. "But, shit. Thank you guys. What the fuck. What even…?" He broke into tears. "I don't know, man. Thank you. This is just—man, I don't even know what to say. All right? Good luck." He took off through the trees, disappearing into the brush.

They watched him go. None of them had felt anything like the squeeze they felt in their chests when he ran off into the woods.

"The water is a good idea," Patrick said, breaking the silence. "Let's get the hell out of here."

They stumbled down the mountain, following Gary until they found a river. Then they dove in, exhausted, letting the cold current carry them a few hundred yards before they clawed their way up the opposite bank and collapsed in a heap in the mud.

Only then did they dare sleep.

18.

"I can't believe you made it," Ben said, throwing his arms around Patrick's shoulders. *"Every other person in the world is dead."*

"I know, Benny Boy." Patrick wiped his tears on Ben's shoulder. He'd been crying for three days. He didn't think he'd ever stop. "Annie and Izzy…"

Ben gripped the back of Patrick's head with his palm and squeezed it gently. "Jesus Christ, Pat. I'm sorry."

Gunshots rang out close by. Ben pulled Patrick inside his garden apartment and locked the door. Then he pushed the sofa and his dresser against the door, setting up a barricade. He motioned Patrick back to the kitchen, away from the windows. He struck a match and lit some candles on the counter. There hadn't been power for over 36 hours. He had a feeling it wasn't coming back.

"I can't believe you walked all the way here. Through that." He gestured to the world outside. "Are you okay?"

"I think so."

"What's it like? Is everyone…? What's happening?"

"It's bad," Patrick whispered, rubbing the tears from his cheeks. "Everyone's going nuts. People are just…killing other people. In the streets. Over nothing. Over a book of matches. Over nothing."

Ben shook his head, his flesh so pale with fear that he was practically glowing in the near-darkness. "My neighbor stabbed some guy in the neck with a knitting needle because he took cover from a shootout in our shrubs. He ran out into the street, bleeding everywhere. He collapsed in the middle of the road, and a pickup swerved to avoid him and hit my neighbor. She just exploded. Then the guy driving the truck lost control and hit a telephone pole. He went flying through the windshield and hit a tree head on. Broke his neck. The whole thing took five seconds."

Patrick lifted the hem of his shirt and soaked up his tears. "What do we do?" he murmured.

Ben shook his head. "I don't know. It's not safe here. Any lunatic can come crashing through the door. Maybe we should hide out at your place. Until things settle."

"If they settle."

"Yeah. If they settle."

Patrick coughed up a ball of phlegm and spat it into Ben's sink. "I don't know if my building will be any better," he said.

"You haven't been back?"

"No."

"It's been three days. Where have you been sleeping?"

"I haven't been. I've just been walking. And running. And hiding. I haven't slept once since the bombs. Every time I close my eyes, I see them. I don't know if I can go back to the apartment. I don't know if there's any point."

Ben frowned. He was shit at emotional support in the best circumstances. And this was the exact fucking opposite of that. "We can try to make it to my roof. We can sleep up there. Should be pretty safe. We can barricade the door, get a few hours of sleep at least. We'll take turns. Then tomorrow we can come up with a plan."

Patrick's eyes shone in the candlelight. "A plan to do what?"

"I don't know," Ben said, frustrated. "Survive."

Patrick shook his head. "Pretty sure I'm not the survivalist type."

"No one will ever confuse you for an apocalyptic hero," Ben agreed. "But let's just try to get some sleep. We'll think better if we can manage it. We'll figure out what to do next."

"I just want to lie down and never get up," Patrick whispered.

Ben hugged him again. "I know, Pat. I know you do. But if you're going to do it, come up and do it on the roof, okay? It's getting rowdy out there." Ben slapped Patrick's back and headed toward the back stairs. He peered out the door, then stepped out onto the rickety deck. He turned back to Patrick. "Okay?"

Patrick sighed. He was so tired.

"Okay," he finally said.

They left Ben's apartment to the darkness.

19.

The Red Caps woke before sunrise, still scared in their bones. They picked themselves up and headed further north. It felt like the only sensible direction to go.

They'd lost everything to the Confederates: their weapons, their food, their bags, and most significantly, the last year of their lives. A year ago, they were dragging Patrick up the Atlantic coast, not sure if he'd live or die. It was a different lifetime. It felt like a different world. Now, they were scrambling across the Carolina countryside with just the clothes on their backs and the panic in their skin. By the time the sun came up, they were back at Highway 74, and the way that things suddenly felt so simultaneously familiar and long-forgotten crashed on them like an ocean wave. It almost felt like the last nine months hadn't happened. It also felt like they'd never get past the trauma of the nine months they had lost. And not a single one of them knew how to ask the others if he felt it, too. So no one said a word.

When they hit the highway, the temporal vertigo put them all on their heels. But they needed resources, they needed supplies, they needed food and weapons and things to touch to make them feel human if they were going to survive another day. This was the moment Patrick remembered the UPS truck, the one he'd smashed with his whole body against when trying to jump to the overpass the day before they were captured. *I rescued an old man's necklace,* he recalled. *It was his wife's. It had a picture from their wedding in it.*

What a strange thing to have happened.

"It's backtracking, I know," he said as the group came back into focus. "And no one is more anti-backtracking than me. But the UPS truck was going somewhere on M-Day. It was loaded with *things*. And I don't have a great memory, mostly because I'd smashed my head into the top of it, but I don't remember seeing opened doors...it's a gamble, but if that truck is still untouched, there's a chance that there are some packages inside that might help us not die tonight."

It was pretty lackluster as inspirational speeches go. "You think that truck is still intact, after all this time?" Ted asked.

"Wasn't intact back then," Brett grunted. "Thing was smashed in from the back."

"By a truck that had wedged itself pretty tight in there, if I remember correctly," Patrick said. "And I may not. But we won't know until we check."

There was some grumbling about going back, but no one else had a better idea about where to find a potential cache of supplies. So they hiked back to the east until they found the overpass where Patrick had shimmied the lamp post in what felt like eons and eons before.

The truck was still there, thankfully, and the doors were still closed. The men spread out and encircled it, checking the entry points. Things had obviously been a mess on M-Day. Most drivers had started melting while still behind the wheel, which meant every road in the country was now blocked with cars that had careened away when their drivers turned to soup. The UPS truck was no exception. The GMC Envoy smashed into its rear had caved in the back panel, making it impossible to raise the rolling door. The passenger door was wedged against the concrete wall of the overpass, and the driver door had been smashed by another car. Although the car had glanced off the side and slid to a stop several feet away, the door had been irreparably damaged. It wouldn't slide open more than an inch and a half.

The truck's interior, however, had not been penetrated. All of its original packages were still unopened inside.

"That's our way in," Patrick said, pointing to the roof. "There's a translucent white panel up there, to let in light. It's intact now—I know because my face smashed into it. It'll be relatively easy to break through."

The Red Caps scavenged a few sizable rocks before helping one another climb onto the top of the truck. Then they rained hell on the panel until it cracked and fell into the truck, leaving a rectangular opening that revealed a quarry of pristinely wrapped packages.

They dropped into the hold and started tearing open boxes. There were so many completely useless things inside—not just for the apocalypse, but for the world that had been before, too. Trinkets and baubles and plastic and cellophane...it all seemed so stupid, to have spent money on plastic cups wrapped in plastic bags, tucked into a plastic box and shipped in a cardboard container. But there were some real prizes as well, which made the whole exercise feel a lot like the Christmas they'd missed out on the last several years. Every few minutes, someone would shout, "Bingo!" and proudly display a set of windshield wipers or a croquet mallet or a zipper case full of backyard barbecue tools. In between swimsuits and spices and curtains and sippy cups, Gary found an extendable baton with a steel core. It drew the biggest smile from him Patrick had ever seen. Jimmy went through some sheet sets and a thermocouple before he found a butcher block full of knives; it took Brett almost thirty minutes to uncover a set of heavy stainless steel wrenches. They also found food: Goldfish crackers, off-brand fruit bars, olive oil popcorn, and huge logs of summer sausage. Richie opened an entire case of Spam, twelve little tins of salty, potted meat.

"Hell yeah," Brett said, looking over his shoulder.

"It's mine," Richie insisted. "I've got dibs."

"Dib this." Brett punched him on the shoulder. Richie dropped the box of Spam.

"Ow!"

But it was Patrick who found the most enviable prize: an 18-inch El Salvador machete from Condor Tool & Knife, with a black carbon blade and Micarta handle. "The Spirit of the Illinois has guided me to this UPS truck," he decided, flipping the blade in his hand. "It wants me to wage war on the Carolinas, its natural enemies, and I will chop this entire region of the United States to bits in gratitude for this gift."

It was so much better than the machete he'd left behind that he wept. "I don't know why I'm like this right now," he said, brushing back his tears, though not a single Red Cap was paying him any attention.

Gary opened a package to find a bottle of Old Grand-Dad bourbon someone had smuggled among an assortment of Christmas-themed dish towels. Patrick congratulated him on the second-best find, though the Red Caps made it clear that the whiskey was far and away the first-best package.

"Agree to disagree," Patrick said, nuzzling his new machete. "But let's open that bottle and see what second place tastes like."

They started a fire next to the highway and ate better than they had in a long, long time. Gary did open the bottle of whiskey and passed it around, but they didn't really talk much. There didn't seem to be a whole lot to say. The last nine months had broken something about them, but it also bonded them somehow. They were like a porcelain vase glued back together after falling off a shelf. They were glad to be out, but the joy of simply being alive had been starved out of them. All there really was to do was eat salty mystery meat from a can while trying to remember how fun it used to be to drink around a fire.

"A toast to Patrick," Gary said, raising the bottle and breaking the silence. "Remembering this delivery truck is the best thing that happened to us."

"Thanks for finding it with your face," Brett agreed.

"Food and weapons. I didn't want to backtrack, but hell. You were right. This probably saved us," Gary said.

But Patrick squirmed uncomfortably. "If I'd thought to notice it a little better the first time, we never would have spent the last nine months in a prison cell. If we'd raided it then, we'd have done this exact same thing—we would have stayed the whole night here, eating and drinking. Telling stories. Laughing. We'd have packed up the next morning, and we would've missed the soldiers completely. We'd have gone on our way, ignorant and happy. We'd have gotten to Fort Doom months ago. I would have been there so long by now that I would have forgotten about how most of this trip went. If I'd stopped to think, just for a second, I would have shifted our whole timeline. We'd be different people in different places. Every single thing that happens from now on will happen because we got caught and imprisoned for almost a year. Totally sidelined while the broken world went on." He looked down at his hands and dug his fingernails together. "That's what I've been thinking about, anyway," he finished quietly.

Gary passed him the Grand-Dad.

"Thanks," Patrick mumbled.

"Well, who the hell knows?" Gary decided. "For all we know, things might have been worse for us if we'd gone straight through."

"Could be the detour saved our lives, and we'll never know it," Ted agreed. "And anyway, it's not your fault, Patrick. We all saw the truck. None of us thought about it."

"We're fine now," Brett shrugged. "I say we take the win."

"You know whose life absolutely was better for how things went, don't you?" Jimmy asked. "That guy you cut loose from the tree. You think he'd still be alive if we hadn't come along?"

"Maurice, too," Gary added. "We stopped them stringing him up. Bet he's glad we showed up when we did."

"Well…this is all true," Patrick said, nodding slowly. "Not a great trade, though. Their trauma for ours. There's no good way for any of it to go."

"That's all there are now, is bad trades," Gary grunted.

Patrick sighed. "Yeah. Well…here's to where we are, in the strangest of all possible timelines." He drank deeply from the bottle and passed it to his right.

"Hear, hear," said the Red Caps.

"Hey," said Brett, taking the bottle and raising it to the group. "We just made it through some shit. I mean, we made it through some *real* shit—together. We got each other through. We should be celebrating." The Red Caps whooped and nodded. "I've got an idea. We've got a mostly-full bottle of bourbon, and by now, our tolerance is shit. Let's drink until we forget the last nine months and leave every goddamn piece of it behind us."

The men cheered. They passed the bottle; they told old stories and old jokes, laughing for the first time in ages. They finally convinced Ted to sing, and even though his words were slurred and his throat was hoarse, it was a beautiful rendition of "Habanera," at least as far as they could tell. When he was done, they clapped and cheered and slapped him on the back. Richie complained about his itchy elbows, and Gary threw gravel at his head. Jimmy told some incredibly gruesome and wildly entertaining tales from his days in the back of an ambulance. One story was so graphic, it made Ted throw up. Everybody cheered. Patrick talked about snorting croke to get across a bridge and sailing a heart-shaped hot tub across the Gulf of Mexico. In its own way, it was more disgusting than the ambulance stories, but at least no one puked.

The last several months burned away from them like the logs on the fire, popping and hissing as they dissolved. The crew ate and drank until their bellies were full, the bottle was empty and the flames had died down to embers. Then they fell back in the grass and snored through their sleep, happy and drunk and free once more.

The next morning, every one of them had a crushing hangover. It took a few hours to get roused enough to move on. When they were finally up and going, they stuffed their food into new backpacks they'd scavenged from the other vehicles, fitting their new weapons wherever they could. They moved sluggishly in the morning heat, heads pounding and stomachs lurching. But they were still laughing about Ted's vomit and Patrick's horrible croke. No one mentioned the Confederate prison.

After a mile or so, they passed a sign that read, NOW LEAVING CHARLOTTE.

"A couple days walk until Asheville," Patrick reminded them. "That's where we'll find the river. We'll snag a boat, float on down, and cruise along for a week or so, until we hit the Gulf of Mexico."

"Good. We could use a vacation," Gary said.

Patrick nodded as he slapped Gary's shoulder. "I think it's going to be smooth sailing from here on out."

20.

It was not smooth sailing from there on out.

They made it to Asheville the next morning. It was a quiet, ruined city nestled in among the mountains, and it was probably beautiful once, but now it looked like a set from some Ridley Scott disaster movie. Buildings were crumbling; bridges were down. The street was full of craters, and there were corpses everywhere, in various stages of decay.

The skeletons were always what made Patrick queasy. Most of humanity had died on M-Day, liquefied by the dust. But the skeletons weren't liquid. Every set of bones had once belonged to a person who had survived the attack but hadn't been so lucky after.

The cities were full of skeletons now. The survivors were becoming extinct.

"If I remember correctly, the river's on the far side of town," Patrick said.

"Then let's get there," Ted said quietly. "This place is giving me the creeps."

"It's so quiet," Gary agreed. "Why is it so quiet?"

"Probably the mountains," Patrick said. "Keeping out the ambient noise." He pushed forward into town, creeping along the silent sidewalks. "Stay on the lookout for supplies. It'll be harder to find anything useful once we're on the water."

They moved slowly through downtown Asheville, picking their way through cars and poking their heads into storefronts. There wasn't much left in terms of survival gear, but they managed to scavenge a half-full box of Hostess cupcakes, a foldable pocketknife, and a few other odds and ends.

Before long, they could hear the quiet rush of the river and began to relax. "Not much farther now," Gary said.

"Good. I hate it here," Ted muttered. He saw an RV parked at the corner of a side street and walked over to check it for supplies. He pulled open the door.

The blood drained from his face.

He closed the door and looked at the others. "It's dusters," he said.

The door exploded open, hitting Ted with enough force to throw him through the air. He landed on his back as six dusters leapt out of the RV, yellow-green foam leaking from their mouths.

"Oh shit," Richie whined.

The Red Caps broke into a run. They scattered across the street, dodging cars and piles of bricks, running as hard as they could. Patrick turned to look for Ted, who was just getting to his feet. Three of the dusters were coming after the Red Caps, but the other three stopped, sniffed the air, and turned to see Ted lying on the ground. Ted scrambled to his feet and took off running up the hill, away from the group.

"Ted! Go to the river!" Patrick shouted.

Ted disappeared over the hill, the three dusters close on his trail. The other three were barreling at Patrick. He turned and joined the other Red Caps running for their lives through the ruined streets of Asheville.

21.

Ted was so fucked.

He kept running, more than he'd ever run in his life. But then, he'd never *needed* to run so much in his life. He had three dusters on his tail, and the real shit part of it was that the further he ran, the more he realized the gut-souring truth that they were faster than he was.

They were gaining quickly…and they *had been* gaining quickly. They growled and snarled, snapping their teeth, desperately hungry and fueled by the concentrated yellow dust in their bloodstreams. They were as determined as death and as hardened as their veins.

Christ, they're fast, Ted thought.

He huffed and puffed, pumping his legs as hard as he could, squeezing through cars, leaping over potholes. His heart seized as he realized with horror that the dusters were close enough to smell his scent. He was exhausted, and he couldn't keep running.

He rounded a corner and saw a bridge… or what used to be a bridge, anyway. The Monkey bombs had done a real number on it. Now it was more like a shaky concrete sculpture of an artist's interpretation of Swiss cheese; there were gaps at the edges of the pavement, as if some gigantic rat had bitten chunks out, and the guardrail on one side had fallen away completely. The overhead trestles were destroyed and dangled down, their sharp ends hovering dangerously like an oversized erector set trashed by a bully and left behind in the sandbox to be mourned. The entire bridge was littered with vehicles—cars, trucks, a few semis. One had jackknifed, its ass-end hanging out over the crumbling edge of the bridge. The sticky residue of melted bodies coated the cement like drips from a grease tray.

With every gust of wind, no matter how gentle, the entire bridge creaked and swayed.

"Shit, shit, shit," Ted panted.

Zombies behind him; a death trap ahead.

He was so fucked.

He sprinted onto the bridge, jumped, and slid over the hood of a Camry, which would have felt like a pretty cool thing to do if not for his current circumstances. The dusters weren't quite so nimble; instead of jumping over the car, they barreled through it, smashing into the front fender and setting the car spinning.

Ted darted around the vehicles. The traffic was enough to slow the dusters down, but not by much. It would only buy him a few seconds at most.

He was running out of time.

As soon as he reached the center of the bridge, they were on him. One lurched forward and rammed him with its shoulder. Ted screamed and slammed into the side of a Ford Explorer. His body burned with pain, but he scraped himself up to his feet and kept running. He leapt over a Firebird, barely avoiding a swipe from the duster behind him as the creature smashed into the car instead. Ted threw himself over the concrete divider. He hit the pavement in a roll, then got to his feet and kept going.

Before he could move, the duster crashed over the divider and knocked him to the ground. The creature clutched at his leg and sank his teeth into Ted's calf. Ted screamed at the pain, at the sheer fucking horror he felt. He kicked the zombie in the face with his free leg; it was like kicking a retainer wall. His foot exploded in pain as his bones cracked. The duster didn't feel anything at all.

"Fuck!" Ted screamed.

He reached desperately for something—a weapon, a deterrent, Christ, *anything*—but his fingers found only asphalt. Ted squeezed his eyes shut and waited for the feeling of human teeth ripping his body apart.

What he felt instead was an absence of pressure. He opened his eyes. The duster on his leg had let loose. It had taken a chunk of his flesh was chewing hungrily.

"*Nope!*" Ted shouted, his brain absolutely screaming with fear.

He flipped over onto his chest and pushed himself up, ignoring the deep, searing pain in his leg, and he sprinted through the dead cars, making his way over to the side of the bridge. The whole thing sloped downward. He had to throw out a hand and catch a cable to keep himself from pitching over the edge. There had been rains high up in the mountains; the roaring waters of the river surged by below, well over capacity and pulling down every piece of debris that got in the way. Over the limp barrier of the drooping cables, a pair of steel pipes ran parallel to the bridge, their anchors more or less intact.

Ted looked over his shoulder. A duster snapped its jaws three inches from his face. "Jesus!" he shrieked. He kept ahold of his line while leaping over the cables and onto the pipes. They groaned under his weight, and he felt the one under his heels snap and fall away. His free arm wheeled as he screamed, desperate to keep balance. He held tight to the line, throwing his weight onto his toes while leaning back to miss the swipes and snaps from the zombie—no, the *two* zombies now—that besieged him, hungry for his flesh. A third was close behind. Ted side-stepped, quickly, moving-moving-moving, one foot over the other, down the length of the steel pipe. It groaned and shifted under his weight. The Flying Monkeys, those savage devices of destruction, had blown out part of the pipe further down; the only thing keeping this one in place were the half-dozen clips securing it to the bridge.

But the bridge was crumbling too, and the clips wouldn't cooperate for much longer.

Ted shuffled away, teetering on the unsteady pipe as the gash in his leg oozed way too much blood. He reached out and grabbed a new cable, pulled on it for support, and stutter-slid his way down the pipe, moving back toward the bank and working desperately to not look down. That last effort didn't pay off—at all. He kept catching glimpses at the river below; each time he saw the surging, frothing waters, his heart sank a little lower, until it hung like a weight in pit of his stomach. He had so much farther to go.

One of the dusters launched itself over the rail of the bridge, its arms flailing and scrambling for whatever purchase Ted had found. But its fine motor skills had been calcified by Monkey Dust, and it couldn't even come close to swiping at the cable. The creature pitched over the edge of the bridge, snarling and slavering, its arms pinwheeling as it took a solid header straight into the water. Ted could hear the snap of its neck when the thing's head smashed against the riverbed. The body floated back up, twisted, contorted, and dead. The water washed it away.

"Fuck me," Ted whispered.

Another duster threw itself across the side of the bridge. It snapped and spat as it scratched at the pipes, trying to claw its way onto them. Ted yelped and continued his hobbled escape, sliding uneasily along the metal tubes, the blood from his leg wound making the surface slick under his feet. He almost tumbled every three or four steps. The loose cable was the only thing keeping him on the edge of the bridge.

He chanced a look back over his shoulder. The duster had found footing on the pipes and was crawling along them, furious and hungry. The final duster did the same, leaping onto the pipes, snarling and clawing with its long fingernails clacking against the metal.

Ted turned and tried to run. His foot slipped immediately; he nearly fell off the pipe. He screamed and clung to the cable, but it had reached as far as it could. The angle of it was pulling Ted back toward the center of the bridge, back toward the dusters. He fought to regain his footing, bawling in fear. He gripped the bridge railing with one hand and aimed the broken cable with the other. Then he let it fly, hoping to knock at least one the dusters off the pipe. But the cable flopped uselessly through the air, its momentum whirling it out over the water as it missed both zombies by a good eight feet.

"Goddammit," Ted sighed.

The cable came wobbling back. Ted reached for it, but missed. He almost lost his balance, falling to his knees in a cold sob. "Stay back!" he screamed at the zombies, which didn't work at all. Tears clouded his eyes as his fingers clutched the pipes beneath him. he began inching backward, sobbing and threatening. "Stay away, you sons of bitches, I'll kill you!"

The dusters didn't seem to believe him, if they even understood what he was saying. They kept on, snarling and snapping their teeth, crawling closer and closer. "Stop it!" Ted cried. "I mean it!" He pulled off one boot and threw it at the nearest zombie, only five or so feet away. It bounced off the dusters head without making it flinch.

The one behind it flinched, though. It watched the boot ricochet off the other duster's skull and go spinning out over the river. Instinct kicked in, and the zombie leapt out after the boot, caught it in mid-air, and sank its teeth into the leather. Then it plummeted into the water, landing in the shallow water with a loud *CRACK*. There was damage, but it hadn't struck hard enough to snap its neck. The monster bobbed to the surface instead, thrashing and furious, with a useless arm trailing from its broken shoulder as it was swept downriver.

There was just one duster left.

But one was more than enough.

Ted was still totally fucked.

"I was Pagliacci!" he wailed. He clung to the pipes on his hands and knees, burying his head between his shoulders, sobbing and shuddering so hard that the brackets began rattling loose. A few even fell out of their mooring. The whole structure groaned and twisted. Ted yelped and clamped down harder. The duster gripped down, too. It locked eyes with Ted, staring him down as the whole bridge swayed.

Something let loose in Ted's bladder. A sudden wet warmth spread across his crotch. It hardly even registered.

The creaking of the pipes gave way to snapping of ties. Somewhere beneath it all, a rumbling *twist-crack* of soft metal sounded out as the pipes that spanned the river valley snapped in half beneath the strain. Suddenly, Ted was falling. He screamed, a pure, raw shriek of terror and incomprehension as the pipes collapsed. He swung down head-first, his hands and feet burning from the iron grip he held on the metal as the whole structure dropped into a freefall.

Somewhere back at the foot of the bridge, one of the brackets held fast; the pipes swung down from that pivot point, dropping toward the river like a hand on a clock. The last duster flailed its claws in surprise, a mistake that sent the snarling creature down into the river. It smashed its skull on the rocky banks and was pulled away down the river, twisted, broken, and leaking yellow goo from its shattered head.

Ted would have been thrilled...if he hadn't been arcing toward his own death.

The pipes fell, and his grip slipped. He slid down the pipes head-first, blood rushing to his brain, the gravity of the world fighting to pull him in. He saw the surface of the river rush up at his face, but he missed the water as the pipe swung clear and sailed back up in the other direction. He was hanging from the pipe now, like a panicked sloth in a collapsing tree. His palms were soaked with sweat, making his fingers slip. He swung by his ankles, upside-down and totally disoriented over the frothing crust of the river...and then his feet gave out, too, and he went soaring through the yellow-green fog. His momentum pushed him out to the bank, and he slammed into the hard, rocky shore.

The air exploded out of his lungs when he hit. His right arm twisted painfully under his shoulder as his head smashed into a clump of solid clay, and the earth beneath him spun.

He had just enough time to think "What the fuck, am I alive?" before it all went black.

22.

"Hey, is that Ted?"

Jimmy elbowed Patrick and nodded in the direction of the bridge. "You see that?" he panted. "That guy on the edge—is that Ted?"

Patrick squinted into the distance. He was out of breath, sweaty and distracted by both the dusters they'd just narrowly escaped and the fact that they were on a sagging old roof they'd climb up to with the help of a terrifyingly unstable stack of milk crates. The roof that was creaking and sagging…and also wet somehow. It was going to give out on them at any second. And how the fuck was he supposed to know if that was Ted? The bridge was a quarter-mile away. He saw *something* clinging to a bunch of pipes hanging off the side of the bridge. But for all he knew, it wasn't even human.

"I don't know," Patrick sighed. "It's a million miles away. It looks like a super-drunk worm.."

Then, the pipes that the bridge-person was clinging to leaned, snapped, and broke in half. Whoever was clinging to them for dear life screamed as they fell away. The pipes made an arc, and then the figure went flying, his arms and legs flailing as he sobbed and wailed. His cry of *"I was Pagliacci!"* carried across the distance.

Patrick blinked. "Oh. Yeah. That's definitely Ted."

They watched in horror as Ted went sailing through the air, and they winced when he slammed into the bank. They could hear the impact from six blocks away.

"Well, Ted's dead," Patrick decided.

Jimmy frowned. "That's a terrible thing to say."

"If it's any consolation, we'll be meeting up with him again soon." Patrick peeked over the edge of the roof at the three dusters throwing themselves against the metal walls of the building. With each impact, the roof shifted a little more. The groaning from the rafters wasn't offering a lot of hope. "They're going to knock this whole building down."

"How can they *do* that?" Richie whined. "This is a *building*."

"A building that got blown half to shit on M-Day," Brett replied.

"And the dusters have reinforced bones and veins," Patrick reminded them. "It's like three Wolverines throwing themselves at a paper bag." Another duster hit the side; this time, the wall dented. The roof groaned louder.

"I thought wolverines were small?" Richie asked, confused.

The other men all turned at the same time, each giving Richie the same look of shock and disgust. "The *comic book* Wolverine, Richie," shouted Patrick. "*The goddamn X-Man!*" He was so exasperated.

"Oh." Richie's cheeks flared red as he shrank back. "I...wasn't allowed to read comics."

"Didn't you watch cartoons?" Brett asked.

Richie cleared his throat and shook his head, embarrassed. "We watched a lot of The Waltons."

"Christ, that explains a lot," Gary muttered.

Another duster slammed into the wall below, and something in the structure finally gave. There was a loud squeal as the roof buckled in the middle, groaning under the strain. The metal tilted under their feet as the men wheeled their arms to keep their balance.

"Shit. We gotta move." Patrick scanned the block. The Monkey bombs had leveled this part of Asheville. Most of the nearby buildings had either collapsed immediately or crumbled since. There were only two buildings left that were close enough to jump to; one of them appeared to be solid brick, the same height as their current location. They could jump to it easily...but the roof had been rigged with rusted barbed wire fencing four feet high all the way around. There was no way over without cutting themselves to pieces.

The second option wasn't much better. It was an older building with a stucco exterior, and it had taken a brutal shelling on M-Day. It was riddled with holes and broken two-by-fours sticking out from the gaps in the walls like busted brown teeth. The water pipes in the building had burst, and though they were empty now, the flood had swamped the walls of the building with thousands of gallons of water before the reservoirs ran dry. Rain and humidity had kept the job going for the years that followed; the stucco was so soft in most places that it practically dripped down the building. The whole exterior was stained brown with rot and splotched with mold. There was no barbed wire, which was a point in its favor. But it was three stories taller than the collapsing store they now stood on top of. There was no way to reach the relative safety of the stucco building's roof.

Dusters, razor wire, or a collapsing third option Patrick really, *really* didn't like.

He sighed.

"I have an idea. No one's going to like it."

"If you ever had a single idea someone *did* like, I'd fall down dead from shock," Gary grumbled. "What is it?"

Patrick grimaced. "Who wants to jump through a wall?"

23.

"This is so fucked," Brett growled.

"It is," Patrick agreed. "But it is *less* fucked than every other option."

Richie peered over the edge of the roof. "What if we just jump to the ground?"

"Two stories down, and then what? You're going to outrun the zombies?" Gary asked. "On the leg you just broke from jumping *two stories* onto broken concrete?"

Richie shrugged. "Maybe…"

The roof continued to shake. Metal pipes in the rafters beneath them broke loose and crashed to the floor. The squeal of twisting brackets pierced the air. "I don't want to rush anybody," Patrick implored them, "but the building is literally falling to pieces under our feet, and we should probably jump."

One of the dusters broke all the way through the exterior wall and slammed into a rusted metal support pole near the center of the room. He glanced off the pole, snarled, and ran at it again and again. The building shook with every blow, until he finally hit the beam so hard it buckled in the middle. The bent pole pulled down a piece of the ceiling. Jimmy slipped and fell, screaming and sliding down the broken panel. He slid off the edge of the hanging metal sheet and threw his arms around wildly. His wrist curled around a narrow exhaust pipe that was fixed through the roof by a thin layer of epoxy. Jimmy flailed as he held fast, his legs dangling out over the open floor. The other dusters crashed through the wall, slavering beneath him, snapping their yellow teeth and spitting greenish foam from their lips.

"Help me!" Jimmy screamed.

"Brett! Richie! Get Jimmy!" Patrick shouted. "Gary, bemme your bag."

Brett and Richie jumped to action. They skidded carefully over to the busted panel and worked on pulling Jimmy out of the hole. But Gary just looked at Patrick, confused. "Huh?"

"Bemme!" Patrick screamed. "Bemme-bemme-*bemme!*"

"*Use* real *words!*" Gary screamed back. But Patrick's frantic grabby hands clutching and unclutching his fingers spoke volumes. Gary slipped his backpack off his shoulders and pushed it into Patrick's outstretched arms. "What's wrong with *your* bag?"

"Yours is heavier," Patrick replied. He tested the weight of the backpack in one hand while focusing the majority of his mental powers on dialing into the distance between buildings.

"So what?" Gary demanded.

"So everything," Patrick countered. "Now be quiet…I'm gonna throw it."

Gary's eyes opened wide. "Why?!"

Patrick didn't respond. He didn't even hear the question. He was consumed by his focus. His aim had to be perfect: the toss, masterly. In the flickering movie theater of his mind, he saw Grandpa Mori in *Three Ninjas.* Or was it *Three Ninjas Kick Back*? "Doesn't matter," he mumbled to himself. *Watch the target grow in front of your eyes,* Grandpa Mori said. *And when it gets as big as a melon, throw!* Patrick leaned forward and willed his eyes to expand the size of the hole in the building across the alley. He put so much force and pressure into his eyeballs that they quivered and felt like they might pop. The hole did not grow larger.

"Movies suck."

Your *movies suck,* Ben's voice snickered in his ear. *I saw your Blockbuster "employee picks" shelf.*

My movies were cherished by millions.

How many millions cherished From Justin to Kelly*?*

That was an ironic choice! Patrick insisted. *I also had* Street Fighter *on there, and it's about to become incredibly relevant, because I'm about to do some Jean-Claude-level shit right now.*

Street Fighter *also sucked.*

I can't even talk to you right now, Patrick thought, annoyed. *I'm glad your weird memory-ghost is back, but I cannot talk to you right now. I'm too busy about to be a legend.*

He took aim, swung his arm a few times, then hurled the bag across the gap. It smashed into the side of the building, at the edge of the hole. The rotten stucco crumbled apart on impact and the backpack barreled through, disappearing inside the building as it nearly doubled the size of the hole in the wall.

"Hot damn!" Patrick chirped. "I'm so good at ninja!"

"Great...let's jump into a building that's literally falling apart," Gary said, rolling his eyes.

"You're welcome to stay on top of *this* building that's falling apart," Patrick allowed. "As for me and my house, we will not serve the horde." He dropped his own backpack off his shoulders and hurled it across the alley. It sailed cleanly through the hole. "*Ninja!* Alright! Who wants to go first?"

"Abso-fucking-lutely not." Gary said.

But Patrick wasn't looking at him. "Brett! You're big."

Brett dropped Jimmy's faint-white body onto the roof and stood up tall, crossing his arms. "So?"

"So, I think you should jump across and hit that wall like the Kool-Aid Man and bust it out a little bit more. What do you think?"

Brett looked doubtfully across the alley. The wet, ruined stucco was practically dripping from the rotted struts. The wall *did* seem pretty flimsy. He stretched his neck and pumped his shoulders. "All right, I'll do it. Fuck it."

"That's the spirit!" Patrick cheered. "It'll be great. Probably."

"Better than getting ripped apart by zombies," Brett muttered. He stepped up to the edge of the roof and gauged the distance across the alley. It wasn't that far, really—maybe six feet, tops. He could jump six feet. "All right, give me some room." The others shuffled out of the way, and Brett took a few steps back. He took a deep breath, said, "Here goes nothing," and ran forward, planting his foot on the edge of the roof and leaping out over the open alley.

It was when he was squarely over a deep, narrow patch of absolutely nothing that Brett just lost his shit.

Maybe he couldn't jump six feet after all.

"*Fuuuuuccccckkkkk!*" he screamed. That was all he had time to say, that one word, but the *weight* of that word, the *pathos* in the way he *said* it, sent chills up the spines of the men standing on the roof. Thrashing his arms and kicking his legs, Brett looked more like a scared dog tossed in a pool than the Kool-Aid Man.

They held their breath when they heard the sound of Brett's flailing meat-body smash into the side of the building. "Aw, Christ...I can't look," Richie moaned, shielding his eyes. Jimmy threw up when he heard the sound—and *he* was an EMT.

"Ho-ly shit," Gary breathed, peering in horrified amazement at the carnage across the alley. "That son of a bitch made it!"

Richie peeked out between his fingers. "What?"

"He made it! Dammit, he made it!"

"I knew he was okay," Jimmy said, dry heaving onto his shoes and wiping brown spittle and pieces of half-digested SPAM from his mouth. "I knew he was fine. I'm a doctor."

"EMT," Richie reminded him.

Brett *had* hit the wall, but he'd hit it with the force of a huge, flying Brett. Just as Patrick had predicted, he'd crashed right through the soppy mess of plaster, leaving a vaguely-Brett-shaped hole in the wall that completely engulfed— and substantially enlarged—the hole made by Gary's backpack.

"Wow. I *am* good at plans!" Patrick said.

"Big words for a man who took a sword to the gut at Disney World," Gary reminded him.

Patrick leaned out over the edge of the building. "Hey Brett—you okay?"

There was silence from the other building.

"Probably knocked himself right out," Jimmy surmised. But then, they heard the grating sound of shifting rubble, and from somewhere within the darkness of the wall-cave, the sound of Brett's best Kool-Aid voice: "*Oh, yeaaaaah!*"

Just then, a duster smashed through another support on the first building, and the roof began to fully collapse. It folded inward from the center, breaking and pulling and disappearing into the depths of the building like a cartoon cave-in. Richie screamed and instinctively did the thing he thought would save his life best, which was to leap up onto the edge wall and throw himself across the alley, screaming, "*Aiiiiiieeeeee!*" like some 1980s cartoon cat. He landed safely nonetheless.

Jimmy went next, figuring that if Richie could do it, any idiot could do it. He was mostly right; he made it in, too, but not without slamming his shoulder against the wall as he went through. And Jimmy, who was not built like Brett, did *not* cut through it like butter.

"Ow!"

The roof beneath their feet was at a hard tilt now; the squealing of metal from below was enough to tell them the roof was officially fucked. Patrick winced as the popping sound of metal supports tearing away from the brick walls cracked through the air, and the entire surface shifted and slipped under their shoes. "Go! Now!" he hollered.

"Go on!" Gary shouted back. He gave Patrick a shove, enough to propel him up and onto the edge of the roof wall.

Patrick wheeled his arms for balance, teetering out over the open drop. His body had gained too much momentum, he had to put it to use; it was now or never. He pushed himself forward on thin, knobby knees and fell across the chasm of the alley. *Jesus Christ*, he thought. *I don't want to die from two stories up.* His gut swirled, and his testicles pulled up tight, into his belly. He closed his eyes and waited for death, but to his great surprise and delight, death didn't come. Instead, he slammed ingloriously onto the cracked floor of the warehouse building, tumbled forward on elbows and feet, and slid to a graceless stop at Brett's feet.

"*Oh, yeaaaaah!*" Brett said again.

He and Richie helped Patrick to his feet as he dusted himself off. He wobbled back toward the hole in the wall and peered across at Gary. The Red Cap was sweating bullets; his face was pale as flour. "Gotta move, Gare-Bear," Patrick shouted.

"Don't fucking call me that," Gary shouted back. He swung his arms, trying to work up the courage. His feet felt like cement blocks. "I'm sorry I pushed you."

"Want me to come back and push *you?*" Patrick asked.

"Come on, Gary!" Jimmy hollered. "That thing's not gonna hold much longer!"

"I know, I know!" Gary snapped. "Fuck!" He stepped up onto the brick rim of the building. The ceiling behind him twisted and screeched, falling and sliding down into the center, and the others could plainly hear the snarling sounds of the dusters, still busily pile-driving themselves into metal beams. One of them must have crunched through another major support, because the ceiling finally had enough; it jerked and wrenched and buckled, and then it fell, the metal crashing to the floor in sheets as the struts clanged against steel. The cacophony was tremendous. Gary found himself teetering on an eight-inch rim with open air in front of him and open air behind.

He closed his eyes and leapt.

His foot slipped as he pushed off, and he fell down instead of forward. He screamed as he plummeted toward the asphalt.

"Grab this!" Patrick cried. He let his backpack fall from his shoulders and grabbed one shoulder strap, clamping his fist around it like a vice. He swung the pack around and prayed to God someone would catch hold of the other strap. Then he leaned out of the building, threw up his right arm, and caught Gary by the wrist as he fell. The momentum of Gary's fall pulled them both down, and Patrick was yanked through the hole in the wall. For what felt like eternity, the two men were free-falling…then Brett snatched the other strap of Patrick's bag, braced himself against an iron fitting in the floor, and stopped their fall. Gary arced down and slammed into the stucco, denting the first floor of the building. "Ow!"

"Should I pull you up or drop you?" Brett strained. "Answer fast."

"Up!" Patrick said.

"Those dusters could bust out any second," Richie added. He and Jimmy rushed forward and grabbed hold of the backpack. The three men hauled in the other two, pulling them up into the rubble, until all five of them collapsed on the floor, breathing hard, sweating, and somehow completely alive.

"See?" Patrick wheezed, his whole body shaking with adrenaline. "That went great."

24.

Ted had decided he would just lie there until he died. And he figured it wouldn't be long. He could feel the life oozing out of him, like thick, heavy sweat glooping from his pores. He'd always thought that when the spirit left a body, it passed through the skin quickly, raised up to the heavens on an angel's wing or a baby's breath or some Precious Moments shit like that. But no. It didn't pass or float. It *oozed*. Slowly.

He was surprised by that.

He knew his body would eventually be found. Hopefully, it would be found by his friends. But if not them, then at least by actual, real humans—*please God*. He wanted so, so badly to be found by actual, real humans. *Don't let the dusters find me*, he thought through the thick, viscous coating of his oozing spirit. *Please don't let that happen to my body. I sang Pagliacci.*

Because he was determined to be found by actual, real humans—preferably his friends—he wanted to make himself presentable. The position he'd landed in made him look like some sort of weird, broken sex-eagle. Ted sent every ounce of force he could muster to his right knee, willing it to straighten and thereby close the indecent gap that spread like a mouth from the bottom of his groin. But his knee didn't respond. In fact, *nothing* in his body responded.

He was beaten, broken, and soon would be dead. And he would look like a weird, broken sex-eagle when it happened.

I take it back—don't let my friends find me like this, he begged.

"I found Ted!" It was Patrick's voice, from just over the hill. "He looks like some sort of sex-eagle!"

Ted closed his eyes, and he wept.

"What the hell is a sex-eagle?" Gary demanded, stomping over the hill. Then he saw Ted's poor, twisted body lying awkwardly on the bank. His face softened. "Oh."

"I'm not a sex-eagle!" Ted cried.

"Big words for a sex-eagle," Brett snorted, joining them.

"Hey, there are *way* worse things to be than a sex-eagle," Patrick said, patting him gently on the shoulder. "I mean, look at Richie. He looks like a living egg. He's an extra-virgin who might be a natural eunuch for all the world knows."

"Hey!" yelled Richie.

"I'm just trying to make him feel better," Patrick assured him.

"Hmph," Richie replied.

Jimmy elbowed his way to the front of the pack. "Hold on, now—don't try to move...your spinal cord might be damaged."

"I *can't* move!" Ted whined.

"You shouldn't know that...it means you're trying," Patrick said. "Stop trying." He couldn't help but be impressed by the calm, methodical way Jimmy inspected the injured patient. As he prodded Ted's various bits and bones with the wooden handle of his new carving knife, he was instantly transformed from the serious sad-sack into some weird Marcus Welby-slash-Dr. Quinn, Medicine Woman hybrid. "Well," he said when he finished his inspection, "without the ability to do any scans, it's hard to say for sure. But based on what I can observe, it actually seems that you're...fine?"

"Define 'fine,'" Gary said.

"Yeah—define 'fine!'" Ted sobbed.

"I mean, as far as I can tell—which, again, is pretty severely limited—you seem pretty okay. No broken bones, no apparent fractures...your leg is missing a small piece of flesh, and you're going to have some pretty intense bruising and soreness, but from what I can tell, you're not in any danger. As long as we get that bite wound cleaned."

Ted sputtered. "But—but—but what about internal bleeding?"

"All bleeding is internal," Patrick pointed out. "All good bleeding, anyway."

Jimmy's face went blank. "No. It's not."

Patrick rolled his eyes. "Okay, Marcus."

Jimmy ignored him and continued. "I'm not ruling out internal hemorrhaging, and frankly, I'm not ruling out any fractures or breaks either. For all I know, your brain could be one-third soup inside your maybe-broken skull. But your pupils are responding properly, you seem to have sensation in all the right places, and I've been bending and unbending your arm the entire time we've been talking...you haven't even noticed."

"You have?" Ted's head lolled so he could look down to see that Jimmy was, in fact, manipulating his left arm. Ted's mouth fell open. "Wow."

"You're in shock," Jimmy told him. "You had a harrowing experience with some bodily trauma and your brain is trying to process. It's normal. But you swung down pretty low to the ground when you dropped and landed on a soft-earth bluff that's thick with vegetation and hasn't been mowed in years. Your hands are ripped raw from holding so tight to the cable, but the trade-off is, you're generally, mostly, fine." And then, to avoid liability, he added, "As far as I can tell."

"I don't think you need the caveat," Patrick whispered. "All the malpractice lawyers died on M-Day."

"Oh, that's true!" Jimmy replied happily.

"Am I gonna die if I stand up?" Ted wailed.

"Honestly, I'll be shocked if you *can* stand up," Jimmy replied. "You need to rest. Don't rush it. It may be an hour, it may be a week."

"A *week*?" Gary grumbled, and Richie elbowed him. Gary turned and growled at Richie, who shrank back behind Brett's wide shoulders.

"Just, he might need rest…" Richie whimpered.

"*Just*, there are motherfucking *dusters* swarming this area," Gary glowered. Richie shrank back even more. "He's fine—the doc said so. Let's pick him up and move him off the grid." The others hemmed and hawed.

Everyone looked at Patrick.

"Who, me?" Patrick asked. "Oh. Uh…sure. Okay. I mean, we're pretty well hidden by the bluff, and I have yet to see a duster that can swim."

"Except for the zombie fish monster," Ted pointed out.

"Except for the zombie fish monster, yes," Patrick agreed. "We'll keep an eye out for those. I think we're relatively safe here, for a little while. Let's lie low, be on guard, and give Ted a chance to make his limbs work again. We'll head out before sundown." Gary opened his mouth to respond, but Patrick raised his hand to silence him. "Hopefully *well* before sundown," he added quickly. "But no later. We could all use a second to catch our breath, and it'll also help me figure out how to execute the next step in the plan."

"Which is?" Brett said.

Patrick nodded upriver. "How to get us passage on that boat."

The Red Caps turned and squinted through the mist. Sure enough, a few hundred yards past the bridge, a huge, old-fashioned riverboat was nestled against a flimsy dock, the yellow-crusted water of the river splashing up against its flaking white sides.

The riverboat was huge. It stood four decks tall and was almost as long as a city block. A red, rickety, two-story paddle wheel rose up out of the water like a bundled roll of wood-picket teeth at the stern, and two scratched-black smokestacks towered over the pilot cabin near the bow. It was a boat from the pages of Mark Twain, a once-genteel ship for once-genteel Midwesterners to paddle slowly and pleasantly up and down the Mississippi…but like all things, it had suffered death now, or something like it, and was resurrected like Patrick's own bones, in the same shape, in the same mode, but faded, scuffed, chipped, and cracked.

Still, it was a pretty impressive sight.

"Shouldn't we look for something…faster?" Gary asked doubtfully.

"Faster would be ideal," Patrick nodded. "But gasoline being basically sludge now—unless someone's got a refinery up and running, and maybe they do, people have enough time to build Civil War camps, they should have enough time to make gas. Short of that, any gas-engine boat is going to be either useless or retrofitted, and therefore slower—and less reliable. But a steam engine paddler…that'll get us where we need to go. And, I mean, look at it." He gestured at the steamboat, and not a single man among them could help but be impressed by the sheer fucking size. It made the dock it was tethered to look like a toothpick. "It's an elephant in a world of mice."

"Aren't elephants scared of mice?" Brett asked.

Patrick frowned. "Are they? I thought that was just a made-up *Dumbo* thing."

"I'm pretty sure they're actually scared of mice," Gary said.

"Well then, it's not an elephant in a world of mice. It's a tank in a world of tricycles. Better?"

"Tricycles don't float," Richie pointed out.

"Goddammit, Richie, neither do tanks—it's an analogy!" Patrick screamed.

"I'm so tired of being yelled at!" Richie yelled back.

"*Shut up, Richie!*" the other Red Caps shouted back.

Jimmy wondered about the crew aboard. "Who knows how long they've been docked, and who knows how long before they leave."

"And who knows which way they're going," Gary added.

"Yeah," Patrick nodded. "There's a lot of recon to do." His gaze broke from the boat and returned to his comrades. "If the answer is 'no', say no. But. Brett, Johnny, Richie…would you feel comfortable staying here with Ted if Gary and I go up and see what's what with the boat?"

Brett crossed his arms, insulted to even be asked. "Yeah. We're good."

"I think we're good here too, yeah," said Jimmy, nodding.

Richie didn't say any words. His mouth just opened to emit a "Squee-aak," and it was pretty obviously a no vote. But it didn't matter, because no one was really paying attention.

"Okay," said Patrick. "If you need us back, just scream."

"We'll be within earshot and eyesight the entire time," Gary assured them.

Patrick nodded enthusiastically. "Unless we're eaten by runners or kidnapped by townies or swallowed up by a sinkhole or exploded by a latent Monkey bomb or hauled off into the woods and nailed to a tree by some crazy zealot, we will definitely probably be within eyesight." ·

"Sounds great," Brett said dryly.

Patrick turned to Gary. "I'm starting to think they're tiring of my wit and charm," he said with a frown.

"*Your* wit? *Your* charm?" Gary asked. "No way."

"The mind reels, just thinking about it," Patrick agreed as the two men left their party and walked toward the paddle wheel boat.

25.

"How glad are you that you pledged yourself to my every move, scale of one to ten?" Patrick asked.

Gary snorted. "You want the real truth, or you want the nicer one?"

Patrick smiled. "Mean truths are nice truths because they save you the cruelty of a really kind lie."

"I don't think I followed that," Gary said. "But since you're asking, I've had some doubts."

"I have *no* doubt." Patrick walked with his hands clasped his hands behind his back…he wasn't really sure what else to do with them. They seemed so thin and rickety, like jointed twigs pinned onto a marionette. "You really can go your own way, you know. I don't mean that like some sort of power play ultimatum. I mean truly and sincerely, I'm grateful for you all and your help, and for your company. But you guys should do what's best for you. And after torturous months in hell in Charlotte…it's just gone beyond what any of us thought this journey I set us on would be."

Gary chewed on those words, letting them sit in his jaw for a few steps before giving his reply. "I meant it when I said I wanted to make up for all the bad shit I've done," he admitted. "Honestly, I think pretty much every decision you make is three-quarters crazy and one-quarter stupid. But I owe you a debt for what we did to you, and to your friend—what we did to everybody. So if being annoyed that we're making ourselves zombie bait for a few hours to let Ted get through his hissy fit is part of it, fine." He shrugged. "It's my fuckin' redemption tour. It's not supposed to be fun."

Patrick smiled. "There comes a time in every man's life when he realizes that he's someone else's punishment."

Gary snorted. "Yeah, well. There's another thing too."

"What's that?"

"It's that even though you have terrible ideas, we're still alive."

"Most of us," Patrick said quietly.

Gary nodded. "Most of us, yeah. Which, really…one thing about Bloom was, he got more Red Caps killed than anything. He didn't care. Throw us at a problem, we'll sort it out or get sorted. Didn't matter to him. There were always more men like us, wandering and alone, looking for some sort of power. Always someone to fill an open spot. Bloom didn't give two shits about our lives. But I think you do."

Patrick snorted. He wiped his nose. He looked off over the river. "Yeah," he finally said. "I guess I do."

They continued on, and soon they neared the dock. The green mist melted away, revealing the riverboat in all its battered glory. The white paint was chipped and flaking, the paddle wheel was missing a handful of planks, and one of the twin smokestacks had begun listing to one side. Most of the windows had been smashed out; behind their empty frames was gloomy darkness. It was eerie, this ghost ship from an era past, sitting here in the apocalypse, swaying and creaking on the water.

The name of the boat was painted on its flaking side in huge, faded red letters: BIG MUDDY QUEEN.

"There's no way one single person said that name out loud before they painted it on the side of this boat. It is impossible."

"Different era," Gary offered. "Different…words."

"Sure."

The silence surrounding the boat was eerie. It wasn't just *quiet*…it was as if the riverboat itself were drawing in and suffocating all the ambient noise of the riverfront, draping a velvet curtain over top if it, so that the only sounds that filled the vacuum were the sounds of the boat creaking and the water lapping.

"I don't like this," Gary said without moving his lips.

"No," Patrick agreed, "this is the first four minutes of a 90s horror movie, for sure,"

"You don't leave a boat like this unguarded. I think we're being watched."

"We're definitely being watched. The question is…are we being hunted?"

Gary stopped. He drew the pipe from his belt. "Goddammit, why'd you have to say that?" he hissed. His hand was already slippery on the metal.

They stepped cautiously onto the dock.

"*Stop.*" The word cracked through the air like a shot from a gun. Patrick and Gary froze.

"Fuck," Gary breathed.

"Fuck," Patrick echoed.

A gray figure appeared on the first deck, melting forth from the dark shadows of the cabin, until it resolved itself into the shape of a woman, short and gaunt, with hard angles in her bones and tight dreadlocks in her hair. She held a crossbow against her chin, one eye peering straight as steel down the sights. "You've got ten bolts pointed at you right now." She gave a sharp whistle that screeched through the fog. At the signal, a chorus of knocks went up from around the boat, invisible mercenaries echoing the threat.

"We're not here to be a problem," Patrick said, raising his hands into the air.

"He's holding a weapon," the woman replied coolly in Gary's direction. They could hear the squeak of her finger tightening on the trigger.

"Sorry." Gary dropped the pipe. It hit the dock and rolled off the edge, into the water. "Goddammit," he muttered. But he raised his hands, and together, they stood like a pair of referees calling a field goal in some pre-apocalyptic nonsense football game.

"What do you want?" the woman asked.

Patrick cleared his throat uncomfortably. "Top of the list right now? To not be in the crosshairs of a crossbow."

"Tough," the woman spat. "Next?"

"We honestly aren't looking for any trouble," Patrick assured her. "We need to get to the Gulf of Mexico and we're looking for a ride. Since this is a boat, and boats go to gulfs, we're hoping it might be heading that direction."

The woman tensed behind the crossbow. "Who are you?"

"I mean, I don't think we've met." An unopened can of beans flew through the air, thrown from the third deck. It was hurled by some absolute cannon of an arm, and Patrick ducked just in time. The heavy can flew past his shoulder and cracked Gary in the front of his skull. "*Ow!*"

Patrick sucked in his breath. "Oooo," he winced. "You okay?"

"Goddammit!" Gary yelled, shoving Patrick hard, then touching his hand to his head. There was already a knot, and it was bleeding pretty badly.

"Do you guys have a Band-Aid or something?"

"One more chance," the woman said. "Who are you?"

"I'm Patrick. This is Gary. He's a Red Cap." He turned to Gary and put a hand on his shoulder. "You want me to try to find you some ice?" Gary snarled and swatted away the hand.

"Red Cap?" the woman said.

"You know," Patrick replied, gesturing at Gary. "Train people."

The woman's eyes frosted over. She nodded. "We've heard of you," she said coolly.

"Well, I just want to be clear," Patrick said. "*I'm* not a train person, I'm more of a walking person."

"I can't feel my face," Gary realized.

"Oh, that'll come back," Patrick assured him.

"Fuck off."

"How'd you end up with train people?" the woman demanded.

"Oh. Um." Patrick thought. "Well, I guess they…tried to kill me. And that really brought us together."

"They tried to kill you?"

"Yeah," he nodded enthusiastically. "It was a whole thing. I guess you kind of had to be there. They were ordered to kill me, then they were really sorry, and they sort of saved my life, kind of? After having a very active hand in almost ending it. And now we're—well, friends is a strong word. I don't think they like me very much."

"Less and less every second," Gary growled, wiping the blood from his forehead with the hem of his shirt.

"It's sort of an *Odd Couple* thing," Patrick assured her. "But now they're helping me get to where I'm headed, even though I keep telling them they can leave."

"What's at the Gulf of Mexico?" the woman asked. Her words sounded like echoes in Patrick's ears.

The boat and the riverbank melted away, and Patrick was back in his Chicago apartment, sitting quietly on his couch.

"I would never go to the Gulf of Mexico," Ben decided out loud.

He was sitting in the hallway with his back to Patrick's door, thumbing through travel magazines. He'd picked them up off the floor of the apartment's lobby on his way to the stairwell. This was his new ritual: showing up at Patrick's door with old magazines. "It's so hot. I mean, look at these pictures. It just looks so hot."

Patrick stared at the floor. There was half of a starfish sticker that Izzy had stuck there when she was two and a half. He and Annie were never able to peel it up. Patrick had been pretty mad about it when it happened—not mat at Izzy, but mad that there was a half-ripped sticker glued to the wooden floor that just had refinished two months before. He'd told

Izzy for the hundredth time not to put stickers on the wood as he scrubbed at the stubborn paper with an industrial strength cleaning solvent that was totally useless. Izzy nodded and said, "Otay, Dada." She toddled over to the sticker book, grabbed a rainbow sticker, and stuck it on Patrick's shoulder with her little baby fingers. "Dere you go," she said. "Thanks, pal," Patrick said. He kissed her on the head. Then she peeled a frog sticker out of the book and pasted it to the floorboards. Patrick closed his eyes and sighed. She was two-and-a-half years old then.

And now, the sticker was here. And she was gone.

"This person's sweating," Ben said from the other side of the door. "God, this person is sweating through her shirt. This is supposed to be a professional magazine, this person is a model, and the whole spread looks like she just ran a marathon into a volcano. It's too hot down there. Let's never go to the Gulf, okay?"

Patrick covered the starfish sticker with his toe. It was cheap paper, shiny and smooth and real. He pulled his feet up onto the couch. He dropped a throw pillow over the sticker. He laid his head down on the armrest and cried.

"Food looks good, though," Ben offered from the hallway. "I'd trade my foot for a Po' Boy. Look at that. It has lettuce on it, and I'd still cut my foot off at the ankle to have one of these right now. Do you think Emeril Lagasse is dead? Probably, right? Yeah…probably." Ben rustled the pages of the magazine, making a big, audible show of closing it up. He stood up and knocked on the door one more time. "Leaving some potatoes out here if you want them. They look kind of weird. But I had one this morning. It was okay. Let's do this again, huh? What's that? Same time tomorrow? You got it." He gave Patrick's door a tap-tap-slap-knock, a way of signing off.

"The Gulf of Mexico. What a dumb place," he said as he disappeared down the hall.

"Hey," the woman on the riverboat said, snapping her fingers.

Patrick blinked. The apartment was gone. Ben was gone.

He was standing on the dock.

"What's at the Gulf?" she asked again.

"Oh." Patrick cleared his throat. "Po' Boys," he said. "And family."

The woman shook her head. "Po' Boys and family. Great." She used the crossbow to gesture toward Gary. "Him too?"

"Well, sort of. Him, and the others, back there on the other side of the bridge. But they don't have to stay. I mean, they can, but…I don't know that they'll want to."

"We may want to find our own way after that," Gary confirmed, taking a knee and cradling his head.

"Look, they did this to you, not me," Patrick whispered.

The woman on the riverboat shifted her weight uncomfortably. "You Red Caps don't plan on staying in the Gulf?"

"We don't have any plans on being anywhere," Gary grumbled.

"Is that right? Good to know." The woman considered this. She lowered the crossbow. "Let me talk to Roman," she said.

"Roman?" Gary mouthed to Patrick. Patrick shrugged.

"Oh," the woman added, tossing a look back over her shoulder, "the rest of them are staying." She gestured toward the upper decks of the boat. "And they are *deadly* with their cans."

"No shit," Gary grumbled.

"We'll just wait here, then," Patrick confirmed. The woman dropped her shoulder and stalked off into the boat, but Patrick and Gary could feel the stares of the hidden warriors boring into their skin like slow-moving bullets. "This is nice," Patrick decided. "We never just take time to stand quietly and enjoy each other's company."

"When I start enjoying it, I'll let you know."

"Hey, I'm sorry you took a can of beans to the bean. I didn't throw it. I just didn't get hit by it."

"I know."

"Okay. Because you seem angry at me."

"Oh, do I?" Gary snapped.

Patrick frowned at Gary's forehead. "That looks pretty nasty. Maybe we should clean it." He glanced at the water in the river, lapping at the dock—brown, thick, and layered with chunks of hard green crust. "Or... maybe not."

"I'm not putting any of that Monkey dust water in my bloodstream," Gary spat. "It'll turn me into some monster like the fish thing that got Ted."

"Boy, that thing could run, huh?" Patrick said, almost wistful.

Gary would have furrowed his brow if it hadn't hurt so goddamn much. "You sound pretty fucking sweet on it."

Patrick shrugged. "I grew up on the *X-Men* cartoon. Mutants are not to be feared, but to be embraced, and trained for righteous combat."

"I got a feeling all that weird shit's just gonna keep piling up," Gary said. "More Monkey dust mixing with more nature, making more and more weird creatures. Give it a few years, you could probably have your own fish-mutant circus."

Patrick's eyes glistened. "That's all eight-year-old Patrick ever wanted."

The woman with the crossbow reappeared at the railing. "Hey. He'll see you." She gave a signal, and a second woman appeared from the darkness of the first-deck cabins. She hauled a homemade ladder over the side of the boat and leaned it against the railing so they could climb onboard.

"Great," Gary muttered, stepping across the dock.

"Not you," the woman with the crossbow snapped. She pointed a bolt at Patrick. "Him."

Gary's face flushed red. "It's both of us or none of us," he growled.

"None, then." She signaled again, and the second woman began to draw up the ladder.

"Wait, wait, wait!" Patrick said. He squeezed Gary's shoulder. "It's okay. I'll be fine."

"They'll eat you, for all you know. Literally fucking *eat* you."

"If they try it, they'll just choke on my bones. I am *exceedingly* bony." He tossed his elbows through the air to show how pointy they were. "I'll be okay."

"You'd better," Gary snapped. "If we came all this way just for you to die here, I'll find your corpse and piss on it myself."

"Ah yes," Patrick said, patting Gary on the arm as he walked toward the ladder. "The old Irish goodbye!"

"That's not what an Irish goodbye is."

But Patrick didn't hear him. He was scrambling up the ladder and tripping clumsily over the railing. He fell onto the boat, and three more women rushed forward, rusty blades in hand. They yanked him to his feet and dragged him into the darkness.

"Ah, hell," Gary muttered.

Then he sat down on the bank to wait.

26.

Patrick stumbled through the dark cabin of the riverboat. He just could not believe how bad it smelled. "I knew it would be wet in here, but sweet Jesus, this carpet," he said with a sour face.

"It's not a JCPenney," one of his escorts shot back. "You want skinny plasticoids to spray flowery shit in your nostrils every four seconds, go back to Malibu."

Plasticoids? Patrick wondered silently. *Malibu?*

"This is the fucking end times, and guess what? Carpet gets moldy," another woman shot at him. She tightened her grip on his arm and yanked him forward sharply.

"I'm not complaining," Patrick protested. "I'm just noticing...and what I notice primarily is that the smell makes me want to throw up."

"You get over that eventually," the third woman confided, bringing up the rear of the guard. "The smell never gets *good*, but you'll want to harm yourself over it less."

They pulled him through a cabin and into a gloomy foyer, where a short flight of stairs trudged its way to the second deck through the stifling weight of red-and-black floral carpeting. Patrick shuffled up the steps, shoved on by the women below. He tripped over the top step and banged his shins on the hard floor. He cursed, but he also wondered how such a thick and heavy carpet so be so goddamn thin. The women didn't seem to care much for his clumsiness. One of them jabbed him with the hilt of her machete until he grumbled back to his feet and stumbled on. "I don't even know where I'm going," he said.

"We'll let you know if you take a wrong turn."

He passed a hallway as one of the women slapped his ear with the flat side of her machete blade. "Ow!"

The woman grinned. "Turn left."

"I should have jumped off Cinderella's Castle," Patrick grumbled.

They shuttled him through a dining room filled with eight-foot round tables in various states of disrepair, some of them covered by soiled cloths. Years-old chicken skin was ground into the carpet, and the smell of mildew was smeared over by dust and grease. Through the double doors, past the rusty, useless kitchen; down another dingy hallway, and up one more flight of damp stairs. They emerged in a study of sorts, a semi-circular room with dark wood panel walls and a burgundy paisley carpet. A set of large windows at the back of the room cast a wide opening over the boat's big red paddle wheel. The watery-green apocalyptic light filtered in through the windows, augmented by a series of six kerosene lamps on hooks in the walls. Their flames threw a flickering orange-yellow light on a heavy oak desk in the center of the room. Behind the table, obscured by the glare of the window backlight, his face shifting in the light of the lanterns, sat a man in dark gray slacks and a blue button-down shirt that was really not very dirty, all things considered. One of Patrick's escorts hurried up to the desk and whispered something into his ear. As he listened, his face brightened.

"Ah!" the man said. He pushed back his chair and stood up. He stepped around the table and extended his hand to Patrick, his face bearing a soft smile. "Welcome aboard. I'm Roman. Roman Marwood. Pleasure to meet you."

Patrick clasped his hand and shook. "Patrick Deen. Thanks for the warm welcome."

"Ah. Yes. I see the welt," he said, examining Patrick's cheek. He turned to the women with the machetes, and his eyes flashed. "That'll be all, ladies," he said, a small sharpness on his tongue. The two women slunk back out of the room and closed the door. Roman's face softened once more. "Sorry about that. They love hitting people."

"Could have been worse," Patrick demurred. They could have used the blade."

"Absolutely." Roman returned to his seat, and he gestured at an empty chair on Patrick's side of the desk. "Please. Sit down."

"I've got a pretty fussy Red Cap out there. I'm not sure I have time for tea." Still, Patrick set down his backpack and lowered himself into the chair, crossing an ankle over his knee.

"Caught that can she threw pretty square, right?" Roman laughed.

"He should be able to see straight in a day or so."

"Most people duck."

"I did," Patrick replied. "He...did not."

"It's actually something of a test for us," Roman admitted, shifting back in his chair and matching Patrick's casual lean. "Anyone who knocks on the door gets a can of beans at the head. The ones who duck usually snatch up the beans and run. They're just desperate for food. As we all are."

"You must have quite the pantry if you're throwing beans at everyone who comes to the door."

Roman laughed. "Oh, they're not really beans. We fill old cans with rocks and water and solder them shut."

"Oh. Well, that's not very nice," Patrick pointed out.

"It's not very nice to try to take our food," Roman countered.

"I don't think it's 'taking' if you hurl it at their heads."

"It shows us what they were here for," Roman said dismissively. "They came to take our food; they can't have it. What we have, we've earned, just like anyone else."

"Lot of ways to 'earn' things these days..." Patrick mused. He rubbed his chin as he worked to mentally sort his first impressions of Roman. Well-dressed. Educated. Aging Wall Street bro, or maybe—no, *definitely* a tech investor. But pleasant. Well-meaning. Not entirely in tune with the new world. Probably at least a little racist.

Roman snorted. "Absolutely." He shifted again and leaned forward, propping his elbows on the desk. "Of course, if they *don't* duck, the can connects. And when it connects, it connects hard. Ella has a wicked arm."

"I saw."

"That usually sets them off. They get mad, they rush the boat, they wind up with an arrow in the chest."

Patrick slapped his hand on his knee. "Well, I'll tell you, Roman, that seems like some pretty cruel and needless instigation. Best case scenario, you return to your starving family with a can of definitely-not-food. Worst case, you die arrow-up on the banks of some bullshit river."

Roman's mouth twisted into a frown. "No. You don't get it. I'm not bragging. I'm trying to explain the reality of our times. We're a small pack of survivors, same as every single person who comes up to the boat. But we have something they want, so they see us as a mark. Desperation is a fog; it confuses everything. It makes us *dangerous*. It has to be disrupted. The people who walk up to the boat are desperate—maybe for food, maybe for a ride. Maybe for blood. I have to protect my people. The cans aren't cruelty; they're our first line of defense."

"You could try, like, a series of riddles," Patrick suggested.

Roman smiled again, and Patrick searched his face. He didn't find malice there, hiding in the folds around the corners of his eyes. What he saw was exhaustion. And what he *felt* was exhaustion. "Riddles are for children."

His muscles released their tension, just a notch. "So the people who don't run toward you or away from you, they end up machete-slapped onto the boat?"

"Some of them. Not all of them."

"How'd I make the cut? My boyish good looks? My fresh-faced smile?"

"Carla's a good judge of people's character. She was intrigued by you."

"She's the one with the crossbow?"

"Lots of them have crossbows," Roman corrected. "She's the one with the crossbow you could see." He reached into a desk drawer and drew out a glass bottle with a rubber stopper. Inside was a murky, gold-brown liquid. "Do you drink?"

"As a physiological imperative, yes," Patrick nodded. "Do I drink mystery liquids from dirty bottles offered by strangers? Boy. Yeah, sometimes. What is it?"

"Calling it whiskey would be a little vainglorious. It's more like a minimum viable product." Roman flipped the stopper off the bottle and poured two fingers into a glass. "It's yours if you want it, but I'm not too proud to drink alone."

Patrick eyed the drink warily. "Last stiff drink I had was made of frog's blood," he said, souring at the memory. "Which makes me think I should start asking what's in this stuff before I try it."

"No blood. Just three ingredients: corn, water, and wild yeast. I'm not saying it's Heaven Hill material, but I promise you no animals were harmed in the making of this moonshine."

"Words I never thought I'd have to take comfort in." Patrick gestured at the glass, and Roman measured out a pour. Then, Patrick picked it up and gave the drink a sniff. It was sharp, but not unpleasant.

"To opportunity," Roman said, raising his drink.

Patrick knocked his glass against Roman's. "Do we have one of those here?"

"God willing." Roman took a long pull while Patrick watched his face closely. He didn't squirm or scrunch. He didn't spit it out.

"To opportunity," Patrick repeated as he took a sip. The liquor burned a trail across his tongue, but it tasted familiar...like fireplace nights and early-winter leaves. "Better than frog's blood," he decided.

"Amen. Another?"

Patrick slid his glass across the table. "Hate to pass on an opportunity."

"Right! Back to the point," Roman smiled, sending Patrick's glass back half-full. He topped himself off, too, then settled back in his chair. "I have a pitch. I think you'll like it."

"I can't wait."

"You're with Red Caps. Which means a lot of people out there won't trust you. And I'm not entirely sure I should, either. But to me, that red hat signifies determination. A drive to get the job done. So I think we can help each other.

"I'm told you're trying to get to the Gulf. And it does happen that I'm headed there myself after this stop, or at least pretty close. I run a campus in Mississippi—just outside of Laurel, southeast part of the state. Not too far from Mobile, actually, as luck would have it." His eyes flashed as he took another drink. "About a two-hour drive, in the old days."

Patrick raised an eyebrow. "Well. You have my attention."

Roman smiled. "The farm is a big operation. Big in size, and big in value. It provides sustainability for a large swath of what's left of the South—food, some textiles. It's become a sizeable investment of time and labor...and of wealth, I suppose, depending on how you define that now. It takes a lot of work to keep it free of pests."

"Don't tell me the aphids have mutated...my worldview is hanging by a thread as it is."

"Aphids, I could manage. It's the two-legged pests with bones of steel that I can't figure out how to exterminate."

"Dusters," Patrick said, nodding slowly. "They *are* destructive."

"And persistent. Which is what brings me here. Rumor has it there's a scientist in Asheville who's managed to develop a sort of...repellent. I'm here to see for myself, and to establish a supply chain, if it's true."

"He invented something that can keep runners away?" Patrick asked, surprised. "Do you think it's real?"

"We'll find out tomorrow."

"And let me guess. You'd like some Red Cap protection at this meeting."

Roman grinned. "It *is* what they're known for. But that's only part of it."

"Putting our lives at risk is only the beginning? Love to hear it."

"No more than my crew and I will be putting our own lives at risk," Roman pointed out. "However the meeting goes, we'll need to head back to Mississippi immediately afterward. We had some complications on the journey here that were...unexpected. They set us back a full month. If we don't get back ASAP, the crop supply for the entire southern seaboard might be lost."

"And who will make the whiskey then?" Patrick cried.

"Right?" Roman replied. "The whiskey is a big piece of the business. But not the only one. We provide food, too. Lots of food. All strategically grown. It's Farm 2.0. I have to get back to it before the zombies destroy it all, if they already haven't."

"So we watch your back tomorrow, help guard the boat down the river, and get an otherwise free ride in return?"

"That's the offer."

"I have lots of questions."

Roman grinned. "I figured you might."

"Why us? Why strangers? Where's your crew? This can't be all of them. How dangerous is tomorrow? Do we get crossbows? How far are we going? How bad is it there? Do we get crossbows? Can you feed us? Are you going to kill us in our sleep? Is your farm a cult? Do we get crossbows? Lots of questions."

Roman laughed. "Tell you what. We'll spend time tonight unpacking answers to every question you have. You like what you hear, you all stick with us. You don't like the answers, we part ways, totally cool."

"Totally cool," Patrick nodded slowly. "No supervillain in any movie *I've* seen has ever said *that*." He reached across the table and shook Roman's hand. "We'll talk. And we'll go from there."

Roman's lips curled into a smile. "Looking forward to it."

27.

"I am *not* looking forward to this," Richie said, wringing his hands nervously. "Is it going to be dangerous?"

"Oh, *incredibly* dangerous," Patrick assured him. "He made it sound pretty easy, so you

know it's going to be just absolutely fucked. He also talks like a V.C. bro. You should be warned about that."

"Okay, so. Why are we doing it?" Brett asked.

"Because we spent, like, four hours together. We talked a lot. We did drink a little." Patrick burped. "Excuse me. Here's my takeaway—I don't know how *far* we can trust him, but I think he's serious about this arrangement."

"Throwing in with strangers who don't give specifics about how they lost their crewmates sounds incredibly dangerous," Ted frowned.

"That *is* the one thing I didn't get a satisfying answer about," Patrick agreed. "I don't think we should go into this with our eyes closed. There's danger here. No doubt about that. But walking the rest of the way to Mobile is *also* incredibly dangerous, probably at *least* as incredibly dangerous, almost certainly even *more* incredibly dangerous, and riding on a boat means we can at least sit for some of it."

Brett cleared his throat and spat a huge glob of mucous into the grass. "That's a good point," he said.

"But they brained Gary with a bean can," Ted pointed out, nodding at the swollen knot on Gary's forehead. It had turned purple and was crusted over with a thin veneer of some sort of pus. Gary scowled and pulled the brim of his red cap down lower on his head, covering the bump at an excruciating physical cost.

"It wasn't a bean can," Patrick reminded him, "it was a wet-rock can. And in a way, Gary took that wet-rock can-bullet for me, for which I will be forever grateful." He reached out and touched Gary's shoulder in gentle gratitude. Gary scowled harder. "But yes, their methods are not exactly what I'd like to see from persons comporting themselves in civilized manners. As it turns out, the world is broken and desperate, and high tea has gone out the window. So I think we give them the benefit of the doubt and just internally agree that there might be a lot of doubt not worthy of a benefit."

The Red Caps glanced at each other, each man's face contorted into an indiscernible twist of frustration and confusion. "What the hell does *that* mean?" Jimmy asked.

"I do not know," Patrick confided. "But it sounded high-minded. The point is, we can trust them about as much as we can trust anyone now, and that amount is basically zero. There's not going to be a safe and relaxing partnership with strangers. That sort of thing was hard in enough in the old world. We cannot trust these people. But we cannot trust anyone. The question isn't, is this plan bad for us. The question is, is this plan better bad or worse bad than us walking alone for the next few months. I think it's better-bad. Better-bad is not good. But if we're on a boat with these people, and it turns bad, then we at the very least know who our enemies are, and that we don't need to worry about checking dusters on the perimeter. To me, that sounds better than walking, where we don't know what's coming at us from any given side at every given second. Plus, I think they need us, and that gives us some safety."

The other Red Caps looked at Gary. He was gritting his teeth and working very hard not to show the pain his hat brim was causing. "What do you think, Gare?" Ted asked.

"I think all of the people who were allowed to call me 'Gare' got dusted five years ago, and that if you try it one more time, you'll get a pipe across the face."

"But enough about his sex life," Brett snickered behind his hand. Only Ted heard him. He choked on his own spit. Everyone looked at him and asked if he was okay. Ted held up a hand and nodded, though he continued to cough up a storm.

"Anyway," Gary continued, annoyed, "these boat people are full of piss and vinegar, as my gramma used to say. Women, every one of them, except the head honcho. Not that I'm saying there's anything wrong with women," he added quickly, and the other Red Caps murmured their agreement, just in case any women were around to hear them. "I'm just saying they've got a different approach—that's all."

"Almost like a subset of humanity that was roundly subjugated as a lesser class for centuries of Western rule finally had an even playing field that they're making their own in a way that the historic subjugators now feel strangely affronted by," Patrick said, beaming and resting his chin on his fists. "Go on."

Gary closed his eyes. He counted to five. And he regretted, not for the first time, every bad thing he'd done that had delivered him a penance like Patrick Deen. "I think we should be careful. But it's also the best plan we got. Stay on our toes, and we'll get where we're going in a quarter of the time."

"Good enough for me," Jimmy nodded.

"I haven't seen that many women in one place since the Internet went down," Richie said seriously. "I'm in."

"Tell them about the contact dermatitis," Patrick suggested.

Richie scowled.

"I could use the break," Ted said miserably. He limped in place to remind them that he'd fallen off a bridge and lost a chunk of his leg to a duster. "How 'bout you, Brett?"

Brett snorted. "I was always in. If you dipshits had said no, I'd have gotten on the boat alone. Walking blows."

"There are actually a lot of really great health benefits associated with walking," Jimmy said.

Brett rolled his eyes. "Shut up, Johnny."

"Don't you start that shit too!"

"All right, so we're agreed," Patrick said, stepping between Brett and Jimmy, holding his hands out for peace. "Which is good, because we're three feet away from the boat, they can probably hear everything we're saying."

"We can," one of the women called out from the deck.

"I told you we should have had this conversation before moving the whole group over here," Gary said, annoyed.

"I wanted to see the boat," Ted reminded them.

"And what do you think?" Roman's voice carried out from the upper deck. He leaned over the railing, smiling down.

"Could use a paint job," Brett suggested.

Roman's smile vanished. "Sure."

"It's called the Big Muddy Queen?" Ted asked.

"Great, isn't it?" Roman laughed. "She's one of four sister riverboats; the Delta King, the Delta Queen, the American Queen, and our Big Muddy Queen. Isn't it hilarious?"

"Where'd you find her?" Jimmy wondered.

"She washed up near the campus. Crew must have abandoned her… or maybe stepped off for a bit and didn't live to make it back." He ran his hands tenderly along the peeling white railing and inhaled deeply, as if breathing in the boat's scent. "She was meant to be mine."

The Red Caps looked at each other uneasily. *Normal*, Patrick assured them, nodding encouragingly.

"Carla!" Roman continued, drifting back to himself. "Will you show our guests to their room? It'll be dark in a few hours. Why don't you all get settled, then join us back at the dock for dinner? We'll want to set out tomorrow before dawn. Let's make sure to get plenty of rest." He clapped his hands like a team coach. Then he smiled again, waved, and disappeared into his cabin.

"Sure thing, Dad," Brett mumbled dryly. Carla, the woman who had held Patrick and Gary at crossbow-point, ambled over to the ladder and motioned them up. She wore an olive- green tank top, smeared with engine grease, and googles pushed up on her head like a post-apocalyptic Gadget from Rescue Rangers.

"He likes to hear himself talk," she sighed.

"Don't we all," Patrick replied.

She frowned and looked pointedly at Patrick. "Some more than others."

"Hurtful, but fair."

Carla motioned with her head, and Patrick led the Red Caps up the plank. "Welcome to the boat," she said, casually turning the crossbow in airy circles. "For however long it lasts."

That didn't make them feel good.

•

They set up camp inside the damp, grimy dining room. Once the tables had been pushed up against the walls, there was a fair amount of space—a safe and protective space, which was a luxury the Red Caps hadn't had since the train. That alone was enough to give the accommodations three stars.

Still, it was wet, and it smelled like mold. Half the surfaces were smeared with a paste of Monkey dust mixed with old dust, dark ash, yellow pollen, dead bugs, and chicken grease. The room smelled like a three-hundred-year-old McDonald's that had flooded in 1940 and had just recently been dragged out of the water, propped up on its soggy timbers and opened up for business again.

"If this is a dining room, why is there carpet?" asked Richie, treading sourly across the floor.

No one had an answer for that, so everyone just ignored him.

They staked their claims and laid out their packs, getting themselves all arranged. When the sun went down, they saw bonfires spark to life through the windows of the cabin. The women of the ship had gathered around the dock, building and lighting the fires in what seemed to some sort of ritual. There were six of them all together; Carla had lied about their numbers to Patrick. But what they lacked in group size, they made up for in intensity and effectiveness. There was Carla, whom they'd met; Lucía, a small, strong woman with a face like a cherub and a mouth like a sailor; Melissa and Mary, the two women who'd led Patrick to Roman, slapping him with machetes along the way. They were sisters, it turned out. There was also Ella, built like a steeple, with fire-orange hair, and Adiva, quiet and thoughtful, dressed all in black. They moved quietly, setting logs and fanning flames and readying the strips of meat they'd produced from God-knows-where. A mismatched cluster of frying pans were passed from fire to fire, and soon the air was thick with the savory scent of meat sizzling over an open flame. It drew the men out from their moldy campsite like it was a curling finger. They floated through the boat, hanging on the smell.

The men folded themselves into the empty slots around the fires, awkwardly introducing themselves to the women who ran the ship. "Thank you for the hospitality," Patrick said.

"Thank you for replacing the hyper-masculine morons who got ripped apart by dusters at our last port," said one of the women, also genuinely.

"Well, that's not a story I want to hear," Patrick frowned.

"What happened?" Gary asked.

Carla snickered from across the fire. "Go on, Lucía," she said, the flames flashing in the lenses of her goggles like shining, sanded-down Hellboy horns. "Enlighten them."

Lucía stabbed at the sizzling gray deer meat with a barbecue fork. "We had a bunch of dipshit frat fucks on the boat for most of the trip."

"From the farm," Carla chimed in. "Good at pulling crops. Bad at being humans."

"They begged to make the trip," Lucia continued. "Change of scenery, you know? Wanted to protect the girls."

Carla sucked her teeth. "Roman shouldn't have done it. He knows what happens when new blood takes the boat."

Richie gulped. "What—what happens when new blood takes the boat?" he whispered.

Lucía laughed. "They made it most of the trip. Mostly puked their guts out, but they did okay. Until Knoxville."

The women at the other fires fell quiet, hearing the name of Knoxville invoked. A flow of cold air pushed across the dock, pulling the flames down low.

"We told them not to get off the fucking boat," Lucía said.

"We got a wood guy in Knoxville," Carla explained. "It's our refueling point."

"The Woodman," Ella said. Carla whooped, and the other women followed suit. Those who had glasses in their hands raised a salute, then coughed down the rotgut inside.

"The Woodman is *very* particular," Lucía confirmed. "We know him; he knows us. The boys didn't know shit. The Woodman sure as shit didn't know the boys."

"Rest in peace."

"More peace with them gone."

Another round of whoops. Another round of shots.

"So the boys come along, in their big puffy jackets and their stupid fucking hats. We get to The Woodman, and immediately, they start pulling their dicks out."

"Metaphorically," Carla clarified.

"Calling him an old man, throwing acorns at him, taking twice as much wood as they paid for. Trying to be big men."

"Men are *always* trying to be big men," Mary said.

"But so many of them are *so small*," Melissa cackled back, holding her fingers three inches from each other.

"So the Woodman looks at us, and what—we're gonna stick out our necks for these assholes?"

A chorus went up among the women: "Hell no!"

"*Hell* no. So the Woodman looks at us, and we shake our heads, like they're not with us. And they never *were* with us. They were hired help, treating us like shit one minute, begging for sex the next. All the shit that got programmed into the world that the Monkey bombs debugged in one fell swoop. Hard reset; we're not going back."

"Whoop!"

Clink.

"So, we shake our heads, and the Woodman doesn't miss a beat. He tells the meatheads, 'Pile's around back. Leave me something, will you?' The brainless idiots go on back, laughing their stupid fucking heads off, not stopping to wonder for one second why this guy who trades in one of the most valuable assets you can lay hands on today keeps that valuable shit lying around on the back porch."

Richie sat up, alarmed. He was very invested in the story. "The wood wasn't back there," he guessed.

Lucía rolled her eyes. "No, sport. The wood wasn't back there. The *wood* was where the wood is hidden. You don't carry the wood out; you make your request, and the Woodman has it brought out to you. Or he doesn't."

Ted cleared his throat. "So…what was on the back porch?"

Carla turned, her eyes dark in the night, her goggles crackling with fire. "There *is* no back porch. There's only ten cords of wood in a big duster pit."

"You go in," Lucía added. "The dusters come out."

"They come out of tunnels. It's a whole thing. Think the Roman Coliseum. But smaller."

"And worse," Carla added.

"Way worse," Lucía nodded. "Way messier."

They let that hang in the air while the men's imaginations filled in the gaps. Richie turned pale. He looked like he might throw up again. Ted placed his hands near the hole in his leg as he realized just how lucky he'd actually been.

Brett sort of smiled at the thought of the frat bros getting theirs.

"And now, it's just us girls," Lucia said, snuggling against Carla.

Carla raised one eyebrow. "Or it was until today."

Adiva looked seriously at the men, her dark eyes like oil through the fire. "We'll see how long this next crop lasts."

28.

Sunrise came fast. Or maybe sleep came late. Either way, the second Patrick woke, he desperately needed a nap. "Where's the complimentary coffee on this cruise ship?" he yawned, stretching and shuffling his way out to the deck.

"Here." Ella tossed him a stick. It bounced off his head and clattered to the wooden floor.

"What is this?" he asked, looking down at the stick and yawning again.

"It's a root."

"What kind of root?"

"A flower root."

Patrick scratched his hip and blinked his sleepy eyes. "Is that the tax-onomical term?"

Carla pushed her way out onto the deck, chewing on a stick of her own. "It's dandelion root," she clarified. "It's like morning coffee. But chewy. And kind of gross."

Patrick frowned down at it lying by his foot. "It's dirty," he pointed out.

"Yep."

He sighed as he bent to pick up the small, twisted stick. "Do dandelion roots even have caffeine?"

"Nope."

"Then it's not really like coffee at all, is it?" Patrick said sourly.

Ella shrugged. "It's like decaf."

"I have been funneled into the stupidest timeline," he muttered. But he brushed the dirt off the root and stuck it in his mouth anyway. It tasted like moldy bread and dirt. "Sort of a Folgers vibe to it," he decided.

The rest of the Red Caps followed groggily, stumbling onto the deck and stretching in the early morning mist. "I haven't slept that hard in months," Brett mumbled through a yawn.

"REM sleep! I had *REM* sleep!" Jimmy beamed.

"Good!" Roman's voice boomed from the next deck up, rolling around the Monkey fog like thunder. He leaned out over the railing, the sleeves of his Navy blue sweater rolled up to the elbows. He looked washed, fresh, and alert.

Patrick looked down at his own torn jeans and his greasy shirt. *I should take a bath this month*, he thought.

"Glad to hear you're well-rested, guys!" Roman said cheerfully. "We'll move out after breakfast, get an early start." Carla was already directing the rekindling of the fires. The sisters were cutting through a small pile of potatoes with sharpened pieces of an old street sign. Patrick couldn't remember the last time he'd had two meals in a row that didn't come out of a can.

The men ate quietly, still feeling out their surroundings. The women watched them with bland curiosity, the way they might have looked at a 16-year-old dog in the window of an animal shelter. *They really don't expect us to last long*, Patrick thought.

Boy, he didn't love that.

•

By the time they finished breakfast, Roman had dragged two big rolling coolers up to the edge of the deck and motioned for help carrying them down the plank. Gary and Brett lifted one and Patrick took hold of one end of the other. Together, he and Roman heaved it down the makeshift steps, struggling under the weight. "What's in this thing—a black hole?" Patrick asked, letting the cooler crash down on its wheels when they hit the dock.

Roman gave him a strange look. "Aren't black holes like super small?"

"Yeah, but they weigh 10 solar masses," Patrick said, wiping his forehead on the back of his arm.

Roman reached down and pulled open the lid. Inside were six white contraptions that looked like squat, fat breadmaking machines.

Patrick sighed. "Oh, nice. We're making sourdough?"

"Oooh, I *love* sourdough," Ted whined.

"Everyone loves sourdough," Richie replied. "Name one person who doesn't love sourdough."

"I hate sourdough," Brett said, crossing his powerful arms. "That okay with you?"

"I mean, I didn't mean *everyone*..." Richie squeaked, shrinking back.

Roman grinned. "Not sourdough. Not even close. We're making *science*. At least, someone will be." He patted one of the pearl-colored machines gently. "These are centrifuges. They're bartering chips for our new friend, the scientist."

"They make centrifuges out of black holes?" Patrick asked, still struggling to catch his breath. "Because of how heavy the black holes are...and also these coolers." He felt the need to explain.

"They're only like twenty-five pounds each," Roman pointed out. "I think maybe you should exercise more."

"Oh." Patrick frowned. He pinched his bicep. It was almost exclusively bone. "Hmph."

"Ours is light," Gary smirked. He lifted up the lid and peered inside. "Beakers. Nice." Brett held out a fist, and Gary bumped it.

"So, this guy is a real scientist, eh?" Patrick asked. He picked out a beaker and carefully unwound the mostly-popped bubble wrap that had been cinched around it. He held the glass vial up to the light. It was pretty dirty.

"That's the rumor," Roman said. He gently lifted the beaker out of Patrick's hands and carefully replaced the bubble wrap. "You wouldn't believe what it cost for a cooler full of unbroken beakers."

Patrick raised his hands and stepped away. "Sure. Right. Sorry."

"I mean it—you wouldn't believe it if I told you. You'd call me a liar."

"He wants you to ask what he had to trade for it," Carla murmured, nudging Patrick.

"Do I care that much?" Patrick asked her.

"You do not."

"Okay then."

Brett shrugged his shoulders and turned his neck until it cracked. "How far away is this guy—this rumored scientist?" he asked.

Roman frowned when he realized no one would be asking him how much he paid for the equipment. He placed the wrapped beaker back inside the cooler and closed the lid. "Shouldn't be too far down in that direction," he said, nodding vaguely south. "Three miles. Maybe four. Through the woods down there."

"That's a long way to go in the woods," Gary said. "A whole lot of hiding places for a whole lot of bad things."

"It probably ain't gonna be a cake walk," Brett agreed, spitting into the river. "Feels like the kind of trip not everyone makes it back from."

"No kidding," Roman snorted. "Why do you think you're here?"

29.

Ted stayed behind, due to his entire injured body, but he promised to make himself useful while he was there, stoking the fires, washing dishes, and valiantly defending the ship from any would-be attackers that happened to descend while the main crew was away. "I'll defend this boat with my life," he swore.

Brett snorted. "Says the man who got dropped by a fish."

"Shut up, Brett!"

The rest of the Red Caps set out with Roman, as did Carla, Ella, and Lucía. Adiva and the sisters stayed back to guard the ship. Patrick gave fifty-fifty odds that Ted would annoy them to the point of his own murder before the party returned.

They pulled the coolers down Riverside Drive, a two-lane highway just over the berm from the river's edge. Old, powerful oaks lined the eastern side of the road, throwing long shadows over the asphalt, and making the path feel gloomy, small, and watched. Richie dragged one cooler down the road and Brett rolled the other. The abandoned cars from M-Day were thin on this part of the highway, but the asphalt was showing its years of disrepair and potholes made the way rough going.

"Watch it!" Roman snarled when Richie hit a deep rut. "The glass in that cooler is worth more than your life."

Richie blushed. "Sorry."

Jimmy walked close to Lucía. She carried a scimitar and looked like she knew how to use it. Carla walked with an arrow nocked in her crossbow, sweeping the tree line from time to time. Patrick prayed that she was being proactive rather than reactive with it.

"See anybody?" Roman asked, without breaking his stride.

Carla frowned. "I'm not sure."

"All right," Roman said. "Look alive."

"Or we all look dead," the women responded in unison.

"Whoa," Patrick said. "You have a call-and-repeat? How come we don't have a cool call-and-repeat?" he asked Gary. "I think it'd be great for morale."

Gary grunted his disagreement.

Soon, they approached what they'd come to think of affectionally as Ted's Bridge. "Officially entering duster territory," Patrick told the group.

Roman paused and raised his hand, signaling the others to do the same. He seemed to listen to the breeze, to feel the green fog for vibrations. He stood that way for almost a full minute, turning the knobs of his senses to home in on whatever frequency he was searching for. "All right," he said finally, turning to the group. "Let's go around."

They walked back to a point where the trees started to thin, turning off the road there and pushing into the woods, quickly losing themselves in the brush. Brett cursed loudly as he fought to drag the cooler through the snarling tangle. Richie simply picked up his cooler and carried it through, making sure to whistle and smile at Brett as he passed. Brett made a mental note to feed Richie to some alligators when they got down south.

The trees went on for longer than they expected, and soon they were pulling their legs through thick vegetation, the dark shroud of trees blocking the sunlight like curtains. "I thought Asheville was a town," Patrick frowned. They pushed on through the brush, passing behind houses every few hundred yards and giving each a wide berth. Suddenly, Roman threw up his arm, nearly catching Patrick in the face. Patrick stopped just short of hitting it; Jimmy stumbled into him, pushing Patrick forward until his nose squished against Roman's elbow. Roman's sweater sleeve smelled like chicory and woodsmoke. It set Patrick's mouth watering, for reasons he didn't quite understand and didn't have the time to explore.

"Everybody down!" Roman hissed. He dropped to the forest floor, and all three of his soldiers did the same. Patrick, still reeling from the half-second elbow-smoosh, was slower to react. He sort of stumbled-slash-lowered his body awkwardly into the brush. The other Red Caps followed suit, easing themselves down onto the moist, rotting leaves.

Richie eyed the muck nervously. "Down...on the ground?"

"*Down!*" Roman hissed again.

Richie began to explain that he had sensitive skin and was susceptible to breakouts, but Brett grabbed one of his ankles and yanked it out from under him before he could get started. Richie yelped as he fell ass-first into a snarl of branches covered by tiny thorns. He threw his head back and hollered in pain; Gary clapped a hand over his mouth, pushing back against his screams so roughly that Richie started to gag.

"*Shut the fuck up*," Gary growled in his ear.

Richie mumbled incoherently through Gary's iron grasp. Gary pulled his hand away, and Richie tried again. "I fell in a sticker bush!" he whispered.

"So *move*, dipshit," Brett advised.

Richie glowered. "You did that on purpose."

Brett grinned. It wasn't a pond full of gators, but still, it had been pretty satisfying.

Roman looked back, fixing them all with a cold-iron stare. The Red Caps shrank back into the brush.

Seconds passed. Then a full minute. Patrick glanced around the woods, wondering what Roman was hearing or seeing that the rest of them weren't. He was about to chance a whisper to voice his curiosity when the sound of footfalls crunching over brittle sticks crackled through the woods ahead of them.

The sound grew closer…and closer. It wasn't just one set of feet, but several sets from someones—or some*things*—stalking through the forest, the sounds moving nearer. Patrick's heart ran cold when he heard the telltale rasp that they had come to know so intimately the last few years.

"Dusters," Jimmy breathed.

Roman held his hand up for quiet yet again; this time, there was perfect obedience. No one spoke or moved. They held their breath. They waited.

The forest floor was dense with broken twigs, fallen leaves, snarls of tangled bushes and shade-grown ferns. But the group wasn't sure if any of it would be enough to cover them and keep them out of sight at any reasonable distance.

The dusters stepped into the clearing just ahead. They pulled themselves through the branches like demons being born, wrenching free from the wet tangle of vines and gulping down furious breaths of air. There were four of them, limbs twisted, jaws hanging and skin peeling off their bones. They stalked across the clearing on broken legs, snarling and hacking up wet, yellow phlegm. They were close enough to smell. Their stench was sour and meaty, like roadkill.

The smell was so thick, Richie actually did gag. He pushed his mouth down into his hands to stifle the noise, but he couldn't keep it all back.

The dusters stopped. The one in front lifted his head and sniffed at the air.

The other three creatures lifted their noses, too, inhaling sharply, tasting for scent on the wind.

The Red Caps and boat people all smelled ripe, a combination of sweat and blood and body odor and campfire smoke and God-only-knew what else was soaked into their clothes, their hair, and their skin.

But somehow, the dusters didn't seem to smell them. They lowered their heads again and resumed their shambling across the clearing. They passed back into the trees in a jagged single file, pushing through the branches and losing themselves in the forest.

Patrick let out his breath. *"Jesus, that was close."*

Then the last duster stopped. It made a strange clicking sound, a dry-rattle gurgle from the back of its throat. It lifted its nose and sniffed again.

This time, it turned straight toward them.

"Fuck," Jimmy gasped.

It was a reflex—automatic. He hadn't meant to speak. He hadn't meant to be so loud.

He hadn't meant to say anything at all.

The other three dusters snapped back into the clearing. They growled and snapped at each other like raptors, jostling for the scent of a meal. One of them stumbled forward, twenty yards from the spot where the Red Caps lay half-hidden in the brush. Then fifteen yards…then ten.

Then it saw them.

The duster roared and its packmates stalked forward, reaching out hungrily, desperately, strings of yellow drool hanging from their lips.

Carla leapt to her feet and pulled a three-pound hammer from a nylon holster around her waist, raising it over her shoulder. The dusters staggered into the brush. They moved quickly, blindly, following their stomachs more than their eyes. They shoved through the evergreen arms of a white pine.

The dusters stopped. They sniffed, snorted.

Then they did something unexpected.

They screamed.

They were primal screams, screams of terror and pain. The dusters shrieked like banshees in a bear trap, clawing their way out of the tree and back into the clearing. They screamed and huffed, clawing at each other, scraping off huge chunks of flesh with their ragged nails. Their jaws snapped in frustration and fear as they pulled themselves away from the clearing and crashed back into the brush, heading the way they'd come, disappearing through the reaching limbs and leaving the Red Caps and the boat people behind.

"What…the fuck?" Lucia said.

"No idea." Roman stood up and brushed the twigs and leaves from his sweater. "You guys ever see anything like that?"

"I've never even *heard* of anything like that," Patrick replied. "If I'd known they were allergic to Christmas trees, I'd have gone to the Yukon instead of Disney World."

"Maybe it's like vampires and crosses," Richie said. The entire group turned.

"What?" Carla said.

Richie shrank back. "You know? Like, Santa is their antichrist?"

Ella took a large step away from Richie. "Is this guy for real?"

"I have contact dermatitis," Richie mumbled as an excuse.

They pushed forward again, moving as quietly as they could through the woods. Eventually they broke out into a paved road that curved its way up the mountain. "This should be right," Roman nodded. He led them up the hill and around the bend, checking off address numbers on the hill houses as they went. Apparently, he had an address in mind. "It's the next one," he said.

They rounded the corner and stopped dead in their tracks.

"You've got to be kidding me," Carla said.

If Roman's address was right, the scientist's lab was actually a house—a mid-size ranch-style with pale blue siding and an overgrown yard. The shingles were in rough shape and the shutters had mostly given up their grips, none of which really matter, because they were all decorative anyway. The windows were boarded up from the inside with thick planks; the gutters were hanging off the edge of the roof, and the twisted remains of the storm door drooped like aluminum foil that had been twisted into an art project during Dali week. But none of the crew noticed any of those things.

Their collective attention was drawn to the thick crowd of dusters that milled through the yard like pigs in a pen.

"What are they doing?" Roman asked.

Carla shook her head. "I've never seen them like this."

None of them had. They were used to the furious, frantic, slavering runners. But the docile, shambling, zombies in the scientist's yard…that was something new.

"It's almost like they're…" Roman trailed off. He couldn't find the words. "I don't know what. They're *different*. It's like they're…?"

"It's like they're prisoners," Patrick said. "Like they've been broken."

The Red Caps grunted their agreement.

The dusters were packed into the yard like toothpicks in a box, squeezing and squirming past each other, their low moans tired, resigned; drained.

It was impossible to count them with the way they roiled, but there were at least one hundred in the postage-stamp yard.

"You're sure this is it?" Gary asked.

Roman frowned. "The address is right."

"There's an awful lot of dusters for a lab that makes things to keep dusters away," Patrick pointed out.

Roman nodded. "I was just thinking the same thing."

Then the air was cut with the crackle of radio static squeaking to life. A voice with a metallic ring said, "*Open the mailbox.*"

The crew exchanged glances. The dented green aluminum mailbox rested half-on and half-off a gnarled wooden post at the end of the driveway. Its red flag was up.

"Paper rock scissors?" Patrick asked.

Brett snorted. "I'll do it." He pushed through the group and strode up to the mailbox, slowing as he drew near. The writhing throng of dusters ended just a couple yards away, and their quiet growling unnerved him. He moved more cautiously then, keeping one eye on the horde. He reached for the lid with a trembling hand, his fingers brushing the metal. He gripped the edge, readying to pull it open when something on the mailbox post glinted. He froze.

Slowly, he bent down and peered beneath the mailbox.

A thin black wire ran out through a hole in the bottom and down the wooden post, disappearing into the grass. The wire was fixed to the post with industrial staples that caught the shifting light.

Roman cleared his throat. "Everything all right?" he asked.

Brett ignored him. He touched the wire. A gentle hum of electricity flowed beneath the sheath. The sound inside the mailbox crackled back to life. "*It's not rigged,*" the radio voice said.

Brett snorted. "Easy for you to say."

He touched the mailbox gently, examining it on all sides. The group watched nervously, drawing themselves back, contracting into a fist. "Is it a...B-O-M-B?" Richie asked.

Patrick stared at him. "Why did you spell it?"

"I don't know," he frowned.

Brett shook his head. "It's a low-voltage wire," he said over his shoulder. "It's probably safe."

"How probably?" Roman asked.

Brett shrugged. "Let's find out."

He pulled open the mailbox lid.

"*BOOM!*" shrieked the voice. Richie screamed.

The ear-piercing sound of radio laughter crackled through the air. "*Gotcha!*"

Inside the mailbox sat a small walkie-talkie resting on a power base, its tiny green light blinking lazily. Brett snatched the walkie off its base and tossed it at Roman. "Your scientist is a real asshole," he grumbled.

Roman caught the walkie and pushed the talk button. "Dr. Gustheed, I presume?"

"*You shouldn't,*" the voice said. "*Who are you?*"

"We're your target market. We want to talk about a purchase." Roman opened one of the coolers and pulled out a bubble-wrapped bundle. He peeled away the wrapping and held up an Erlenmeyer flask over the heads of the zombies, high enough to be seen from the front windows. The walkie was quiet in his hand; the only sound was the low, grumbling groan of the horde.

Finally, the voice crackled back to life. "*In through the sewer. Two of you, maximum. The rest of you stay.*" The voice cut out, followed by a click.

The line was dead.

"Sewer?" Roman asked into the walkie. His question was met with cold, dead silence. "*What* sewer?!" he demanded again.

But the voice on the other end was gone.

"I'll take a wild guess," Patrick offered. He pointed down at a storm drain built into the curb, a few feet away from the mailbox post. "Pennywise wants us to go float down there."

Brett slapped Patrick's arm with the back of his hand. "Why would you say that?" he glowered. "Don't say that."

Patrick was stunned. "You, of all people, afraid of *IT*? I'm telling you, I would have bet a literal million dollars that it would have been Richie."

"I—I don't like that movie either," Richie frowned.

"Well, at least now I'm rich," Patrick said. He held out his hand. "Pay me."

Roman knelt down and inspected the drain. It looked normal enough—brick construction under a cement cap, with slimy moss creeping up across the brick. He stepped onto the rectangular cap and pried up the manhole cover. He rolled it into the grass, then took a small flashlight from his pack and shone it down into the hole. "There's a runoff tunnel that leads to the house," he said. He looked up at his crew. "Carla? Are you up for it?"

Carla was already on her way with her hands on her hips, her mouth twisted and annoyed. "I'd rather crawl through the sewer than listen to these idiots," she said, jerking a thumb at Richie and Brett. "Any of you other heroes want to join me?"

"Hell no," Gary gruffed.

"It's…really unsanitary," Jimmy fretted.

Carla grinned at Patrick. "Guess it's you and me."

"Oh." Patrick grimaced. Tight spaces weren't exactly on his top ten list of cool spots to pass the time. Then again, all the zombies were on the outside, so maybe inside was the better place to be. Plus, it seemed like Carla could do a solid job protecting them both. "Sure." He dropped his bag and kicked it over to Gary. "If I get eaten by a spider-clown, get this to Ben, will you?"

"If you get eaten by a spider-clown, I'll be halfway to Canada before your blood hits the asphalt."

Patrick snorted. "Coward."

"Take this," Roman said, handing him a flashlight.

Patrick slipped it into his back pocket. "Thanks."

The sewer hole was cold, wet, and slimy—and dark. Narrow iron bands were affixed to the bricks, situated vertically every eight inches or so, forming a slippery ladder. Carla went first, moving quickly with a penlight between her teeth. She swung down into the horizontal tunnel and swept the light around. "Storm runoff, not sewer," she confirmed.

"How about spider-clowns?" Patrick asked.

"Inconclusive," she replied. She clicked off the light.

"Very funny," Patrick grumbled.

He lowered himself onto an iron rung. His sneaker slipped, and his whole body clenched with fear. His foot swung out over nothingness; his fingertips dug into the cement cap. "I hate this," he decided. He resituated his foot, jamming his heel against the metal and curling his toes in toward the brick. Slowly, carefully, he lowered himself into the sewer, his sweaty palms hot against the wet iron.

Down he went, until his foot found the lip of the runoff tunnel. He eased down into the darkness, grasping for something, anything, to give his hands purchase. A hand whipped out of the darkness and yanked him forward. Carla clicked on the light and flashed him a grin.

"I love this adventure, and I'm glad we met," Patrick said.

"Then how come you're sweating so much?" she smirked.

"Because I was lying, I hate everything about this."

"Figured."

Carla shone her light down the length of the tunnel. It was about five feet in diameter, large enough for them to stand, if they hunched. The walls were uneven, clumsy earth, and shards of rust-colored pottery crunched beneath their feet.

"Looks like someone broke up the clay pipe that ran through here and dug it out to make it a usable passage."

"Looks like it was a hand job, which is a phrase I *instantly* regret using," Patrick grimaced. "I mean it looks like they dug it by hand. With a shovel. Not. You know."

"Hey—no kink-shaming here," Carla said, shining the light around. "Think it's structurally sound?"

Patrick took her flashlight and investigated the rough-hewn walls of the tunnel. He ran his hands along the slimy earth, pressing in here and there. "Seems solid enough," he decided. "Can't be more than, what—a hundred feet to the house? Should be safe, I think."

"Now, if only you were an engineer, I'd take some comfort in that."

"I *am* an engineer," Patrick said.

Carla blinked. "No kidding?"

"Hard to tell, I know, because I left my pocket protector at home, but yeah."

"All right," Carla shrugged. "Let's go."

They crept through the dampness, the brittle clay breaking beneath their feet with every step. They pushed through the spiderwebs and the thread-like roots that dripped down from above, wiping sweat and condensation from their necks. They crunched over desiccated rat carcasses and slow-scuttling beetle shells, watching for traps, holding their breath.

"There," Carla said. She caught the end of the tunnel in her flashlight beam. It was a huge, ragged gap in the house's concrete foundation, a hole that looked like it'd been gnawed through by huge metal rats.

They peered through the hole, shining their lights into the basement of the house.

"What do you think?"

"Well," Patrick said, sliding his light around the darkness. "I don't love the bars."

The hole opened into a steel cage, a custom-made prison cell with two-inch bars cemented into the floor and bracketed into the ceiling with iron joists. One section of the wall was lined with hinges, but that gate was locked shut by a padlock the size of Patrick's fist. He leaned cautiously into the hole and examined the inside of the access wall. "Doesn't look like a trap, though. There's no closure that'll slam down once we're in, as far as I can tell."

"Great," Carla nodded. "You go first."

"I thought you were the one protecting me?" Patrick said.

"I can protect you better if I'm not in a cell."

Patrick swallowed. "Fine. Turns out I do great in prison cells anyway."

He gripped the broken edge of the hole and pulled himself into the basement. He climbed through into the cage. His right foot slipped on the wet dirt as he climbed, and he lost his balance. He fell clumsily onto his left foot inside the cage and stumbled forward, flailing across the darkness and banging his forehead into the steel bars on the far side. He fell to his knees, then slumped onto his side. "Flawless victory," he said, dazed.

"How did you make it this far alive?" Carla muttered, shaking her head. She slipped easily through the hole and began inspecting the bars. There was no way through without being let in from the other side.

"Well," Patrick said. "Now what?"

"*Boo!*" A woman in the darkness clicked on a flashlight, held under her chin. Crazy shadows leapt across her face. Carla screamed. She immediately flushed with embarrassment, scowled at Patrick and said, "Not a word."

"No words," Patrick agreed. "Just sweet, blissful glee."

The woman with the flashlight laughed at her own prank. She pulled a string, and a bare lightbulb threw a harsh yellow light across the basement. The space was larger than it had seemed from outside the wall. It bent into an L-shape, and from here, they could see the addition, which was lined with metal shelving units. Every inch was covered with beakers, vials, and jars, some empty, some filled with liquids of muddy colors. In the center of the lab space were two broad tables, upon which sat what appeared to be standard scientific equipment—microscopes, scales, Bunsen burners, tongs.

The whole house smelled like pine needles.

"Who are you?" the woman asked. She had straight, mostly-gray hair pulled back in a tight ponytail. Her green eyes sparkled behind huge tortoise shell glasses held together with electrical tape in three different places. She was short, just barely scraping the five-foot mark, and her well-worn lab coat hung nearly to the floor.

"I'm Patrick. This is Carla. We're—well, boy…this is complicated. We're new to each other. She seems pretty normal, adjusted for post-apocalyptic terms. And I'm just trying to get back to my friend, Ben, so my group, and her group, it's sort of a *Perfect Strangers* sort of thing, and I don't *want* to say that I think we're the Balkies, but boy…now that I say it out loud, I really think we're the Balkies." He rubbed his chin and frowned furiously at the floor. He turned and wandered toward the back of the cell, mumbling, "This has given me a lot to think about."

Carla sighed, exasperated, and stepped up to the bars. "We're people who are just trying to survive. We're people like you. You're a scientist, I'm a farmhand, he's a—" She gestured at Patrick, grasping for inspiration. "I don't know, a Muppet who made a wish to become a real boy? He says he's an engineer, but that seems unlikely. We've made a long, difficult trip to find you. We lost a lot of people. If you've done what they say you've done, you can save a whole hell of a lot of people back home. And we aren't beggars. We brought you a barter—a good one."

There was a long silence as the older woman stared at Carla, reaching into her eyes with her mind, working like a safecracker, digging with her picks and listening for the pins to fall.

"I was just asking your names," she said finally.

Carla's hands fell away from the bars. "Oh," she said. Her shoulders softened.

"I'm Dr. Philbin," the scientist said.

"Philbin? We were told we'd find a Dr. Gustheed."

Dr. Philbin's mouth drew into a tight line. "Susannah is no longer the custodian of this lab. Hasn't been for years. I don't miss her!"

Carla raised an eyebrow. "Okay…"

"Philbin," Patrick cut in, making his way back to the front of the cage. "Any relation to Regis?"

"*Goddammit!*" the doctor screamed. "Coming up in school, it was 'Are you related to Regis?' Every day at work, it was 'Are you related to Regis?' I won a fucking *Nobel Prize*, and still, it's 'Are you related to Regis?' There is a one thousand percent chance the man died on M-Day—those fleshy cheek pouches were not meant for survival. He's dead as any of them, and here we are, in a Regis-free world, and you want to know, am I related to Regis?!"

Patrick wriggled uncomfortably. "But…are you?"

"Yes! How many Philbins do you think there could have been in the world? Of *course* I'm related to him! He was my father's cousin, but who gives a shit? *I* invented *cassmium cream!*"

Patrick leaned over to Carla and whispered, "What's cassmium cream?"

Carla shrugged.

"Well, I love your bloodline," Patrick assured Dr. Philbin. "And cassmium is…my favorite of all the creams—except for ice," he added quickly. "Ice cream is…well, you know how good ice cream is."

"I think we could all just use a second to take a breath," Carla said, making her voice even. "Dr. Philbin, can we call you by your first name? Would that be okay?"

The older woman snuffled, and she made a point of not uncrossing her arms. "Certainly," she said. "My name is Regina."

Patrick offered his hand through the bars. "Great to meet you, Reeg."

"Oh my God!"

"What?!" Patrick cried. "I am genuinely thrilled beyond belief to be in the presence of a brilliant scientist who both won a Nobel Prize *and* is related to the hardest working man in showbusiness! His work on *Pinky and The Brain* alone was just…" Patrick kissed his fingers like a chef and tossed it into the air.

"He was never actually *on Pinky and The Brain*," Dr. Philbin said, annoyed.

"I know, but his presence was so vital. So crucial. So weird." Patrick hugged himself with absolute joy. "Really, when I tell you it's an honor to meet you, I'm an engineer, so the Nobel thing is way above and beyond. That alone has me walking on sunshine. No kidding. And plus, Reeg? I mean. Wow."

Dr. Philbin seemed to relax a bit. Some of the color faded from her cheeks, and she let her shoulders let go of their tension. "He was really sweet at reunions," she said.

"Oh man, I bet."

"All right," she said, letting out a calming breath. "What did you bring to trade? More than just an Erlenmeyer, I hope."

"Quite a few Erlenmeyers, actually. And some other beakers," Carla said.

Dr. Philbin scowled. "I'm up to my eyeballs in beakers."

"How are you with centrifuges?"

That got her attention. "Do you mean *actual* centrifuges, or the makeshift kind of centrifuges where I tie eight modified graduated cylinders to a noisemaker with yarn and spin them around like some sort of first-grade science experiment?"

Carla blinked. "I mean actual centrifuges."

"Oh!" Dr. Philbin said. "Then, none."

"Lots of the other kinds, though?" Patrick guessed.

"So goddamn many," she admitted.

"Man. Regis would have loved that."

"You know what?" the doctor said. "I think he probably would have."

Carla worked *very* hard to not hit either of them. "Anyway, those *real* centrifuges? The ones you don't have? We brought you six of them."

Dr. Philbin pressed her palms together and looked very much like someone who was trying to play her life cool, but who was doing a terrible job. "This is…not *un*interesting to me."

"Not uninteresting means it is positively interesting," Patrick pointed out. Both women looked at him with the same blunt stare. Patrick cleared his throat. "Language," he explained meekly. "Language makes what I said true."

"Anyway," Carla said, returning to the doctor, "they're yours, in exchange for…whatever your zombie repellant is. If it works."

"Oh, they're not zombies," Dr. Philbin replied, pushing her glasses up her nose.

"*Thank* you!" Patrick cried. "They follow like *none* of the precepts, especially, and, I think, most notably, *they're not dead!*"

"Hey, can we not do semantics about raving mad lunatics who want to eat us off our own bones right now," Carla snapped, "and instead—I don't know, maybe try to not be locked in this literal prison cell for another fucking second?"

"Look, I don't want to be in here either," Patrick said, crossing his arms. "I'm way over my prison quota this year. But I won't let the reputation of zombies be tarnished by the weird, ravenous, drug-addicted, hard-boned racists trying to eat us alive every sixteen hours. I didn't let Ben get away with that nonsense, and if you think your odds are going to be any better, hoo boy!"

Carla raised an eyebrow. "Who says they're racist?"

Patrick shrugged. "I've only seen them in the South. I'm connecting the dots."

"Ah." Carla considered that. Then she nodded. "Fair."

Dr. Philbin nodded thoughtfully. "Yes," she murmured. "Yes." She stared off into the distance for several long moments. Then she said, "I'll see your offerings. If they're adequate, we'll have a deal."

"Science shit for zombie repellant?" Carla said.

Dr. Philbin made a sour face. "Sure. Science *shit*. For *zombie* repellant."

Patrick shook his head. "If you think I can drag those coolers through a rat-bone sludge-tunnel without breaking every single beaker inside, you've got another thing coming."

"No," said Philbin. "Not that way." She fished a key from her coat pocket and unlocked the cell door. It swung wide open. She pointed up the stairwell. "That way."

Patrick gulped. "Sorry…out the front door, that way?"

She nodded. "Mm-hmm."

"I don't know if you know this, but your front yard is so thick with dusters, it looks like the American Prairie in 1932."

Carla blinked. "What?"

"You know. The Dust Bowl. So many dusters, it looks like the Dust Bowl." Patrick blinked. "Was it the thirties? Why are you looking at me like that?"

"We'll talk about it later," Carla said. "Right now, the grown-ups are talking. Regina, the plan *is* a little concerning, given what's out there."

"Think of it as a trial run," the doctor said. "I'll send you out with the repellant. A little 'try before you buy'."

"I'm concerned it'll be a 'try as I die'," Carla said.

"Life is a wonderful adventure, isn't it?" The doctor grinned with every tooth in her head. She turned and headed up the stairs, gesturing for them to follow her.

Patrick looked at Carla. Carla looked alarmed.

"I don't suppose Roman would be anxious to honor our deal if I dove back through the tunnel and escaped into the sewer system and started a new life beneath the streets of Asheville like one of those lizard-people who control Manhattan, would he?" Patrick asked.

Carla shook her head slowly, her eyes wide, unblinking. "No, I do not think he would take you back to your friend if you dove down into the sewers and became a gross mutant thing," she said, her voice thin. "But I don't think it's a smart idea to step out this lunatic's front door and wade through a thick soup of runners. So the lizard-person thing actually sounds good, if you can get on board with not getting back to the Gulf."

Patrick gripped the iron bars and gently banged his forehead against the jail cell. "None of this would be an issue if Ben hadn't done what I tricked him into doing when I thought I was going to die," he sighed. He stayed that way for a few beats, his forehead pressing against the cold bars. His mind projected every outcome it could conceive. Almost all of them were incredibly bleak. But one of them opened up the path back to Fort Doom.

One of them brought him back to Ben.

"Fuck it." He let go of the bars and stepped through the gate. "I'm stringy and mostly bone. If these runners want a bite, they can choke and go hungry and die."

Carla didn't know what to do. But the sewer was awful and Roman was impatient. So she followed Patrick up the stairs and prepared herself to watch him get torn into pieces and swallowed, still screaming and alive.

30.

Patrick stood before the door. "This is seriously a prank, right? You're going to open the door, and I'm going to pee in my jeans, and you're going to laugh, and Carla's going to laugh, and I'm going to cry, and then you'll close the door and we'll all have fond memories of the time Patrick was so scared, he inked. Right?"

"You poor boy," Philbin said, pinching his cheek. Patrick didn't like that. He slapped at her hand. "This is your leap of faith. You want the key to the thing that will ward off the dusters? Only the penitent man will pass." She pulled open the front door.

The plodding swarm of half-human dust-creatures filled the yard, so close to Patrick that, even with the storm door closed, he could smell the stench of their failing flesh.

"That reference doesn't even make sense here," he pointed out sourly. "I can see the path, I can *see* the fucking *path*, and if I kneel, I'm pretty sure my entire *face* will get eaten by these addle-boned monsters."

"Ye of little faith," Philbin beamed.

Patrick sighed. "What's this magic potion that's going to make me impervious to death-noms?"

"Magic potions are for children's books," Philbin said happily. She pulled a hunter's vest off the coatrack near the door. Then she forced Patrick into it and gave him two pats on the chest. "This is science, and we prefer wearables."

Patrick frowned. "I thought scientists preferred injections. What on Earth is a 'wearable'?"

"Things that you *wear*," Philbin said. "Things that are *wearable*. They were about to be all the rage, before M-Day. Apple was about to introduce a watch. Ha! Can you imagine? An iPhone for your wrist! *What?!* It was going to revolutionize everything. If the Jamaicans hadn't done their thing, we'd be a computer- and phone-less society right now."

"We *are* a computer- and phone-less society right now," Carla pointed out.

"Hmm...good point," Philbin mused.

Patrick tried to do the math in his head, but the last few years had been such an absolutely nonsensical blur. "What year is it?" he asked.

"2016!" Philbin exclaimed. "Can you believe it? If not for M-Day, this would have been our most progressive and evolutionary year in human history!"

"I can't imagine that's true," Patrick said.

"Sounds wrong," Carla agreed. "What's in the vest?"

Philbin's smile was so big, the corners of her lips threatened to swallow her eyeballs. She patted Patrick's chest again. "This man's salvation," she said.

"I've never felt less safe," Patrick informed her.

"It's been fine knowing you," Carla said.

But Philbin was radiant. "You'll see," she said, touching Patrick's cheek fondly. "This vest is your grail, and you're about to drink your way right through the leap from the lion's head." Her eyes got misty.

"You have *got* to stop mixing your Indiana Jones metaphors," Patrick grumbled. "Let's just get this over with. I'd rather get eaten by dusters than let Harrison Ford's memory be so disrespected."

He pulled open the door. The sound of moaning dusters crashed against them like a wave, and Patrick's newfound resolve evaporated as quickly as it had appeared. "Christ, there's a lot of them." His knees wobbled; he had to grip the doorframe to keep himself on his feet. He patted the pockets of the vest and felt small vials tucked away in each one. With every pat, a puff of pine-scented air wafted into his nostrils. "If you're so good at keeping these things away, why are there so goddamn many of them on your doorstep?"

Philbin smiled. "If you have the power to keep something out, then you also have the power to keep it *in*." She reached past Patrick and unlatched the storm door. "You'll see when you go."

Patrick frowned. "I don't really care about Harrison Ford's memory as much as I let on," he admitted. "Maybe I'll just stay inside and we can watch 'Fresh Prince' or something. You get MeTV here?"

Philbin pulled a revolver from her lab coat pocket and pressed the barrel against Carla's temple. "If you're not out that door on the count of three, I will paint the television with your friend's gray matter," she beamed. She cocked the gun. "One."

Patrick squirmed. "Well, we don't…actually know each other…very well, so…"

"Are you serious right now?!" Carla cried. She leapt forward and shoved Patrick, hard. He crashed backward through the storm door and fell head-first into the swirling mob of leaky, hungry dusters.

"Sorry about that," Philbin said. She lowered the hammer on the revolver and slipped the gun back into her pocket. "It always goes this way. People get so nervous. That's why I always ask groups to send two."

"Hey—no need to apologize to me," Carla snorted. "It's not the tenth time I've had a gun put to my head, and it gave me a good reason to throw him to the wolves."

"Everybody wins!" the scientist clapped.

"Would you have shot me, though?"

"Absolutely."

"Mm," Carla sighed. "The world is pretty fucked."

"Oh, yes," Philbin agreed. "Totally, totally fucked."

31.

Patrick closed his eyes and waited for death.

But death didn't come, and that was surprising.

He opened his eyes, expecting to see an angry swarm of dusters snapping their jaws and descending on him like the locusts in a Biblical curse. Instead, he saw nothing but greenish-yellow sky.

He sat up. *What the hell…?*

The dusters weren't just not converging on him; they were frantically clawing to get *away* from him. They were clawing, fighting, biting each other in a desperate attempt to get as far away from Patrick as possible.

Jinkies, he thought. *It really works.*

He stood up and brushed himself off. He turned to see Carla and Philbin peering out at him through the storm door and tried to give Carla a scowl for throwing him to the wolves. But she was too amazed for it to take, and he was too amazed for it to look right. In the end, they just gaped at each other like fish, totally dumbfounded.

Patrick turned toward the street. The rest of the crew looked pretty much like he did. The dusters had parted before him like the Red Sea.

"What did you *do?*" Jimmy hollered.

Patrick shrugged. "I fell?" He headed toward the curb, marveling at the dusters who literally climbed on top of each other to get as far away from him as possible. He nearly tripped over a black hose laid across the driveway a few yards from the curb. It stretched in both directions and seemed to encircle the entire house. It was anchored to the ground every few feet by landscape stakes, the rubber punctured with a thousand tiny holes. It looked as if someone had taken the time to stab the whole hose through with a sewing needle, again and again and again. A quiet hiss rose from those holes and the now-familiar pine smell floated out on the stream of that hiss. Whatever was in that hose was being released into the air around the house, an impenetrable wall of anti-duster science.

The stuff that kept them away was the same stuff that kept them locked inside.

Patrick logged some ethical questions about Philbin's experiment in the side-burner part of his brain. He crossed into the street and walked up to the group of Red Caps and riverboat people. "I think she wants the coolers."

The crew stood there, gaping at him in open-mouthed wonder.

"Holy shit," Roman breathed. He stepped forward and grabbed Patrick by the shoulders. "It works." His amazement melted reformed into something like jubilation as he shook Patrick's shoulders. "It *works!*"

They loaded him up with the coolers and he made his way back up to the porch. He pulled the coolers up the steps and knocked on the storm door. "Hey. Your stuff works."

Philbin laughed through the screen. "Told you so!" She pushed the door open and beckoned him in. "Welcome to a brand-new world."

32.

Patrick shrugged out of the hunting vest while Philbin attended to the coolers, pulling out the new equipment and cooing at the beakers like each one was a newborn baby.

"Hey. You're still alive," Carla said.

"Yeah," Patrick answered. "Thanks for your help."

"I'm all about that self-preservation. Besides, you're fine."

"I am," he agreed. "Somehow." He unzipped one of the pockets of the vest and pulled out a small glass vial filled with a bright purple liquid. The vial was capped with wire mesh woven so tightly that it kept most of the potion inside the vial, even when Patrick tipped it upside-down. He sniffed the cap, and his nostrils swelled with the scent of pine.

"Don't touch that—it's radioactive," Philbin said.

"What?" Patrick jerked. The vial slipped from his hand and shattered on the floor. "Oh." He stared down at the spreading purple puddle. "Oh! Fuck!"

Philbin grabbed a towel from the kitchen and mopped up the spill. "Just kidding." She scooped the broken pieces of glass into the towel and tossed the whole mess in the trash. "But you should never just go around touching science. You never know what might kill you."

Patrick grasped his hammering chest and slumped back against the wall. "I do not like this," he decided. "Not anything about what you're doing here. You, them, it—whatever, I do not like it. I want to go home."

Philbin appeared not at all put off by the rebuke. She beamed and said, "Oh? And where's home?" as if they were new friends having tea.

It was such a simple question. Such a simple, impossible question.

"These days, it's in Alabama," he sighed, thinking of Ben. "I am loathe to admit."

"Hmm..." Philbin said thoughtfully. "Loathe, indeed."

She closed the coolers and wheeled them over to the basement stairs. Then she headed into the kitchen, rummaged around in an overhead cabinet, and emerged with a small Ziploc baggie filled with ten vials of the mysterious purple liquid. "Everything here's in order. This should last you four or five years, at least, if you dilute it properly," she added quickly. "It's *incredibly* potent. Put it in an atomizer, any old perfume bottle lying around, and one spritz will clear a radius of...oh, I don't know—I'd say three or four feet, depending on weather conditions."

Carla snatched the bag, and she and Patrick inspected the vials. "What *is* it?" they asked simultaneously.

Philbin smiled that eye-swallowing smile again. "I call it Dust-Away Spray. It's actually pretty ingenious," she said proudly. "Think of them as smelling salts, but a few hundred times more powerful."

"It smells like Pine-Sol," Patrick countered. He opened the bag and took a sniff. "But just barely."

"Barely, to you—sure! But to the dusters? It's like mainlining an ammonia solution through the nose."

"That's not what mainlining is, *doctor*," Carla rolled her eyes. "And the name Dust-Away Spray is terrible."

"I don't want to perpetuate offensive labels, but have you considered Zom-Be-Gone?" Patrick wondered.

Carla snapped her fingers. "I hate to say it, but that's so much better."

Philbin ignored them both completely and chattered on. "It's a chemical solution that takes advantage of a breakthrough discovery we made some time ago, just after M-Day—maybe three months on? Revolutionary, really. If there were still medical journals, we'd be on the cover of every single one!" she gushed. Then her face fell, her shoulders sagged, and she sighed. "I wish there were still medical journals.

"What was this 'breakthrough discovery', exactly?" Carla asked.

"And who's 'we'?" Patrick added.

"Oh." Philbin's frown deepened. "My former colleague, Susannah. Dr. Susannah Gustheed. A brilliant otorhinolaryngologist."

Carla's brow pinched together. "I'm sorry, a...what?"

"An otorhinolaryngologist."

"What is an...that?" Patrick asked.

"An ENT. Ears, nose, and throat specialist. She was a surgeon, but such a keen mind. She used to tell people she was a physicist, which of course wasn't true, but she had such a knack for the interconnectivity of environment to body. There was something of a physicist in her. Just ex-traordinary. One of the best minds of our generation. I knew her from before…we would bump into each other at conferences. Over time, we became…well, friends, I guess."

Carla leaned over to Patrick. "We just asked for her name," she whispered.

Patrick held his finger to his lips. "I think she's working through something."

"We began our work on the Monkey dust right after M-Day—as soon as the dust settled, as it were. We studied it, experimented with it. We had no idea why we were immune when so many others were not. I *still* haven't cracked that one," she said wistfully.

"Lifelong consumption of trace amounts of cremated human remains," Patrick said. "Please, go on."

She gave him a quizzical look as she continued. "Well, we still don't know much about the Monkey dust, to be honest. But three of the chemical compounds we isolated are synthetics that I've never seen before. I don't understand how their structure hold together, and I don't have the equipment to properly analyze them. But I assume they're what makes the dust fatal. Taken as a whole, the compounds in the dust seem to bond to each other when introduced into the bloodstream. For most people, the reaction is an incredibly accelerated deterioration of the blood vessels."

"Meaning?" Carla asked.

"Meaning blood acts as a catalyst for a chemical reaction with the Monkey dust that turns it into a sort of acid that eats you from the inside out, starting with your blood vessels. That's why on M-Day, people turned into puddles."

Patrick bit his lip and fought against his brain as it tried to show him a vision of what Izzy must have looked like: there, on the schoolroom floor, dissolving from the inside…feeling that pain, confusion and fear burning and spreading like molten ore through her head, through her chest.

He bit back his impulse to throw up. Swallowing it down was easy enough.

He'd done that twenty times a day for the last five years.

"But some people experience it differently," Dr. Philbin continued. "And, in fact, in essentially an opposite way. Many of us who have survived will find it not *dissolving* our veins, but *hardening* them— petrifying instead of liquefying, but more intense than that. For these victims, bones don't just become stone; they become something much, much harder."

"Diamond?" Carla asked.

At the same time, Patrick said, "Adamantium?"

Carla gave him a look that made it very clear she had decided that he was a very lonely virgin. It hurt Patrick's feelings a little, until Dr. Philbin chimed in and said, "Of the two, adamantium. One thousand percent, no question." Patrick smiled happily. Carla still looked at him with pity.

"Why the dust liquefied 99% of the population and instead solidified part of the remainder, well…I have some theories about that. I'm still working, but oh, I have some theories!" She leaned in conspiratorially. "But that portion of the one percent…the folks whose veins turn to Vibranium…that's the space that Susannah broke wide open."

Patrick noticed the look on Carla's face. It was the look of someone whose soul had been sucked out of her body and had been replaced by a dusty bellows to keep her lungs breathing. "You're not loving this, are you?" he asked.

"I've literally never been so bored," she said. "Can we go?"

"Definitely not." Patrick turned back to Dr. Philbin, who, sure, had forced him into a pack of bloodthirsty monsters ten minutes earlier, but was now speaking a language he hadn't shared with anyone else in almost half a decade: The language of intensive scientific interest. "You can go. I'm weirdly riveted."

Carla squeezed her hands into fists and tensed her neck to keep the rest of her body from shaking. "No," she sighed. "Roman likes you. I have to pretend to like you."

"People say it's so much harder to make friends post-apocalypse, but I don't know why," Patrick gushed.

"Fuck off."

Once again, Philbin seemed oblivious, completely lost in her own story. "For those people, the dust doesn't solidify just their veins; it substantially alters *them*. This has so many potential implications! I mean, we may not even be technically able to consider these dusters *human!*"

"No kidding," Carla grunted.

"They may be a whole new branch on our evolutionary limb! Study is required, of course, but…it's *exciting*, isn't it?"

Carla twirled a finger through her hair. "It's a real gas."

Philbin beamed. "Ultimately, the Monkey dust fills their veins until they burst; the hardened structures become a new, impenetrable system, hard and hollow like tunnels…they channel and amplify information sent through them. The circulatory system, the nervous system, the muscular system—all of them are radically, irrevocably altered! Changed and enhanced so *finely!* It's like…like a Fisher-Price keyboard becoming a Steinway!"

"I don't know music, but that sounds impressive."

"It is!" she gushed.

"This is truly fascinating," Patrick said honestly. He nudged Carla, adding an, "Eh?" But his elbow only found empty air.

Carla had left the living room and was currently searching through the kitchen cabinets. "You *have* to have alcohol in here," she yelled from the other room. "You cannot subject people to shit like this and not expect to give them a bottle to brain themselves to death with."

Philbin frowned. "Is your friend okay?"

Patrick shrugged. "Is anyone?"

"That is such a good point," Philbin mused, pressing her hand against her heart.

"So...oboes," Patrick prompted. "How does an oboe come to perceive the scent of pine as the odor of ammonia?"

"Maybe your friend's right," Philbin said, turning a bright shade of red. "I'm blathering about incredibly esoteric science. It's just that most people don't stay. When they come and buy my compound, like you have. They grab and they go, and then there's no one here but me." She pulled off her glasses and pushed her fingers into her eyes, trying to clear the salty film that coated them. "Susannah's gone; it's just me, and there's no one who..." She paused and took a deep breath. Then she laughed. "There's no one. You know?"

Patrick frowned. "Trust me; I do know." He shifted uncomfortably, then he patted her awkwardly on the shoulder. "I really do."

"Thank you for understanding," she sniffled. She rubbed her nose on the sleeve of her lab coat, and she put her glasses back on her nose. "I'm sorry to have made you so uncomfortable, with my emotions and my incessant droning about the technicalities of Monkey dust."

"Oh, don't apologize to me," Patrick said. "I *love* technicalities! I'm a mechanical engineer."

"Oh my God...then you get it!" she sobbed, lurching forward and throwing her arms around Patrick's shoulders. She wept into his chest as Patrick patted her on the back.

"I really do," he repeated.

"I'm going to see if there's any wine in the cellar," Carla grumbled as she stomped down the basement stairs.

Dr. Philbin cried a while longer. Then she released Patrick and stepped back, drying her eyes again. "I'm sorry," she sniffled. "I'm just overcome. I've been so lonely for so long."

"Since Susannah," Patrick said.

Dr. Philbin nodded and snuffled loudly, clearing her throat and setting herself right again. "To answer your question about oboes and ammonia:

scent contains particles. When you smell something, it's because actual particles of that something are entering your nose. It's not some sort of ethereal connection; it's a physical response to a physical stimulus."

Patrick blenched. "That changes every single public restroom experience I have ever had— dramatically."

Philbin laughed. "Tell me about it. Your nose works because particles that carry scent go into your nostrils and hit the olfactory epithelium. They slam up against *millions* of olfactory receptor neurons. The particles stimulate those receptors, which send signals to the brain that say, 'This is what *this thing* smells like.' Now, imagine that the neural network that sends those signals to your brain is no longer a child's toy, but something *much* more impressive."

"A Steinway," Patrick said.

"Yes! What was once a toddler's keyboard is now a piano worthy of Rachmaninoff himself! Do you understand what I'm saying?"

Patrick squinted. "I think you're saying I'm ready for Carnegie Hall."

"In a sense, I'm saying you're *not* ready for Carnegie Hall, but those dusters *are*. Where you and I smell nothing, or dull somethings, they smell *Clair de Lune* by Claude Debussy!"

"I always thought Debussy stunk," Patrick nodded wisely.

"I'll assume you're joking, since you're a guest in this house," Philbin said dryly.

"I am joking," Patrick quickly assured her, raising his hands in defense. "I don't know *what* he smelled like."

"Tobacco and sweat," she replied, matter-of-factly. Then she added, "It was a less fortunate time, hygienically speaking."

"Less fortunate for hygiene than now?" Patrick frowned.

"You would be surprised."

"Okay. So. The dusters are the Beethoven of bodily functions. So they—what?—play the notes of the smells? Better?"

"Exactly," Dr. Philbin said, clapping her hands. "They smell the most impotent scents many times more powerfully than we do! *But!*" She tapped her temple knowingly. "They still retain their scent memories. So if they smell something they were familiar with in their pre-duster lives—let's say, coffee, for example—they'll smell that coffee *way* most intensely than they ever did before. But it's not shocking to them, because it's expected at the same new level as all smells."

Patrick squinted. "So because every scent they smell is intensified, they're used to smelling intensified smells of things they expect to smell. Though I would imagine there's some period of...acclimation."

"Exactly right!" she chirped. "During the transformation process into a duster, the poor soul goes through what must be agonizing stages of discomfort as they adjust to their new reality. The more gradual the transition, the more gradual the adjustment. But once they're there, it seems things regulate, somewhat."

"Sure," Patrick nodded. "But if you introduce a completely new smell…"

"Precisely!" Dr. Philbin trembled so violently, she seemed ready to explode. "You get it! Introduce a *very* small but very *new* scent into their olfactory library and it will shock, stun, and repulse!"

"We don't smell ammonia every day, and that's what makes it so potent," Patrick mused.

"It's part of the reason, at least! And that is *exactly* what I've done with my Dust-Away Spray. It's an entirely new olfactory experience for them," Dr. Philbin nodded.

"Then why does it smell like Pine-Sol?"

Philbin shrugged. "That's for me. I wanted a mechanism that would make it easy for me to know if there was some sort of problematic leak, similar to sulfur piped into the natural gas lines of old. I need to be able to detect if my own lab is breaking down, so I add terpenes from a conifer resin—alpha pinene, beta-pinene, limonene, bornyl acetate. Add a few drops of that mixture and the whole thing smells lightly of pine trees to the average non-duster human." She smiled and breathed deeply, as if inhaling the imagined wonder of Christmas. "Think about snorting an entire lot full of granulated Christmas trees. That's about one-third of the experience for dusters."

"So pine is the opening act and ammonia is the headliner."

"You could say that."

"Which explains why the dusters in the woods bugged out when they smacked into a pine tree on their way to eating our faces."

"Yes—a very fortuitous Pavlovian response! Any duster who comes into contact with my Dust-Away Spray is thereafter unable to bear the smell of a conifer. I can't tell you how many times I've benefitted from that."

Patrick glanced out the window at the throng of changed, mindless addicts pushing past each other on the postage stamp-sized property. He thrust his chin in their direction. "What about them?"

Dr. Philbin shrugged. "They're useful test subjects. I'm always tinkering with the formula, making it better … or trying to, anyway."

"You lure them in, then turn on the gas, keep them trapped, and make them breathe the stuff you design to be more and more painful for them?"

"No ethics lessons, please," Philbin insisted. "They would rip your meat from your bones if you gave them half a chance. I've seen dusters tear through my friends and neighbors. You know how hard you have to bite down with regular human teeth to tear out a chunk of flesh? 140, 150 pounds of pressure per square inch, just to tear it loose, much less the added strength required eat a whole skeleton half-clean." She tapped her finger against the window pane. "These are no longer people, unfortunately; they are monsters—real-life monsters. If it helps your sympathetic heart, I never keep one group here for very long. I haven't killed a single one. I keep them fed and sheltered—I take quite good care of them, actually, all things considered."

Patrick held up a hand. "Wait a second…what do you mean you *feed* them?"

"Well, they need to eat to survive."

Patrick's brow clenched. "And what exactly do you f—"

"Whoops!" Philbin cut him off as she raised her wrist and checked her watch. It was completely shattered. "Time to go!"

Carla emerged from the basement. "Thank God," she grumbled. "Let's get out of here."

Philbin ushered them to the door. "Make sure you open that bag—you want the dusters to really smell it."

"But wait—what do you feed the—"

Patrick's insistence was overridden by Dr. Philbin's pushy dismissal. "Don't be strangers, and do come back when you have more centrifuges! Good luck, darlings!" Then she shoved them out onto the porch and locked the door behind them.

"Well?" Roman asked. The crew members were tapping their feet, annoyed.

"All good, I guess?" Patrick said, holding up the Ziploc and pushing through the dusters. "Just a little disagreement on the topic of feeding normal humans to the zombies for science."

Roman nodded. "Ah."

"And speaking of normal humans," Patrick continued, "We happen to be three of them. What say we *run* back to the boat, yeah?"

Everyone agreed that was probably best.

33.

They made excellent time to the river, only to find that back at the riverboat, everything was on fire.

"Sorry! Ahh—sorry! Ahh—sorry...ahhhhh!" Ted screamed, alternating between apologies and panic as he ran around the deck of the ship, swatting at the flames with blankets.

Patrick stood on the road, his mouth agape. "Only Ted could figure out how to burn something down while it's surrounded by water."

Roman shouted orders to his crew as they sprang into action. Ella and Lucia dashed onto the burning boat and into the kitchen, reemerging less than a minute later with rusty pails in each hand. They started tossing river water on the flames they could reach. Carla stormed up to the top deck and started kicking through the burning railings, breaking them off the boat. Roman pulled down the lean-tos they'd pitched on the harbor and used the canvas to beat down the flames inside the cabin. Ted kept running around, shrieking and swinging his blankets at various fires until he himself somehow caught fire, the sleeve of his t-shirt turning to flames. He screamed himself hoarse, dropped the blankets on the deck, and threw himself over the side of the boat.

The rest of the Red Caps just stared.

Patrick shook his head in disbelief. "I...guess I'll go get Ted."

Brett stepped up and pulled off his shirt, revealing a set of upsettingly powerful muscles that rippled under his somehow-tan skin. "Nah—I'll do it. The more I can hold over his head, the better." He set off at an easy walk toward the water, his casual attitude in stark contrast to the general emergency of the situation.

Patrick, Gary, Jimmy, and Richie all hurried to the fire and pitched in where they could. They helped with buckets and blankets; at one point, Richie tried kicking through a burning railing, but his ankle popped when his foot made contact and he hobbled away while sucking air in through his teeth, wincing, "Ow, ow, ow, ow!" Carla knocked that particular bit of wood away from the boat with a quick sway of her hip.

"I loosened it for you!" Richie cried, hobbling down a flight of stairs.

With everyone in motion, it didn't take long to put out the fires. They were spotty and localized; ninety percent of the boat was untouched and unharmed. It looked like a small fire demon had taken bites out of the other ten percent.

"What the hell was *this*?!" Roman yelled when they'd reconvened on the shore. "Where are the girls?"

Ted was soaking wet, and out of breath. "First off—let me say, I am so sorry…this was my watch, and I take full responsibility. Again, I am *so* sorry."

"You said you'd defend the boat with your life," Brett reminded him. He pulled a half-smoldering two-by-four from a pile of fire wreckage and gave it a practice swing. "You ready to pay the piper?"

"Don't you fucking dare!" Ted hollered, ducking behind Patrick for protection.

Patrick turned his head and whispered, "You might want to hide behind someone big."

"He wouldn't dare hit *you*," Ted whispered back.

"Oh, no—Brett's well known for his deference to authority," Patrick said, rolling his eyes.

"I recognize no authority," Brett smiled. He was having a great day.

"Focus," Roman said, snapping his fingers. "Where are the others?"

Ted cleared his throat. "Well, uh…they're the ones who did this."

Roman's face fell. "What?"

Ted picked up a sooty blanket and wrapped it around his sopping wet shoulders, huddling against himself for warmth. "I was on the top deck," he explained, "just, you know, trying to heal. I didn't see the sisters and the other one all morning—they were just wherever on the boat. Then suddenly, they climbed down the gangway with a box full of bottles with rags stuffed inside."

Carla gasped. "Oh shit."

Roman raised an eyebrow in her direction. "Anything you'd like to share with the group?"

Carla blew a big gust of air out of her cheeks. "Well…Mel and Mary, they've been running their mouths lately, about…" She glanced at the Red Caps, then refocused her eyes firmly on Roman. "You know…everything."

"They're *always* running their mouths," Lucia said.

"I know," Carla admitted. "That's why I didn't think anything of it. But the last few days, they've been…I don't know. Quiet. Weird."

Roman's nostrils flared. Fire danced in his eyes. "You knew they wanted to leave?"

"Shit, Roman—we *all* want to leave!" she sputtered. "And we all want to stay! It's not as if we had our choice for the best possible life, this would be it. But it's better than most. So yeah, we all want to stay *and* we all want to leave. But I didn't think they'd actually do anything about it. I guess they've just had enough and…"

Her voice trailed off.

"I can't believe they would try to burn down the boat," Ella said.

"I can't believe they would try to burn down *me*," Ted moaned.

"Oh yeah—because you're some great prize," Richie rolled his eyes.

"Go scratch your dumb elbows 'til they bleed," Ted snapped.

"Shut up—that was *one time!*"

"God, that was gross," Brett said. His shoulders cringed at the memory. "Disgusting."

Roman's face had turned a dark shade of purple. His fingers shook as he ran his hands slowly through his hair. "Carla," he said, his voice trembling, "where did they get Molotovs?"

"I don't know," she answered honestly. "I mean, my guess is Adiva. If anyone can put together a firebomb, it's her."

"Her room," Ella suddenly started. "All those bottles…she used them as vases."

"For dead flowers," Lucia added. "I thought she just had some weird goth-girl thing. But she was storing up Molotov bottles."

"Dead flowers," Roman said, almost as an afterthought, his hands still tight against his skull. "Dead flowers in dead peat. Dead peat in old bottles." He laughed. Then he laughed more. Harder and harder, louder and longer, until the whole river basin seemed to rumble. "Ella?" he said, his voice shaking with laughter, tears dripping down his cheeks. "Be a doll and go get the bottle from my desk, please." His fists were still clenched around his hair.

Ella's eyes widened. She stepped sideways, as if skirting a rabid dog. "Sure," she said uncertainly. Then she sidestepped up the ramp and disappeared into the riverboat.

Gary leaned in closer to Patrick. "What am I missing here?"

"Peat," Patrick whispered. "Peat is really flammable."

Roman flashed him a look. "Go ahead—share with the whole group," he said, laughing again.

Patrick cleared his throat uncomfortably. "Um...okay. I was just saying that dried peat is really flammable. Put some dried peat in a bottle and stick a dead flower in it, it looks like a Tim Burton Valentine. Take out the flower, add a rag soaked with high-octane alcohol, I would guess you've probably got a pretty good bottle bomb."

Gary blinked. "What the fuck is peat?"

"It's like...swamp earth, kind of," Patrick answered. "Cool stuff, actually. Great at holding carbon. Bad at not catching fire."

Ella emerged from the ship. "I can't find it," she said. "It's gone."

Roman nodded. His laughter sounded hoarse now, scratchy. He pulled harder at his hair, his fingers turning white from the pressure. Patrick turned away; there was something about watching a grown man slowly tear fistfuls of his own hair out by the roots that really turned his stomach. Then, Roman relaxed. He released his hair, smoothing it back. When he lifted his head again, his face was bright. "Well, gentlemen, your timing is even better than we thought! A new crew for a new adventure." He slapped Gary on the back then strode confidently up the platform.

Patrick leaned in close to Carla. "Um...is he okay?"

"No," Carla whispered back, shaking her head sadly. "He is most definitely not okay."

Roman turned and smiled at them from the deck. "Let's go, team! Let's get this burned-out, broken-down old gal ready to launch. In the morning, we head South."

Then he disappeared into the cabin, slamming the door behind him.

34.

The next morning, they woke with the sun and made final preparations for launch. Ella headed down to the lower deck to fire up the furnace while Carla stowed their rations and supplies in nets nailed to the walls. Lucia passed out slices of summer sausage and stale bread. By the time they were done with their cold breakfast, Ella had the smokestacks coughing smoke and the boat was ready to go. Roman gave the word, and the big, broken paddle wheel began to churn through the water.

"Shit," Gary said, watching the huge wheel make its slow but powerful rotations. "She actually works."

"You know what they say," Patrick replied, patting the side of the boat. "Can't keep a good Muddy Queen down."

It was sort of thrilling to be on the water, even if they were moving slowly. There was something about the musty river breeze and the slap of the yellow-brown water against the ship's flaking paint that made the trip feel like a real adventure.

Patrick squinted into the sky. "This feels like we're going north. Are we going north?"

Gary nodded. "Far as I know, sun still rises in the east, so yeah. We're going north."

Patrick blinked. "Not exactly what I thought heading south would be like."

Roman came trundling down the stairs, rolling up the sleeves of his button-down. "We have to go north to go south," he grinned. "We'll take the French Broad up to Knoxville, then the Tennessee will take us south."

"Sorry," Richie said, looking confused, "which broad?"

Roman laughed. "This one!" he exclaimed, gesturing down into the water. "The French Broad River. It links up to the Tennessee River around Knoxville."

"We're riding the Big Muddy Queen on the French Broad?" Brett asked. He snorted. "Well, that's it...I'm turned on."

Carla rolled her eyes. "There's a sock in the hallway. Knock yourself out."

"Way ahead of you," Brett winked.

Carla wrinkled her nose and groaned.

"So...what's the plan?" Patrick asked, desperate to change the subject.

Roman smiled, his teeth glinting in the light. "Home," he said. "The plan is return home." He sat down on a bench and patted the space next to him. Patrick reluctantly sat; he couldn't help but feel like an obedient puppy. "We've got to wind around a bit to get there—up to Knoxville, which should be pretty smooth sailing."

"Smooth sailing sounds positive," Patrick said.

Roman nodded. "Absolutely."

"So then why do you need us?"

"'After the Tennessee, things get a little dicey." Roman looked at the group and cleared his throat. "Could we have the room?"

Roman's crew roused themselves and headed inside, making for the boiler room to check on Ella. The Red Caps looked questioningly at Patrick; he nodded. They stood grumpily and wandered off. "Guy sits down outside and asks for the room," Brett grumbled.

Roman watched them wander away. "Easier one-on-one," he explained.

"It all sounds the same in my ears," Patrick said.

"So. The dicey part...it comes pretty soon after we split from the Tennessee." Roman reached into his shirt pocket and pulled out a well-worn knob of paper. He unfolded it and smoothed it out on the bench between them, wiping his palm over the surface. He pushing it down, but that didn't do a thing for the wrinkles. "This isn't a great map, but it's accurate... mostly." It was a withered page, torn from a Rand McNally, printed in a time when books of maps were a navigational necessity. It pre-dated M-Day by half a decade at least.

Patrick exhaled sharply. "I haven't seen a map like that since my buddy Clark and I took a road trip from St. Louis to San Diego in...boy. Was it 2004? Maybe 2005?"

"Clark...the friend in Mobile?" Roman asked.

Patrick felt a sudden wave of sadness wash over him. "No. Different friend. Different adventure."

"Before the smartphone," Roman nodded.

"Those were days, huh?"

Roman smiled. "Those were days."

"I miss trips like that," Patrick confessed, "when you could cross the country and not get your hand nailed to a tree or have your own buffalo served to you in a soup."

"But if you haven't had a flesh-eating armored townie sprinting for your jugular, have you even really lived?" Roman countered.

"Well, we went to Tijuana on that trip, so we pretty much checked that box."

"Gotcha." Roman stood quietly for a few moments, watching the bank slip by. "Do you think he's still alive?"

"Who, Clark?" Patrick shrugged. "Maybe. Probably not. I'm sure he survived the dust, but…he's not really built for survival. More of an indoor person."

"Ah."

"Though of course, I am too. And I'm still here." Then he added, "Most of me." He motioned toward the map page. "May I?" Roman handed it to him. Patrick carefully examined the soft, faded paper. "So this was your original route?" Patrick asked, pointing to line drawn in red marker that traced a meandering path along the Mississippi River and through the Rust Belt, down to North Carolina.

"Yep. And this one's the path back home." He pointed to a blue line that branched off and spilled more or less due south, running through the Tennessee-Mississippi-Alabama border and continuing on down through along the western Alabama edge. On the map, the blue line ended about three-quarters of an inch above Mobile.

"It's a hell of a lot shorter," Patrick observed.

"'Hell' is exactly right," Roman said. "It's shorter, but it's hell. This river here," he said, tapping the map at the Alabama border, "that's the Tenn-Tom Waterway. That's the key. It breaks off from the Tennessee River up here, see? The Tenn-Tom is where we run into trouble."

"What kind of trouble?"

"Some real *Mad Max* shit. That waterway's a major corridor of commerce. Probably even more so now than it was before. And where there's value, there are leeches, from the boardroom to the bedroom. That's what my old man used to say."

"He sounds neat."

"The man could really pick a stock," Roman sighed. "Absolute genius." He shook his head and cleared the memory away. "Anyway, the whole Tenn-Tom is full of pirates."

"Like, Disney pirates? 'Cause if it's Disney pirates, I am gonna have a *lot* of fun."

"No, like hill people pirates."

"See, now that sounds less fun," Patrick frowned.

"When we were planning our trip here, I sent some of my guys on a recon of the waterway. Their debrief showed three big points of concern." Roman pulled a pen from his shirt pocket and clicked it open. "The first is here," he said, drawing a circle around the point where the Tennessee River diverged into the Tenn-Tom. "You want on or off the Tennessee, you have to pay the toll."

"And I'm guessing you'd rather not pay the toll."

Roman nodded. "First rule of business: never pay the tax."

"I thought the first rule of business was greed is good."

"Same rule," Roman said.

"Oh. That's true."

"The second blockade is here," he continued, drawing another circle about an inch or so southwest of the first. "The Jamie Whitten Lock. Built to lower ships down off the Bay Springs Lake. There's a gang holed up there now, running the lock. My guys couldn't get close enough to see much detail. But a boat of, say, five or six people went into the chute…and an empty boat came out."

"What happened to them?"

"Nothing good, I assume. My guys said the locals around that part of the river speak about the Whitten Lock crew only in whispers. Everyone's scared to death of them. So whatever they're doing, it's bad. I'd wager it's very, *very* bad."

"Sounds…bad," Patrick frowned.

"The third pain point is down here," Roman continued, circling a space not far from their destination.

"What happens there—Buffalo Bill takes all your skin and sews himself a wetsuit?"

Roman shook his head. "I've got no intel on this one," he admitted. "Some group camped out on the bridge over the water there, but my guys couldn't get close. It's out in the open, my guys were too exposed. So it's a total question mark."

"Excellent."

"And between those three points, the river's swarming with smaller, faster boats with some pretty heavily armed dudes trying to board every boat that passes. My guys say they're efficient."

"So if we make it past the gate and the lock, we could still get torn apart by raiders."

Roman nodded. "Most people do."

Patrick blew out a long gusty breath. "And you're sure you can't be convinced to go back the long way?"

Roman shook his head. "No way. It took us way longer to get here than we planned. *Way* longer. We can't take that time again. We were supposed to have been home by now. You know what our absence means to my farm? You know what *any* absence means *anywhere*? Every time you leave a place, a power vacuum opens up, and some upstart asshole slips in, takes control." He put his hands on Patrick's shoulders and looked him square in the eyes. "That campus is everything. A takeover there would destroy the entire southern U.S. economy. I'm not kidding. That's how integral we are to the supply chain. We have to get back. People's lives depend on it." He released Patrick's shoulders and returned to the map. He traced his finger along the thin blue line. "This is how we get there. This is the route. Three groups of pirates; three serious blockades, any one of which might mean our death. I need your help to survive it."

"Hmm," Patrick said. He gazed out at the water while the gears turned in his mind. "How good are your people with those crossbows?"

"They're surgical," he said proudly.

"Good. We're going to need animals. A lot of animals. Dead ones."

"Sorry?"

"Now, look, I'm a champion of living creatures," Patrick insisted, waving his hands through the air, "I'm practically a vegan, minus bacon, eggs, honey, and all the other meat. But we're going to need a lot—I mean, a *lot*—of dead animals."

Roman frowned, but he nodded. "Done. What else?"

"You have any tools on board?"

"Sure."

"I'll need to see them. How much do you like this boat?"

"I *love* this boat."

"But do you want to keep it?"

"I'd prefer it," Roman said.

"But do you still need it to be seaworthy after we get back?"

Roman thought about that. "I mean, it would be ideal. But no, I guess not necessarily."

"Great. Then I regret to inform you that I have a plan."

"I don't think I'll like the sound of it."

"I doubt you will."

"So what are we going to do?"

"It's actually pretty easy," Patrick shrugged. "We're going to out-pirate the pirates."

35.

Gary grumbled and slapped a mosquito on his neck. "Anyone know what this genius plan is all about?"

They had reached the Tennessee River at Knoxville the night before, docking the boat a dozen miles west of the city proper. The Tenn-Tom wasn't much farther, so they'd pulled off and docked to make the preparations for Patrick's plan. He'd divided them up into teams with specific instructions, which was how Gary found himself trundling through the exurban woods of Tennessee as part of a two-person hunting party.

"By 'anyone,' I assume you mean me, since I'm the only other person in earshot," Carla replied, lifting her crossbow to her shoulder. "Now shh." She stared thoughtfully down the sights.

"What the hell are you aiming at?" Gary squinted into the woods. He didn't see shit.

"*Shh!*" Carla said again. She tilted the crossbow a few centimeters to the left and pulled the trigger.

The rabbit was dead before Gary could say, "Jesus."

Carla crunched through the leaves, slinging the crossbow over her shoulder. "If anyone knows, shouldn't it be you? He's on your team."

Gary snorted. "He's not on my team. He's a substitute."

"Or *you* are."

"And we may be on the same team, but we're not friends."

"Then why are you traveling together?"

"Because I tried to kill him for a pretty long time."

Carla was intrigued. "You tried to kill him for a pretty long time?"

"Yeah, I tried to kill him for a pretty long time," Gary said, annoyed. "I was mean, I was violent...I did a lot of bad shit, and this is my penance."

"Okay."

"I didn't know he'd be so goddamn weird, though."

"He *is* weird, right?" Carla agreed.

"So goddamn weird," Gary repeated.

They approached the carcass. Carla's arrow had lodged in a tree, pinning the rabbit like an insect in a glass case. "Bag," she beckoned with one hand open.

Gary sighed and slipped off his backpack, wincing as he unzipped it. The stench of dead animals was already strong, even though the kills were fresh. They smelled like blood, mostly, iron and tang, but there was also a hint of spoiled milk, and some unspeakable gaminess that made him both sickened and hungry at the same time.

Carla wrenched the bolt out of the tree trunk, then used her boot to slide the dead rabbit into the bag. "Five," she said proudly.

"Yeah, yeah." Gary zipped the bag shut and threw it back over his shoulder. "Why am I even on this mission? I'm not a hunter."

"I know. You tried to kill Patrick for a long time, and he's doing great."

"This is why I don't open up to people," Gary grumbled.

"Who knows why he sent you to hunt?" Carla said. "Maybe he's playing some weird Six Sigma StrengthsFinders leadership game with you. You know, helping you find your power language and breaking you down to build you back up so you can interview for the V.P. job next quarter."

"So you worked in the corporate world," Gary said.

"Financial services litigator," Carla said. "God, I miss that job. You think the apocalypse is brutal? You should have been in a courtroom with Goldman Sachs three times a month." She inhaled deeply, then let loose her breath with a satisfied sigh. "No blood tastes sweeter than Goldman Sachs' blood."

"How do you know what other blood tastes like?"

Carla looked at him blankly. "How do you not?"

"And how does a bank lawyer get so good with a crossbow?" he demanded.

"Just because I'm educated doesn't mean I don't come from Arkansas," she replied.

They pushed on through the woods, tramping through brush in erratic loops that Gary figured were random nonsense, though Carla insisted she was following trails. The fact that she then bagged a sixth rabbit—and then a fox, and then another fox, all in a span of thirteen minutes—didn't change his mind one bit.

"So...you like working for Roman?" Gary asked.

"I don't work for anyone," Carla said sharply. "I play my deck for survival. This is the hand with the high cards right now."

"And Roman is the King."

"Yes, he is. You'll see, if we actually make it back to the farm. You won't believe how gnat-speck small your control over anything has been until you see what Roman's built on that campus in the last four years. He basically *is* a king. That power is working for me. If it stops working for me, I'll shuffle the deck."

"So what're you, then? A queen?"

Carla scoffed. "Hell no. I'm a ten."

Gary shook his head. "We're out here hauling dead animals, and Roman's at the boat, soaking up the sunshine. Must be good to be the king."

Carla gave him a side eye. "Yeah. You've got the look," she decided.

"What look?"

"The look of someone who thinks he wants to be a king."

Gary's eyes flashed. "You don't know anything about me."

"I know your eyes are little baby black holes of hunger. You think it's better at the top. But believe me, king is not what you want to be. Not in the world before, and not in this one, either."

"Oh yeah?" Gary snorted. "Why's that—too much whiskey? Too much power? Too much fun?"

"Because even in a world of a thousand people, there are a million other Garys out there, all waiting for their chance to stab the king in the neck," she replied. "Read a book."

"I read books," Gary lied.

"Quiet, pig."

Gary started. "Hey—fuck you, lady. I don't come around here calling *you* mean names."

"*No*," she hissed, her eyes flashing. "*Quiet!*" She pointed into the brush ahead of them. "*Pig.*"

Gary followed her finger and saw the backside of a wild hog that was rooting through the mud beneath a black walnut tree. "Oh."

Carla raised the crossbow to her shoulder. "We bag this one," she whispered, "and we can head back. He's going to be *so* heavy for you."

"Shut up," Gary glowered.

She aimed the bow and waited patiently for the hog to present its side. Her palms started to sweat. She couldn't remember ever seeing a pig tear at roots so aggressively. It gnawed at the twisted bark, working hard to tear it apart. It hauled back and slammed its head forward into the thick trunk, again and again and again. Then it dove right back down into the roots, ripping with its tusks and digging in with its knuckles.

Something about it wasn't right.

"Come on, come on," she muttered. The pig kept on with its furious onslaught, and the tree trunk began to crack. The hog dug in and pushed its powerful legs so hard, they sank another three inches into the earth as its whole body twisted to the side.

Carla flashed her teeth. "There you are."

She fired the bolt at the hog's heart. It hit the side of the animal like a stick hitting reinforced cement. The arrow snapped in two as the sharp metal tip bounced uselessly of the hide.

"Oh. fuck." Gary's face turned white as death. He grabbed Carla's collar and pulled her back. "*Run!*"

"What—?" Carla asked, totally bewildered. She stumbled after him, losing her footing, slipping in the leaves.

"Come on, come *on!*" Gary shouted, sprinting ahead. "*Run!*"

The hog had been in such a lather over the tree, it hadn't even noticed the arrow that had broken against its shoulder. But it heard the hunters turn and run off, shouting into the woods. Its head snapped in their direction. It took one sniff in the air, spun its legs in the mud, and sprinted toward them through the tangle of leaves and vines. Branches snapped as it snorted angrily, letting fly long banners of yellow-green spittle from between its dust-stained teeth.

"Jesus Christ, will you fucking *move?!*" Gary shrieked.

Carla finally got her feet beneath her and pushed off after Gary, her powerful legs quickly catching him up. "What the hell is going on?!" she demanded.

"It's a duster!" Gary wheezed, already out of breath.

"*What's* a duster?" Carla asked as they both launched over a fallen tree and hit the soft ground running. The hog was charging them down, snarling and squealing, gaining ground fast.

"The *pig*! The fucking *pig* is a duster!"

"How can a pig be a duster?!"

Gary shook his head. His cheeks were turning redder as he huffed and puffed. "Animals are dusters now! We saw a fish just like it! Now *go!*"

They tore through the trees, Carla pulling ahead, Gary doing his best to keep up with the sack full of animal corpses on his back. The hog staggered as it ran, zigzagging on what appeared to be a broken front foot. Every few steps it crashed into a tree or slipped in some leaves—the only reasons it wasn't on them in the first ten seconds. They caught a lucky break when the pig stuck one hoof in a rabbit hole. The huge animal pitched forward and slammed into an old oak tree, the crown of its head smashing into the trunk so hard, the tree cracked in half. It teetered over, splitting from its base and crashing down into the forest. The earth shook when it hit the ground, but the two managed to keep their feet under them. The pig was so dazed from the brute force impact, it lay stunned on the ground for almost a full minute.

Not that a minute was going to do them much good.

"What do we do?" Gary panted.

"We should climb a tree!" Carla shouted over her shoulder, still pumping her arms and running way faster than Gary. "They can't climb trees!"

"No—they just knock them down!" he hollered back. They broke into a clearing, and Gary spied a small river over the hill. It was narrow, but it looked deep, probably a feeder to the Tennessee. "Can they swim?"

"No, they can't *swim*," Carla said. She meant it sarcastically, but Gary missed it. He peeled off and made a beeline for the river. Carla looked back and saw where he was headed and called out, but by then Gary was too far away, slip-sliding down the hill and careening toward the bank. The hog was back up on his hooves and pounding the grass, more furious than ever now, closing in with unthinkable speed. Carla had no choice but to turn back and push forward, cocking a useless bolt into her useless crossbow as she ran, because what else could she do?

The boar saw them split, and the decision of which meal to follow was simple. Gary was obviously the easy prey, tumbling down the hill and splashing clumsily into the cold water. The animal tore off after him, yellow bubbles frothing from the corners of its mouth.

Gary stumble-swam out toward the middle of the river, gasping for air, struggling to turn himself onto his back, to float on the backpack like a sick turtle thrashing on a balloon. He shifted into a floating position more or less, his arms paddling like noodles, though they kept him mostly above water. *Thank Christ*, he thought, sputtering river water and trying to slow his heart. *I'm safe.*

His head bobbed up as he glanced back at the riverbank. He watched the boar thunder down the hill. He watched it ram into the river at full force. He watched it disappear under the water. Then he closed his eyes and smiled. His lungs burned, his chest ached, and his arms were hanging by threads. But he had outsmarted the duster-pig. He laughed and laughed and laughed.

Then he heard rustling, and he opened his eyes.

The hog's face was twenty feet away and closing in.

And that was how Gary learned that hogs can swim.

His screams echoed through the valley, scaring birds out of their trees for hundreds of yards in every direction.

But they didn't scare the pig. It simply opened its jaws and lunged.

Carla watched all of this helplessly from the top of the hill. "Oh my God," she said numbly as the hog went in for Gary's throat. "I just sarcasmed someone to death."

36.

"Why did Patrick give us a shopping list?" Jimmy frowned. "Doesn't he know how the apocalypse works? You don't just drive to the store and get everything on your list, you know?"

"Quiet," Brett said, "I'm reading."

"Yeah, and he needs all his concentration," Lucia said. "Some of the words have two syllables,"

The team of three stood at the edge of a wide suburban parking lot that was littered with dead cars, rusting shopping carts, and a few hundred brownish-greenish glop piles that used to be humans.

"This is the most depressing Home Depot has ever been," Jimmy decided. "And that's saying a lot."

They skirted around the edge of the lot, watching the doors beneath the tattered orange awnings warily. "Think there's anybody inside?" Jimmy asked.

"Always assume there's somebody inside," Lucia replied. "Always assume you're being watched by an army."

Jimmy and Brett exchanged looks. *Is she more badass than we are?* Jimmy's look said.

She's definitely more badass than you *are*, Brett's face replied.

They darted between banged-up cars, keeping low and trying to stay out of sight of anyone who might be inside looking out. The only windows were the two banks of doors, one at either end of the building, so they swung wide around the edge of the parking lot, where they could approach from the blind spot to the side of the building.

"No one in their right mind would hole up in a Home Depot," Brett decided. "You don't live at the Home Depot; you raid the Home Depot, take the hatchets and the hammers, then go live it up at the Chuck E. Cheese across the street."

Jimmy snatched the shopping list from Brett and read through it again. "I don't care about the hatchets and the hammers. I just hope they left the rest of this stuff."

"Should we keep making small talk out here in the open, or should we get a fucking move on?" Lucia said, rolling her eyes and scooting toward the entrance.

Jimmy frowned as he watched her go. "Today is going to be a hard day," he decided.

They crept up to the busted-out doors with their backs pressed against the wall and their weapons in their hands. "All right, I'll go first," Brett whispered as he moved toward the doors.

Lucia grabbed his arm. "Why do you get to go first?" she demanded.

"Because *I* know Home Depot."

"We've all been to Home Depot, Tim Allen."

Brett smiled confidently, crossing his arms. "But not like *I've* been to Home Depot."

"Brett used to be a plumber," Jimmy explained.

"Oh wow," Lucia said. "You plunged other people's shit professionally, or was it a hobby?"

"Professionally, baby. Construction-level. I laid a lot of pipe." He winked.

"Ugh," Lucia grimaced. "Gross. But you know what? Do go first. Tell whoever's in there how good you are at Home Depot while they beat the shit out of you with a wrench."

Brett gave her a salute. The he slinked up to the doorway, holding the two-pound hammer he'd brought as his weapon of choice. He took a deep breath, rounded the window bay, and stuck his head through the open-door frame.

"It's okay," he called from half-inside thee door. "There's no one here."

"Yeah, sure—you scouted the entire place in three seconds," Lucia snorted.

Brett pulled his head back out of the doorway, smiling a toothy grin. "You'd be amazed what I can do in three seconds," he said.

"Did you just brag about premature ejaculation?" Jimmy frowned.

Brett winked. "Oh yeah." He motioned them over, and they both reluctantly joined him. "See? There's no one manning Returns."

Jimmy blinked. "So what?"

"So, if you're protecting a Home Depot, you're going to put men with eyes on the door, and the Returns section is already walled off, so it offers the best line of sight with the best protection. Unless you build yourself a brand-new barricade—and you can see that ain't been done—then you're gonna put half your people at Returns, to watch this door, and the other half at Checkout, to watch the other door. Then everyone else can live their dumb, joyful lives in the back, doing…I don't know—forklift Olympics or some fuck-all."

Carla sighed. "Despite the fact that half the people here and half the people on the other side would account for the entire group of people and wouldn't leave anyone do to 'fuck-all' in the back, that makes a lot of sense. I hate that I'm saying it."

Brett tapped the side of his head smugly. "Eighth Wonder of the World up here."

"Shoot me in the face," she bristled, pushing past him and into the store.

"Dude, I don't think she likes you," Jimmy whispered, patting Brett on the shoulder.

"You stupid virgin, of course she likes me," Brett said, slugging him back, but much harder.

Jimmy wilted. "Ow."

They explored the building, shining flashlights down the aisles and taking quick stock of what was left. There had definitely been people living in the Home Depot at some point; old food wrappers crunched under their feet, and they had to step around several large sleeping nests made of gathered rags and tarps. The aisle with the outlets and light switches had even been used as a toilet at one point. "Makes sense," Brett said, "because electricians aren't worthy of respect." But whoever had been camping there seemed to have cleared out.

"I don't like it," Jimmy decided. "It feels spooky. Why would anyone leave this place? It's like a fortress."

"A fortress with the doors blown out isn't much of a fortress," Lucia pointed out.

"Besides, who wants to live in a big-ass bunker with no windows?" Brett asked. "It's like a tomb that's a million times too big. Come on…read off the list."

Jimmy pulled shined his flashlight on Patrick's hurried scrawl. "Okay. First thing: lengths of pipe. Lengths? Lengths of pipe." He squinted at the handwriting. "It's either lengths of pipe or Luigi pipe. Probably not Luigi pipe, right? They probably don't have those. Right? It's probably lengths."

"Probably," Lucia agreed with a sigh. "You're a doctor, right? Aren't you supposed to be good at bad handwriting?" She snatched the paper and read the first line. "Lengths of pipe."

"How many?" Jimmy asked.

She tapped the marking next to the words. "He drew the infinity symbol, so…a lot, I guess?"

Brett led them purposefully toward the plumbing section. "Did he say what size pipe, what material—any details at all?"

"Nope. Just 'pipe.'"

Brett rounded the corner and stepped into the plumbing aisle and whistled. "I guess we'll just have to choose, then." He shined his light up at the racks. They were fully stocked. "Not a top-ten apocalypse essential, I guess."

They pulled a dozen twelve-foot lengths of PVC and half-a-dozen lengths of copper. Lucia found some loose bungee cords on the floor a few aisles over to bundle them with before setting them next to the door. Then they set about checking off the rest of the list: caulk, a few tarps, some duct tape, four buckets, white paint, a packet of rags, half a dozen cans of spray adhesive, and a few more odds and ends. In thirty minutes, they were done.

They stood in front of the pile. Brett's eyes narrowed. "This seem strange to you?"

"What, that he ordered more than we can carry?" Jimmy asked, rubbing the back of his neck. "Yeah. Feels pretty frustrating,"

"He wasn't expecting us to find everything," Lucia guessed. "That's what's strange. But this place has…*everything*."

Brett nodded. "The tools section is mostly stripped, but otherwise… it's like this place ain't been touched."

"In five years, no one's thought to look through a Home Depot for tarps?" Jimmy said.

"Hell, look at this," Brett said. He jogged across the aisle and pulled a white box off the shelf next to the cleaning supplies. Then he flipped it over and showed them the front of the box. It was emblazoned with a big red cross.

"A first-aid kit," Jimmy said, surprised.

"Mm-hmm." Brett flipped it open and showed them the contents inside. "Still full, too."

"Okay. That does feel off." Lucia drew her machete from her belt and walked slowly backward toward the door, her eyes darting around the dark warehouse. "Yeah…something's not right, here. We should go."

"Yeah," Brett agreed. "Time to fly." He started loading things into the buckets, and Lucia began dragging the pipes toward the door. But Jimmy didn't follow suit. He perked up and turned toward the back of the store. "Hey!" Brett snapped his fingers. "Jimmy. What's up? Let's go."

"Hold on," Jimmy mumbled. He held a finger to his lips for quiet. "Do you guys hear that?"

Lucia heaved the bundle of pipes over the doorframe and went back for a bucket. "Hey, genius, if you're hearing noises, guess what? That means it's doubly time to get the fuck out."

Brett agreed. "Yeah, Jimmy—let's go."

"Hold on..." Jimmy turned his head, pricking up his ears. "I could swear I heard someone calling for help."

"So what?" Lucia said. "Let's *go*."

Jimmy shook his head. "I'm a *doctor*."

"He's an EMT," Brett clarified. "Hey, why is it you're only a doctor when you want to be an asshole?"

"If someone needs help, I have to help them. I took an *oath!*"

"You know who needs help?" Brett muttered. "*Me*. Grab a bucket. This shit is heavy."

Jimmy was already gone.

"Hey." Lucia crossed her arms and motioned toward Jimmy with her chin. "Go get your boy."

"Yeah, yeah," Brett grumbled. "Goddammit."

He dropped his bucket and stormed off after Jimmy, leaving Lucia alone at the front of the store. She dragged the rest of the buckets out through the doors and separated everything into piles, so they'd be easier for the three of them to divvy, grab, and go.

Then she went back inside.

The seconds passed slowly. They turned into minutes.

Jimmy and Brett didn't come back.

"Jesus hell," Lucia muttered. Her heart started to pound as the familiar feeling of fear began to prickle up her spine. *You should leave*, she though. *Self-preservation. Survival of the fittest. Not your crew, not your problem. Just go. Save yourself. Just go.*

"Yeah, yeah," she spat. "I should go."

She tightened her grip on her machete and stepped into the opening of the aisle. "I swear to God, if I die in a Home Depot, I'll kill myself," she promised.

Then she headed toward the darkness Brett and Jimmy had disappeared into.

37.

Carla felt bad. She didn't really like Gary all that much, but she didn't want to see him get eaten by a zombie pig, either—and *definitely* not while she was watching. She had enough death on her conscience; she wasn't looking to add to expand her portfolio of ghosts. And the thought of being haunted by an asshole like Gary was too much to bear.

By now, the demon creature was basically on him, snapping its jaws and closing in for the kill. Gary had swum a few clumsy backstrokes over to a fallen tree, throwing his arms around it presumably because drowning was worse than being ripped apart by a raving, razor-toothed pig. It didn't matter either way. It would all be over any second now.

Carla had one shot.

She reached into her pocket and pulled out a small vial of bright purple liquid. "Good thing I nabbed you," she sighed. She dropped to one knee and tore off a piece of her tattered sleeve. She cinched it around the shaft of an arrow, then slipped the arrow into the crossbow. Then, she pulled the rubber stopper off the vial with her teeth and dribbled some of the Zom-Be-Gone onto the rag. The pig had reached the log. She heard Gary's screams intensify as the animal smashed its hooves against his legs, scrambling up his body. His chest was suddenly foamy with the sickly yellow pus pouring from the pig's mouth.

Gary squirmed under the weight of it, catching a knife-sharp tusk against his chin that sliced his flesh open. The pig lapped at his blood with a swollen green tongue.

Carla plugged the vial again. In one smooth motion, she cocked the crossbow, pulled it to her shoulder, aimed down the sight, said a quick prayer, and pulled the trigger.

The bolt sailed across the hill.

"Oh, shit," Carla muttered.

She had moved too quickly. She hadn't been steady.

She had inadvertently aimed for the log.

She missed.

"MOTHER GOD!" Gary shouted as the arrow went *phunk* into his right forearm. The bolt came out the other side of his arm, a few inches below the elbow. "*Ahhhhh!*" he shrieked. "You fucking shot me! Goddammit, Carla, you fucking *shot* me!"

"Sorry!" she hollered down from the hill. She felt like she should say more, but she was at a loss over just how bad the situation had gone. "Sorry," she said again, quieter this time, hoping he wouldn't hear it.

But the hog had stopped thrashing. It was standing half on Gary's chest, half submerged in the river. Its wet, bristly head lifted into the air. The tonic-soaked rag was stuck partly within Gary's soft tissue, but even the blood-and-gore-soaked bit that poked through carried more than enough of the strange purple potion.

The hog inhaled three huge sniffs, and that was all it took. The scent filled its nostrils and sent a firestorm of chemicals deep into its lungs. The chemicals coursed through its reinforced circulatory system, filling it with ammonia that seeped into its brain. The hog flailed and snarled and pawed at its own snout, trying desperately to work out the confusing new toxin. It fell into the water and thrashed there in the current, too focused on the pain to remember to swim. In a flash, the wild pig disappeared below the water, sputtered a few dozen bubbles to the surface, and went quiet.

"Holy shit," Carla murmured. "It worked." She leapt up and clapped, pumping her fists in the air. "Gary, it *worked!*" she shouted.

But Gary didn't hear her. He had passed out cold on the log.

38.

Lucia was halfway down the lightbulb aisle before she realized the guys had taken both flashlights. She stopped dead in the dark, and she snorted at the wall of bulbs that rose up on either side. "Isn't it ironic?" she said to herself. "Don't you think?"

She moved more slowly into the dark recesses of the store, letting her eyes adjust and keeping a tight grip on the machete. She felt safe enough, hidden between the impossibly high rows of shelving, but soon she reached the halfway point of the aisle, where the shelves gave way to a wide, open walkway that bisected the warehouse. It was a good five or six strides across that opening to the protection of the next set of shelves. Lucia peered out from between the shelving units and searched for movement, *any* movement, from the guys, from a stranger—hell, she'd even have taken a duster attack at this point. At least she'd know what she was up against.

The not-knowing was paralyzing.

She didn't dare call out for Brett and Jimmy. She'd seen them both go down the lightbulb aisle, but where they'd headed from there was anybody's guess. The machete felt small and useless in her hand. She wished she'd brought her crossbow; she was good with a machete, but she was a goddamn artist with a crossbow. It had seemed stupid to bring a range weapon on a mission to raid a store, where any combat was certainly bound to be a close-quarters affair. But now that she was in it, she realized that the Home Depot was just enormous.

She was still debating her next move when she finally heard it: a muted, but very distinct, call for help. It was coming from further back in the store.

Lucia checked the walkway for movement one last time, then she darted across the floor and dove into an aisle full of plumbing fixtures.

She peered out between two model toilets and saw the outlines of what may have been Brett and Jimmy standing at the far edge of the kitchen appliance showroom, their backs pressed against a refrigerator. They had turned off their flashlights, making it difficult to see details. But when the voice called for help again, the bigger shadow moved quickly over to the back wall of the building, and Lucia recognized by the smooth, loping gait that it was Brett. The fear in her chest broke like a water balloon, and she scurried down the aisle to meet up with him against the wall.

"What's happening?" she hissed, creeping up behind him.

"I'm about to find out," he whispered back. "Stay here a second. Don't let Jimmy do anything stupid."

"I need to help!" Jimmy buzzed from behind the refrigerator. "I'm a doctor! I took an oath!"

Lucia groaned. "We know."

Brett moved quietly over to the short hallway that led back to the Employees Only part of the store. The security door that sealed it off from the main space was still intact, as was its rectangular wire mesh security window. He slipped up to the door and peered through the window, standing there for several long moments and taking in what there was to see. Lucia and Jimmy shifted impatiently, ready to jump out of their skin. After what felt like ages, Brett reemerged from the hallway and the three gathered in the darkness beneath the collection of storm doors.

"Well, guys," Brett said, scratching his head, "things just got weird."

Lucia snorted. "Sorry? Things *just* got weird?"

"Oh, yeah," Brett nodded. "*Real* fuckin' weird. Go see for yourself."

Lucia glanced at Jimmy, who only shrugged. The two of them left Brett and padded down the hall. Lucia peeked up through the window.

"What...the actual fuck."

"Told you," Brett hissed from the storm doors.

There were lanterns burning in the employee area, the gas-powered Coleman kind. They were spaced around the perimeter in a circle, and there were enough of them to bathe the whole room in light. There were people in there, eight or nine of them at least, though it was hard to tell the exact number; they all kept climbing up and down a set of three different extension ladders that descended into a massive pit in the center of the floor. It looked like the photo of a sinkhole Lucia had once seen on the news, a big crater that had opened up beneath the highway in Peru or Argentina a year or two before M-Day. Except this sinkhole wasn't in a South American suburb.

It was in a Home Depot breakroom.

The people going up and down the ladders were bringing tools down into the pit. One man disappeared down the ladder carrying a Sawzall. A woman with bright red hair wound three extension cords around her neck before she climbed down the ladder. An older man with short-cropped silver hair and big, puffy white eyebrows eased his way down another ladder while shouldering a pair of gallon jugs filled with something Lucia couldn't quite make out. Down they went with their loads, and back up they popped, empty-handed. Everyone was busy; everyone had a job.

One man's job was to act as a coatrack. Both of his arms were laden with bright orange vests with the Home Depot logo stamped on the back. As Lucia and the men watched, the others began to form a line in front of the human coat hanger. One by one, they stepped up and slid an orange vest off one of his arms and pulled it on over their shirts. Every time someone put on the vest, they stood face-to-face with the man holding the vests and made a secret salute with their arms. First, they held the left arm out in front of them, parallel to the ground; then, they placed their right elbow on top of their left hand, arm raised straight into the air, as if they were signaling nine o'clock. Then, the arms switched; the right arm went parallel to the ground, and the left arm raised up above it—three o'clock. Then, they placed *both* arms parallel to the floor, one hovering over top of the other. Finally, they smashed both arms together, so that they ended the salute standing like Indian caricatures in old, racist Disney movies from the 1960s.

"What in the absolute hell are they doing?" Lucia mumbled.

Jimmy shook his head. "I think they're making a box. You know. Like the Home Depot logo."

Lucia's eyes grew wide. She turned back to the window and watched the last few people go through the arm motions.

It really did look like they were making a box.

Brett joined them at the door. "Fuckin' weird, right?"

"What did we walk into?" Lucia demanded.

"I don't know," Brett admitted, "but that sign is giving me the heebie-fuckin'-jeebies." He nodded at the wall over Lucia's shoulder. She turned and saw the white sign with block lettering. The Home Depot logo was situated at the top of the sign, and beneath it, their slogan: YOU CAN DO IT. WE CAN HELP. Except the word "WE" was crossed out in black Sharpie, and someone had written "HE" instead.

The sign now read, YOU CAN DO IT. **HE** CAN HELP.

Lucia turned to the others. "We're leaving. Now."

"Right behind you," Brett said.

They heard the voice again, closer this time, and clearer: "Help! Please! Somebody! Help us!" It was a woman's voice, full of pain and fear and desperation.

It was coming from inside the pit.

"You guys…" Jimmy said, shaking his head. "Come on. We can't just turn our backs. Who knows *what* the hell is going on down there? They might hurt her! They might *kill* her! You saw the Sawzall!"

Brett stiffened. He turned back to Jimmy. "They have a Sawzall?"

Jimmy nodded. "One of them brought it into the hole."

"Damn," Brett said. He rubbed his jaw. "That's not good."

"What's a Sawzall?" Lucia asked.

"Like an electric knife. But for bigger, harder things. Tree roots. PVC."

"Human bones!" Jimmy added. "They're going to chop up her *human bones* with a *Sawzall!*"

They all peered back in through the window, doing their best to stay out of sight. The men and women in the orange vests were now descending the ladders, every one disappearing into the hole. As they filed down, the woman's cries for help intensified, becoming terrified screams until her voice gave out. When the last ounce of hope left her, and her loud crying softened into a gentle whimper that was somehow much, much worse.

A door opened at the far end of the room, throwing a brilliant rectangle of light into the room. Lucia shielded her eyes; through the glare she could make out the silhouette of another person walking into the storeroom from the alley back behind the building. The door slammed shut. Once their eyes adjusted again, they watched in horrified fascination as a woman stepped slowly to the edge of the pit, her arms outstretched over the people below. She, too, was wearing a branded orange vest, as well as a ridiculous hat made of duct tape. It stood more than two feet tall and was secured by a short bungee strap under her chin. Blue mosaic backsplash tiles were stuck into the duct tape hat like jewels. The overall effect was that of a ninety-nine-cent queen's guard bearskin hat and crown jewel cosplay mash-up.

"Okay, well, I suddenly feel less threatened," Lucia decided.

"Someone took the time to make that," Brett said, disgusted.

"It's as if Pee-Wee Herman kept prisoners in the basement of the Playhouse," muttered Jimmy.

"Pee-Wee Herman *did* keep prisoners in the basement of the Playhouse," Brett said.

"Oh shut up."

The woman lifted her hands higher as the people in the hole began clapping in slow rhythm. The beat moved faster and faster as she raised her hands higher and higher, until the claps reached a frenzied applause. Then the woman made a motion for silence, and the clapping abruptly stopped. From the hole, a chorus of voices shouted, "The power of The Home Depot!"

And then there was silence.

"What…is happening?" Lucia whispered.

The woman with the duct tape hat placed her hands on her hips, slipping her thumbs through the belt loops in her jeans. She did it slowly, and with great ceremony. "In the Builder's name, we gather," she said.

"Long live His holy Depot," came the response from those assembled in the hole.

"My friends, my colleagues…my fellow handy hobbyists." At that, an excited tittering rose from the pit. The people down there were very excited to be counted among her fellow handy hobbyists. "Today, we meet to honor the Builder and His mercy, as we have done every new moon's eve since the fall of civilization, in accordance with the Great Blueprint, which we believe the Builder himself has inspired."

"I wrote part of it!" one chipper voice rose up proudly from the pit.

The priestess rolled her eyes. "Yes, Larry, we all know you wrote part of it."

"I was inspired by the Builder to detail His holy schematic for the New Society to be Built Upon the Quikrete of the Soul!"

"We were all there," she replied testily.

"The Builder flowed through me like runoff through a storm drain!"

"*We get it, Larry!*" she snapped. Some of the others in the hole shushed Larry. Larry stopped talking. "Tonight is the eve of the blood moon cycle. We honor, therefore, both the blood that was spilled that day, and the blood that was not."

"We were spared!" cried a voice from the pit.

"Jesus Christ, shut the hell up, Larry," said a different voice in the hole.

"Can we muzzle him?" asked another.

"Did you just say 'Jesus Christ'?" said someone else.

"Uh…no? I said…uh…'Great Builder, shut the hell up, Larry.'"

"Oh. I thought you said Jesus Christ," the other someone said.

"No, I said Great Builder."

"Oh. Well, taking the Builder's name in vain is punishable by death."

"What? No, wait—!" But then there was the gushing sound of metal on meat, and that particular voice fell silent, forever.

Up on the lip of the hole, the priestess was growing impatient. "Can we just get on with it?" she demanded.

"Sorry! Just punishing a blasphemer, in accordance with the Blueprint," said the someone else from the hole, sounding very pleased with herself.

"Anyway. As I was saying. We honor the blood that was spilled, and the blood that was not. Remember, oh my handybrethren, that on the day of the Great Collapse, the bombs did fall. Oh, how the bombs fell!"

"They fell so hard!"

"They fell so *many!*"

"That doesn't make sense, Bob."

"Shut up, Mary!"

"Many bombs fell hard," the priestess agreed, getting things back on track. "But the showroom floor of Home Depot Store #730 was unharmed! Our goods, untouched! Our doors, unbreached! Our people, unharmed!"

"Most of them."

The priestess closed her eyes and took a centering breath. "I'm getting to that, Bob. Thank you." She cleared her throat and tried to regain the energy she'd been building, but it was a struggle. "Lo! It was nigh the end of the onslaught when a Monkey bomb fell through the roof here, in the back room. And did it destroy a single item?"

"No!" the chorus shouted happily.

"And did it injure a single handybrother?"

"No!"

"No! We were spared in that moment, and we suffered only a hole above and a crater below!"

"A hole above, a crater below," the chorus murmured reverently.

"Then a second bomb fell through the roof! Here!" she said, pointing to the center of the pit. "Directly next to the first! And was a single item destroyed, or a single life lost?"

"No!"

"No! Just a larger hole above, and a bigger crater below!"

"The second hole, the second crater," the people whispered.

"And then the third and final bomb fell through the roof! And it landed *here!*" She thrust a powerful finger toward the far end of the pit. She was really working the room now. "And my handybrethren, did *that* bomb cause loss of property or life?"

"No!"

"Nooooo! Because we, the people of Home Depot Store #730, have been spared! We, among most, have been allowed not only to live, but to *flourish!* We were *chosen* by the all-seeing, all-knowing Builder! We are his project; he is our master craftsman! By his mercy, we are milled, planed, fastened, and stained! By his love, we are insulated!"

"Blow insulation on me, Lord!" cried Mary in a fit of pique.

"By his will, we are the New Church, upon which the New Society to be Built Upon the Quikrete of the Soul will be placed!"

"I never understood that syntax," Larry admitted.

"We!" the priestess screamed, ignoring him. "We are the mortar that will hold together the bricks of this new world! We are the two-and-three-quarter-inch nails upon which the world will hang its dreams! We are the Scott-brand fertilizer that will coax the downtrodden back to life! We are the TrafficMaster carpet squares that will cover the bare floors of Before, where no feet shall tread again! We are the Builder's apprentices! We can do it! He can help!"

"We can do it! He can help!" they all cheered.

The priestess let them roar for a few moments, then she held up her hands for silence. "And yet, my handybrethren…and yet. In his infinite wisdom, the great Builder saw fit to trade the gift of our future with the sacrifice of three beautiful souls. Three of our own, who died on that day, not from the bombs themselves, but in Reckless and Careless Accidents, in accordance with the Builder's wishes. There was Terry, the floor manager."

"Terry," the chorus whispered sadly.

"Terry was not looking where she was going, and she fell into the hole and died."

"Rest in Accomplishment, Terry," they chanted.

"There was Linus, the intern, who rode his skateboard to work that day, and was excited to do a 'sick jump' over the pit. But no one warned him about Terry's dead and broken body, still in the hole, and when he saw it, he was startled, and he did not make his jump."

"Rest in Unpaid Accomplishment, Linus," they intoned.

"And there was Gerald, the snack counter vendor, who tragically, and ironically, slipped on a hot dog bun. He, too, perished in the hole."

"Rest in Fullness, Gerald," they said.

"It is these three souls we honor tonight, on the eve of the blood moon cycle. We remember the three lives taken by taking three new lives. We offer to you, wise Builder, a sacrifice of three heathens, that you may know our gratitude."

"We're not heathens!" came the frantic woman's voice.

"No? Then why did we find *this* in your bag?" The priestess triumphantly thrust a Lowe's credit card into the air.

"That's not even mine!"

"*Quiet the heathen!*" the priestess shrieked. There was a round of shushes from below. There were many, many shushes. "Good. Now, fire up the generator!"

A battery-powered generator roared to life inside the pit, and the sound broke the trance of the three visitors watching through the door. They pulled away from the glass and pressed their backs to the wall. "Holy shit," breathed Lucia. "What do we do?"

"We have to stop them," Jimmy replied.

"We don't know how many of them there are."

"But we know we have the high ground," Brett said.

"But what do we *do?*" Lucia asked again.

"Easy," Brett snorted. "You don't fight the whole snake. You just cut off the head."

"Okay. Okay. So we grab the head lunatic and hold her until they let the others go."

"Huh? No, that's not what I'm saying."

"What *are* you saying?"

Brett looked at her like she was an idiot. "I'm saying we grab the head lunatic, and we bash in her head."

He pulled open the door and charged the pit.

Lucia and Jimmy stared after him in shock.

"Is he always like this?" Lucia asked.

"Only sometimes," Jimmy frowned. "He does a whole weird, righteous violence thing."

"Oh." Lucia cleared her throat. "Righteous sounds...good."

"No," Jimmy said flatly. "It is always very, very bad."

39.

Patrick had his doubts about the plan.

To be honest, he almost always had *some* doubts about all of his plans. But they very rarely nagged at him. This one, though? He wasn't quite sure about it. There was something off that he couldn't quite shake—a kind of dread or hopelessness that he couldn't put his finger on…something that tugged at his sleeve and whispered, "Maybe try something else?"

But there was nothing else.

They were a short-handed group of bumbling survivors who barely knew each other, and they were going head-to-head against at least three separate blockades of well-trained, blood-hungry pirates. There were no real options. Sailing in on their sweet, old-fashioned Mark Twain paddle-wheel would be like bringing a Nerf shooter to a gunfight.

So Patrick had a pretty bad plan, but it was the only plan he could see having any chance of success. And when a bad plan is the only plan, he reasoned, then it's also the best plan. He satisfied himself with that knowledge as he crouched in the dark, sweltering boiler room, punching holes in the metal pipes with a sharp rock and a hammer while trying not to think about their chances of success.

Actually, he reasoned, the idea wasn't so much bad as it was silly. It was a *very* silly idea, in fact—a Monty Python sketch of a plan. It was also exactly the kind of plan he would have thrown himself into entirely just a year and a half earlier.

But he felt older, now. Slower. Stiffer.

Sadder.

If he took time to shine any light at all on the dread knotting his stomach, he was pretty sure he'd see that the cold, black tendrils of it hadn't started with the pirates. But they certainly ended there. The beginnings of the dread-creature those tendrils belonged to lived way back beyond the river, behind the walls of Form Doom. Patrick knew Ben had gone back there, and he knew the Doomers wouldn't leave Mobile. So he tried to imagine that when he eventually made it back there—*if* he made it back there—he'd find them all there, working in the garden, laughing by the fire. Still…he couldn't shake the feeling that the dread-creature knew something he didn't. The gloom of it covered his heart like a shadow. He tried to ignore the feeling, to wall it off in his chest instead of giving it oxygen. He just kept beating a hammer against a rock to make holes in an old, tired boiler.

"Ben would hate this idea," he said aloud.

"Oh, I especially hate this idea," Ben said miserably.

"That's how you know it's good!" Patrick cried happily. They were standing on the roof of Patrick's old apartment building. They'd smashed through the bookshelf barrier that Patrick had set up against the rooftop stairwell door before clamoring over fallen HVAC ducts to get out through a Monkey bomb hole and onto the soft, gravelly roof.

Patrick bounced on his toes a few times. "You know, I'm starting to think this whole thing might cave in and kill me in my sleep."

"Wow, you're really selling it," Ben rolled his eyes.

"No, Benny Boy—come on! 24C is perfect for you! The woman who owned it was a fussy old widow, she would have wanted it to go to another fussy celibate!"

"First, I'm not fussy," Ben insisted.

"Interesting first point to refute."

"And second, I'm not celibate."

"If you were getting laid, you wouldn't be so fussy. Now listen," he said quickly before Ben could respond, "living on your own isn't good for you. Look at you—you're all skin and bones."

"I have three times your body mass," Ben said smugly, crossing his arms.

"Yeah, but I was born this way. But you! You were born to beef!"

"I never know what you think you're trying to say," Ben frowned.

"I'm saying, move in here and let's live like kings. There's no reason for you to stay in Ukrainian Village. That's a terrible neighborhood."

"I like Ukrainian Village."

"No, you liked Ukrainian Village, until two weeks ago. Then your entire apartment building fell down and basically buried you in your garden unit."

"Now I have the penthouse," Ben said smugly.

"You can have the penthouse here!" Patrick cried. He gestured wildly to the ruined Chicago landscape. "Look at this place! Look! You can see the lake!"

"Not from 24C," Ben reminded him.

"Oh, who cares about the lake. You can see the Sears Tower!"

"It's called the Willis Tower now."

"Oh, no it is not…and it never will be. You'll have a great view. And if that building across the street ever falls over, you'll be able to see the river!"

"Oh, wow," he said dryly.

"Look," Patrick said, sitting on an old heat exchanger. "You shouldn't be on your own. Your place is all exposed. You stay there, and one day you'll wake up with your throat kicked in. Here, you'll be safe! No one will bother you 24 stories up. We'll set cool booby traps in all the stairwells— it'll be like Home Alone, but vertical. And we'll be neighbors," he added. He looked down at his hands and picked at the flakes of dry skin in the center of his palm. "I think I'm the only person still alive in the whole building. Did you know that?" His sincerity was a surprise, even to him. "It'd be nice. To have a friend here. You know?"

"Hey, look," Ben said, shifting uncomfortably, "if you start crying, it's gonna be so awkward that I'll throw myself off the building, because death is preferable to me seeing your feelings, so I'll just save you the waterworks and tell you, I'm sold. I want the apartment. Are you kidding me? It's a fucking fortress. That old nut job built a panic room that's bigger than my whole apartment. I'm in."

"Oh." Patrick brightened. "Well, great! Then why'd you say you hate the idea?"

"I don't hate the idea of taking over the apartment," Ben clarified. "I very much hate the idea of how you think we're going to get in there."

"Ah," Patrick said. He nodded sagely. "Yes. That makes a lot of sense."

"I am not—and I cannot repeat this vociferously enough—am not going to tie a rope around my waist and try to kick through the window by swinging down from the roof."

"Vociferously is a very good word," Patrick said admiringly.

Ben leveled a finger at Patrick's face. "Don't you dare try to compliment me into jumping off a building. Don't you dare."

"Hmm," Patrick said, rubbing his chin. "I guess I could go back to crying…"

Ben narrowed his eyes. "You do that, and I jump. Without the rope."

Patrick waved his hands through the air, clearing the negativity and trying for a reset. "Just listen. It's the only way."

"It can't possibly be the only way…there's a door."

"Which she reinforced with three-inch-thick steel! Trust me, there's no getting through that thing. The only way into that apartment is through the window."

"Then why don't you go?" Ben glowered.

"I already have an apartment—24E…you've been there. This is your apartment. It's for you."

"And it'd be an excellent housewarming gift for me if you were the one to crash through the window to get it," Ben told him.

"It's scientifically improbable," Patrick said sadly. "I wish I could, Benny Boy, I do. For you? I'd do it. But it's scientifically improbable that I could break through that window."

"Because you're built like a water balloon animal?"

Patrick nodded. "Sadly, yes. And you, Ben. You are beef." He hopped up from the heat exchanger and pulled open the door to the stairwell. There was an old cinderblock on the landing that had been used as a door-stop over the years. Patrick hefted the block with both hands and struggled it over to the edge of the roof. "You are beef," he said again, panting, "and when beef rides rock, nothing can stop it."

Ben stared blankly at the cinder block. He looked up at Patrick. He blinked. "What?"

"You'd probably break through the window just fine on your own, as long as you concentrated your force with your feet and kicked through. But just in case you get a bad jump and wind up slamming in butt-first, we're just going to send a cinder block down with you."

Ben couldn't believe his ears. He gripped the top of his skull with both hands and took a deep breath. "And how exactly do you plan on 'sending' a cinder block down with me?" He tried to keep his voice even.

"I'm so glad you asked," Patrick said seriously. "Remember the Slim Pickens scene in Dr. Strangelove?"

"Oh, fuck this," Ben snapped.

"No, don't fuck this! Ben, it's going to be fine!" Patrick insisted. "People do this sort of thing all the time!"

"Who does this sort of thing all the time?"

"People!"

"When?!"

"At times! Listen—I'm an engineer! This is what I do! I've worked out the math. And look!" He reached into his backpack and produced a black nylon rope. "You know where I had to go to get this rope? REI! Ben…I went to REI!"

Ben raised an eyebrow. "You hate REI."

"I hate REI! But I went. And it's not like it was just hanging on the shelf! It's not like I could just walk in and buy a rope! I had to make friends with five different granola bros. They never even worked there—they've just made it their fortress! I had to make small talk for an hour with five granola bros, just to get access to the building!"

"You hate small talk even more than you hate REI."

"I know! And one of them had made these god-awful hemp and raisin banana chips, and they kept making me eat them. Ben...it was horrible. Truly. I would rather go through that window ten times than go back to REI."

Ben rubbed his chin. "I do know that to be true..." he said slowly.

"Look at this thing." Patrick unraveled the rope and held it up for inspection. "This is a BlueWater Assaultline Non-Dry static climbing rope. This is a rope they used for forest rescues. This is a rope they tie people to helicopters with before they dangle them a thousand feet in the air. This is a very good rope, and it will not break."

"I actually wasn't thinking about the rope breaking until you said it wouldn't," Ben frowned.

"And it won't!" Patrick said happily.

Ben exhaled deeply. This plan was so stupid, and way more dangerous than just living out the rest of his miserable days in the exposed garden apartment on Hoyne. But as insane as the plan was, he was loathe to admit that he did trust Patrick.

He just had never had to think about if he trusted him at "jump off a roof" levels before.

"Let's pretend I'm dumb enough to do this," he said carefully. The look of pure ecstasy on Patrick's face was instantaneous, and distracting. Ben had to look away. "I'm not saying I'm doing it! But if I did, how would it even work? If I jump off the roof, I go down vertically. To crash through the window, I need to go horizontal."

"Ben," Patrick said, trying desperately to temper his excitement that the conversation had gotten this far. He gestured to the surfboard that was propped up against the stairwell. "Why do you think I brought the surfboard?"

"I have no idea why you brought a surfboard. When I asked you earlier why you were bringing a surfboard, you told me not to ask stupid questions."

"Oh yeah. I did say that, didn't I?" Patrick remembered with a smile. "Heh."

"Boy. I do hate you."

Patrick shook his head and waved his hands. "Listen: The surfboard is a fulcrum. Here." He ran over, grabbed the surfboard, and lifted it over his head, nearly taking out a dead power line. Then he trotted it back over to the edge of the roof and shoved one end beneath the heat exchanger, leaving the other end to stick out over the edge of the roof by about four feet. "We tie one end of the rope around the heat exchanger. The other goes around you and the cinder block. All measured out, okay? You walk out on the surfboard like this." Patrick pantomimed walking, because there was no way in hell he was going to walk out over 24 stories of open air without a harness. "See?"

Ben screwed up his mouth. "What is—is that walking? Are you pretending to walk?"

"Yeah—this is supposed to be walking, do you get it?"

"Yes, Patrick, I fucking know how to fucking walk!" Ben exploded.

"Okay, well, then you should have no problem walking off the edge of the surfboard. We'll wrap the rope around the fin, there—again, painstakingly measured to precision—and that's it. You really don't have to do any work. You just sort of fall off the edge of the board, the rope will catch, it'll swing you back, and the cinder block will do the rest. Bingo-bango, smash-crash—you've got a new penthouse apartment."

"Where did you even find a surfboard in Chicago?!"

"Shh, Ben, shh. Too many questions."

Ben sighed. He looked at the surfboard. He looked at the rope, then looked over the edge of the building, at the sidewalk that was just barely visible through the swirling green mists below.

He looked at Patrick.

"I'm not doing this. I'm sorry. I am never, ever going to jump off this building."

Four minutes later, the rope was secured, and Ben was standing on top of the cinder block on the far end of the surfboard, 400 feet over the city street. "I hate you," he told Patrick.

"But you're going to love your new apartment," Patrick beamed. "I can't wait to come over for brunch. Ready?"

"No!"

"Great. Deep breath, close your eyes."

Ben squeezed his eyes shut. The rope was cinched so tightly around his chest, waist, and hips that he thought he might actually be sliced into pieces when it pulled taut. Despite this, the magnitude of tightness actually gave him some comfort. The end of the rope terminated at the cinder-block, in a knot that Patrick promised was "the best knot—don't worry."

"If I die, I want you to know that I'm going to haunt you so fucking bad," he said.

"I expect nothing less."

"Not in a normal way, either. In a murder way. No chains rattling and lights flickering bullshit. I'm going to reach my ghost hands into your chest and tie your arteries in a knot."

"Seems cruel, but fair," Patrick agreed.

Ben sighed. "All right. Let's do this, I guess."

"All right!" Patrick clapped his hands excitedly. "You are an unstoppable force, Ben-plus-cinder block. Ready?"

"No."

"Good. Oh, one last thing."

"What?!"

Patrick took a deep breath. "I'm only assuming the old widow reinforced the door with three-inch-thick steel; I didn't actually try to break it down. It's theoretically possible that we might be able to go in through the door, but I'm almost positive she would have reinforced it, so there's no use injuring ourselves trying to break it down, and this is going to be fine, bye!" He gave Ben a shove.

The string of curses that Ben screamed as he fell into open air was absolutely historic.

"And that worked out fine," Patrick remembered, as the bright rooftop dissolved and the sooty boiler room crept back into place around him. Ben loved that apartment. It had become his home. A real home. And he had been fine after crashing through the window. Mostly.

A smile crept across Patrick's face. Maybe this riverboat plan wasn't such a bad one after all.

He'd had more fun with worse.

He put the rock against the boiler wall and hammered away, whistling happily while he worked.

40.

Brett was having so much fun.

He wasn't *really* planning on bashing in the priestess' head—not with a two-pound hammer, at least. But he figured he could sure give it a good knock, maybe break one bone, two at most. He wasn't typically so juiced to put someone in traction, but this monster was about to offer up three human sacrifices, and that little detail worked like Windex on his conscience, leaving it squeaky clean.

He sprinted into the back room and dove for the priestess. He gave the hammer a good swing, throwing his whole shoulder into it. It felt so good to be whacking homicidal lunatics upside the skull that he laughed as he swung. It was a full-chested laugh that shook his body so hard that his aim went wide, and instead of smashing the Home Depot dipshit in the temple, he smashed through her stupid hat instead. He cracked half a dozen jewel-tone tiles that adorned it and sent the whole crumpled mess of duct tape flying down into the pit.

The woman gasped at him. "My *hat!*"

Brett threw up his arms and said, "I know!" Then he pushed her into the pit, too.

She landed so hard on her back that they could hear the wind knock out of her lungs like a blacksmith's bellows were working in her throat. Everyone in the hole winced as they looked up at Brett. Then they got agitated.

"You killed Dina!" one man shrieked.

"She's not dead, *Bob*," snapped a woman.

"Give it a minute," Brett said. He took stock of the situation in the pit. There were eight lumberyard lunatics in total, counting Dina the Priestess.

They were all in the back of the pit, near the ladders. In the front of the hole, close to Brett's feet, was a crude table made of eight-by-fours laid across two sawhorses and lashed together with towing straps. There were three people tied to the table: a woman in her early thirties, her eyes swollen, her cheeks streaked with tears; and two children, a boy and a girl—twins, by the look of them, and no more than seven or eight years old. The children's mouths were stuffed with disposable rags. The looks of terror in their eyes drove nails into Brett's stomach.

He clenched his fists so hard, his wrists cracked. "Boy. You all fucked up *bad*."

He jumped down into the hole and got to work.

Out of concern for the children, who had already been traumatized enough, he didn't kill anybody.

But it might have been a kinder mercy if he had.

The priestess was on her back, wheezing for breath, probably having cracked a rib or two on impact. Brett figured a single word from her might have the power to inspire the caulk-gun cultists to fight, so he jammed his heel down on her jaw, hard. Breaking it had the pleasant double effect of both removing her ability to speak *and* causing two of the orange vest acolytes to double over and vomit on their own shoes.

He leapt at the others before they could process what was happening.

The hammer did a lot of the work.

He smashed one man's collar bone, felling him like a bag of cement. He hit another woman's shin so hard, the bone popped out through the back of her leg. She went down, too. The man holding the Sawzall had a momentary flush of adrenaline, which caused him to fire the thing up and lunged at Brett with the blade going full speed. But he forgot he was tethered to the generator; when he jumped, he went soaring, but the Sawzall stayed put. His face changed from fury to confusion to terror, all within the span of three seconds, all while flying through the air at Brett. Brett swung the hammer at the man's gut with all this strength, dealing incredible damage to the poor bastard's organs…and his pants, which he immediately soiled.

The two pukers were still gagging on their own bile. Brett calmly walked up between them, grabbed their heads, and smashed them together. They dropped to the floor like popped balloons.

The last two handy helpers had seen enough. They ran to the ladders and climbed up as fast as their shaking arms and legs could carry them. Brett flipped the hammer in his hand, to feel out the weight, then he threw it at the woman scrambling up one ladder. It caught her in the center of her back, on the ridge of her spine. Something cracked there. She moaned as she crumpled off the ladder, hitting the dirt floor hard with her shoulder.

The last man made it to the top of his ladder and laughed with relief as he went over the edge of the pit. But Brett leapt up, planted his foot on the third rung, then jumped again, and grabbed hold of the man's ankle, just as it slipped over the top of the ladder. He yanked the man's foot, dragging him backward. He screamed as his chin hit every rung on the way back down into the hole. Brett rolled him over onto his back. His nose was bloodied and broken, and he was crying. Brett knelt down and stroked the man's hair. "Hey man," he said, his voice calm, and quiet. "Look." He grabbed the man's chin and turned his face toward the sawhorse table. "You see them?" The man whimpered incoherently, which Brett took for a yes. He brought his mouth down close to the man's ear. "Those are fucking *kids*," he said.

Then he picked up the Sawzall, switched it on, and brought it to the man's ear.

Jimmy and Lucia peeked over the top of the pit. "Stop, Brett—what the hell are you doing?" Jimmy yelled.

Brett switched off the Sawzall. He looked up at Jimmy. "What? They were about to sacrifice *children* to the fucking *God of Home Depot*."

Jimmy shook his head. "Well, yeah, but…" He looked around help-lessly at the eight broken bodies writhing in pain. "Now I have to help *them!*" he whined. He did some quick mental triage. "And they are…I mean, come on, Brett, I've seen videos of Afghanistan that looked less horrific than this."

"Good thing we found a first aid kit," Brett said. He walked around the scattered bodies and made his way to the sawhorse table. He untied the prisoners and gently pulled the rags from the children's mouths. "You guys okay?" he asked, checking them for injuries.

The kids trembled so violently, it was hard to tell if they were nodding or just shaking with fear.

"Thank you," the woman said, her voice cracking with grief and grat-itude. She took Brett's bloodied hand in her and squeezed it. "God sent you here to save us."

Brett snorted as he helped her up. "It wasn't God who sent us," he said.

The woman gathered her children close and hugged them tight. "Then who?" she whispered.

Brett smirked. "If I had to pick one person, I'd say the apocalypticon."

41.

"I can't believe you shot me."

Carla rolled her eyes. "Oh my God, Gary—will you stop saying that? I'm *sorry!* I didn't mean to shoot you."

"I thought you were this *amazing marksman*," Gary said sarcastically as he shifted his grip on his injured arm. The makeshift bandage was already soaked through with blood, and a thin stream of red dribbled from the fabric as they walked. His arm was swollen; his fingers wouldn't move and the pain was starting to intensify. "Now I'm gonna have to have my arm amputated."

"Better than having your head amputated by a zombie pig, isn't it?" Carla snapped.

"Hmpf," Gary glowered. "You told me they couldn't swim."

"I was joking!" she said for the hundredth time.

"I know, and it was very fucking funny."

"I'm sorry…I thought you were smarter than a third grader! My mistake."

"We didn't all grow up with Jed Clampett for a dad," he spat. "Christ. This thing really fucking hurts."

"We're almost there—look, you can see the smokestacks," she said, pointing over the next hill with her crossbow. "Your friend Jimmy's a doctor, right? I'm sure you'll be fine."

"EMT," Gary grumbled. He stalked through the field, woozy from the loss of blood and weak from the fear and the running. "I guess I should say thank you."

"Some people would, yeah," Carla said. "When another person saves their lives and stops a mutant pig from ripping their throats out and eating them to death."

"I guess so," he agreed roughly. He cleared his throat and spat again. It became clear that he wasn't going to make the apology official. All things considered, Carla would have to be fine with him leaving it unspoken. "Hey—where'd you get that stuff, anyway? You swipe it from Roman?"

"No, and don't you dare start telling people I did," she snapped. She stepped in front of him and blocked his path. "I'm serious, Gary. No one knows I have it. *You* don't know I have it. Got it?"

"Then where'd you get it?" he asked again.

"I swiped it from the doctor's lab. I went down while she and Patrick were having some sort of goo-ga lovefest over some boring science shit. It's not part of Roman's stash. It's mine. And it's secret."

Gary eyed her suspiciously. "Why?"

"My things are my things," she said flatly. "I am my own person, and my things belong to me. Not him; not anyone else. Me."

Gary searched her eyes for more, but Carla wasn't offering anything else. "Fine," he finally said. "Because you saved my life."

Carla nodded. "Goddamn right I did."

They pushed on over the hill. Gary nearly fainted on the way down to the boat, so Carla gripped his good arm and helped him hobble to the riverbank. She called out and Ella popped her head over the railing. "You made it."

"For the most part," Carla agreed.

Ella looked at Gary's arm thoughtfully. "What happened?" She climbed down the gangplank and helped support Gary from his other side.

"Run-in with a wild hog. It was a duster."

Ella raised an eyebrow. "*What* was a duster?"

"I'll fill you in later," Carla shook her head. "Lucia back yet?"

"Yeah, just a little bit ago. They're eating."

"Go get the doctor, will you?" They stepped onto the boat and eased Gary down onto the floor, leaning him back against the railing.

"He's not here," Ella said. "He stayed behind."

"Stayed behind where?"

"Ask Brett," Lucia said, barging out of the dining hall. Brett followed, wiping his mouth on his sleeve. "This psychopath slaughtered a dozen people at a Home Depot."

"Almost none of the words in that sentence are true," Brett insisted. "Except that it *was* at a Home Depot."

Ted and Richie came around from the other side of the boat, padding over like dogs. "What's going on?" Ted asked.

Lucia was fuming. "Your lunatic friend beat the shit out of a bunch of unarmed weirdoes—with a hammer!"

"They had a Sawzall," he reminded her.

Carla held up her hands. "Wait. What?"

"There were all these people in the back of the Home Depot," Lucia explained angrily, "doing some cult thing, and they were going to sacrifice this family. Brett just jumped down in the hole like he was Rambo and started wailing on everyone with a hammer!"

"They were going to sacrifice a family?" Carla repeated

"With children," Brett added.

Carla blinked. "So what's the problem?"

"What's the...Carla! He *broke* some woman's *jaw* by *stomping* on it!"

"And this woman was going to kill children?"

Lucia was exasperated. "Well! Yeah!"

Carla nodded slowly. "Okay...so?"

"It was...I don't..." Lucia sputtered. She made big, frantic motions with her arms. "I don't know—it was upsetting to watch!" She stormed off into the boat, shoving Brett out of the way.

"She's processing," Brett assured them.

"Where's Jimmy?"

"He stayed behind to tend the wounded." Brett peered around Carla and saw Gary sitting in a growing puddle of his own blood. "What happened to you?"

"She shot me with an arrow," Gary replied, nodding up at Carla.

"On purpose?"

"Probably."

"Oh, it was *not* on purpose!" Carla cried. "Shit. When's Jimmy back?"

Brett shrugged. "I don't know. There were a lot of them."

"The wound needs to be disinfected," Roman said, emerging from his cabin overhead with the last bottle of alcohol hanging between two fingers.

He dropped it over the railing to Ella. "It'll need to be cauterized, too," she said.

"He's not going to like that," Ted pointed out.

"He's right fucking here," Gary muttered, hobbling over to the gangplank. "And no, he does not like it."

Roman rested his elbows on the upper railing, leaning over as if he were taking in the sights on a dinner cruise. "Besides hammers and arrows and broken jaws, how was the day? Everyone hit their objectives?"

"All good here," Brett said. It had taken some organizing, but with the help of two shopping carts they'd lifted from the parking lot, he and Lucia had managed to haul back everything on Patrick's list.

Carla hoisted up the knapsack full of animal carcasses. A wet, red stain had started to spread across the bottom. "Enough dead animals for a pet cemetery in a bag that we are definitely going to have to burn."

Richie frowned. "Hey...that's my bag!"

"I love the energy of this new crew," Roman decided. "It's like we're optimized for success."

"Speaking of new people, where's our fearless planner?" Carla asked.

"That's slander," Patrick responded, emerging from the boiler room steps. His shirt was filthy; his skin was streaked with sweat and his hair was sticking out at all the wrong angles. His hand shielded his eyes from the low light of the sun. "I have three fears: quicksand, antelopes, and the Bermuda Triangle."

"Antelopes?" Ted asked, confused.

Patrick shook his head and held up his hand. "I won't discuss it." He noticed the bloody backpack, and his face lit up. "Ah! Our gore!"

"Killed and delivered," Carla said, tossing the bag at his feet.

"It smells terrible!" he said happily. He turned to Brett. "Were you able to find anything on the list?"

"We found *everything* on the list," Brett grinned. He gestured out to the riverbank at the store of goods piled into the shopping carts.

"Wow," Patrick said, stunned. "I can't believe it."

"You can do it," Brett assured him. "He can help."

"Stop it, Brett!" Lucia called from somewhere inside the boat.

Patrick gave him a questioning look. "Okaaay...I'm going to assume that's a whole...thing...that you can fill me in on some other time." He rubbed his hands together excitedly. "This is great! We have a lot of weird jobs to do, and I had a hallucination that makes me think that it all just might work."

Carla raised her hand. Patrick pointed at her. "Yes, Carla?"

"Are you actually going to share this plan, or what?"

Patrick nodded sagely. "Gather 'round, sweet cherubs, and let the sponges of your minds drink from my waters."

They exchanged a round of uneasy glances. "Hey, Pat. You okay?" Ted asked.

"It was very hot in the boiler room and I am *very* dehydrated," he admitted. "I've got about eight minutes before my kidneys shut down, so listen up. Here's how we're going to survive the death run."

42.

"You think his plan will work?" Carla asked, stabbing a rabbit carcass with her stick. She lifted it up like a banner on a flagpole, then she slopped the dead rabbit against the side of the boat and smeared its blood around the wood.

"It's working on me," Lucia said sourly, scrubbing the boat with a bloody fox. Thin ropes of red, clotted gore crisscrossed the boat like a bleeding spider web. "I wouldn't touch this thing with a ten-foot pole."

"You're touching it with a five-foot pole," Carla pointed out.

"And I'm about to puke my guts out," Lucia complained. Suddenly, she stood straight up and dropped her stick. The fox plopped into the river. Ella covered her mouth with both hands. Then she ran to the shoreline edge and starting hurling into the water.

"Huh," said Carla, watching with interest. "I guess maybe it *will* work." She flung her used-up rabbit carcass into the middle of the river, stuck a fresh one on the end of the stick, and went back to work, whistling while she painted.

A few dozen yards away, Ted and Richie were having the same conversation. "I don't know," Ted said, looking down at the canvas tarp they were spray painting black. "It just seems like a lot of useless theatre to me."

Richie looked at him, confused. "Didn't you do opera?"

"So?"

"So isn't *that* theatre?"

"No, you simpleton! Pagliacci isn't *theatre*, it is *opera*, it is *high art!* Theatre is just…costumes and paint!"

Richie was confused. "Don't you use costumes and paint in opera?"

"Oh, fuck you, Richie!" Ted exploded, throwing his can of spray paint on the ground.

"What? What'd I do?"

"Just finish the skull!" Ted screamed. He stormed up the gangplank and pushed his way into the boat, singing "Vesti la giubba" and fighting back tears, slamming the door behind him.

Richie looked on in amazement. "Jesus," he muttered, shaking his head. "Theatre people."

Patrick and Brett heard the door slam all the way down in the boiler room. They both looked up. "Should we go up there?" Patrick asked.

Brett craned his neck and listened. "Nah," he finally decided. "When Ted starts singing, it's best to just leave him alone."

"That's great, because when Ted starts singing, I *want* to leave him alone." They turned their attention back to the maze of pipes that they'd constructed. They'd connected six main lines to the holes Patrick had hammered into the boiler, shooting out to all sides of the riverboat hull, with some branching into forks. The far end of each pipeline pushed an inch or so out of the hull, through holes Brett had carefully cut to size. "This'll work. Right?"

Brett shrugged. "It's your plan."

"Yeah, but I mean, this part specifically. You think we can make enough steam?"

"No, *you* think we can make enough steam. You're the science guy. I just set the pipes."

"I think we can make enough steam," Patrick assured himself.

"We just gotta seal the joints, and the pipes'll be good."

"Good," Patrick nodded. He fetched the caulk they'd taken from the store and got to work. "I apologize in advance if we did all this work and we still die."

"Apology not accepted."

"Cool."

A few dozen feet over their heads, Roman stood at the windows of his captain's cabin and watched his crew busy themselves below, moving like notes in a symphony. "This team is really synergized," he said happily.

"If they don't work together, we all die," Gary grumbled. "That's pretty good motivation."

"We all might die anyway," Roman pointed out.

"So you brought me up here to cheer me up."

Roman beamed. "I thought you could use a breakout to rest your arm. How's it feeling?"

"It hurts like a motherfucker."

"I bet." Roman watched Carla as she scrubbed the main deck rail with a bisected fox. "Sorry I can't offer you anything for the pain. We used the last of the whiskey on the wound."

"I don't think it helped," Gary frowned, inspecting his arm. The redness had spread well beyond the bandages.

"Hopefully your doctor will be back soon. Maybe he can save it."

Gary flushed white and fought back the urge to vomit. He was struggling with every breath to keep the thought of amputation out of his brain.

"Everyone's asking everyone if Patrick's plan will work," Roman continued. He turned from the window and gave Gary a curious look. "But you haven't asked."

"No point," Gary snorted. "No one knows the answer, so what's the point of asking?"

Roman turned back to the window, and he clasped his hands behind his back. "Absolutely."

Gary eased himself down onto a chair, holding his swollen arm close to his chest. His eyes filled with tears from the pain of it, but he gritted his teeth and blinked them back, falling into the chair with a grunt. "How come you're so hell-bent on taking the shortcut back?"

"'Cause the longer we're out here, the more limbs we'll lose," he said, watching his crew. "Not just arms and legs."

Gary frowned. "What do you mean?"

Roman peeled himself away from the window and joined Gary in the center of the cabin. He slipped easily into his desk chair, propping his elbows on the desk and tenting his fingers under his chin. "The people we rely on are limbs, in a way—right? The people who rely on us. The danger to my crew—and to your friends—it's serious. And it gets more and more dangerous every second we're out here. In the world. Exposed. The pirates on the Tenn-Tom are no joke. But draw the journey out by an additional six weeks, eight weeks...the easier path becomes just as deadly anyway, if not more so."

"You lost men on the way here," Gary said flatly.

"Eight, in all. Four at a woodcutter's in Ohio; two got hacked to pieces by an old witch in Missouri; one went out to hunt and never came back. Carla found his body torn open and mostly eaten. Another got caught in a rope trap some sick assholes strung up under a bridge on the Mississippi. A messy, simple thing...they got a loop around his neck and yanked him right off the deck. Pulled him up fifty feet. All we could do was watch him strangle."

Gary shook his head. "Jesus."

"It's bad in every direction," Roman sighed. "And we stand to lose a lot. The campus...that's another limb, you know? It's a major producer. Probably the biggest economic driver in the world at this point. Every day away is another day some would-be kingpin is thinking he might take a run at a hostile takeover."

"Have people tried to take your farm before?" Gary asked.

Roman gave him a strange look. "Everyone is always trying to take everyone's farms," he said. "Don't you understand that? There's no security against the world other than the security we provide ourselves. And I can't provide shit from three states away."

"Then why'd you even come? Why not just send your people on their own?"

Roman snorted. "Can't trust people with your farm...can't trust people with your zombie repellant." He reached into a desk drawer and pulled out the bundle of ten vials. He slipped one from the package and held it up to the light, inspecting the purple liquid inside. "This wonderful little innovation and my farm are intertwined. Dusters are a problem that's only going to continue to get worse. More despair means more addicts, more addicts mean more dusters. God, and now it's the animals, too? The world really is going to hell." He set the vial down on the desk and rolled it thoughtfully beneath his fingers. "The future of the farm lives in this bottle. Probably the future of the world."

"If we die on the Tenn-Tom, it'll all be for nothing," Gary said.

Roman snickered. "If we die on the Tenn-Tom, I won't give a shit."

"Fair enough," Gary grimaced.

Ella appeared at the door and knocked on the glass. Roman beckoned her in. "Got some kids to scout around for us," she said. "They just came back. Said they found a body."

"Good—tell Patrick," he said, and Ella disappeared down the stairs. Roman noticed Gary's confusion and simply said, "The *pièce de résistance*, my friend."

"Can't wait," Gary said dryly.

Roman slapped his hands on the desktop, stood up and moved to follow Ella.

Gary blurted out as he passed through the door, "All right, well...do you?"

Roman looked back over his shoulder. "Do I what?"

"Do you think Patrick's plan will work?"

"Oh." Roman shrugged. "Three dangerous blockades. One crazy plan. I guess time will tell."

Then he headed downstairs to see about the body.

43.

Over at the first blockade, a man who called himself Sharksbane crossed his arms and flexed them as hard as he could without looking like he was flexing. He looked down at his biceps and admired how big they'd gotten. They were way bigger than they were yesterday. Three times bigger, at least.

"Hell yes," he said quietly. The fish tails were working.

He heard someone rustling up the rope ladder behind him. He took a deep breath and bore down, flexing even harder. Not just in his arms, but in his neck, too. He wanted to look huge, in case it was   .

"What's happening to you? Are you pooping?"

Sharksbane let out his breath and shook out his arms. It wasn't Bridget. It was fucking *Steve*. "No, I'm not pooping again," he snapped. "I mean, now. Shut the fuck up, Steve."

Steve eyed him strangely. "Sure…hey, listen, I just came up to tell you, shift change is gonna be late."

"Oh, come on!" Sharksbane cried. "That's the third time in like two weeks! Who's on tonight?"

Steve frowned. "It's Lucas."

A thousand capillaries in Sharksbane's brain exploded. "Lucas," he hissed through gritted teeth.

"Yeah. So. Ya know. It's just…he's gonna be late. Okay?" Brian was about to leave, but he noticed his companion stroking his own bicep lovingly, in extreme contrast to the fury that showed on his face. "God, are you still on the arms thing?"

"They look good, don't they?" Sharksbane said admiringly. He held up his arms and showed them to Steve.

"They look the same, Brian. They always look the same."

"They do not!" Sharksbane snapped. "And don't call me Brian, I told you to call me Sharksbane."

"But your name is Brian."

Sharksbane bit down so hard he cracked a tooth. "Ow," he whined, rubbing his jaw. "My name is Sharksbane. You don't want a pirate name? That's fine. You can be Steve. But this is a new world. I'm a new person. I'm a Tenn-Tom pirate, and my name is fucking *Sharksbane*." *And Sharksbane is seriously cut*, he added to himself. He smiled down at his arms. They were so much bigger today.

"Rivers don't even have sharks," Steve pointed out.

"Not anymore." Sharksbane winked, then flexed again. "Sharksbane!"

"Sure, dude. Look. No one else wants to tell you this, but you're going a little hard on this whole…" Steve moved his hand around in a circle, encompassing the entirety of Sharksbane. "…thing." Then he remembered something, and he straightened up. "Hey! Listen. You're not still eating the fish tails, are you?"

Sharksbane guffawed. "Of course I'm still eating the fish tails. How do you think my arms got so big?"

"Dude. You gotta lay off those things. Weren't you at the meeting? They think there's mercury in this water. You might be eating mercury, Brian."

"Mercury's a planet, you dipshit!" Sharksbane laughed. "Now get the hell out of here, you're distracting me from the watch."

Steve rolled his eyes and sighed. He headed back down the ladder. "Stop eating the fish," he said seriously. "It's dissolving your brain."

"I'll dissolve *your* brain with my fucking muscles," Sharksbane muttered quietly.

"What?" Steve asked, poking his head back up.

"Nothing."

Sharksbane picked up his spear and resumed his patrol of the gate. He hated the spear. The stupid thing was so heavy. And he hated patrol. Shore patrol wasn't too bad, but gate patrol sucked; the whole thing was just a bunch of big, dead trees lashed together with bungee cords and weighted down with cinder blocks. "Gate" was such a stupid name for it. It was a dipshit-level beaver dam that opened. Big deal—he could have built a better gate in his sleep. One with sick-ass welded metal and spikes and shit. Or maybe just a huge slab of concrete that opened and closed on hydraulics, like those badasses downriver had at the lock. Sharksbane had seen their gate once, from across their lake. It was so cool. It was like *Mad Max* meets *Mad Max II*. Those guys knew what the hell was up. He'd never actually talked to any of that crew, but he just knew they were sick as hell. He'd fit in way better down at the lock. Those guys knew the value of muscles, for sure.

Of course, if he wanted to join the lock pirates, he'd have to change his diet.

If the rumors were true.

"I could eat anything," he said out loud. "I'd eat stupid-ass *Lucas*." He spat into the water below. The spittle dribbled down his chin and made his beard wet. "Goddammit!" he cursed. "How do guys spit so cool?"

A bright light caught his eye. He snapped to attention, nearly blinding himself with the point of the spear. Big Nick was up at the mouth of the river, waving his torch in big, wide arcs.

A boat was coming.

Sharksbane hurried to the front of the gate and planted the butt of his spear on top of the log beneath him. On the other half of the gate, another watchman hurried over and took up his position, too. Sharksbane looked over and was relieved to see that it was Tom. Some guys were real dicks on the watch, but Sharksbane respected Tom. He didn't talk much, and he had good muscles. Also, sometimes people called Tom "T-Bone," which wasn't necessarily a great pirate name, but it was a step in the right direction.

"Toll time!" Sharksbane chirped excitedly. He looked over at Tom. "Toll time!" He loved saying that. "You feeling good, Tom? You feeling ready?"

Tom nodded. "Yep."

"Excellent. Excellent," Sharksbane said, nodding too. He always felt a little jittery on the night watch. The morning was fine, and afternoon was fine, but night felt different. It wasn't that he was scared. It was just different.

"Excellent," he said again, whispering it to himself.

Then the boat emerged from the darkness.

Sharksbane was so surprised, he dropped his spear in the river without even noticing.

The riverboat was on fire—that was the *most* surprising thing, at least at first. Sharksbane had seen burning boats before, but he and his crew were usually the ones setting the fires, and when those boats burned, they sank. But this boat was burning and *moving*. The railings were on fire, there were flames in the cabin windows, and even the hull of the boat was filled with flickering orange firelight that seeped out through cracks in the wood. But the paddle wheel was turning, the smokestacks were belching, and the boat was being driven into the Tenn-Tom.

Then he noticed the mist. Not the smoke; there was plenty of that, though, rising into the darkening twilight sky. It wasn't Monkey fog, either.

The entire boat was surrounded by a shroud of pale gray mist.

The eerie cloud seemed to form just ahead of the prow, materializing out of nothingness. As the boat pushed through it, the mist clung to the sides of the boat, then it vaporized as the boat moved on. It was ethereal, otherworldly—as if the boat were churning forward on the backs a thousand roiling ghosts.

"Holy shit," Sharksbane whispered. He inhaled sharply. "Ghost boat."

Tom must have been thinking the same thing, even though he didn't say it out loud, because when he held up his spear and shouted, "Stop!" at the boat, both the spear and his voice were shaking so badly that not even Tom's good muscles could save him from coming off as totally ineffectual.

"Stop!" Sharksbane echoed, more loudly. He was surprised to hear his own voice shaking even more than Tom's. The two guards looked at each other.

"What *is* this thing?" Tom hissed.

"I think it's a ghost boat!" Sharksbane hissed back.

"That's stupid!" Tom said.

"I know!" Sharksbane agreed.

The boat drew closer to the gate; it wasn't slowing down. The rest of the gang was watching the ship's approach in similar awe from their small shoreline village. No one said a word—not even Lucas as he stumbled out of Bridget's camper. Lucas always had some smart-ass thing to say. But he didn't say a word.

Fucking Lucas, Sharksbane thought.

Bridget stepped out of the camper on Lucas' heels. Every other member of the crew's eyes were glazed over and dumbfounded at the sight of the burning ghost ship, but Bridget's eyes were burning with a fire of their own. She began snapping orders, pulling on her boots and stomping toward the water, while everyone else just stood there with their mouths open and gawked. That's why Bridget was their captain. That was what made it worth eating ten fish tails a day. She was why the muscles would pay off.

Sharksbane realized that the orders she was snapping were being snapped at him. He hadn't been paying attention. *Goddammit!* he thought.

"*Stop* it!" Bridget screamed. "Do your job and *stop* the goddamn thing!"

Sharksbane wanted to stop the boat—desperately. He wanted to do a good job, to please Bridget. But he had no fucking clue how to get a flaming ghost-boat to stop.

Tom sprang to action instead. He planted his feet, raised his spear, and hurled it at the boat. It sailed across the bay. It struck the boat.

It bounced off the hull and fell into the water.

"Why do we even *have* spears?!" he yelled.

"I don't know—the boats usually just stop!" Sharksbane replied.

"We've never had to stop a ghost ship before!"

"I *told* you it was a ghost ship!"

"I know!"

The riverboat was close now, close enough to see the decks illuminated by the fire. "Tom!" Sharksbane said, his voice trembling. *"There's no one on board!"*

"Look!" Tom gasped, pointing up at the ship. "Is that…is that—?"

"Yes," Sharksbane said, swallowing hard. "It's a…a pirate flag."

The huge black banner flapped loudly in the quiet night, the crude white skull and crossbones waving in and out of view like a demon behind a curtain. Its grotesque mouth was stretched and open, filled with jagged teeth. The nose holes were flared angrily; the eye sockets burned like deep-black pits of hellfire.

But Tom shook his head. "No," he rasped. "Not the flag. *That.*"

Sharksbane followed Tom's finger. He was pointing past the flag, to the huge twin smokestacks that rose on either side of the main cabin. A small fire on the roof of the cabin illuminated the stacks in a soft orange glow that flickered in and out of the darkness, but Sharksbane could just barely see that, yes, there was *something* up there, in the space between them. Something that he couldn't quite make out…

The boat drifted closer, and the roof fire flared, and the thing between the smokestacks flickered into view. Sharksbane's stomach lurched as he recoiled in horror. "No," he whispered. "No, no…"

It hung between the smokestacks, splayed by taut ropes cinched around the wrists and ankles. It was spread open like a butterfly in a display case, caught in the air like a fly in a web: a rotting human corpse.

"There's no one on the ship!" Tom cried. His voice was tight with panic. Sharksbane recognized that pitch, the same as the voice screaming in his brain. It was the sound of abject terror. "There's *no one on the ship!*"

"Demon ship!" Sharksbane gasped, stumbling backward as the boat churned closer.

Bridget screamed in the background; some of the men on the bank were shouting, too. But their voices all blended into a cottony murmur. "Ghost ship!" The riverboat was nearly on them now, pushing through on its cloud of brimstone smoke, its thirsty, lapping flames burning, but not consuming. It was so close now, Sharksbane could hear the creaking of the ropes that held the body, that perverse figurehead of death and decay. The skull of the pirate flag, huge now—grinning, winking, licking its lips.

Devouring the night.

"*Demon ship!*" Sharksbane screamed. "*Come to swamp us to hell!*" He fell back, covering his head as the ship rammed the wooden barrier. He landed against the lever that opened the gate, and under his weight, the latch gave. The gate fell open, letting the river rush past the dam. The ghost-boat flowed with the river, slipping between the watchmen on their perches and leaving the exasperated pirate crew behind.

Sharksbane watched in stunned silence as the ship sailed down the Tenn-Tom. He gasped in horror when he saw a figure standing at the back of the boat, its head just visible over the spinning red paddle wheel. It was the skeletal figure of the Grim Reaper himself, his eye sockets flashing with fire, his ivory teeth twisted into a leering grin.

"Oh my God," Sharksbane breathed. "It's the Dread Pirate Roberts."

Then he passed out cold and fell into the river.

44.

The riverboat rounded a bend, and the first pirate checkpoint slid quietly away into the night.

"We're clear!" Jimmy cried, throwing off the skeleton costume. A chorus of cheers went up around the boat as the rest of the crew members picked themselves up off the floor, emerged from behind boxes and came out from under tables.

"I cannot believe that worked!" Lucia said, laughing with relief as she pushed her way from the dining room out onto the deck. "I mean, I *cannot* believe it *worked!*"

"Amazing!" Roman clapped, flashing with a wide, winning grin. "So immersive! So *experiential!*" He threw his arm around Patrick's shoulders and squeezed him close. "Incredible work—some *real* outside-the-box thinking. Absolutely incredible."

"You guys did all the hard work," Patrick replied, gesturing to the rest of the crew. "I just knocked some holes in a boiler. You really pulled it off!"

"A hell of a plan, though," Roman said, ignoring Patrick's modesty and smiling at him from ear to ear.

"Literally a hell of a plan!" Ted added. "We must look terrifying!"

"I was *not* expecting that much steam to funnel out through the walls," Patrick admitted.

Brett snorted happily. "Told you."

"You told me I was the science guy, and you were just there for the pipes," Patrick reminded him.

"Yeah," Brett nodded, "and the pipes worked awesome."

"The whole fire thing actually looked real," Richie said admiringly.

"The fire *was* real, dipshit," Brett said.

Richie frowned. "You know what I mean—setting it in the buckets…I thought it would look stupid. But man, I saw it up from downstairs and it looked like the boat was really on fire!"

"The Grim Reaper was a nice touch," Patrick told Jimmy.

"I can't believe they had like twenty of these things just sitting back there in boxes," Jimmy said, admiring the Grim Reaper mask with the LED eyes. "I didn't even know Home Depot *sold* Halloween stuff."

"Have you never been to a Home Depot?" Patrick asked. "That's like 80% of its business."

Roman darted into the boat, ran up the stairs, and reemerged on the upper balcony. "My friends," he shouted into the night, his voice carrying over the churn of the paddle wheel, "I must confess!"

The others quieted down and looked upward. Something was wrong.

Roman's face was somber and sad. "I need to apologize for something."

"Well, that's a first," Lucia said under her breath. Carla elbowed her in the ribs.

"I lied to you guys," Roman said sadly. "When Gary came back from the hunt with his injury, we used the whiskey as an antiseptic. One that seems to have worked, by the way. My own recipe…you're welcome."

"It ain't fallen off yet," Gary glowered.

"It still might," Jimmy reminded him. "But so far, it's looking pretty promising."

"Nice!" Roman continued. "But anyway…I'm sorry. When that happened, I told you all that was the last bottle of shine." He lifted his hands, revealing a full bottle in each. The crew cheered as Roman laughed. "I'm sorry!" he insisted. "I was saving them, in case things went really well…or really badly! And by God, this went *really well!*" More cheers erupted from the crew. Roman let them howl for a few moments, then motioned for them to quiet down. "Now…we've put the fear of Satan in those pirates, and that was that was incredible. But intel suggests the river only gets harder from here. We've got another group of pirates to worry about tomorrow at the lock, and by all accounts, they're the real deal. So I don't want anyone celebrating *too* hard. Okay?" A general moan of disappointment spread through the crew. "But we *are* going to celebrate, because what just happened was incredible! Lucia, grab some glasses, please. Tonight, we drink to the Hell Ship of the Tenn-Tom!"

Everyone on the boat went wild and the celebration began.

•

A few drinks in, and the Red Caps had started swapping old stories from the train, exaggerating their heroics and playing up their own charm. Patrick watched with amusement as Ella and Lucia made an absolute art out of the eyeroll…but he also thought he noticed a chink in Lucia's armor when Brett stood up and regaled them with a tale about a time in the Sonoran Desert when a mountain lioness had leapt onto the train, and Brett and Gary fought her off with pool noodles. At the climax, Brett picked up Richie and started swinging him around like a foam noodle, drawing a definite glimmer in Lucia's eye. Patrick smiled to see it.

Humanity may have been down, but it wasn't quite out.

The world can break to a billion pieces, he thought, *and people can still fit themselves back together.*

"Quite a night!" Roman had appeared so quietly that Patrick jumped at the sound of his voice.

"One of the best wakes I've ever been to," Patrick joked.

Roman snickered. "Nervous about tomorrow?"

"I feel nervous about *all* tomorrows, just as a rule. Today's tomorrow has the added benefit of involving bloodthirsty maniacs."

"True," Roman said. "Though death by pirate is a pretty exciting way to go, from a eulogy perspective. I figured you'd like that."

"Yar, ye've got me pegged," Patrick said.

Roman drifted toward the far end of the boat, and Patrick followed, the two men sipping their whiskey in the warm, calm night. "You know, there's no reason to think we won't fare as well tomorrow night," Roman said as they reached the bow of the ship.

"There *is* a reason to think that, and it's called the hot hand fallacy," Patrick pointed out.

Roman sighed. "That's one way to look at it."

"Sorry. I don't mean to be a downer."

"You do seem to be missing your essential good humor," Roman pointed out.

Patrick turned his back to the water and leaned against the railing. "It's strange to feel so celebratory and still be so far from the end of the mission." He looked up at the pilot's cabin and saw Carla standing alone, her head poking up over the wheel. He raised his glass, and she raised her middle finger. "Did you bring her a glass?" Patrick asked.

"I told her to drop anchor and join us. She said she wanted to get us closer, to make sure we hit the lock before nightfall tomorrow. Couldn't argue with that."

"She's smart," Patrick said. He turned and rested his wrists on the railing. "You have a good crew."

"I have a tenuous crew," Roman corrected him. "Talented, and tenuous."

"To good leadership, then," Patrick said, raising his glass.

"Aye-aye," Roman said, acknowledging the salute. They downed the rest of their drinks in silence, with Patrick's good humor remaining at bay.

The sounds coming from the other end of the boat suggested Richie had just caught himself on fire and was flailing around the deck, screaming about his contact dermatitis while the others chased him and tried to put out the flames. As they gave chase, the boat eased to a stop fifty feet from the shore.

Carla appeared, shaking out her cramped hands after her work at the wheel. "You guys just gonna let Richie burn?" she asked.

"It's an interesting thought," Roman said.

"I'm just wondering how long it's going to be before he remembers we're surrounded by water," Patrick replied. They heard Richie yell. Then they heard a loud splash. Patrick nodded, satisfied. "There we go."

Carla nodded at the dwindling reserves in Roman's bottle. "Got anymore glasses?"

"Have mine," Patrick said. "I'm going to head down for some shuteye." He handed her his glass.

Carla looked at it and frowned. "It's empty."

"That's how I know I'm done with it," Patrick said. He gave them both a genial wave, then he headed inside to go make a nest for the night.

"He seems...off," Carla told Roman as Patrick disappeared.

"He's okay," Roman said. "Nothing to worry about."

"Oh, I wasn't worried," Carla replied as she shook the last remaining drop from the glass onto her tongue.

The last thing Patrick heard as he retired from the party was Richie, clamoring over the side of the boat and shouting, "My pants are still in the water!"

45.

Patrick smushed his head down on a pile of old towels in the musty dining room and drew his tarp up to his chin. "Good night tonight," he said aloud, closing his eyes. "This is all going shockingly well."

"It's all going unshockingly terribly," Ben insisted.

Patrick opened his eyes. He was standing in the abandoned lot on East Illinois, across from the AMC River East 21, where he and Amy had watched the movie Ted a few weeks before M-Day, a pretty disappointing choice for a last movie ever. They'd walked out of the theater and had seen a billboard for a new development coming to the abandoned lot, some 47-story luxury apartment that they could never afford. They'd joked about how they'd move in anyway—live a stone's throw from the horrors of Lower Wacker and see terrible movies every night for the rest of their natural lives.

But now, the lot was totally abandoned, overgrown with weeds, choked with trash and dusty rubble from the building that had toppled on M-Day. It also contained one especially angry Ben Fogelvee, who was on his hands and knees with his face three inches from the ground, his nose brushing a beansprout. "One bean!" he yelled. "One fucking bean! Unbelievable." He jumped up to his feet and stormed around the lot, throwing his hands up and grumbling under his breath.

"Hey—it's not one bean; it's one bean plant!" Patrick corrected him happily. "We'll get at least five beans from that thing!"

"Five beans. Awesome." Ben rolled his eyes. "We can beat each other to death with sticks to see who gets to starve to death very slightly slower."

"Five beans is almost a soup!" Patrick cried.

Ben frowned and kicked the ground. "I'm sick of soup."

"Aw, Benny Boy…don't be like that!" Patrick threw his arm around Ben's shoulders. "Sure, it's just one bean plant now, but someday it'll be thousands of bean plants!"

"It won't be."

"Yes…thousands of bean plants—millions, even! From here to Fullerton, as far as the eye can see. Beans! Beans for days! Beans for weeks! Beans for miles, and it all starts with our little bean here, whose name, I think, should be Bean."

Ben blinked. "You want to name a bean Bean?"

"You know! From Ender's Game!"

"Ender's Game?"

"Yeah…you love Ender's Game!"

"Doesn't Bean die in Ender's Game?"

"Who can remember?" Patrick shrugged.

"Have I even read Ender's Game?" Ben wondered.

Patrick frowned. "I thought you loved it."

"I'm not sure I even know anything about it," Ben realized. He thought for a second, then he added, "Oh my God, what books have I read?!"

"Look, before you start spiraling about that, can you finish spiraling about this?" Patrick asked, pointing at the bean. "Bean needs his father."

"Why am I Bean's father?"

"Because you're the most disappointed that he's not living up to expectations," Patrick said. "You know, like dads do!"

"When we have conversations like this, it makes me think the Jamaicans were on to something," Ben sighed.

Patrick crouched down and admired the little bean sprout. It was a thin, curly thing, pale green with two delicate leaves. It looked like a sneeze might obliterate it. "I think Bean's a warrior!" Patrick decided. "Look at those gams. He's got great gams!"

"Plants don't have gams," Ben said irritably. "Don't use that word, it's weird."

"You don't like gams?"

"I don't like the sound of the word 'gams' coming out of your weird mouth."

Patrick frowned. "I know you're upset about killing Bean's family, but you don't have to take it out on me."

"I did not kill Bean's family!" Ben exploded. "Bean's family chose death!"

"And little Bean chose life," Patrick breathed, wiping away a tear of joy. "You're looking at this all wrong, Benny Boy. We grew a bean sprout!

That's amazing! A couple of weeks ago, this was a seed! Now, it's a plant! A plant with leaves! We have made life!"

"That's great, but we planted fifty of those stupid things, and only one sprouted."

"It's not a great hit rate, I'll grant you," Patrick said, tapping his lips. "In fact, I'd categorize it as 'less than ideal.' But one is a good start! This one plant can become twenty other plants! And those twenty other plants will become a thousand other plants! Give it a few cycles, and we'll be swimming in beans, Ben! Swimming in beans!"

"I don't even like beans that much," Ben realized.

"Listen. Most people never grow a single thing in their entire lives. You grew Bean. You're one up on humanity."

Ben gestured hugely at the world. "There is no more humanity!" he said.

"True," Patrick agreed. "Humanity, much like the beans in this field, is having a bad run. But we're here, and Bean's here, and you and I are the Beans of humanity, and Bean is the Patrick and Ben of bean sprouts! Don't you see?" He wove his fingers together and held them up for Ben to see. "We're all connected!"

Ben rolled his eyes. "That's great, Morpheus. But what are we going to eat?"

"Hell if I know," Patrick shrugged. "Let's go raid the Billy Goat, see if there're any mummified cheeseborgers under the fryers."

"I've always wanted to smash up the Billy Goat," Ben admitted.

"I know you have, Ben," Patrick said, patting his arm. "I know you have."

Ben turned and walked down Illinois Street, continuing the conversation they'd had that day, talking to a version of Patrick that seemed so alien now, as the Patrick of three years later looked on, watching the memory move away without him. The pair of friends disappeared around the corner, and River North disappeared with them. Patrick was sitting in the dining hall, alone.

Bean never made it to harvest season. He didn't even make it through that week. They returned to their rubble lot two days later to find their one fragile bean sprout gone. No sign of it anywhere.

Told you, Ben had said sourly. *Humanity's great hope is unshockingly terrible.*

Patrick shuffled back down into his nest and pulled the tarp up over his shoulders. He closed his eyes and tried not to think about Ben, or plans that only went well for a while before falling apart.

46.

Tap.

Tap-tap.

Tap-tap-tap-tap-tap-tap-tap-tap-tap.

"What?!" Patrick cried, lurching awake. He'd been dreaming about buffalo. "Stop tapping me on the head!"

"Oh hey—it worked," Carla said dryly. "I've been trying to wake you up for five minutes. I thought you were dead."

"I'm solidly pre-death," Patrick yawned. He sat up and scrubbed the sleep out of his eyes as he looked around. It was morning, but just barely. Only a few of the Red Caps had made it back to the dining hall the night before. Richie was under a table, sleeping on a pile of crumbs while fussing and scratching his arms in his sleep. Brett was snoring away on top of that table, his head and his feet hanging off either end, a thick line of drool spilling from his open mouth and pooling on Richie's chest. Gary was huddled under his blanket in the corner, distancing himself from the pack like a wounded animal. "Must have been some party."

"They had like three drinks each," Carla said, rolling her eyes. "Come on. Get up."

Patrick rolled over onto his belly and groaned as he pushed himself up into a kneeling position. "Why?" he asked, rolling his neck on his shoulders and wincing at the cracks. "What's up?"

Carla gestured toward the ceiling. "His Highness would like a word."

Patrick struggled up the stairs, tripping three separate times. But he persevered through his sleepiness. At long last, he reached the summit and fell into Roman's cabin.

"Morning!" Roman beamed.

Patrick looked at him with confusion. The riverboat king was once again dressed in a clean button-down shirt—pink gingham this time—which was tucked neatly into a pair of gray chinos. He looked like he'd had a shower, a shave and a leisurely morning with the local paper. "How is it possible you're always so—*awake*? And…" He waved a hand in the general direction of Roman's shirt. "…pressed?"

"Stimulants!" Roman replied happily. "There's not enough to go around, but if you can keep it quiet, I'm happy to share."

Patrick shook his head. "Thanks, but Officer Dan told me never to do drugs."

"Who's Officer Dan?"

"My D.A.R.E. officer from sixth grade."

"Sixth grade?"

Patrick nodded. "He showed us a *very* graphic slideshow. Not suitable for children. Or adults. Boy, now that I think about it, I don't know how on Earth that presentation got approved. But it sure made an impression."

"I bet." Roman picked up a battered Thermos from his desk, unscrewed the lid, and poured Patrick a glass full of a dark brown liquid. "Here. Officer-Dan-approved. Probably."

Patrick wrinkled his nose. He did not reach for the glass. "What is it?"

"It's coffee."

Patrick snorted. "Sure. Like moonshine is whiskey, except it tastes like motor oil and might leave you blind. You know, it should be illegal to say the c-word in this stupid, awful timeline. And I do *not* mean 'cunt.'" He swiped the cup and examined the contents. "Which knock-off is this? Chicory? Dandelion? I swear to God, if it's an old Starbucks VIA, I will lead a mutiny on this ship."

Roman shook his head. "That's for the hired help. But you? You're C-Suite now! CSO. Chief Survival Officer. You know, I've been watching all morning. There've been half a dozen board-and-hoard boats going up and down the river. Even without the fireworks, they're steering clear of the Queen."

"Probably has something to do with the corpse dangling over our heads," Patrick said, shifting uncomfortably. "Still not sure I'm feeling great about that part."

"It's pretty gross," Roman agreed. "But highly effective. Also, we didn't kill him; he was already dead."

"Yeah. And he's helping! He probably would have wanted his corpse to be helpful," Patrick nodded. "That's the fiction I tell myself and then don't probe any further in order to keep my sanity about the whole thing."

"And it's that sort of mental nimbleness that's made you part of the executive team." He pointed proudly at the glass in Patrick's hand. "And the executive team drinks *that*. 100% Costa Rican coffee. Real beans. Real coffee. Real caffeinated."

Patrick's heart stopped. His hands started to tremble. He had to put the glass down so he wouldn't drop it. He tried to speak but his voice caught, and all that came out was a squeak. He cleared his throat and tried again. "This is…*actually* coffee?"

"I mean, it's cold brew, which kind of sucks. I'd drink it hot in a Mississippi summer. But for the boat, I figured a French press would be a lot easier to manage, and cold water, obviously, there's no stove up here, so…" Roman stopped. "Patrick, are you crying?"

"The last time I saw coffee grounds, I was snorting them in exchange for passage across a bridge," he sobbed. "And they were all white and wet, because I'd spent three months sucking every last caffeine molecule out of them."

"Boy," Roman said. "That's a pretty weird thing to hear."

"I never thought I'd see coffee again," he said, wiping his eyes. He reached out gingerly, cradled the glass of coffee in his hands, inhaled the cold, chocolatey-spicy scent of it. Then he closed his eyes and exhaled. "I take it back about the mutiny," he decided. He swirled the glass. He took a sip.

He sobbed for five whole minutes.

"Well, this has gone weirder than expected," Roman announced, giving Patrick an awkward pat on the shoulder. "There, there."

"I can't believe I'm drinking coffee. How did you get this?"

"I told you: my campus is legit. We have a lot of trading partners. The world may be a disaster, but we still have commerce. And being so close to the Gulf, we have a pretty good import-export business."

Patrick nodded slowly. "You know, I haven't actually spent much time thinking about the state of other countries," he admitted through sniffles. "The world seems so completely and utterly shut off. Or I guess I should say, *we* feel so shut off. From everything."

"Not from everything," Roman said. "And not from everyone. A few more years and we'll have a global economy again. Some version of one, anyway. Marwood Farms is leading the way—mark my words!"

"I do, I mark them," Patrick assured him. He knocked back the rest of the drink in one gulp. The cold coffee had a honey texture and a sweet finish. It flooded through his digestive tract, sparking at his nerve endings, practically shooting light out of his fingertips. It was real coffee. And it was so good. "Thank you for this."

"No sweat! And when we get to where we're going, I promise you a hot cup of pretty crudely roasted but freshly ground coffee every morning, for as long as you're with us."

"Which, sadly, won't be long. But I'll gladly take it while I can! Plus, you never know."

Roman raised an eyebrow. "Never know what?"

Patrick spun the empty glass in his hands. "Your farm...the way you talk about it...it sounds like a real place."

"It *is* a real place," Roman assured him.

"Yeah, but I mean, a *real place*. You know? A place that might actually be permanent. With a future."

"That's the plan."

"A permanent place with a future isn't the worst kind of place to end up," Patrick mused. "Fort Doom is nice, and who knows what all they've got going on there now. It's been almost a year. But I don't know. Once I'm back, maybe the gang will be ready for a change of scenery. We could all do worse than the leader of the next global economy."

"Absolutely," Roman grinned. "And I could use a good engineer...and whatever your friend Ben is. Or does. I'm sure I can use one of those, too."

"He fusses. Sometimes he writes. But mostly, he fusses."

"I'm sure we can find a use for that."

"Then it's a definite possibility," Patrick said. "Assuming we don't get murdered tonight."

"Which is actually why I asked you up here," Roman remembered. He screwed the cap back onto the Thermos. Patrick watched the coffee disappear with a sad ache in his heart. "How would you feel about a scouting mission?"

"It's been a few years since my Webelos days, but I can hold up three fingers as well as anyone else," he said, holding up two fingers. "Need someone to scope out the pirates?"

"I'd be helpful to know the state of things. A little industrial espionage. My guys didn't get a whole lot of specifics on their recon...the more we can know about their setup, the better. I know it's a lock and a dam, but that's not a whole lot to go on. A little more intel might help us figure out if this ghost-boat trick will work a second time."

"Or if the boat will even fit through the lock."

Patrick nodded. "Sure. No problem. I'll take Carla with me."

"Take Ella," Roman said quickly. "She's quiet, and good with a knife." He dropped the Thermos into his desk drawer and slammed it shut.

"Oh." Patrick's face fell. "Yeah. Sure." He nodded once, then pushed his hands into his pockets and slipped out the door.

He just managed to keep himself from saying aloud, *Who better to take on a dangerous mission than someone you've spent no time with at all?*

47.

"He wants *you* to go?" Ella said, her voice quiet and even, but her face giving away her surprise. "I don't know anything about you."

"That is *exactly* what I said!" Patrick cried. "Well, it's what I *thought*. I should have just said it."

"I should be out here with Carla," they both said in unison.

They looked at each other and shrugged. Then they started walking south. Now that it was light outside, the boat had maneuvered a bit further along the lake, pulling into position closer to the lock. Judging by Roman's map, the Big Muddy Queen was tucked into a cove about a mile and a half from the Jamie Whitten Lock, hidden from the pirates' view by the wooded hills. Patrick and Ella set off into those hills, Patrick using a baseball bat for a walking stick, Ella moving quickly and lightly, with a hunting knife on her hip.

"I didn't mean Carla would be a better person to scout with," Patrick said as they neared the top of the hill, finally breaking the silence. "We just went on a mission together already once and we have kind of a rapport. Plus, she shot Gary through the arm, which is something I'd like to laugh with her about, but in a quiet, respectful away, out of Gary's earshot. This seemed like a good opportunity to do that."

"Okay," Ella replied. She kept moving, working her way through the trees as if she'd lived in the forest her entire life.

Patrick struggled to keep up, his breath already coming in hard. "Is there any sort of quasi-apology you'd like to say to *me* about the time when you said *you'd* rather be out here with Carla?" he asked, winded.

"No," she said.

"Okay, then. Good talk."

The forest was quiet. Unnervingly so. There were no birds chirping, no squirrels rustling, no demon pigs crashing through trees. It was as if the world had pushed a mute button. Not even the sound of Ella's footsteps registered as more than a whisper.

There wasn't a noise in the world, aside from the bluster-crunches of Patrick's clumsy steps.

"Am I being extra loud?" he whispered, suddenly very self-conscious. "I'm just walking like normal—does it sound like I'm walking extra loud?"

"It sounds like you've only seen how people walk in movies and this is the first time you're trying it yourself," Ella said curtly.

Patrick frowned. "You're annoyed to be out here with me. I see that. Sorry. I'll try to walk quieter." He took a careful step forward, placing his foot gently on the earth.

A branch snapped under his foot. The resulting crack echoed across the lake.

"I think that could have been *way* louder," he whispered happily.

Ella ignored him, her eyes scanning the canopy. Then she moved silently to the base of a large pine. She disappeared into the needles, and it was a good several beats before Patrick realized she was climbing the tree. "Oh. You're going up. Okay." He looked around at the dense woods. The midday sun made the Monkey fog glow, the trees casting shadows like gravestones through the air. He lifted the baseball bat and set it on his shoulder, his fingers tightening around the grip. "I'll probably just stay down here. I'll just…be here. While you do that. I guess."

Ella dropped onto the ground behind him, and Patrick screamed. "This way," she said.

"Oh my God—you were so fast! I almost hit you with this bat!" Patrick gasped, though they both knew that wasn't true.

Ella guided them across the landscape, shimmying up a tree or climbing up a cliff every few hundred feet to get their bearings. They skirted around inlets and shot the narrow gap between lakefront cliffs to their left and an exposed clearing with a hiking trail and campgrounds to their right. Patrick followed behind, walking where he was told, trying not to be too much of an inconvenience. "Sorry I'm so jittery," he told her at one point. "I just had coffee for the first time in like three years. It's making me feel weird."

"Stop," she said.

"Boy, your lips to God's ears, huh? If I could *stop* feeling jittery, yes—that would be ideal. But the jitters are also a nice reminder that I had coffee today, and I don't want to deprive myself of that glorious memory, so in that way, I'm just grateful, you know?"

"Patrick," she hissed. "*Stop*."

He hadn't noticed, but Ella had stopped in her tracks. She was holding out her hand to physically stop him, but he had missed that, too. "Oh," he said as he stopped moving. He cleared his throat. "Sorry."

"Don't be sorry." The deep voice with the Southern drawl came from a thick-set man who stepped out from between the pines. He held a machete in one meaty paw; in the other, he flicked the blade with a finger the size of a sausage—*ting-ting-ting.* He wore a black leather duster with a black cowboy hat pulled low over his eyes. "If you hadn't trundled through here like a sow feelin' heat, we might not have had the opportunity to introduce ourselves. Ain't that right, Tommy?"

"That's right, Chester," said another man, skinnier and taller, emerging from the fog on Patrick's right. He had stringy orange hair and a scraggly beard that traveled down his neck, and he looked to be missing some teeth. Like Patrick, he was carrying a baseball bat, but his had a dozen or so nails driven through it, which made Patrick's bat just seem silly.

"But now we have the opportunity. We like meetin' new people. Ain't that right, Tommy?"

"Sure do, Chester."

The two men closed in on Patrick and Ella. They smelled sour, like sweat and rot and dead animals. The stench was so strong, Patrick's eyes began to water. When the one called Chester got close enough that Patrick could smell his breath, he thought he might start gagging. Patrick's nostrils filled with the smell of raw liver and onions when he said, "What'd you bring us for a friend-warmin' gift?"

Patrick coughed. "I might have some gum in here somewhere," he sputtered. Chester's face fell. He cracked Patrick's skull with the machete handle—not hard enough to knock him over, not hard enough to draw blood, but hard enough that he'd have a welt for a few days.

"Son of a bitch!" Patrick cried, stumbling back and landing in Tommy's arms. Tommy shoved him forward and giggled. "Try again."

"How about you?" Chester pointed at Ella with the machete and moved in slowly. He touched the neck of her t-shirt with the point of the blade, then pulled it to the side, revealing her freckled shoulder. "You got a gift for me, pale beauty?"

Ella lowered her eyes. "Yeah," she said quietly.

Chester moved in closer. He reached for a loose strand of Ella's red hair and tucked it behind her ear. Then he brought his lips close to her cheek and said, "I love to hear that."

Tommy's giggles rose to hysterics. He hooted and hollered and jabbed Patrick with the end of the bat. Patrick's shirt snagged on the nails, ripping in two places. "Today's gonna be a good day!" Tommy howled.

"For one of us," Ella said. She pulled the knife from her belt, and with the speed of a cobra, she made four quick slashes in the air. The first sliced through Chester's wrist above his machete grip, opening up a spurting geyser of blood. The second cut through his shirt and left a deep red ribbon from his shoulder to his chest. The third carved a channel in his gut, and the fourth sliced his mouth open from the corner of his mouth to his cheekbone.

She was finished before he even knew she had started.

Chester gazed down at his blood-soaked body, bleeding from four deep, precise wounds. "What the *fuck*?" he gurgled through the blood filling his mouth.

Patrick and Tommy had both watched the quick mutilation in stunned horror. Tommy was first to recover. His face melted from open-mouthed shock to clenched-teeth fury. He shoved Patrick aside and ran at Ella, hoisting the bat above his shoulder. "You fucking bitch!" he shrieked as he swung the nail-bat at her head.

Ella didn't flinch. She simply turned, raised the knife, and plunged it straight down into Tommy's shoulder, leaving the handle sticking up like a second neck.

Tommy screamed as he dropped the bat and fell to his knees. He screamed again as he gripped the knife handle and tried to yank it out. And he screamed even more when Ella stepped up, planted her foot on his neck, and wrenched the four-inch blade from his clavicle.

"You okay?" she asked Patrick as she wiped the blade clean on her jeans.

Patrick gaped. "Uhh…me? Yeah. I am…I am comparatively awesome," he stammered. He looked at the legs of her jeans, which were covered in rust-colored stains. "I also understand the unique color patterns of your jeans a lot better now," he added.

Ella slipped the knife back into its sheath. Then she headed off into the trees. "Let's go."

Patrick hesitated. He frowned down at the two men, writhing in piles of leaves soaked through with their own blood. "What about them?" he asked.

"They're dead," she called over her shoulder.

"Not…dead," Chester rasped, pink foam blood bubbles forming on his lips. "Help me."

"Help us!" Tommy screeched.

They both reached for Patrick's foot. Patrick stepped backward, awkwardly, moving out of their reach. "It's just…you hit me with a machete… and she's kinda my ride. So I'm gonna go?" He made a pained face as he walked backward. "Yeah…I guess I'm gonna just…go."

"They're dead," Ella reminded him. Her voice was muffled by the trees.

"Good luck. I guess." He hemmed and hawed, and then he pushed into the trees, following Ella, leaving them groaning and dying. "Okay bye."

Patrick trotted through the woods, and he finally caught up with Ella when she climbed another tree to check their bearings. "So that was something," he said, already out of breath again. "Should we talk about it?"

Ella didn't respond.

"It's just that they're kind of just bleeding out, maybe we should help them or…*help* them? You know what I'm saying?"

Ella dropped down from the tree and clapped the sap from her hands. "I know what you're saying," she confirmed. "But it's not in our interest to help them. Either way. They would have killed, robbed, and raped us. Maybe even in that order. Who knows how many others they've killed, robbed, and raped. They deserve to die. That way, they won't kill, rob, or rape anyone else. Get it?"

Patrick nodded. "I do get that."

"Their screams likely scared off anyone else who might have been clocking us. If they didn't, their bodies will."

"Okay," Patrick said slowly, nodding, "that also does make sense. But the whole 'put them out of their misery' thing still seems—"

"It seems short-sighted," Ella interrupted. "The longer they bleed, the longer the scent of their fresh blood attracts predators and keeps them off *our* scent. If what you learned from Dr. Philbin is true, then the duster predators have a supernatural sense of smell. A duster-wolf might be able to smell blood for five miles, even ten. Leaving them to bleed out clears our path of any potential predators. Okay?"

Patrick considered this. "Okay," he finally said. "But only because it's inscrutable logic. And because they were very bad people."

"Great. Now focus. We're almost there."

They emerged through the trees and stood at the top of a short cliff overlooking the lake. On the far side of the water sat the Jamie Whitten Lock and Dam.

"That's it?" Patrick said, surprised.

"Guess so," Ella replied. She glanced at Patrick. "Not what you expected?"

Patrick shrugged. "It looks like a lock."

"It *is* a lock."

"I know, but it's an *apocalypse* lock. Run by pirates. I thought there'd be more...I don't know—bones?"

"They may not want to scare people away. Which means they're likely drawing people in." She opened her bag and pulled out a pair of field binoculars.

"True. I mean, to be honest, I'm relieved. I also thought there'd be twisted metal and gasoline torches and blood pools and stuff, but they obviously have some respect for nautical ingenuity. And you know what? I say, good for them."

"There *are* bones," Ella said, peering through the binoculars. "Here." She handed them to Patrick.

He frowned as he put them up to his eyes and nudged the dial. "Where? I don't see any—oh," he said as the lock came into sharper focus.

From water level, everything may have looked on the up-and-up. The building was clean, and drab, made from big slabs of concrete and shaped like an oversized lifeguard tower. It appeared to be a normal, boring building from a normal, boring time. And the lock itself was unremarkable too, as much as extraordinary feats of human inventiveness can be described as unremarkable: huge metal gates with massive concrete struts powered by a pulley the size of a construction crane. Not a single piece out of place.

But from their vantage on the cliff across the lake, the building told a slightly different story.

The roof was absolutely chockablock with bones. Some were attached to other bones; some were even parts of partial skeletons. But most had been separated from their origins, from their flesh, though most still had some gristle near the joints. They were scattered without any concern for organization, though there was a fairly impressive pile of spines stacked up neatly on one side.

One lone pirate sat in the middle of the roof, his considerable bulk straining the fabric webbing of the old beach chair. He wore a pair of postcard-pattern Jams shorts, a light blue tank top, flip flops, sunglasses, and a wide-brimmed straw hat, despite the fact that the weather could have been described as "partly sunny." He held a large femur in one hand, using it to stoke a fire in a clay brick pit about two feet wide and four feet long. By the shape of his lips, he appeared to be whistling.

"How can you have so many bones and still be so chill?" Patrick asked, his face souring. "If you're going to play with human bones, you should at least be forced to feel some anxiety about the trajectory of your life."

"Any idea how many of them are in there?" Ella asked.

Patrick searched the building. "No," he decided. "I can see some movement in the windows, but no idea how many."

Ella took back the binoculars and examined the building. "Seems like a lot, judging by the bone count."

"Compared to the normal number of human bones I think it's normal for other humans to have, I'd say there are infinite people inside," Patrick blenched.

"Hold on. We're about to catch a break," Ella said.

"Can't imagine where you're going with that, but let's have it," Patrick said miserably.

"Look." She pointed down at the lake. There was a rowboat with four passengers cutting through the water, heading toward the lock.

"Oh." Patrick's face became pale. "Oh, no." He started waving his arms, though the people in the boat had their backs to them. "Hey! Heeeyyyyy!" They didn't turn around. "Come on! We have to stop them!"

"They're too far in. And too far away."

"Throw your knife at them or something!" Patrick exclaimed, pacing in tight circles. "You're strong—hit them with your knife!"

"Calm down," Ella said.

"*You* calm down!" Patrick cried. It was a stupid thing to say, of course, because he'd never met anyone calmer than Ella in his entire life. "We have to *do* something!"

"We are doing something," she said. "We're learning. Which is what we're here to do."

"Oh, be serious," Patrick snapped. "I'm not going to 'observe' a murder I could have prevented!" He began scouring the area, looking for a good throwing rock. He picked one up and hefted it a couple times. It wasn't heavy enough, and he let it drop. He picked up a second stone, a bigger one about the size of a baseball; it had a good weight to it. He swung it in his arm, trying to work up a good momentum. Then he ran up to the edge of the cliff and hurled the stone with every ounce of force he could muster. The momentum nearly sent him over the edge. Ella quickly grabbed his arm to keep him on the land.

The stone flew out over the lake, arcing down toward the boat. Patrick held his breath.

The stone actually hit one of the rowers in the shoulder.

"Oh! Yes!" Patrick exclaimed, pumping his fists in the air. "Oh my God! Yes! I did it! That thing's, like, a *mile* away! I *did* it! I—hey! No, wait! Hey! *Heeeey!*" His excitement turned as he watched the rowers double their efforts, paddling harder toward the lock. "No—stop! Come back!" he screamed, waving his arms and jumping around on the ledge of the cliff. "What are they *doing?!*"

"They're paddling away from the lunatic who's pelting them with rocks," Ella sighed. "Obviously."

"What?! No! That's not what I was—hey! *Heeeey! They're going to kill you! Heeeeey!*" But it was hopeless. The damage was done, and the rowers were hauling toward what they assumed was the relative safety of the lock.

As they neared the dam, the door to the concrete building opened, and two women stepped out. "Oh no," Patrick moaned, his heart sinking. He trained the binoculars on the pirates. Like the bone holder, the women wore jeans, t-shirts, flip-flops, and hair ties. They looked completely normal and not at all threatening. "These pirates look like real people!" Patrick gasped.

"They *are* real people," Ella reminded him. "Real people with problematic habits."

"No; *vegans* are real people with problematic habits," Patrick said angrily. "These people are monsters." He moved the binoculars toward the boat. "Don't go in there—they're *monsters!*"

The monsters were all pleasant waves and kind eyes as they welcomed the rowboat to the lock. Patrick could see their lips moving as they made polite small talk with the travelers, who, for their part, pointed frantically back at the cliffs, working themselves into a lather. The two women nodded sympathetically and gestured toward the lock.

The lock was an open-air hallway with massive concrete walls and a steel gate at either end. The lakeside gate was open; the far gate was closed. In order to be transported from the lake to the river, the boat would have to enter the channel, with the gate closing behind it. The water inside the channel would be released slowly, gradually lowering the boat down to river level. Then the far gate would open, and the rowboat could continue its journey down the Tenn-Tom, unharmed.

At least, that was how it was supposed to work.

"And that's what they're probably telling them right now," Patrick said aloud, not realizing that he'd been thinking about the technical workings of locks silently to himself. Ella looked at him, confused. But she didn't ask any questions.

They watched helplessly as the rowers paddled into the channel. Patrick moaned again as he watched the two women turn and follow them into the lock, directing them to hug the eastern ledge on which they walked. He could see now that one of the women had a machete tucked into the back of her jeans…a machete she reached for as she followed the boat, as the gate began to draw closed.

Before it shut the killers in with their prey, Patrick saw the second woman reach behind the gate post and pull out a cattle prod. She jammed it into the rear rower's shoulder. There was a blue spark as his whole body slumped over in its seat. The first woman lifted the machete above her head and brought it down onto another boater's neck, and the gate closed, blocking Patrick's view.

But he could hear their screams.

"I think I'm going to be sick," Patrick said, covering his mouth.

Ella looked at him, confused. "Why? You can't even see what's happening."

He gestured at her, trying to keep his words inside his mouth so they wouldn't let the vomit escape. Ella shrugged and took back the binoculars. The man on the roof had been roused from his repose by all the ruckus. He hauled himself out of his beach chair and waddled over to the edge of the roof. He peered down into the channel and watched the two women work. When he was satisfied with their progress, he reached down and grabbed ahold of a garden hose cart stashed nearby. He grabbed the hose and started lowering it down into the channel.

"What's he doing?" Patrick asked Ella, who was watching through the binoculars. "Hosing down the river?"

"It's not a hose," Ella said, dialing in the binoculars. "It's a chain."

The end of the chain disappeared into the channel, hidden from their view by the gate. But after a minute, the man on the roof started cranking the wheel on the hose cart, reeling the chain back in. He seemed to be struggling with it and had to stop twice to let his arm rest. But eventually the chain came back over the lip of the roof. It was fastened to the ankles of a lifeless body.

"That's one," Ella said coolly.

"One? One what?" Patrick demanded.

"One body."

"What do you mean, one body? One *living* body?"

Ella shook her head. "No."

"Oh, I don't like this at all," Patrick decided, feeling the bile rise up into his throat. He pushed his hands into his hair and began to pace. "This is bad. This is so bad. And I should not have had coffee."

"Hold on…we're going to get a second," she said.

"A second to do what?" Patrick asked.

"No, a second body. I wonder if they leave any survivors. Guess we'll know soon enough." She offered Patrick the binoculars, which he adamantly declined. She turned her gaze back to the lock, watching the man on the roof with great interest. "He's so relaxed," she observed.

"He's got Baby Boomer Buffett brain!" Patrick cried as he continued his frantic pacing. "That whole generation is broken. They'll skin you for a margarita."

Ella didn't reply. She kept watching as the man dragged the two bodies toward the fire pit. As he was positioning the second body, he perked up, as if someone was speaking to him. He ambled back over to the edge of the roof, where he engaged in a conversation for a few more seconds, then he shrugged and lowered the chain back over the side. He soon found himself dragging a third body over the edge of the roof.

"Got three," Ella said.

"So…they're just killing everyone," Patrick fumed, stomping around on the cliff behind Ella.

"I don't know if you missed all the bones on the roof, but yeah, they're killing everyone," Ella pointed out.

"I'm a glass-half-full person!" Patrick cried. He flailed around even more, feeling completely helpless. Eventually, he slowed to a thoughtful pacing, with his hands clasped behind his back. "I'm sorry. I'm not usually this worked up. My attitude toward imminent death has actually been described as 'too casual.' But now…I don't know what's going on with me."

"You don't know if your friends in Mobile are alive, and you'll never find out if you die on the Tenn-Tom." Ella responded. She lowered the binoculars and looked at Patrick with her calm blue eyes. "It's stirring up your anxiety."

Patrick frowned. The lucid dreaming was getting to him. All the memories of Ben flooding back…no, more than *just* flooding back; *taking over*. Plunging him into a memory well, every flashback becoming real again, urgent, as if his brain were bear-hugging his whole body and throwing him through a time portal—not firing synapses to relive those moments, but dragging Patrick himself, his whole human self, into the past to *relive* them, going through them again, not able to deviate from the script of the past, and not wanting to, either. Not in the slightest.

For all of his spatial intellect and engineering mental precision, he had never trusted the details of his personal memories. He knew that at some point, Izzy had started walking, but he didn't remember her very first steps. And of course he knew that she had started talking, at one point, but he didn't remember her exact first words. He remembered his wedding day, how Annie had looked when they danced, but he didn't remember the ceremony or whether or not the doors had opened to reveal her in a flood of sunlight, like they always do in the movies. He remembered the crush of the bones in his hand as Annie pushed against him to deliver their first and only daughter, something he would only realize was true after they both were gone from the world. But he didn't remember Izzy's face when she finally slid into the world, didn't remember if she'd had angry fists or a furious brow, didn't remember which attendant had asked him if he wanted to cut the cord. He barely even remembered cutting the cord himself. What Patrick remembered instead of the details of these fundamentally personal moments were the colors and the feelings they inspired, the irreversible impact they made on his sense of reality. The *bursts* of Izzy's first steps and words; the *swell* of his world on the day he married Annie; the *unknowing, unknowable flood* of watching his wife deliver their baby; the *gravity* of scissors in his hand while the whirlwind of existence spun around him like a hurricane.

Patrick's most crucial memories were Post-Impressionist. His reflection was color, and strokes, and ambient light.

But these memories of Ben…they were cinematic, with crisp dialogue, with exact choreography, with specificity that was the same every time. He could rewind it and rewind it and rewind it, and it was all so exact, so unwavering and true.

"It's not just anxiety," Patrick sighed. "It's something else. I don't know what. It's like…you know how there's a future? I mean, there's always something else, for however long, and so you think, 'Well, everything that's happened before, everything that's happening *now*, it's all part of a timeline.' Everything that happens will flow and merge into the present and the trail into the past, and it's all one big line, so your brain doesn't catalog memories like a photo album. But it mixes them into the paint on the palette of everything you remember, and it makes these paintings that are part then and part now. You know?"

Ella blinked. "I do not."

"Well, it's like that," Patrick continued, rolling over her words. "When there's a future, there's always more paint to add to the palette. You don't have to work with the colors you have when you know there will be new colors to add later. I think that's how my brain makes memories." He stood at the edge of the cliff, his toes off the rock, watching the lake and the lock and the trees and the dust, and not really seeing any of it at all. "I have impressions of things more than memories. But ever since Disney World…I'm seeing these memories that are *sharp*. And *clear*. And they're not about my daughter, or my wife. They're not about the only two humans who ever existed in the history of the planet that I want to be able to hold in my mind. Those two are still fuzzy. They're impressions that don't get any sharper. What I see when I have these spells is memories of my friend Ben." He sat down on the cliff and dangled his legs over the edge, watching the lock glumly as the man on the roof fussed with the bodies.

"Why can't I remember my wife and my daughter in anything but smudges of light and color? And why can I remember Ben so sharply."

Ella raised the binoculars back to her eyes. She refocused on the man on the roof. "Because your friend is also *them*," she said, like it was the most obvious thing in the world.

Patrick wiped his nose on his arm. "What?"

"Ben was your friend before M-Day, right? And your wife and kid knew him?"

"Yeah."

"Memories get all mashed together sometimes; the feelings all connect up. Because your friend knew your family, he carries them as part of himself now. You access that through your memories. They merge into one thing; he carries them with him, and you carry him with you. He's like a talisman for everything you feel about them."

It made more sense than Patrick would have guessed. "And you know this how?"

Ella rolled her eyes. "This is Psych 101. I thought you went to college."

"I never took Psych," Patrick sighed.

"Lucky me," Ella said.

"I think I just have a brain tumor."

"What you have is PTSD."

"What I have is a brain tumor and a stomach hole and lucid dreams from probably sepsis."

"It's PTSD," Ella said, sounding annoyed. "My brother served in Afghanistan. He came home with it. Dreams like hallucinations, from trauma. Then the world blew up, and now everyone has it. At least a little. You? Your family died, and you and your friend didn't. Your residual pain is manifesting in hallucinations, probably mixing with survivor's guilt that it was them instead of you. You've got the real deal disorder."

Patrick raised an eyebrow. "So you're thinking no on the brain tumor?" he asked.

"You don't have a brain tumor. Just trauma brain. Now...do you want to know what's happening at the lock or not?"

"Not," Patrick replied sourly. The thought of trauma and hallucinations and stress and manifestation made his stomach hurt. Adding a thick layer of human dismemberment over top of that felt like a bit too much to bear.

"Too bad." Ella said, pressing the binoculars to her eyes. She saw the top few inches of the far lock gate open up as the ghouls below released one lone survivor out into the horrible, deadly wild. "They're letting the last one go."

"I can't believe they just murdered three people," Patrick said. He didn't know what to do with his arms. He tried crossing them, but it felt way too aggressive for the despair he was feeling, and he didn't want to give the appearance of adjusting to it. Instead, he hugged himself tightly and prayed for this whole experience to be over soon.

"I think they're going to barbecue them," Ella said.

Patrick blinked. "I can't tell what's worse: that it's happening or the very casual way you just said it."

"Want to see?" she asked.

Patrick shook his head. "I do not." He relaxed his arms and shook the blood back into his hands. "So… apparently, you're a bladed weapons expert; do you think we could take them? Crew versus crew?"

Ella was quiet as she studied the scene. Patrick's insides roiled to think of what she was seeing through the lenses of those binoculars. He was from St. Louis; it had given him a very specific idea of how barbecuing worked. For instance, he knew that one of the first steps to cooking something on a grill is to butcher that thing into grill-sized pieces.

He sat down near the edge of the cliff in case he became sick.

"I don't know," Ella finally answered. "If there aren't many more of them, then we may be able to take them. But I'm worried about the lock. I'm not sure our boat will even fit. If it does, it'll be tight. *Really* tight…we'll be boxed in, and that's not great."

"And if there are a lot more of them, we might have a problem."

Ella lowered the binoculars. "We definitely have a problem. Here." She lifted the glasses up to Patrick. "You want to see this."

"I'm sure that's not true," Patrick frowned, but he took the binoculars anyway. He focused in on the roof of the building. This time, his stomach turned for a whole different reason. "Well shit." A hatch opened from the roof. People were pouring out of it like ants from an anthill. By the time Patrick got the binoculars focused, there were a dozen of them at least, with more emerging every few seconds—an entire legion of cannibal pirates clad in Hawaiian shirts and madras shorts and straw hats and flip-flops. "That can't be good."

"It's not survivable, either."

"Good Lord, there must be thirty of them now," Patrick said in horrified awe as the last few stragglers climbed out through the hatch. "How are there so many people who have decided it's okay to eat other people?"

"Broken world," Ella said.

"I don't think the flaming boat with the splayed corpse trick is going to get us past this one."

"No. The boat can flame all it wants. If we enter that lock, we're done for."

"So, we can fight a horde of cannibals, or we can backtrack across the country, or we can walk for a few hundred miles. Am I missing any of our options?"

"No. But 'fighting a horde cannibals' is a nice way of saying 'get eaten by a horde cannibals.'"

Patrick scratched his itchy palm. The gears in his brain were starting to turn. "What do you think we should do?" he asked.

"I think we should walk," Ella confirmed "But it doesn't matter what I think."

"Because Roman won't want to lose more time."

"No. He won't."

"But if we go forward, we'll be killed and/or grilled."

"Seems like it."

"Okay," Patrick said slowly. The pieces of a new plan were starting to emerge. "I'm becoming acutely aware of the fact that people really hate it when I say this," he continued as his brain began sliding the pieces together, "but I think I have an idea."

48.

"Every idea you have is terrible, but this one is *truly* the dumbest shit I've ever heard," Gary fumed.

"Well, you haven't really known me that long," Patrick pointed out.

"This would destroy the boat," Carla pointed out. "You want to destroy the boat?"

Patrick pointed at Roman. "He said I could."

"To be clear," Roman said, stepping forward and waving his hands in the air, "I said I wouldn't need it to be seaworthy *after* we were done with it." He gave Patrick an uneasy glance. "We are far from done with it."

"It would only destroy the boat a *little* bit," Patrick promised, holding up his hand as if taking a vow. "Probably. Maybe. Probably."

Ted was having a hard time wrapping his head around the whole thing. "So…you want to trap a *zombie pig* on the boat—with all of us *also* on the boat. You want us to be trapped inside the boat with a zombie pig. Do I have that right?"

"It doesn't have to be a pig," Patrick clarified. "It could be anything—a raccoon or a fox. A pig would be great, but I bet even a handful of squirrels would do the trick."

"A pig would destroy the boat!" Carla repeated.

But Patrick disagreed. "Not if we set up a perimeter of Zom-Be-Gone. We lure a duster animal onto the boat and into the main cabin; we're all stationed inside with vials of Zom-Be-Gone. We sprinkle it around, and we'll have the animal trapped. We've already seen it work, over at Dr. Philbin's Muppet Lab. The potion acts like a fence—run the animal into the room and by the time it realizes it's trapped, the last person rushes in and closes the door behind them, also holding a vial of duster-juice, and boom, it's trapped. And I would imagine," he added, "angry as hell."

"Then we bring the boat into the lock," Roman said, nodding slowly. "Like a Trojan horse. We sail into the channel and let them close us in. They board the ship, open the door, and all hell breaks loose."

Patrick smirked. "All we have to do is step aside. The animal smells its way out, and off it goes. Angry—and hungry, presumably."

"Ready to tear into anything and everything it sees," Roman said, a grin spreading across his face.

"It's still risky, obviously," Patrick admitted. "Even if it all goes to plan, we only saw two of them go in after the rowboat. That leaves a *lot* of cannibals."

"But if we can corral the animal inside the boat, can't we corral it again outside the boat?" Roman said.

"In theory. Maybe not for long…but probably long enough to do some real damage."

"Sure, so we take out a few," Gary grumbled. "But then the pig swims off." He glared at Carla. "Our secret weapon is gone, and the rest of them are on us."

"But we'll have knocked them back on their heels," Roman said. He rubbed his hands together excitedly. "We'll take them by surprise. They won't know *what* to do."

"And how are we going to open the second gate?" Ella asked.

"Great question," Patrick nodded. "One of us will be stationed on the upper deck. I'd suggest Brett."

"Why don't I get to do the thing with the pig?" Brett frowned.

"Because while we're inside the lock, you're going to jump onto the roof and take care of the Grill Master."

"Oh," Brett said, brightening. "Hell yeah."

"Then we just draw them out," Patrick continued. "They're either going to have to come through the roof hatch or onto the boat. Either way, they'll be single-file and pretty easy to take."

"What if they don't all come out?" Lucia asked. "What if they realize what's happening and hunker down inside?"

"We've got enough peat left over for a few Molotovs," Ella realized. "Drop them in through the hatch and that problem is solved."

"Once it's clear, we slip inside, open the gate, and we're on our way." Patrick dusted his hands off. "Easy peasy."

Roman could hardly contain his excitement. He was practically vibrating. He slapped a hand on Patrick's shoulder and squeezed. "I think it'll work."

"It gives us a fighting chance, at least," Patrick said.

"It's risky," Johnny pipped up from the back of the room.

Carla sighed. She cleared her throat and walked into the center of the group. "It *is* risky," she agreed, giving Johnny a nod. "But our other options are to go back upriver or to go forward on foot. The land journey is a crapshoot; we have no idea what's out there. It might be better, but it also might be a whole hell of a lot worse."

"Better the devil you know than the devil you don't," Ella said.

"Yeah. And we *do* know what sort of devils are upstream. We lost people there already. I don't see this as any worse."

"It's worse because *these* lunatics are *eating people*," Gary snarled.

"But you'll be dead by the time that happens, so you won't care," Patrick pointed out.

"Also, these are *unsuspecting* people, without a secret weapon," Roman pointed out. "And we will have a very mean, very powerful, and very hungry secret weapon."

"Sorry...can I say something?" Richie asked, raising his hand and clearing his throat. Everyone was annoyed to hear from him, but he pushed. "How are we going to *get* this secret weapon? I mean, how do we get a zombie animal onto the boat?"

"We don't *get* it onto the boat," Patrick said. "We *lure* it onto the boat."

Richie frowned. "Okay...so how do we *lure* it onto the boat?"

"We're going to need some blood," Patrick said. He turned and raised an eyebrow at Gary. "It's easiest if we can use blood that's already on the outside of a body."

49.

"This is so fucking stupid," Gary grumbled, holding his injured arm as he trudged up the hill.

"That's some pre-apocalypse thinking right there," Patrick replied as they pushed through the trees. "Would it have been stupid to lure a super-powered wild animal onto a hundred-year-old boat in 2008, with a few vials of pine tree essential oil as our only weapon? Yeah. Of course. It would have been very stupid. *Immensely* stupid. The absolute stupidest. But now? In this, the worst of all possible timelines? It's not stupid. It's inspired!"

"We're all going to get killed," Gary grumbled.

"Okay, but you're a pessimist," Patrick pointed out. "You only think that because you're wired to."

"How do you do it?" Gary asked, grunting with frustration, exertion, and pain. "How do you come up with all these dumb ideas? And how do you convince yourself to follow through?"

Patrick snorted. "The Urge to Solve. You don't become an engineer if you're not cursed at birth with the incessant and terrible and wonderful Urge to Solve."

"Ever consider the idea that there's some things you *can't* solve?"

Patrick thought for a few seconds. "Not really," he admitted. "I mean, I don't think *I* can solve every problem. But I think every problem *can* be solved. The fun is in figuring out if you can be the one to unlock that door."

Gary cleared his throat and spat into the leaves. "So you think this is fun?"

Patrick sighed. He stopped walking, and Gary took his cue, slumping back against the trunk of a tall, old pine. Patrick crossed his arms and propped himself up on a mossy boulder. "I don't think this is fun. I don't think *any* of this is fun," he sighed. "Just like everyone else, I've lost everything—we've *all* lost everything. Before M-Day, we all had specific ideas of what it would mean to lose everything—losing jobs, loved ones, our houses…our time. But now we've really lost *everything*. We've lost every single thing we could possibly have considered losing, and that was just for starters. We had no idea back then what we had that we could lose. But now *everything* is gone. Even the world." He knocked his fist against the stone, "It's here, but it's gone, you know?"

Gary cradled his injured arm closer to his chest and lowered his eyes. The fire in his gut seemed to settle a bit. "Yeah. I know."

"'Nothing' *then* has the same definition that it has now. But stupid ideas then aren't stupid ideas now; happiness now doesn't come close to happiness then." Patrick gestured out at the world. "Do I think *this* is fun? No. I do not think that this is fun. Do I find some personal pleasure in finding creative ways to try to solve problems that are literally life and death? honestly don't know, Gary. But I'm interested in solutions. They make my brain crank in ways that nothing else in this busted-up, broken world does. I don't think that's happiness, and I don't think it's fun. I think it's a stretch of a muscle that spends most of its time going to atrophy because almost every decision is fight or flight, not think or sink. When I get a chance to think, I know it's almost always going to result in something new and weird, but every new thing *has* to be new and weird. This is not the world we think we remember. Someone picked up the planet and shook it up and slammed it back down eight feet to the left, and none of the old rules apply anymore. So, please, *please* stop telling me that every idea is bad. Maybe they *are* bad, and maybe they'll prove to be bad, but they're the only ideas anyone is offering. Meanwhile, they're keeping us all alive in the face of insanely fucked-up circumstances that we've never seen before. So please stop telling me my plans are bad and start working with me on making them better!" Patrick punched downward on the rock beneath him for emphasis. "Ow!" He jumped off the stone and stomped around the forest, shaking out his hand and muttering curses to himself.

Gary shook his head and spat into the trees. "Maybe when your ideas stop putting us in added danger, we'll stop complaining."

Patrick took a deep breath. He felt so tired these days. He felt so old. "Sure," he said. "Fine." He continued into the forest, pushing over the hill and down into the clearing below.

"There's nothing down there," Ben said.

Patrick turned to his friend and frowned. "What are you talking about? There are like a dozen mattresses down there."

The low-country mountain fizzled away, replaced by the roof of the Mattress Firm at Milwaukee and Wabanasia in Wicker Park. The trees dissolved into brownstone houses, new-brick strip malls, and the proud, tall spire of the Northwest Tower a few blocks to the south. The Monkey dust was thinner and the hot sun glared down, making them squint.

"I don't care if there are a million mattresses down there...what are we doing here?" Ben cried.

"There's no way this building could hold a million mattresses," Patrick pointed out. "You'd need a warehouse the size of Rhode Island for that."

"Who cares about mattresses?!" Ben exploded.

"I think lots of people care about mattresses," Patrick replied. "Definitely most people. Quite possibly all people."

"Not this people."

"Yeah, but are you really 'people'?" Patrick asked, sizing Ben up with a squint. He lifted his palm and twisted it in the air. "Eh."

"I thought we were coming for food, or water, or some badass weapons," Ben grumbled, crossing his arms. "For fuck's sake, Pat—the U-Spy Store is like half a mile that way!"

Patrick was stricken. "Ben," he said seriously, holding a hand to his chest. "Benjamin. Benjamina. I love the U-Spy Store—you know I do. To even suggest that I might come all this way and not ransack the U-Spy Store for something less than? You wound me!"

"I know you love the dumb U-Spy Store—that's why I'm saying it! To knock some goddamn sense into your head! Let's go smash in the door and get some cameras we can't plug into walls anymore, because that'd be more useful than dropping into a stupid Mattress Firm! From the roof! This is the apocalypse, Pat! People are out here killing each other for shoes! I saw a woman last week who brained some poor guy to death with a trash can lid because she wanted his flip-flops, and they were six sizes too big!" Ben shoved his fingers into his hair and pulled in frustration. Sometimes he thought about shaving every bit of it off just so he wouldn't have to give Patrick the satisfaction of knowing he was driving Ben to stress-induced baldness. "There are so many things we should be scavenging for right now. Why in the hell are we going mattress shopping?!"

Patrick had pried open a skylight with the claw of a hammer; now he sat down on the roof, swinging his legs down into the rectangular hole and scooting himself closer to the edge. "You're cranky. I see that. You know what I think? A good night's sleep will go a long way."

"I'm going to push you off this roof," Ben realized.

"Oh, stop it. Annie and I bought a mattress from here, maybe a year ago? Not long before the bombs."

Ben's body stiffened and he took a step backward. "And you need a new one already? What have you been doing in there alone?" he asked, horrified.

"Nothing, you clod," Patrick said, rolling his eyes. "The mattress is fine. Not as good as Sealy would want you to think, but fine."

Ben frowned. "Then, again: Why are we here?"

"Because when we came here to look at mattresses, I made the very astute observation that there was a row of vending machines in the corner. One for snacks, one for drinks, and, for reasons I'll never quite come to grips with, one for pillowcases. So while we certainly could be out there, slap-fighting all the other pairs of panicked know-nothings over the last six kernels of mummified popcorn at the closest Garrett's, I thought we might slip in undetected to mine the sweet, corn-syrupy goodness of America's packaged noms in the quiet, peaceful bliss of a place where no one has ever, ever, thought to go looking for Pop-Tarts."

"Oh," Ben said. He thought about this for a moment. "Why do they have Pop-Tarts at a Mattress Firm? It feels unholy. And God, why do you think a year after the last refill is the right time to right time for us to eat them?"

"Actually, I'd assume it's been more like six or seven years. I cannot imagine they went through inventory at any sort of worthwhile rate."

Ben soured. "What's the shelf life of a Pop-Tart?" he wondered.

"Benny Boy, the Earth will be swallowed up by the sun before Pop-Tarts hit their expiration date," Patrick assured him. "Food science is a wonder. A delicious, carcinogenic wonder. Or it was, anyway." With that, he shuffled over the edge of the skylight and dropped down into the store below.

Ben watched him go, then heard a series of unfortunate sounds that he was pretty sure meant Patrick had misjudged his trajectory, grazed the edge of a mattress, and slammed into the floor.

He peered over the lip of the opening and saw Patrick splayed out on the floor.

"You dead?" he asked.

"In one sense, yes," Patrick groaned, scraping himself up from the concrete floor. "But in another, more nuanced sense, I've never been more alive."

Ben blinked. "There is a mattress literally directly beneath this opening. How in God's name did you miss it?" He tightened the straps of his backpack, then he hopped through the skylight and dropped into the Mattress Firm. He landed with a gentle bounce on a Beautyrest Harmony Lux. "You are the worst at the apocalypse," he decided aloud.

"I wasn't so great at the world before, either," Patrick mumbled, working the ache out of his shoulder. "At least I'm consistent."

He twisted his bones back into place, then set off for the corner of the store, where three dark, dusty vending machines stood like huge ancient tablets just waiting to have their spider webs brushed off by Indiana Jones. Ben hopped off the Beautyrest and trotted after him. "Jesus," he whispered, his eyes widening, his pulse quickening. "That's more food in one place than I've seen since M-Day."

"I told you," Patrick smiled, grinning at the glass-and-metal boxes that were filled with packaged candy bars, breakfast pastries, popcorn, trail snacks, and, indeed, in the case of the machine on the far right, pillowcases. "You can apologize anytime you want."

"I won't," Ben assured him.

"That's my boy." Patrick twirled his hammer in the air, caught it, heaved it back, and smashed it through the glass front of the pillowcase machine. "This is the most vandalism I've ever done," he said, thrilled.

"You broke into the wrong one," Ben pointed out. He tapped the candy bar machine. "Food's over here."

"Haven't you ever trick-or-treated?" Patrick asked. He reached into the vending machine and pulled out a two-pack of pillowcases. He tore it open with his teeth and tossed one of the cases to Ben. "Load 'er up."

Ben nodded grudgingly. "All right. This one time, you did something right."

"A-thank you," Patrick replied, bowing with a flourish. He moved to the machine in the middle and smashed it open. They stuffed Snickers, Milky Ways, M&Ms, and Kit-Kats into their pillowcases until the only thing left in the metal spiral arms was a row of Mounds, because some things were worse than starvation.

"This is a solid haul," Ben decided, hefting his bag. "Way better than Halloween."

"That's because you grew up in Eureka. And in Eureka, Halloween—much like everything else—has always sucked."

"At least it wasn't Jeff County," Ben grumbled.

"I love that all these years and one apocalypse later, we can still make fun of where each other grew up," Patrick beamed. "We are so St. Louis!"

Patrick had saved the Pop-Tart vending machine for last. Not only did it hold a treasure trove of death-proof pastries; not only did it have the more savory necessities like trail mix and the popcorn mixed in, but it also held the single most life-sustaining snack on the planet, as far as he was concerned. He hadn't dared let himself hope that he might see the familiar purple-and-yellow bag at a Mattress Firm, but now, here he was, his face pressed against the glass, and there wasn't just one telltale purple bag…there were two completely full rows of pristine jewel-tone delicacies behind the very frail and smashable glass. Fourteen bags in all.

And for the first time in days, Patrick wept.

Ben sidled up beside Patrick and glanced into the vending machine. "Whoa!" he said. "They've got Takis!"

Patrick nodded, tears of joy streaming down his face. "Yes, Ben," he whispered, his voice thick with gratitude. "They've got Takis."

He lifted up the hammer. He was about to bring it down on the glass when a raccoon popped up, inside the vending machine, its angry little paws on the glass, baring its teeth and hissing and foaming from its small but horrifying mouth.

Patrick screamed. Ben screamed. Patrick screamed again.

"What the fuck, raccoon?!"

"Kill it!"

"Get away from the Takis!"

"Kill it!"

The raccoon swiped at them, its dirty claws streaking the glass with alley mud and dumpster juice. It hissed again, and the hair on the back of Patrick's neck prickled to attention.

"Patrick! Kill it!" Ben shrieked again.

"I can't! It's alive!"

"Change that!"

"I'm not going to kill a thing!"

"It's trying to eat us!"

"It's trapped in the machine!"

"That only makes it angrier!"

"I'm not going to kill a thing!"

"It's not a thing, it's a monster!" Ben cried.

"Monsters are things!" Patrick shrieked.

"Only technically!" Ben shrieked back.

They both stumbled away from the machine. The raccoon lowered itself off its hind legs, watching them with furious black eyes. Though it had stopped hissing, a deep, horrible growl rumbled out of its throat. Its teeth were still bared and dripping with foam.

"I think it's rabid," Patrick whispered.

"Why are you whispering?" Ben asked.

"I don't know," Patrick whispered.

"It doesn't speak English."

"Shut up. Let's go."

Ben blinked. "What? Really? You're going to leave Takis behind because you don't want to hit a rodent with a hammer?"

"I don't think they're rodents," Patrick pointed out.

"You have a hammer!" Ben shouted.

"Absolutely not." Patrick shook his head. "I'm not killing a living thing. I don't need that kind of karma on my soul."

"You don't believe in karma," Ben reminded him.

"That's true," Patrick agreed. "But just in case I'm wrong." He tossed his hammer into the pillowcase full of candy and slung the whole pack over his shoulder. "I want Takis more than anybody. More than anybody. You know this."

"I do know this," Ben nodded.

"And even as that person, for whom that is true, I'm saying, let's sew up our riches and cut our losses and call it a day, huh?" He headed for the door.

Ben watched him, confused. "Hey," he said, as Patrick neared the glass door. "Why the hell did we climb up onto the roof instead of just smashing in the door?"

Patrick shrugged. "Because you always wanted to be Batman. And this seemed like a very Batman-able opportunity."

Ben gasped. "Batman would have gone in through the skylight."

"But I don't think he would have killed a raccoon," Patrick said, unlocking the door and pushing it open. "And even if he would have…I'm not about to start making nature mad."

"Aren't we specifically out here to make nature fucking mad?" Gary sneered, spitting into the leaves.

Patrick blinked a few times, hard. Wicker Park evaporated, and the river woods snapped back into view. Gary was ambling down the hill, skidding in the loose underbrush.

"Wasn't it your specific idea to come out here and make some abominations of nature very fucking angry?"

Patrick closed his eyes. He squeezed the bridge of his nose. His head ached. His body was tired. When Izzy was small, she used to talk about her body like it was an iPhone. "My battery is green!" she would say, when she was full of energy and ready to cause chaos. But when her battery was yellow, it was time for a snack—or maybe in very rare cases, even a nap, suggested by Izzy herself.

No matter how tired she was, though, her battery never got red.

"My battery is red," Patrick said, pulling himself away from the Mattress Firm memory and settling uncomfortably into the now. "We can do this, or we can go back. Back to the boat, back up the river, back to the road, back to being separate and wandering, back to anything. I don't care, Gary. This is all a means to an end. I don't know the best way to do things. I'm thinking three steps behind the world. We don't have to be out here. I just want to go back to Fort Doom. I just *need* to get back to Fort Doom. I don't know if anything I'm doing is getting us closer or not. If it's not, it's all been for nothing. This is just—" he said, dismissing the woods around them. "This is nothing. It's all a snowball rolling downhill. I'm trying to keep us all inside until we smash onto the valley floor and wonder how we lived. But that living…that's the important part. I have to get back to Fort Doom. I *have* to get back to Ben."

Gary shuffled into the clearing, favoring his arm, a scowl twitching across his mouth. "Well," he said grumpily. "Run me through the plan again."

50.

Gary closed his eyes. He tried to take a breath. "Don't know why I asked," he said.

"Want to call it off?" Patrick asked.

Gary glowered as he considered his options. In the end, all he could do was shake his head. "No. It's a stupid plan, and we're all gonna die, but if we don't, then it'll probably work okay. And if we do die, it was bound to happen soon anyway."

"That's the apocalyptic spirit," Patrick sighed.

"You've got the go-away juice?"

"It's called Zom-Be-Gone, but yes," Patrick said, pulling the vial from his pocket. "Duster-tested, Roman-approved. Anything goes wrong, we pull the cork and spill this stuff like gossip at a gossip party."

"Huh?"

Patrick shook his head. "I don't know, I'm very tired."

"I see that." Gary frowned and turned to survey the forest. "So how do we attract this pig, or whatever dusted-up wild animal is supposed to come devour me alive?"

"Ella thinks the senses of the dusted animals are heightened enough that we shouldn't have to do much. Just stand upwind for a while and wait."

"If that's true, why aren't we getting constantly ripped apart by duster animals?" Gary asked.

"I was wondering that myself," Patrick admitted. "I think we're living in the heyday of the apocalypse. The number of animals that have ingested enough Monkey dust to go Super Saiyan is still extremely limited. But give it a few years…" He trailed off.

"And then, watch your fucking back," Gary finished.

"In the near future, it's going to be better to not bleed," Patrick agreed.

"Feels pretty bad to bleed right now."

"About that…we're going to want to take off the bandage."

Gary's face darkened. "Goddammit," he mumbled. But he set to work unraveling the dirty, bloody cloth from his arm. He peeled it away, grunting from the pain of the semi-formed scab tearing away from his skin.

Patrick looked at the wound. His face drained to an Elmer's glue white. "Gary," he said quietly, "that does not look good."

A full third of his arm was purplish-black, from a few inches above his elbow all the way down to his forearm. The wound itself still bled a little, but it also oozed an off-white pus that dripped down his elbow, leaving milky streaks across his skin. The wound was outlined with a fiery red ring, and the overwhelming stench was like rotten mushrooms.

Patrick took a few steps back and covered his nose. "I think it'll get an animal's attention," he said, trying to stay positive.

Gary frowned. "Jimmy said it would be touch and go."

"Did he say that today?"

"Yesterday."

"Did it look like this yesterday?"

Gary frowned. "No. Not quite as bad."

Patrick's eyes watered. The smell of Gary's necrotic flesh was overpowering, even in a forest thick with the musty rot of autumn. "It's probably fine," he lied. "And it's good that it's so…actionable. You know? For what we're doing. I mean, the sooner we can get past this cannibal dam, the sooner we can get back to Roman's place. It sounds like he's got a good thing going there. He might have penicillin. So let's hope for an animal and…you know…" He nodded at Gary's arm. "…let's also hope for the best."

They stood in a clearing in the low valley, a sloping uphill forest separating them from the boat. When an animal showed up—*if* an animal showed up—they'd have to be ready to haul ass back up the hill, which wasn't exactly an ideal situation, what with Gary's injury and Patrick's general fitness. But the trees were thinner in the valley, and considering the way the wind was blowing, they'd have a better view of an animal charging on the scent. It would hopefully buy them the precious extra seconds they needed to drag themselves over the hill and tumble back down to the lakeside.

Gary seemed to be reading Patrick's mind. "Why'd you come out here with me? Why didn't you send Ella? Or Carla? Someone who's…" He trailed off as he gave Patrick's wiry, angular body a once-over. "…fit?"

"Because if I'm sending anyone on a suicide mission, I'm sending me."

"And me," Gary added.

"Well, yes. I've come to find you expendable."

"Clearly."

Movement in his peripheral caught Patrick's attention. "Hold on," he said, holding up a hand. He turned toward the trees up the valley to the north, the breeze whipping up the tail of his shirt from behind. "Am I crazy, or are those trees shaking?"

Gary frowned at the trembling copse. "It's not you."

"Okay." Patrick tightened his grip on the Zom-Be-Gone. "Get ready."

But Gary shook his head. "No. Something's wrong," he said.

"What do you mean?"

"I mean, something's different. The trees shook when the pig attacked, but…"

Patrick tensed. "But what?" he urged.

Gary swallowed the tremor in his throat. "But not like that," he said.

The huge pines thrashed like stalks of wheat in a thunderstorm. Birds shot out from the forest in such multitudes that they turned the sky black. The ground beneath Patrick's feet began to vibrate with the quick drumbeat of something hitting the ground hard, harder and harder as the creature came nearer. The earth rattled so violently, Patrick had to fight to keep his footing.

"I guess we caught something," Patrick said over the rumble, the color draining from his face.

"I don't think it's a pig!" Gary yelled.

The forest broke apart as a massive black bear exploded through the tree line with its paws beating down the valley, its eyes bloodshot and red with fury. Yellow-green froth flew from its lips. The bear's legs moved like brick pillars, solid and straight and reluctant to bend, but it didn't slow the dust-fueled predator as it threw itself into the hunt. It streaked down the hill, its thundering roar reverberating like an avalanche.

"Oh shit," Patrick whispered.

Gary couldn't make words. The abject terror that coursed through his body left him unable to do more than shudder a string of fractured syllables. He pulled his arm in, to protect it. A warm, dark stain spread across his crotch.

Patrick held out the vial of Zom-Be-Gone. "Gary. Take this." Gary looked at him, confused. "Take it!" He shoved the vial into Gary's numb fingers. "And now run, as far as you can—that way," he said, pointing west. "Away from the boat and away from the dam. It'll follow your scent. Go as far as you can, for as long as you can. When the bear gets close enough, pull the cork and dump the liquid. Got it?"

Gary stared at him with dumbfounded eyes. "Close *enough?*" he asked. The bear was close now.

Very close.

"Goddammit, Gary—just do it!" Patrick cried. He shoved Gary in the right direction, then he turned and headed south. *Everyone was right,* he thought as he sprinted down the valley. *This was not a good plan.*

He glanced back over his shoulder, glad to see that Gary had managed to actually move, at least. He disappeared into the trees, and Patrick wished him all the luck in the world. He was going to need it. Because the bear that pummeled the earth beneath its stone-solid paws didn't waste a beat changing trajectory to follow the smell of Gary's blood into the forest.

The bear was only twenty seconds behind, and closing the gap fast; he'd be on Gary any moment. *Move,* Patrick urged himself. *Or you're going to die.*

He pushed himself down the trail, his lungs burning, lactic acid setting fire to his muscles. It occurred to him to wonder how someone so out of shape had fared so reasonably well in post-apocalyptic times, but this wasn't the best time to dwell on such questions. So he pushed the thought deep down into his brain and ran for his life instead.

Suddenly, the entire forest shook with the angry roar of the duster bear. It was an earth-trembling growl of frustration, and Patrick felt just a bit lighter, knowing Gary had done his job, distracting the bear for a handful of precious seconds. *Attaboy, Gary,* Patrick thought.

He forced the sense of relief into his legs, and it gave him a burst of speed that almost sent him tumbling head over heels down the trail. The extra push was good; if Patrick was right, the bear's next move would be to chase down its consolation snack.

He didn't have to turn to look behind him to see if he was right. He heard the bear explode from the forest and thunder down the path behind him.

Keep not looking, keep not looking, he urged himself. *Goddammit, this is the dumbest thing I've ever done…please, please keep not looking.*

But he couldn't handle the terror of the uncertainty, so he did the new dumbest thing he'd ever done, which was to look back over his shoulder.

The bear was coming after *him.*

It was farther away than it sounded, which was good. But it was running like it had a V8 engine, and it was gaining ground fast. The animal's black fur was matted with dirt and blood; a chunk of flesh on its tan nose had been torn off at some point, giving its snout a blood-chilling skeletal look. One of its ears had been bitten off; a bone stuck out through its fur near the back hip, but it didn't seem to register. Thick drool spilled from its mouth, and when it roared, pints of the stuff poured out and spilled onto its powerful chest. The creature was twice as large as any bear Patrick had seen at the zoo, as if the Monkey dust were an ooze from Dimension X that had mutated him into a hellish Rahzar-bear hybrid from *Teenage Mutant Ninja Turtles: Curse of the Jamaican Apocalypse*.

Even at this distance, Patrick could see the hunger in the bear's eyes.

Shouldn't have done that, he sighed to himself as he refocused on the ground ahead. His worn-out sneakers, the same shoes he wore when he left Chicago two years ago, flapped dejectedly against the soles of his feet. He felt every stick, every rock, every crack and crevice as he sprinted down the hill. The adrenaline forced his nerves to bury their pain to keep him running on; otherwise, he'd have stopped, and if he stopped, he would be ripped apart by the dagger-claws of a chemically-modified super-bear.

His heart pounded. It skipped every other beat. It wasn't used to this. It was going to burst.

Any second now, Patrick's heart was going to literally explode.

"Too many cans of beans," he wheezed as he turned to follow the curve of the lake.

And then, breaking through a narrow line of trees, he saw it: The Jamie Whitten Lock and Dam.

Shit, he thought. *I'm not going to make it.*

The bear was hot on his tail. Patrick threw himself forward, ignoring the fire, the magma that had spread through his body and had turned it into a disjointed pile of animated noodles. The bear crashed into the trees behind him, smashing them clear off their roots, sending them flying. Three-hundred-year-old sour gums were hurled into the river, skidding like stones, and half-sinking in the upended waves.

More trees slammed to the earth, one of them hitting hard just a few feet to Patrick's right. The best thing to do, he realized, was to stop running. Stop hurdling trees. Stop shaking himself into unstable atoms with fear.

Just stop, he thought. *It'll be over fast.*

Patrick gave into his exhaustion. His legs slowed.

He closed his eyes.

"*Oh, be serious,*" Ben groaned. "*You're going to stop now? Really? Then what was any of this for?*"

Patrick opened his eyes. He was standing at the southern edge of Lincoln Park, staring down the empty, cold corridor of skeletal trees, their bare branches stretching out into the yellow-green mist, bare even though it was spring. Late spring, if Patrick's notebook could be trusted. There should have been way more leaves on every branch. But the Monkey dust had blotted out the sky like an Old Testament plague, and where there were leaves, they were small, delicate, and uncertain about whether or not to try life in this awful new world.

"This was for me to realize how stupid this is," Patrick frowned. "Apparently."

But Ben shook his head. "Absolutely not. Nuh-uh." He trudged into the park, and Patrick reluctantly followed. "You brought me all the way to Lincoln Park—Lincoln Park—which is a place I didn't like to go when the world was normal, because it had way too many rich idiots, and it's somehow even more depressing than that now, since everyone on the planet is dead, and we risked our literal lives to get here, because the only reason we made it past Clark and Division is because you hiccupped and the fucking Warriors cosplay nerds got scared of a sound and ran away. You brought us up here, you can't possibly want to call it off."

"It's just—look at this place," Patrick said, gesturing out at the park. "It's like someone pulled the skin off of all the trees and left their skeletons behind."

"Oh my God, are you scared of trees?"

"No, Ben, I'm not scared of trees."

"Guy survives the apocalypse, but can't bear the sight of trees."

"I'm not scared of trees!" Patrick insisted, stomping off toward the lake.

Ben hurried after him. "Well, you've got something going on that makes you hate jokes," he said. "And something that makes you want to give up as soon as we get to where we're going." He caught up with Patrick and buried his hands in his pockets. They trundled through the brown grass as Ben asked, "What's going on with you?"

Patrick raised his head to the dismal sky, breathing in deeply through his nostrils. His eyes were creek beds, trembling before the break of a dam. "Tomorrow is Izzy's birthday."

Ben raised an eyebrow. "Already?"

Patrick shrugged. "I think I'm counting the days right. If I am, it's tomorrow." He stopped walking. He knitted his fingers together behind his neck. The first few trickles of water filled his eyes. Memories of mylar balloons and princess cakes and bouncy houses and bubble machines spun through his mind like a storm. "She'll be seven." He stopped. He lowered his head. He pressed the heels of his palms to his eyes. He corrected himself. "She would have been."

Ben frowned and patted Patrick on the back, gripping his shoulder and patting his back again, confused about how best to comfort his friend.

"I don't know what to do here," he confessed miserably. "Jesus Christ, this is sad."

Patrick sniffled and raised his head. His cheeks were marked by slick channels where tears had dampened into his dry skin. He didn't see the sense in words, so he just nodded.

"Pat…what're we doing out here? We should be home…doing something to celebrate…putting up weird crayon signs or making a gross cake out of beans and old t-shirts or something. Why are we here?"

Patrick closed his eyes. "I thought we'd find some——" His voice cracked. He cleared his throat and started again. "I thought we'd find some heart-shaped leaves," he said.

"Yeah. I know," Ben said. "You said, 'Let's go to the park and find some heart-shaped leaves,' and I said, 'What, are you serious?' and you said, 'Yeah, it'll be fine,' and I said, 'Why in God's name would I risk my life for leaves?' and you said, 'It's important,' and I thought you meant, like, we could use them to make medicine or some shit, but I'm starting to think that's not true," he added, crossing his arms.

"What about my background would make you think I know how to make medicine out of leaves?" Patrick asked with a sigh.

"I don't know," Ben shrugged. "You use to use the internet."

Patrick slipped his hands back into his pockets and resumed his slow ambling across the park, just to feel the movement. "When she turned three, we went to a park for her birthday. She got a ton of presents, and she played with them all, but after a while, she toddled off away from the pavilion, away from everybody, away from the party. She walked over to this tree and reached down and picked up a leaf it had dropped. This heart-shaped leaf. She sat down right in the wet grass and she just stared at this leaf with the sweetest smile on her face. It must've been ten minutes she sat there, just smiling at this leaf, waving it around, talking to it. All these other kids are playing with her toys and throwing themselves around the playground, and she's sitting quietly alone with her leaf. I eventually went over, and she looked up at me and smiled and said, 'It's a love leaf!' She thought the tree had given it to her for her birthday. She loved that love leaf more than any of the toys she'd gotten. And there were some very expensive toys," he added. "Every year after that, she wanted love leaves for her birthday. She wanted other things too— Paw Patrol and princess and Spider-Man stuff. But she also wanted love leaves. Twelve love leaves, specifically."

"Why twelve?" Ben asked, padding quietly alongside.

"Twelve was her favorite number."

"Twelve isn't anyone's favorite number."

Patrick smiled. "It was Izzy's."

"Why?"

"It's how many eggs come in a carton."

Ben laughed. "Sorry, what?"

"I have no idea," Patrick shrugged. "She didn't even like eggs. But man, she loved those cartons."

"She was so weird," Ben said.

Patrick nodded. "The weirdest." He sniffled and gave his head a shake. "I thought maybe we'd find twelve love leaves today. I didn't figure it'd be like…" He gestured at the scraggly branches around them. "…like this, with the trees all dead. I haven't been paying attention." He slapped Ben's arm with the back of his hand. "Come on. Let's go home."

But Ben shook his head. "Fuck that," he glowered. "We came out here for love leaves, and goddammit, we're not going home without love leaves."

"So you want to never go home."

Ben scoffed. "After the work I've put into that old lady's apartment? After I swung from the roof and crashed through a window to get it?! Oh, no, we're going back. We're going back hard. I'm going to die in that apartment. But we're not going home yet."

"We're not going to find the leaves," Patrick insisted.

"We can do anything we put our stupid minds to," Ben countered. "Listen to me: The worst and hardest thing that you could ever experience, you've already experienced. Life doesn't get darker or more fucked-up than it got on M-Day, especially for you. What you lost…that's the worst thing that could possibly happen. Do you understand that? There is nothing worse than that. And you made it through, so now every other hard thing is only annoying."

Patrick shrugged. "I wouldn't say I've made it through."

"Well, you're making it through, at least. If you can do that, you can do anything."

"I can't make leaves grow."

Ben agreed. "Probably not. Your track record with nature is well-documented." He gripped Patrick by the shoulders and turned him until they were face to face. "But you have accidentally led us to the only living tree in the entire city of Chicago."

Patrick gasped. Standing there, across the park, on the other side of the lagoon, was a tall Eastern Redbud, its branches ruffled with small, purple buds and limbs fringed with huge, green, healthy heart-shaped leaves.

"Oh my God," Patrick choked. His legs began to wobble, and he sank down to his knees. Then he lowered his face to the dry grass, and he cried.

Ben knelt down beside him. "Giving up is bullshit," he said, squeezing Patrick's shoulder. "We go forward. And we make motherfucking magic."

Patrick lifted his head from the grass. Ben faded away, and Lincoln Park faded with him, replaced by the forest.

He was exhausted. His legs felt like twigs, brittle and ready to snap. His chest was on fire, and it felt like someone was digging into his ribs with a bowie knife. Going further was impossible.

But it still wasn't as hard as losing Annie and Izzy.

"We go forward," Patrick snarled.

He pushed the last bits of his energy into his feet, willing them to take him forward. The bear swiped down at him from behind, and the tips of its claws just barely clipped Patrick's left shoulder blade. Patrick heard his shirt rip and felt trickles of blood pour down his back. But he didn't feel the pain—*couldn't* feel the pain. Not yet.

That'll come soon enough, he knew. For now, adrenaline was on his side, and he let it surge through him.

The dam was in sight.

He leapt over a narrow ravine, a split in the bluff that was an easy jump. But the bear was blinded by its anger and plunged its great paw straight into the crack in the earth. The animal lost balance and gave a screaming roar as it twisted and crashed into the ground.

Patrick didn't look back. By the time the bear had picked itself up, he was rounding the curve of the lake, and suddenly his sneakers were beating against the concrete walkway in front of the dam. The building was on the far end of the walkway, past the lock. There were still a few hundred feet to go, and the bear was back on its feet, moving faster than ever.

Even so, a smile crept across Patrick's lips.

He was going to make it.

He threw himself into the last sprint, flying on a current of exhaustion and exhilaration. The bear hit the concrete, its claws scraping against the hard surface just as Patrick sprinted past the lock. He could feel the hot breath of the bear on the open wound on his back.

But he was going to make it.

Just one last push.

There was a stack of crates piled up next to the building. With the last ounce of energy he could summon, Patrick leapt up onto the boxes, then lurched himself up toward the roof. He gripped the edge and hauled himself over the top of the building as the bear smashed full-speed into the wall below. It broke open, and the bear crashed through it, into the pirate lair. The air was suddenly full of screams as the angry bear dove into the building and tore through the people inside. The wall buckled; the ceiling began to fall away. Patrick rolled toward the center as the whole roof shifted and broke apart. He pushed himself to his knees and scrabbled to the far side, catching quick glances at the bloody confusion below. Streaks of brown fur and bright-red blood flashed through the widening gaps in the buckling structure. The bear hurled itself around the bunker, slamming into the walls, cracking the struts, smashing the concrete to pieces, bringing the whole building down on the people inside.

Patrick scrambled to the far side of the roof and threw himself over the edge, down into the water on the other side of the dam. He plunged into the shock of the cold river. Water filled his lungs. Darkness seeped into him.

And everything went quiet.

51.

Something coarse ground against Patrick's face. It pulled him from the black well of his unconsciousness like a fishing line yanked to the shore. He lurched upward, shocked, confused, and cold. His mouth was full of pebbles and sand; he pushed them out with his tongue. They dribbled out through his lips and onto the sandbar.

The water came next. His lungs were full of fluid, and he fell into a vomiting fit, spitting up brown lake sludge and retching his own bile with it. He collapsed again, heaving onto the ground, the freezing cold water of the Tenn-Tom biting at his ankles and sending spider legs of numbness up his limbs.

How long had he been unconscious—hours? Days? There was nothing in his memory but what felt like years and years of cold, quiet darkness.

He pushed himself over onto his back, desperate to relieve the pressure on his lungs. He let his head fall to the side. He squinted into the gray light.

Based on what he saw, he'd only been out for a few seconds.

The concrete cabin that sat atop the dam was still upright, but just barely. The walls looked like they'd been hit by mortar shells; people inside were still screaming. The roar of the bear made what was left of the roof shake…and then the supports gave up the ghost, and the rest of the ceiling caved in, crushing the life out of whichever cannibals hadn't already been ripped to shreds by the angry animal.

The roof's collapse put too great a pressure on the foundation of the dam itself, which had already been rocked by the fury of the bear. As the entire cabin crumbled, the dam beneath it cracked. Water sprayed through the fissures, just a little at first, in thin streams, then more and more as the cracks split wider. Soon, the entire dam was spouting mist and white foam like a overfilled teapot at a full boil.

The bear thrust up from the concrete wreckage, its fur matted with gore and dust. Its snout was smeared with blood. It bellowed into the air, a deep, primal roar of triumph. Then it pulled itself out of the rubble with its powerful paws and bounded off into the forest, leaving a trail of thunder and carnage in its wake.

Jesus, Patrick thought, turning his head so he could heave up another flood of water and bile. He wiped his mouth with the back of his hand. *What did I do?*

The cracks in the dam split out to the edges, and the whole wall shattered into a thousand pieces of concrete and rebar as the entire force of Bay Springs Lake exploded into the lock. The surge of water flooded the valley, swamping the banks ten feet high, crashing over Patrick and pulling him down into the water again. He groaned as the water crushed his chest, threw him down into the depths of the mad tidal wave, and scraped him against the bottom of the river. Then it pulled him up again and spun him into a whirling current of white-capped lake and yellow-dusted air. His head surfaced as he gulped down air before he was pulled back down and swept away by the roar of the water.

The flood wave was so powerful, it smashed the Highway 4 bridge to pieces and kept on rolling. The cement and steel might have been made of spun sugar, the way they dissolved into nothingness from the force of the water.

It was another three hundred yards at least before the overrun slid Patrick to the shore and let him be, with his body wrecked, his lungs soaked, his muscles unwound, and his skull shaking. His chest still held water; he could feel it gurgle every time he took a breath. He was deep in pulmonary aspiration. His blood wasn't getting enough oxygen; his brain was fighting for consciousness and fading fast. He didn't have the energy to pull himself further up the bank. He didn't have the energy to cough. He was the closest to death he'd ever been.

He was too overcome to have any feelings about it. His brain was struggling simply to make connections.

His eyes felt heavy. He was so tired...

He turned his head to see a slice of the water rushing behind him. The water was tinged red with blood, and the corpses of so many pirates bobbed by, some of them intact, but most of them in snarled, stringy pieces.

He wasn't sure how to feel about any of that, either.

The lake was a frothing, churning chaos.

Water was flooding through the newly opened gap, and the lake was emptying into the basin, pulling all the boats downstream along with it like bath toys in a tub with the water circling the drain. Gary had hobbled back to the Big Muddy Queen and had told the crew what had happened. They had stoked the fires, pulled the anchor, and steamed toward the dam.

But they'd only just made it out of their cove when the dam broke.

The water surged past them, slamming against the boat. The passengers cried out as the ship was spun around, dragged forward by the suction of the water. "*Roman!*" Carla screamed, gripping onto the second deck's railing.

"*Hold on!*" Roman yelled back. His body was lodged against the starboard corner of the stern, the veins in his arms straining with his iron-tight hold on the railings as the steamboat twisted and bucked atop the violent tow. The Big Muddy Queen was dragged down the lake, its bow tipping dangerously. If the front railing hit water, or if the Queen spun to its broadside, the whole boat would tip, and every human on board would be sucked into the lake. The only thing keeping the boat from being ripped apart was the paddle wheel, which provided a stable drag that eased the pressure on the rest of the boat, just enough.

But they were still heading toward the broken dam, with chunks of concrete and rebar jutting up through the water like crude and monstrous spike strips, ready to tear the hull to pieces.

"*Get ready!*" Roman shouted against the roar of the water. The Red Caps huddled together near the stern, locking their arms and clinging to the railing. Carla lost her footing and hit the floor of the upper deck, smashing her chin on the wood. She groped blindly for something to hold onto. A hand seized her wrist, and she looked up to see Ella, holding onto her with one hand and holding tightly to the anchor chain with the other. Carla barked out a cry of relief. Ella looked at her solemnly and shook her head. "Not salvation," Ella said.

Carla's face sank, and so did her heart.

And then the boat hit the dam.

The whole structure crunched and rocked. Ella lost her grip, and Carla went sliding away down the tilting deck, slamming into the railing and bruising her ribs. She gasped for air, and the boat buckled. Ella went sliding off in the other direction, out of sight behind the cargo boxes. The Queen was hit from behind by a surge of water that ramped up over the concrete fingers. The craft scraped over the barrier, then tilted down and dropped ten feet, crashing clumsily into the water below. The bow hit first, threatening to tip the boat, but the weight of whatever was left of the paddle wheel set the stern falling back to the water. The ship landed with a bone-shaking crash, wobbled a bit, then settled into survival, though it seemed to sag from exhaustion as it steadied on the water before following along in the wake of the downstream pull.

"*Clear!*" Roman's voice rang from the lower deck. "Roll call!"

Carla stumbled clumsily to her feet, every bit of her body trembling, her hands slipping their grip on the railing, her feet trembling on the water-soaked deck. "Carla!" she shouted.

One by one, the calls went up from around the boat. *Ella. Lucia. Richie. Jimmy. Ted. Brett. Gary.*

All were accounted for.

All but one.

"Someone get upstairs and steer this thing," Roman shouted as he scanned the waters. Lucia scrambled up from the floor of the deck where she'd been taking cover and headed up toward the cabin. Finally, Roman spotted what he was looking for. "There! Starboard!" he yelled, leaning over the railing, pointing at a body floating in the drift. "Someone grab Patrick and see if he's still alive."

52.

Brett hauled Patrick's body over the railing and threw it down onto the deck. It landed with a heavy, wet *WHUMP*.

"He's dead," Brett announced.

Richie gasped. Carla dug her nails into Ella's arm.

The whole group formed a ring around Patrick's lifeless body. "Fuck me," Gary grunted.

"I'm not dead," Patrick wheezed. He rolled over onto his side and coughed up a few liters of river water. "And someone tell Gary, I'm saving myself for marriage."

The whole boat exhaled. Jimmy slapped Brett's shoulder with the back of his hand. "What?" Brett shrugged. "He looked dead."

"Well, hot damn!" Roman said, beaming proudly. He strode up to the wet Patrick lump and dropped to one knee. He put his hands on Patrick's shoulders and squeezed them gently, his eyes going misty. "What in the ever-loving hell was that?"

"Drug bear," Patrick said, his eyes closed tightly. Every bone in his body felt like a piece of elastic, overstretched and loose. He tasted fish, and his shoulder blade was on fire with a river of lava. "I need a doctor."

Jimmy was already laying out some sort-of clean bandages next to Patrick's prostrate body. "You need a psychologist. What were you thinking?" he tutted. He shooed the others away. They reluctantly withdrew, giving the EMT space to work.

"Had to draw it away from the boat," Patrick groaned.

"You could have thrown a fish into the woods instead."

"Sure," Patrick said. "Where was that idea an hour ago?"

"The boat's in pretty bad shape," Jimmy updated him. "We got dragged over the concrete wreckage of whatever you did up there. Cracked the hull in a few places, they said. Lucia's down there right now, trying to patch it up, at least enough to carry us for another day or two." Jimmy eased Patrick up onto his side and inspected the claw marks. They were deep. Too deep. "Looks like we'll need to stitch you up again."

"Don't use shoelaces," Patrick grumbled.

"I think Roman has some fishing line."

"Thank God."

Jimmy set to work, cleaning Patrick's wounds and checking him for internal damage. He had Richie go and fetch the fishing line and a hook. Jimmy tied the line to the hook and slid a branch between Patrick's teeth. "Sorry about this," he sighed. Then he sewed up the claw marks while Patrick screamed into the wood.

Darkness pulled him under long before the job was finished. When the stitches were set, Jimmy and Brett carried a softly snoring Patrick into the cabin and laid him across his nest.

Patrick didn't stir. He didn't shift. He didn't dream.

He sank into a black space as thick as cold tar, not concerned in the least if he'd ever resurface.

53.

A stiff hand plunged into the heavy oil of slumber and grabbed Patrick by the arm, yanking him back to the surface.

"What?!" Patrick screamed, bolting upright. Roman raised his hands and backed away, alarmed by the speed and intensity of Patrick's waking. Patrick was confused. He was on the boat. It was bright outside. How much time had passed—hours? Days? Minutes?

"How long?" he asked through a dry, cottony mouth.

"Hard to say. Eighteen hours?" Roman guessed. "Seems like you needed it. And sorry to wake you. But we have a situation." He offered his hand.

Patrick blinked the sleep out of his eyes, and he fought to push the exhaustion in his joints down deep into his bones so he could spread the burden across his whole body. He'd somehow slept for an entire day, had missed the nighttime completely, and was back up with the sun bright, but not as high as it had been when he'd laid down. And he felt as tired as ever. He took Roman's hand and let himself be pulled up to his feet. His head spun, his shoulder blade ached, and his left arm felt half-dead.

"We've been making good time," Roman reported. "We made it through the Tenn-Tom and hit the Tombigbee River sometime last night. And now we're almost at the next checkpoint."

"The one we don't know anything about," Patrick remembered groggily.

"We know it's a few hundred yards away," Roman frowned. "And there's something else…"

Patrick raised an eyebrow. He trudged out of the cabin, clumsy with sleep. He pushed through the door and stepped out onto the deck, shuffling toward the front of the boat, scratching the sleep from his eyes. Then he looked up and saw the bridge, down on the horizon. "Oh."

"Yeah," Roman agreed. "'Oh.'"

The highway overpass was built up on a small embankment, but lower than it should have been. With the river newly flooded, the space between the surface of the water and the underbelly of the bridge was fifteen feet at the absolute maximum. There wasn't nearly enough clearance for the Big Muddy Queen to pass beneath. "Honestly, the fact that we've made it this far without hitting a bridge is pretty incredible," Patrick decided.

"People love to blow shit up," Roman said. "Didn't blow this one up, though. So what do you think?"

"Well, I'm not sure I can take it down. I'm fresh out of bears."

"Too bad."

Patrick sighed. "I think we have two options. Option one: stop the boat and abandon ship. Leave it behind, slip off into the wild, and head to the farm on foot."

"Sure," Roman agreed. "Option two?"

"Abandon ship, send it full steam ahead, and see if it hits hard enough to take down the bridge."

Roman raised an eyebrow. "You think it can?"

"Not particularly, no. It's not really even an idea, it's just a variation on option one. Because unless you've got a secret stash of explosives you haven't told me about, either way, this boat isn't making it past that bridge."

Roman nodded. A smile spread slowly across his face. "You know what? I don't hate it," he decided.

"Which one?"

"The one where we ram it all to hell."

Patrick blinked toward the bridge. He rubbed more sleep away from his bleary eyes, until he was pretty sure he could make out the shapes of actual human people standing on top of the bridge. "The boat might take some of them with it," he said.

Roman snorted. "So? They'd do it to us. Look, they've got the waterway roped off." He pointed out the webbing that stretched from shore to shore beneath the bridge. It appeared to be a line of tennis nets tied together. "They're blocking the waterway to do what—loot the boat? Take the women and chop off our heads?" He shook his head. "No. I'm okay with taking them out."

Patrick folded his arms. The bone-weariness was heavy in his body. "We don't know they're planning anything like that."

"You think they're stopping traffic to laud us all with kisses and encouragement?"

"I'm just saying we just don't know what they're doing. We don't know who they are, and we don't know what they're doing."

"Says the man who just led a zombie bear into a cabin full of strangers."

Patrick frowned. "We knew what *they* were doing; we saw it. And the bear sort of forced my hand."

"Listen," Roman said. "You've lived through this apocalypse the same as all of us. It shouldn't have to be a shoot first, ask questions later world. But it is. That's how we survive. That's how we *have* survived."

"True," Patrick conceded. "But I think you gave me another idea. How do you feel about a third plan?"

"I get the sense I won't love it quite as much."

"Let me off the boat here— Carla, too. Let us walk down and scope it out. See if we can see what they're about before we try to kill them."

Roman deliberated, bobbing his head slowly back and forth. "Why put in the time? We might as well just leave the boat, take option one."

"Sure," Patrick agreed. "But something tells me you're set on mutual destruction."

Roman couldn't help but smile. "I do love an adventure."

"So let me at least check it out," Patrick said. "You turn on the special effects, get the smoke going, light the fires. Take some of Richie's blood out of his body and smear it on the boat. But let me go in first, yeah? We don't have to be the people good people are afraid of."

Roman frowned. "Okay," he said. "Go tell Carla. We'll get you to shore so you can see what you can see."

Patrick extended his hand. Roman gripped it. They shook. "Thank you," Patrick said.

"I should be thanking *you*," Roman countered. "Humanity isn't what it used to be."

"No. But maybe someday."

Roman exhaled. "Yeah. Sure."

54.

"Thanks for making me a part of this," Carla said sourly. "I hated the warm safety of the boat."

"That boat's not so safe," Patrick insisted. "I went down below decks. It looks like Swiss cheese down there."

"Thanks for that, by the way."

"Hey—I didn't tell you to get swept over a bunch of jagged wreckage."

"No, you just produced the wreckage and caused the current that swept us over it."

"It's a subtle difference," Patrick acknowledged.

"Also, the hull doesn't look like Swiss cheese. It looks like Swiss cheese with tape over the holes."

"I think you'll find that on a surprisingly short timeline, the difference is irrelevant."

They trundled along the riverbank, advancing cautiously toward the bridge. They'd left their bags on the boat, opting for lightness over utility in case they had to make a quick retreat. But Patrick held his machete and Carla had her crossbow slung over her shoulder, with a few extra bolts in one hand. "So we're just going to walk right up to it?" she asked, biting her lip nervously.

"We can try to sneak if you want," Patrick replied. "But I'm pretty sure they clocked us before we got off the boat."

Carla looked up at the bridge. There were three people standing there, all with binoculars held up to their eyes and pointing directly at her and Patrick.

"Oh."

"Just be ready to run," Patrick said.

Carla nodded. "Yep, yep. Just another day…"

They closed in on the bridge, projecting confidence, feeling exhaustion. The three figures huddled together and had a quick conversation. They seemed to agree on something, their heads all nodding excitedly. All three of them reached back behind their necks in unison and lifted hoods over their heads.

"Are they wearing robes?" Carla asked.

"There's nothing wrong with robes," Patrick replied. "I'd give anything for a robe right now."

They stepped into the shadow of the bridge and stopped, uncertain of the next move. They started discussing their options, but ultimately, the three figures on the bridge made the decision for them; one of them raised a hand in a sign of welcome, then crossed to the end of the bridge with their arm outstretched and started stumbling down the embankment.

Patrick tightened his grip on the machete; Carla dropped the crossbow off her shoulder and into her hand in one smooth motion.

The figure drew closer, stumble-sliding down the loose earth, shuffling and working hard to stay upright. They seemed determined to keep the welcoming hand in the air, making a generally very awkward show of it all. The hood was much larger than it needed to be, and the man wearing it couldn't see the ground beneath his feet. The stumbling gave way to slipping, and the slipping became a tumbling, and suddenly he was flailing down the embankment, screeching in surprise. His arms pinwheeled as his body dragged a rut in the earth. He came to a skidding stop at Patrick's feet.

The two other figures on the bridge above began to clap. "Extraordinary grace!" cried one. "Well done, Brother Wildgardyn!"

Patrick closed his eyes. He put his hand to his head. "Oh no," he muttered.

"What?" Carla asked.

Patrick pinched the bridge of his nose. "We should have rammed the bridge."

The man on the grass lurched upward, and the hood flopped backward, off of his head. "Great Centralizer around!" he screeched, hopping from one foot to another. "Brother Patrick! Is that you?!"

"No," Patrick said miserably.

"It is!" cried one of the other monks from the bridge overhead. "It is, it is! It is Brother Patrick, of the Order Patri-Benicus!" Patrick was incredibly dismayed to learn that he instantly recognized the voice of Brother Triedit.

"Gasp!" said Brother Haffstaff, pronouncing the world as he slapped his hands to his cheeks. "Brother Patrick! How full are your bazoombas?!"

Carla stared at Patrick, bewildered. "Bazoombas?" she asked.

"The mammaries!" Brother Wildgardyn said helpfully. "You know." He gestured in circles toward his own chest. "The boobulars."

Patrick placed his hands on his hips, rolled his head back on his neck, and looked up at the sky, silently begging for a god— *any* god—to strike him dead on the spot. "I don't have boobulars."

"Improbable!" Brother Triedit shouted. "The centerwine flowed into you and through your mammarian corpuscles! Surely you have felt its effects!"

"Show us your mams!" Brother Haffstaff encouraged.

"Shall I investigate your mams?" Brother Wildgardyn inquired happily, rubbing his hands together in excitement.

Carla raised her hands and took two steps backward. "What is happening?"

"A reunion!" Brother Triedit said happily. "Our long-lost brother is returned to us! Brother Haffstaff, this calls for a celebration! Go forth and find ye a frog to milk!"

"Do not find a frog to milk!" Patrick yelled.

"I *certainly am* going to find a frog!" Brother Haffstaff cried gleefully, skipping across the bridge and into the field beyond.

Patrick turned to Carla and jabbed his finger into the center of his forehead. "I will give you one thousand dollars if you shoot me with an arrow right here, right now. I'm not kidding. One thousand dollars."

Carla shook her head in stunned amazement. "Who *are* these people?"

"That is Brother Wildgardyn!" Brother Triedit shouted down from above. "He likes chamomile tea now! And I am Brother Triedit. We are but humble servants of the Post-Alignment Brotherhood, and I have the honor of serving as Holy Father. We aim to adulate the Great Centralizer, so that we may be worthy of the transmutation of our current selves into the femalular sex so that we might procreate and spread the Word of the Aligned into future generations."

"I feel the urge to adulate right now," Brother Wildgardyn wailed, "but I haven't prepared a totem!"

"There, there, Brother Wildgardyn! I shall adulate in your name." Brother Triedit reached into his robe pocket and pulled out a hawk feather, holding it up to the sky. "I adulate the Great Centralizer with this fallen remnant of a raptor, which I furtively plucked from a fallen bird's nest on my semi-regular morning traipse." He stuck the tip of the feather between his teeth and ripped off the edge with his incisors. Then he spat the separated fluff into the air and said, "Nom!" as he bit off a second piece, then a third piece, then a fourth, eventually destroying the entire feather and spitting each bite with a "Nom! Nom! Nom!" When he was left with just an inch of the feather's stem, he stuck it into one nostril, pinched the bridge of his nose, and exhaled sharply, shooting the little tube out into the river. "In Its Name, I adulate."

"Oh, *very* well done, Brother Triedit!" Brother Wildgardyn exclaimed, clapping like a maniac. Tears came to his eyes, and he wept. "It is such an honor to be in the presence of your light."

"*Oo-mee-kar-ohh Nahm-ee-toos,*" Brother Triedit said gratefully, with a bow.

"*Mar-so dey-lo Tohm-ih-nay,*" Brother Wildgardyn replied, drying his eyes on his robe.

"How in God's name do you know these people?" Carla muttered to Patrick, not taking her eyes off of Brother Wildgardyn. She tightened her grip on the crossbow.

"They ate my buffalo," Patrick bristled.

Carla blinked. "Your what?"

"And you!" Brother Triedit said, interrupting them. "What is your name, femalular consort of Brother Patrick? Are you also with the Order of Patri-Benicus?"

Carla lifted the business end of the crossbow. "I'm Carla. And if you try to touch me, I'll put a bolt through your dick."

"Gasp!" Brother Wildgardyn said again. He approached Carla slowly, holding his hands up to prove he was no threat. His eyes searched her face intensely and some kind of understanding dawned on him. "Is it you, Brother Ben?!"

"*Brother Ben!*" Brother Triedit screamed. "*You have been transmuted! Oh, Great Centralizer around! You have transmuted our dear consort! Its Will Hath Been Done!* Brother Haffstaff! Come back! Come quick! Brother Ben has grown such small but interesting mammulars!"

"Hey!" Carla shouted.

"Brother Haffstaff—come see, come see! Oh, we *must* prepare a feast! A great feast of celebration, with spotted clams and twiggy noodles! And once we have supped, in honor of the Great Centralizer's grace, we shall all copulate with New Ben!"

"Oh, just you *fucking try it,*" Carla seethed, her eyes flashing dangerously.

Patrick had heard enough. He turned back upriver and cupped his hands around his mouth. "Roman!" he yelled. "Ram the bridge; you were right!" He waved his arms wildly. "Ram the bridge!"

"Oh, I *do* love how your hormones rage!" Brother Triedit gushed. "Please don't despair, Brother Patrick. Our order prohibits the drinking of centerwine beyond our friary borders, but even some frog's blood alone, without the boysenberry, and you'll evolve just as Brother Ben has done!"

Patrick exploded. "Look, she is *obviously* not Ben, you absolute lunatics! She's like four inches taller, she actually has hair, and she's clearly a woman who looks nothing like Ben—and *is* obviously *not at all* Ben!"

Brother Wildgardyn stepped back. He inspected Carla more fully, analyzing her whole structure. "It's true," he breathed. "This femaluar being is a radically different shape than Brother Ben, if my poor memory doth serve. The bone structure is maybe quite different." Finally, he nodded, satisfied. "The Great Centralizer works in mysterious ways. He has made you wonderful, Brother Ben. Your new form is a wonder."

Carla looked at Patrick. "Can I shoot him in the dick?"

"Please do."

"Wait!" Brother Haffstaff burst back onto the bridge, out of breath. In his hands he held a bored, fat bullfrog, its legs dangling below his fists. "Brother Triedit! If I may!"

"You may, dear brother! *Ohm-lay kar-say dom-lee-ayy.*"

"*Tar-koh lar-moh somlee-ay,*" Brother Haffstaff replied through labored breaths. "This person claims to be Brother Ben—"

"I do not!"

"—But might it not be a devilish trick of Toomralan?"

"Gasp!" said Brother Triedit.

"Gasp!" said Brother Wildgardyn, louder.

"You would intone the name of the evil mage?!" Brother Triedit demanded.

"I apologize for my abruptness, and I will confine myself in the mobile Centrification Chamber for atonement." He nodded at an old, slime-covered porta-potty situated just a few dozen yards east of the bridge. "But if this woman is correct, and she is *not* Brother Ben, might we incur the wrath of the Great Centralizer by idolatrizing her?"

"Brother Triedit!" Brother Wildgardyn called up from below. "I have such faith, but what Brother Haffstaff speaks…it *is* the sort of test that the angry spirit of Toomralan would put against us."

"Oh, for the comfortable protection of our blessed friary!" Brother Triedit wailed. "Toomralan has no such power within the sacred lands of our order!"

"We will return home soon, Brother Triedit!" Brother Haffstaff said encouragingly. "And we are here for very good reason! Your dreams prophesized for us a bridge wherein we would strengthen our numbers—and look!" Brother Haffstaff gestured with the frog toward a pile of sticks in the center of the bridge. Two pairs of legs stuck out from beneath the woodpile. "We have already convinced two lonely males to close themselves in the Cocoon of Imminent Centralization! In just twenty-seven more days, they will increase our numbers by two! You have made great wonders here!"

Brother Triedit began to cry. "I have," he nodded. "I have, and you all have helped."

"I have helped quite insistently!" Brother Wildgardyn chirped from below.

"Yes, brother, you were the *most* insistent when it came to knocking these two men about the head with large sticks to inspire them to consider the Way of the Order."

"And I believe they may yet be alive," Brother Wildgardyn added.

"We must all have faith," Brother Triedit agreed.

"And that faith tells me that we will have two new brothers in but another month," said Brother Haffstaff, "despite the blueish hue of their current ankles."

"I believe these encouraged believers will re-find their breath," Brother Triedit said, wiping tears from his eyes. "Thank you, Brother Haffstaff, for fighting back against the darkness of my doubt. You may now engage in the holy sacrament of Recentralization."

"I will need the use of my hands," Brother Haffstaff remembered. He looked down at the bullfrog. The bullfrog looked out at the world. The creature was really quite bored.

"You must milk his blood!" Brother Wildgardyn reminded him from below.

"I know the process!" Brother Haffstaff retorted. But the Ceremonial Limestone was trapped somewhere under the Cocoon of Imminent Centralization, and it was blasphemous to open a sacred frog with one's teeth. Only the Ceremonial Limestone could be used for this purpose. And it was a mortal sin to disturb a Cocoon of Imminent Centralization during its incubation period, a very serious offense that was punishable by sleeping on a mattress covered in honey for forty nights, which—Brother Haffstaff could attest, having received this punishment once before—was a *much* more agonizing experience than most people expected. Therefore, he was not about to disturb the Cocoon, but nor could he retrieve the bullfrog's blood by any other means. So he did the only rational thing he could do, given his situation: He popped the bullfrog into his mouth and, after a few very challenging tries, swallowed it whole.

"Now," Brother Haffstaff said, blinking back tears, and working *very* hard to hide the suffering his corporeal body was experiencing as it worked to shuttle a fat American bullfrog through his normal-sized American in-

274

nards, "I will Recentralize you, Brother Triedit." He held his hands over Brother Triedit's head. Brother Wildgardyn watched with rapturous attention from the riverbank below. Brother Haffstaff whispered the words of the Recentralization ceremony, a complicated passage of Latsish that he stumbled on a few times, but actually felt pretty good about, on the whole. He reached into his pocket and pulled out a small tool that was given to every member of the Post-Alignment Brotherhood upon acceptance into the order, a colorful plastic food clip. "I do this with a heavy heart, and only with the strength of the Great Centralizer." He lifted Brother Triedit's robes, reached deftly underneath, and snapped the clip onto his scrotum. "I weep with you for the discomfort I am causing to your testicular sack-agery," he whispered sadly, for he well knew the uncomfortable closure of the Realignment clip.

"No," Brother Triedit winced, shifting his weight and trying to make the discomfort lighter. "No, Brother Haffstaff, you have done well in the eyes of the Great Centralizer. I am a fortified man, and I will recentralize very soon, I think. Very, very soon," he added, biting back the pain. "But what of Sister Carla-Ben?"

"Ah! Yes!" Brother Haffstaff said, relieved to be returning to a different subject than the Holy Father's nards. "I believe that we may truly know of their base nature by engaging in a ceremonial bone-steal!"

"A bone-steal!" Brother Wildgardyn cried, clapping his hands. "What a marvelous idea!"

"We haven't had a bone-steal in ages!" Brother Triedit said.

"Not since the early days of the Great Alignment!" Brother Wildgardyn confirmed. "I believe that if we remove the bones of Ben-Carla, we may then engage in a trans-dimensional exploration with the Spirit of the Cosmic Earthworm to determine whether the bone structure is original, or if it was manipulated into its current state."

"Marvelous!" Brother Triedit hollered. He immediately drew in a sharp breath and lowered his arms, patting his nethers gently. "Marvelous," he said again, more quietly. "We shall extract Ben-Carla's entire skeletal structure and send it up to the outer spatial regions of the galaxy in a basket powered by balloons and a Honeywell fan with a very long extension cord, as is prescribed by our sacred texts."

"We shall!" Brother Haffstaff agreed.

"We shall!" Brother Wildgardyn added.

"Brother-Sister Ben-Carla, please come up to the bridge, and lie upon our cocoon of sticks," Brother Triedit said, gesturing magnanimously down to the woman on the riverbank.

But his gesture landed upon an empty spot in the grass. The brothers all turned, confused, wondering where their brethren had gone. It was Brother Haffstaff who eventually spied them, several hundred feet upriver. "There!" he cried, pointing at the two dots that were Carla and Patrick as they boarded their smoking, burning boat. "They have absconded!"

Brother Triedit shook his head sadly. "This is a sad day for the Order of Patri-Benicus," he assured the others. "Brother Patrick has been taken in by the wiles of the evil mage. And that cursed cuss's name is Carla."

Brother Triedit spat. Brother Haffstaff spat. Brother Wildgardyn spat, but his mouth was dry, and the spittle dripped off his chin and dropped onto his robe. "Doggonit," he muttered, scrubbed the spot with his sleeve.

Brother Triedit and Brother Haffstaff turned their attention to the Co-coon. They hoped against hope that the Great Centralizer wouldn't forget to undead their new recruits.

55.

"So...are we going to talk about that?" Roman asked, watching his dearly beloved *Muddy Queen* sail downriver, consumed in flames, burning in gray-black smoke, heading straight for the low-slung bridge.

Patrick glowered. "It's best if we don't."

"They ate his buffalo," Carla explained.

"I'm going to have questions about that later," Roman decided.

The whole crew watched with conflicting emotions as the boat hit the bridge. Lucia had done her best, but the patches in the hull had started to leak. The *Queen* had taken on quite a bit of water, and it was dragging the bottom of the river, so the impact wasn't quite as spectacular as they'd hoped. The front smokestack knocked a few sizeable chunks of concrete out of the overpass, and the whole thing made a terrible groan, but that was basically it. The brothers watched from the other bank and looked dismayed at the mess the whole thing made of their tennis nets. Patrick found a small bit of joy in that.

The impact caused the fire buckets on the main deck to knock over, and it wasn't long before the wood caught fire. The flames spread across the railing, and the smoke emanating from the boat turned black.

"Hey, what happened to the body?" Patrick asked, nodding at the empty air between the smokestacks.

"Oh. I don't know," Roman said. "I guess it must have broken free when we hit the dam."

"Huh."

"Yeah."

"I hope we're not held cosmically accountable for any of that. The body was dead when we got it, after all."

"As we've said."

They watched as the flames roared, spreading across the ship, consuming the rails, the cabin, the hull. It peeled away the paint and melted off the blood; it twisted the *Queen* into an unrecognizable shape, with only the steel of the smokestacks left upright and unbothered by the lake of fire below. For almost an hour they watched the boat burn, until the decks collapsed, the vessel caved in, and the smokestacks crashed down into the river, landing sideways like open storm drains lying atop the Tombigbee banks.

"How far from here to the farm?" Ted asked, staring out nervously at the field that yawned before them in the darkening twilight.

Roman raised a questioning eyebrow at Ella. She glanced up at the setting sun and did some quick mental math. "Less than a hundred miles," she decided. Roman smiled.

"Pretty close, really."

"What kind of land between here and there?" Brett asked.

"Pure Mississippi," Roman replied, rubbing his hands together. "Fields and swamps and rivers and roads."

Richie gulped. "*Dangerous* swamps?" he asked.

"The gators stay mostly south of here," Roman said.

"Mostly?" Richie asked.

"They get erratic sometimes," Roman shrugged. "But, hey! We can handle a bear, we can handle a gator!"

"The bear did most of the handling," Patrick pointed out.

"Absolutely," Roman nodded. "Anyone who'd rather get back on the boat, please feel free." He gestured toward the Big Muddy Queen, which was now little more than a smoldering pile of kindling mounded up in the river.

"Seems easy enough," Patrick admitted, rubbing his hands together, looking each of the Red Caps in the eye, in turn. "The farm is the goal, right? He built something good there. He built something safe. A few more days, hell or high water, we get to see if it's real, or if we've all hitched our wagons to a consumptive horse."

"A consumptive horse?" Ted asked, confused.

"A horse with tubercu—never mind," Patrick waved his hands, clearing the air. "The point is, we're so close. Compared to where we started? We're so close."

"If it's real," Brett reminded him. He glanced at Roman. "No offense," he added, though he didn't sound like he meant it.

"If it's real," Patrick agreed. "Maybe it is, maybe it isn't. If it isn't, we're *still* better off than we were before, on the zombie-fish beach. And if it is? Well, then we can really make something of this world. And it's not just Roman speaking its praises; it's Carla and Ella and Lucia, too."

"It exists," Carla assured them. She lowered her eyes and dug at some dirt beneath her fingernail. "Safest place I've ever been—pre- *or* post-apocalypse, really."

"One hundred miles," Jimmy repeated. "What's that? A four-day walk, maybe five?"

Roman grinned. "Depends on how tired you are," he said. "My crew can do it in three."

"Two," Ella corrected him, staring through the group with her sharp eyes.

"Well, what are we waiting for?" Patrick asked. "The longer we stand here, the greater the chance of the Mammarian Monks over there coming back over and trying to touch our nipples."

"That's very upsetting," Richie said squeamishly, tugging his shirt down to protect his chest.

"Then here we go."

They trudged forward, chasing the sunset, pushing toward the Mississippi border, leaving the Brotherhood to the frogs on the river.

56.

The crew didn't move as quickly as they'd hoped. Everyone was exhausted, physically and mentally, and Gary's arm had gotten so bad that he couldn't take a step without grunting in pain. Jimmy forced them to set up camp after just a few hours so he could do a proper inspection of Gary's wound. When he peeled off the bandages, the air filled with the stench of rotting meat, and everyone in camp had to turn away, because the flesh was so black and putrid. "You'll be all right," Jimmy choked out between gasps for air. He patted Gary's knee, then he scrambled away to find Roman.

"Well?" Roman asked.

Jimmy shook his head. "It's bad. It's very, very bad. It's septic and necrotic. I have to amputate."

"You can't be serious."

"If I don't, he'll be dead tomorrow. It's so far gone, that honestly, even if I *do* remove it, he might *still* be dead tomorrow. I can't tell how far it's advanced. But this needs to happen now if he wants any shot at surviving."

Roman nodded. "Okay. Do it."

Jimmy cleared his throat uncomfortably. "Well, it'll be up to Gary, obviously. I'm sharing this with you as more of a courtesy and because HIPAA can't really be enforced anymore—"

Roman reached up and gripped his fingers around the back of Jimmy's neck, drawing him in close with force. He stared him in the eye and did not blink as he said, "Gary is an asset to this team." He applied more pressure to Jimmy's neck. "Move ahead with the procedure."

Jimmy gulped. "Sure. Makes sense." He ignored the beads of sweat that were rolling down his spine. Roman released him, and Jimmy skittered back over to where Gary lay, coated in sweat and murmuring about sea creatures in the sky. It was almost certainly too late. His forehead was burning hot and the arm was essentially biologically dead. Even so, Jimmy started a fire and laid the blade of his knife in the flames. He was pretty sure it wasn't sharp enough to see the job through. But it was the only knife he had.

"Would this work better?" Jimmy raised his eyes and saw Patrick standing across the fire, holding out his machete.

The entire structure of Jimmy's body collapsed, and he sank, burying his head in his hands, exhausted, helpless, and sad. "You're reading my mind," he said, laughing bitterly, though he didn't know why. He wiped the sweat from his eyes and looked back up at Patrick. "To answer your question...no, actually. Not from a surgical standpoint. Worse, probably. But quicker. And that's going to be the best we can do."

Jimmy reached out as Patrick handed him the machete. Jimmy considered the chipped edge of the metal, running his thumb over the rivets. He frowned at the damage. "You've had this for like two weeks."

"Well, I've been busy."

"It's already kind of dull."

Patrick crossed his arms and glowered. "I lost my knife sharpener in the apocalypse. Do you want it or not?"

Jimmy nodded. "It'll work." He kicked his hunting knife away from the fire and set the machete down in the flames, with the handle resting near his boot.

"Mind if I join you?" Patrick asked. Jimmy motioned for him to sit. Patrick lowered himself onto the night-damp grass and drew his knees up to his chin. "Have you ever done this sort of thing before?"

Jimmy's mouth fractured into a sad grin. "I was an EMT. I mostly took vitals and applied tourniquets. I used a defibrillator a few times. I reset a dislocated shoulder once." He stared into the fire, and his eyes were dark with fear. "No. I've never done this sort of thing before."

Patrick nodded slowly. "Mm-hmm," he said. He tilted his head to one side. He looked at Jimmy. "Did you ever watch *ER*?"

Jimmy frowned. "Like...George Clooney, *ER*?"

"Yeah. George Clooney, Noah Wylie, that Sherry someone who I had a *massive* crush on in middle school."

"Sherry Stringfield," Jimmy nodded. "Boy, there was something about her, wasn't there?"

"She could have set my broken bone, you know what I'm saying?"

"I hate that I do," Jimmy sighed.

"Anyway," Patrick said, waving his hands, "so that's a yes. You watched *ER*."

"Yes, I watched *ER*. Why?"

"Well. There was a later episode where that short, bald, angry doctor got his arm chopped off by a helicopter rotor. Did you see that one?"

"It's coming back to me."

"I don't imagine that's the way that doctor would have preferred his arm to be removed—with a quick chop across the bow—"

"Chop across the bow?" Jimmy interrupted.

"I don't know medical terms," Patrick shrugged. "But that's how it happened, and he ended up fine."

"They reattached his arm."

Patrick's brow furrowed. "They did?"

"For a while," Jimmy nodded. "But it didn't really take, so eventually he had it amputated again."

"See? It all worked out," Patrick said, getting back on track.

"Then he got a new robot arm," Jimmy said sadly. "He used that for a while. Then he got killed by a helicopter that fell off a building."

"Jesus." Patrick frowned. "*ER* really jumped the shark."

"What was your point again?"

"I'm afraid to make it now."

Jimmy stared into the fire. The machete blade was starting to glow. "That was TV. Fiction. This is real life. And even if it had been real, they were in a hospital full of surgeons. We're in Mississippi and there's no one left alive."

"Not entirely true," Patrick said. He shuffled around the fire and crouched next to Jimmy. "*We're* alive. And we do what we can. We do what we have to do, in the way that we can. Gary doesn't have Eriq LaSalle. He has someone better. He has you. Will you be able to give him a robot arm? No. And that will be very disappointing for him. But you care about him, and you're doing your best, and you're absolutely right: Fuck fiction. This is the real world, a fucked-up world, and you're going to fuck him up back to life."

Jimmy stared at Patrick. "I have no idea why those words are as motivating as they are."

"Give in to the process," Patrick said, patting Jimmy's hand. "Now let's go save a man by destroying him substantially."

Brett and Ted carefully carried Gary over to the fire. His skin was slick with sweat. The dank smell of rot wafted up from beneath his bandages, and he was whispering a string of words that none of them could understand.

"Richie, give me your belt," Jimmy said, holding out his hand.

Richie frowned. "But I need my belt."

"I need it more."

"But...my pants will fall off."

"So what?"

"Give him the belt," Brett said, elbowing Richie.

"But my pants will fall off!"

"Gary's *arm* is going to fall off—give him your fucking belt!"

"Okay, okay," Richie said sourly, fumbling with his buckle. He pulled the belt off and tossed it at Jimmy. His pants slipped down over his hips, and he had to bunch them with one hand to keep them up. "I want it back when you're done."

"No, you don't." Jimmy took his knife and punched a new hole in the belt. He carefully tightened it around Gary's arm, just under the shoulder, and cinched it tight. He lifted the arm and rotated it out to the side. "Toss me that can," he said to nobody in particular, nodding at an empty bean can that lay close to the fire. Ted tossed it over, and Jimmy jammed a stick into the can and carefully placed it into the fire. Then he looked at Patrick. "Ready?"

Patrick swallowed. The only thing he was ready to do was vomit in the grass. But Jimmy needed him, so he bit back the urge to puke. "So ready."

Jimmy pulled the machete out of the flames. The blade glowed yellow for a few seconds, then faded to a dull red as it cooled in the late-spring breeze. "Hold him still."

Patrick scooted closer to Gary, pressing a knee against each shoulder, locking his head in place. He put pressure down on Gary's right shoulder. Brett stepped up and pinned Gary's left arm to his side, pressing his weight down on Gary's legs. Roman watched from behind them, chewing nervously on his thumbnail. Carla and Lucia turned their backs and wandered a few yards away. Ella stood next to Roman, expressionless.

"Okay," Jimmy said. His face was as pale as the moon, and his eyes were filled with fear, but his hand was steady. He knelt next to Gary's arm and tore the sleeve open with his teeth. With the bicep exposed, Jimmy placed the edge of the machete against Gary's skin, lining up his swing. "Okay," he said again. He took a deep breath. "Christ. I'm sorry, Gary."

He brought the machete up over his head, then hacked down as hard as he could.

Gary's eyes shot open. His scream filled the air like a hydrogen bomb. His limbs jerked with unexpected strength, and Patrick and Brett bore down with all their weight to keep him still. Blood and gore splattered across the grass as he thrashed, the heels of his boots carving deep grooves in the earth with each desperate kick. "Hold him!" Jimmy yelled. "I'm almost through!" The dull blade had gotten lodged deep in Gary's arm, and Jimmy had to press down with a sawing motion to finish the cut. Gary turned his head and saw the blade and the blood. Then he became still. His eyes rolled up into his head and he fell back into the grass.

"Still alive," Patrick assured Jimmy, watching Gary's chest rise and fall. "Go on. Finish it."

Jimmy yelled as he sawed, working the machete hard. Finally, he broke through and completed the cut. The arm separated. Jimmy tossed it to the side. "The can! Right now!" he snapped at Ted. Ted hoisted the stick with the red-hot tin can out of the fire and handed it to Jimmy. The EMT who was now a makeshift surgeon looked up at Patrick and Brett. "He might wake up," he warned them.

Both men nodded.

Then Jimmy pressed the glowing hot metal to the bleeding stump. The heat cauterized the wound with a loud sizzle, the strangely redolent smell of charred meat filling the air. Gary did wake, briefly; he shot upward and gave one last scream. Then he passed out again. This time, he remained unconscious for the rest of the night.

Jimmy fell back into the grass, out of breath and out of strength. Patrick locked eyes with him and nodded in reverence. "Nice work, Jimmy," he said.

Jimmy nodded back. He didn't have the energy to speak.

"Uh...what do we do with this?" Richie asked, nudging the severed arm with the toe of his shoe.

"Get it out of sight before he wakes up," Patrick said.

The Red Caps drew blades of grass to see who would dispose of the arm. The job fell to Brett. He picked up the arm and carried it off into the woods as easily as if it were a piece of firewood. He was even whistling. But when he came back, he wouldn't say what he'd done with it, or how it had all gone.

He never spoke about it at all.

57.

They waited in place for two days to see if Gary would die.

He woke screaming early the morning after the amputation, and woke everyone else up, too. They'd taken turns watching over him through the night, but Richie nodded off during his shift, and Gary had woken up alone, confused and scared. The whole camp descended on him, doing their best to work through their own bleary heads to calm him, comfort him, make him feel at peace with the revelation that he'd lost an arm without having much say in the matter. That whole day was spent tending to his needs: checking the wound, checking the fever, checking in, checking up—checking to see if he was checking out. He was angry with everyone and furious Jimmy. He was in excruciating pain and he was in absolute denial.

He wavered in and out of consciousness, curing every person he saw with terms most of them hadn't heard since their schooldays, images so visceral and graphic that Richie couldn't stop blushing. The women formed a protective triangle around the camp so the men could deal with Gary's anger. He asked for his arm—he *demanded* his arm— and threatened to cut off all of *their* arms. He raged, he sobbed; he laid quiet as a stone, staring up at the yellow-green sky with fury and hate.

Later that night, his fever broke.

On the second morning, he stood up on his own.

The others called a quick conference and agreed to pack up and move on, all except for Gary, who said they could all go fuck themselves to hell. In the end he tramped along behind them, because there was really nowhere else to go.

The walk to the farm was a weary grind. They were bone-tired, and the thrill of navigating a riverboat down a hellish waterway had evaporated as soon as they'd picked up their gear and stepped off the gangplank. Before, they had been on an adventure; now, their trip was a chore. They moved slowly and quietly, no one much in the mood to speak, with the three women surrounding the Red Caps like mother wolves protecting a sick pack. But the way was easy, at least; they were a big enough group that other survivors scattered like cockroaches when they crossed the horizon, and only twice did they come across settlements that might prove a challenge. These, they skirted by a margin wide enough to make it appear they weren't worth raiding. Even if they *had* been raided, the assailants wouldn't have found much of value—except, of course, the ten vials of Zom-Be-Gone, if they'd even been able to figure out what they were. Roman would have smashed them under the heel of his boot before he let anyone else have them either way.

It was on the fourth day of the journey that Roman started to return to his normal self. He began slapping the boys on their backs, thanking them for their hard work and assistance on the journey, at one point even "discovering" one *actual* last bottle of moonshine in his bag and demanding that everyone take a mouthful. "That's how you know we're close," Carla explained to Patrick, observing Roman's sudden shift in mood.

A few hours later, they crested a high hill, and the ground beneath them opened into a wide, flat valley. A four-lane highway ran through the basin, a busy road at one time, judging by the number of billboards. Their decaying graphics advertised Ole Miss and Pearl River Resort and Hog Heaven BBQ and Beaver Creek Distillery and all sorts of things that had once seemed important for reasons none of them cared to think about. But the highway had been cleared of cars, from the crest of the valley all the way to the horizon, something Patrick hadn't realized would be surprising until he actually saw it…and then he couldn't stop thinking about how unnerving it was. Abandoned cars were part of the white noise of this post-apocalyptic world. Now that someone had clicked off the sound machine, the world felt eerily silent.

There were old farmhouses down in the valley, clapboard buildings that looked like they'd been ruined long before the great ruining of M-Day. They stood next to silos that had fallen over, or were about to, and they all had barns, though each was missing many vertical planks from their wooden walls in the peculiar kind of disappearing-timber malady that only seems to afflict old barns.

The fields had been planted with a patchwork of crops. Patrick saw soybeans, corn, cotton, and wheat, and a few other plants he couldn't readily identify. There were people in the fields, inspecting the plants and aerating the earth, maybe two dozen of them, looking at this distance like aphids prickling their way across the fields. Most of the activity, though, was buzzing around the largest structure in the valley, a sprawling U-Store It with what had to have been more than a hundred storage units. The storage sheds had flaking off-white walls and green roll-up doors. The units around the exterior were shaped like a giant U, with four more back-to-back rows filling in the interior space. There was an office at one end of the lot, a long, narrow building with sheet metal walls. A ten-foot fence surrounded the entire business. It was topped with barbed wire, probably an original feature, with wire mesh electrified using a few dozen car battery jumpers rigged up to just as many generators—*that* feature was definitely a post-M-Day improvement. Fifteen or so people patrolled the outside of the fence, holding crossbows or arrow bows or baseball bats or iron pipes; another thirty or forty people milled around inside the fences, wandering from one storage unit to another, chatting, working, being busy. Being lazy.

Just a few hundred yards beyond the storage unit stood the only house that seemed to have survived the plague of residential neglect. It was an architectural anomaly in this valley spattered with farmhouses: a two-and-a-half story painted lady Victorian, with four gables, an embarrassment of windows, and a rooftop widow's walk atop a four-story tower that stood front and center. Except for the cheery blue and yellow paint, which had been recently refreshed, it looked like Hitchcock's inspiration for the Bates family home in *Psycho*.

"Gentlemen," Roman said, his eyes flashing dangerously as he grinned down at the world below, "welcome to my farm."

58.

"It's no five-star resort," Roman told Patrick, rolling up the door on one of the storage units, "but I think you'll be comfortable here."

A light clicked on when the door reached the top, and Patrick gasped. It was another thing he hadn't really realized he didn't really register anymore—electricity. "Bemme!" he whispered.

Roman smiled with obvious pride. "A few solar fields over the next hill. We buried the lines to hide them from would-be anarchists—and so the dusters wouldn't chew them to shit. We're fully powered here at the Marwood campus."

"This place really is something," Patrick marveled. "I mean, not just this storage unit specifically…although it's a very wonderful storage unit." The tiny shed contained a desk, a working lamp, a small dresser, a rolling chair, a mini-fridge, and a queen-sized mattress fitted with what appeared to be clean sheets. It was by far the nicest room Patrick had set foot in since M-Day. "I mean the whole farm—the storage units, the fields. The house. That's a weird-looking house, though! Is that where you sleep?"

Roman flashed a smile. "The house is a decoy," he explained. "We get more than our fair share of bad actors coming through here and trying to take what we've built by force…which means we spend a lot of time protecting what's ours. One of the ways we do that is with that house. Most people see it and naturally assume it's where we sleep—or at the very least, where *I* sleep. The number of times that house has been raided in the middle of the night…I've lost count. It must be in the dozens."

"Pretty smart," Patrick nodded admiringly. "Though this is an unexpected place for a Haunted Mansion."

"I wanted something jarring. Something to make people really notice it. The more out of place it looks, the more people are convinced that it's important."

"Interesting. Is that why you chose this spot for the farm?"

"Oh, no; the farm was here. Or the cornfield was, at least, and this storage business. But the house was a transplant. We brought it in."

Patrick raised an eyebrow. "Brought it in?"

"Moved it halfway across the state," Roman said proudly. "The transport was masterminded by an old friend."

"That'd be an impressive feat for the old world. Seems totally impossible in this one."

"He was a very strong asset to the team. A good man to have around. And a good man. An engineer, like you."

Patrick was flattered. "What happened to him?"

Roman hesitated. A sadness washed behind his eyes. "He didn't make it," was all he said.

"Right." Patrick cleared his throat and changed the subject back to the house. "So when people go inside the house. What happens next?"

"They don't come out." Roman slapped Patrick on the back. "Spread the word to your men, will you? Don't go in that house. We'd like to not lose any of you." He winked, and then he wandered off down the corridor between the storage units. "Get settled in," he called over his shoulder. "I'll be back in a bit to give you a tour!"

"Sure," Patrick said. He frowned up at the old Victorian mansion, wondering how many ghosts it held. "Looking forward to it."

59.

Brett crossed his arms. "Well, now I want to go into the house."

"Boy, do I understand that impulse," Patrick said, nodding sympathetically. "But when someone who's paranoid enough to move an entire three-story mansion across a state to use as a Disney prop tells you to stay out of the house, you should probably stay out."

"Yeah, yeah," Brett grumbled.

"Thank you," Patrick said. "Because if anyone's going in, it's Richie."

"Hey!"

"Look, you're just the most expendable," Patrick shrugged. "It's not a problem. *Someone* has to be!"

"I hate you," Richie decided.

"You hate that he's right," Brett grinned.

"I hate to break up this little snuff-fest," Ted broke in, "but can I ask a question?"

"No," Gary said gruffly from the corner of the storage unit. They had gathered in his room, and he was pretty sour about it. They'd meant it as a courtesy, to include him in their impromptu safety meeting without forcing him to travel. But he was still in incredible pain, and he was also still pretty unglued about losing his arm, so when they showed up he told them all to go eat dicks in hell. They'd eventually persuaded him to act as host, but he refused to let Jimmy in unless he got to rip off one of the EMT's arms to make things even-Steven.

Jimmy elected to stay outside.

"Okay, well, I'm going to," Ted said, ignoring Gary. "I'm just wondering; what do we *do* now?"

The Red Caps turned toward him, blinking. "What do you mean?" Jimmy asked.

"I just mean…we're *here*, right?" Ted explained. "We held up our end of the bargain with Roman. So I guess the original plan was to escort Patrick back to wherever he's going—that comes next. But…" He gestured broadly toward the storage center. "This is a good, safe setup. I haven't seen this many people with weapons since 'Platoon.' We have our own rooms; I finally feel safe. So, what I'm saying is…are we planning on leaving all this to drop Patrick off with his friends? Or are we maybe in a good place where we should think about…staying? No offense, Patrick," he offered quickly.

"None taken," Patrick assured him. "Truly. I never asked for this escort. I've been grateful for it and I thank you all, but it was never my Plan A. If this is the end of your line, I respect that completely." The thought of continuing on without the crew both thrilled him and filled him with dread. It meant he could get to Ben that much quicker…but also that much more alone in a cold, dark world. "It's your choice."

"I'm not feeling too motivated to move on," Gary spat.

Jimmy squirmed against the exterior wall of the storage unit. He may not have been invited in, but he was still part of the meeting. "We give Patrick our word," he reminded everyone, peeking into the storage box.

"You're not allowed to speak," Gary shot back.

"We could escort him to Fort Doom and then come back," Jimmy explained.

Richie snickered. "So *he* encourages *you* to do the hard shit of cutting off Gary's arm, and now he's like your best friend?"

Jimmy frowned. "I just think we're all a team."

"He gave me shit every step of the way for my dermatitis!" Richie exploded. "*I get hives! It's a serious condition!*"

"He also killed a hundred cannibals by ramming them with a bear," Brett pointed out. "Just so we could get past."

"Oh, be serious—it wasn't a hundred," Richie said, rolling his eyes.

"So, you're in the Patrick column?" Ted asked, raising an eyebrow at Brett.

Brett snorted. "I ain't in any column. I'm as happy here as I am out there. I'm good with anything. But it seems worth mentioning that this fuck-ball weirdo led us through a whole lot of shit and kept us alive."

"Thank you?" Patrick guessed.

"He also led us *into* most of that shit," Gary reminded them.

"Yes, he did," Richie nodded.

"Can't argue with that," Patrick agreed.

"Stay out of this," Gary snarled.

"Sure thing," Patrick said, tipping Gary a small salute. "This is probably a conversation best held without me anyway. Gentlemen and Richie, I bid you adieu." He bowed very low, scraping his knuckles against the cement floor. "Ow. And if it helps, I'm planning on leaving tomorrow, and I absolutely do not expect any of you to give up the safety and security of Roman Ranch just to take me across state lines."

Gary pressed his mouth into a thin line without responding. Brett gave Patrick a nod, and Richie stared venom right through him. Ted shrugged helplessly, and that was that. Patrick walked out of the storage unit, patting Jimmy on the shoulder as he passed. "Thank you for the kind words," he said.

"You're welcome," Jimmy replied. Then he added, "I don't like that you called me Johnny on purpose."

Patrick sighed. "Yeah. I get that."

And so, on his own, he wandered out into the lot and went to explore the fields beyond the fence and ponder what would come next.

60.

Patrick didn't work too hard to try to forge any sort or relationships with the rest of Roman's team now that they were on the farm together. There was really no point, since he wouldn't be there long, and they all looked like they took themselves way too seriously, like they were extras in a Predator movie. There was no need to introduce himself to the women guarding the storage lot entrance; they knew he was with Roman and stood back and let him pass.

"Much obliged," he said, slipping between the sentries.

The sun was on its way toward setting, and the Monkey clouds were taking on their dusky burnt-orange glow. Patrick wandered out onto the highway, walked down the dashed center line for a while, then turned and meandered into the fields. He was pretty sure the crop in front of him was soybeans; he'd eaten enough edamame to recognize the pale, stunted pods. Further down the road was corn, and beyond that, cotton. There were two more crops he couldn't even guess at on the other side of the highway, plus a pretty expansive vegetable garden full of cabbage, zucchini, tomatoes, sugar snap peas, cucumbers, and plenty more. He hadn't seen this much food since a Monkey bomb fell on his neighborhood Jewel-Osco.

"He undersold it, didn't he?"

Patrick jumped when he heard Carla's voice, so close behind his ear. "What are you, a cat?!" he exclaimed, catching his breath.

"What are you, a mouse?" Carla teased, clearly pleased with herself.

"Mice have ultrasonic hearing," Patrick frowned. "I'm more of an armadillo."

Carla planted her hands on her hips and gazed out at the patchwork of crops growing in the valley. "It is so much food, isn't it?"

"It is," Patrick nodded. "I mean, he did say he wanted to be the next big economic driver, but I thought that was just some sweet aspirational talk. He didn't paint the full scope of all this into his word picture."

"It's part of his strategy," Carla sighed. She turned and sat down on the edge of the highway, her boot heels digging into the loose gravel embankment. "Don't tell strangers what you have so they don't covet it and raise an army against you. If those strangers become friends that you eventually welcome in, they're pleasantly surprised to see such abundance. Or something like that."

"Pretty smart," Patrick admitted. "A place like this is worth protecting."

Carla nodded. "It is." She scooped up a handful of asphalt gravel and started tossing tiny pieces into the fields, aiming at the fledgling soybean pods. "It's also a place worth staying."

Patrick sat down next to her on the road. "Are you talking about me or are you talking about you?"

"I'm talking about me," she said. "I'm *explaining* about me. Roman is…not a good person. He's full of bluster. He's careless and he's selfish, and there's a meanness inside of him that you haven't seen yet."

Patrick drew his knees up to his chin. "I can sometimes sense it, though."

"Mm." Carla tossed another pebble. It hit a yellow-green pod square in the center and knocked it off its vine. "He's…not a good person," she said again. "That's why Melissa, Mary, and Adiva ran off. They were saving themselves. And I keep wondering why I don't save myself. But we come back here…to all this…" She stared out at the land, at the fences, at the heavily-armed security guards, at the homey storage units. "This is the best place I've been since M-Day. Best place by a long shot."

"A person could be very comfortable here," Patrick agreed. "In post-M-Day-adjusted terms."

"Yep."

The distant, watery disc of the sun touched the edge of the horizon. The world would be dark again soon.

"So you're going to stay?" Patrick asked.

Carla nodded. "I am." She gave Patrick a sideways look. Her eyes glistened with hope as she asked, "Are you?"

But Patrick shook his head. "I have to get back," he said.

"To your friends."

"Yeah. To Fort Doom."

"And to Ben."

Patrick nodded. "Mostly to Ben."

Carla sighed. "I don't even remember what it is to love someone like that."

Patrick chewed on his bottom lip. "Ben's a friend that became family long before the bombs dropped. My daughter, Izzy…she called him Uncle Ben. I used to worry about how we'd eventually break the news that he isn't *really* her uncle, because to her, he was as much a fixture in our family as my sister and her wife, and my brother-in-law and his. Turns out, we never had to have that conversation." He sniffed back against the sting of the cool night air in his nostrils. "At the time, it felt like something we'd have to explain. I wish I'd known then that it was something to celebrate."

Carla looked over at Patrick. She reached out and placed her hand on top of his, squeezing it gently. Patrick started, surprised at this new warmth, and Carla started to pull her hand away. But Patrick held on and squeezed back. The warmth was new, but it was nice.

They settled into each other. Carla's shoulder pressed against Patrick's arm, and he could smell the heat on the back of her neck.

"I don't know what I'd do without Ella and Lucia," Carla said. "I really don't. It took me an apocalypse to realize that a found family is just as real as blood."

They sat there for a while like that, holding hands and not knowing what to think about the world, watching the sun get swallowed up by the earth. When they heard the crunch of boots walking up the gravel slope of the highway's shoulder, they dropped their hands. Patrick wiped his palms on his jeans.

"Anything going on here I should know about?" Roman asked, his smile as big as the moon. "Hope you don't mind if I borrow our brilliant engineer for a bit, Carla." He reached a hand out to Patrick and helped him to his feet.

"Of course not," Carla said, pushing herself up. She locked eyes with Patrick. "Find me later," she said. It wasn't a question, and there was a strange dire edge beneath the words, a fear that cracked the air like glass. Patrick frowned when he heard it as Carla's warning echoed in his head: *Roman is not a good person.*

He nodded. "I will," he promised.

Roman watched them with his wide grin. "Sweet little lovebirds," he laughed. Then he slapped Patrick on the back and directed him back toward the gate. "Come on, there's something else I want you to see."

They walked back toward the storage units, leaving Carla alone in the darkening night.

61.

"You've traveled a lot…have you seen many other farms like this?" Roman asked as they passed back into the storage lot.

"I haven't seen *any* other farms like this," Patrick admitted.

"You know why?"

"The Monkey bombs took all the green thumbs?"

"No. It's because people are lazy. They want to be taken care of."

Patrick frowned at that. "I don't know if that's right…"

"Let me explain the human condition to you," Roman said, throwing an arm around Patrick's shoulder. "Most people are baby birds with their mouths open to the sky, waiting for someone to vomit down their throats so they can say, 'Thank you.' Government performed that function *very* well for the length of the American experiment, and in that government's absence, I am more than happy to fill in. Behold." He gestured grandly to the crops beyond the high fences. "The new and improved nanny state! It was ripe for disruption long before M-Day, and now I've filled the gap. We can provide anyone with the basic necessities of survival, oh yes…but unlike the old, resource-depleting entitlement programs of yesteryear, here there's an exchange value for value."

"Why do I feel like I'm suddenly trapped in an election cycle?" Patrick asked miserably.

"Because all those old white men knew that this is what it comes down to: dependency. We take that same approach here, but we amp it up. The survivors of M-Day are dependent on our food—we have control of that. But we don't cash it in as votes."

"How generous?"

Roman laughed. "This campus is a *meritocracy*. People here must earn the right to promotion. This system—*my* system—gives even the lowest, most insignificant members of the community a way to earn their keep."

The hairs on the nape of Patrick's neck crackled to life. A shivered rippled through him.

Roman led him to the long office building just inside the entry gate. He strolled up to the door and rapped sharply three times. "Open up!" he barked. "I brought a visitor!" The door pushed open, bathing the lot in a warm orange glow as the flickering firelight from inside washed out through the open doorway. A woman with thick hair and thicker glasses peered up at them as she considered Roman's call. "It wasn't locked," she said sourly. "We don't lock it." She looked at Patrick, frowning. "Is he here for the test?"

"He certainly is," Roman said, herding Patrick inside.

The light came from lanterns positioned throughout the building; Patrick noticed the eerie shadows they cast across the dull white walls. "Juice is a precious resource," Roman explained. "We have a field full of generators, but between the living quarters and the machinery we run in here, well, the lab lights do suffer a bit. Just to save power. But trust me—what we lack in light, we make up for in scientific illumination."

The building was divided into three rooms, each one larger than the last. The first room contained the U-Store It service counter, which had been covered with scientific equipment—beakers and burners and spinners and testers. The next room had once been a customer waiting area; the cheap cabinets with peeling Formica countertops were still lined against two of the walls, and had probably once held a Keurig, some cheap Kirkland coffee pods, maybe some teabags and a hot water machine. Now, the counter was covered with books—textbooks and notebooks—and there was an old-fashioned calculator, one with large buttons that ran on a solar-charged battery. A display of clean pipettes and beakers sat on the other end of the counter, and a wire magazine rack now held several dozen brightly-colored powders with crude masking tape labels. A mini-fridge hummed angrily on the floor beneath the pipettes; two rolling carts stood at the ready near the far side of the room, their surfaces covered with glass and metal instruments Patrick did not recognize.

But the main attraction of this second room was the huge plexiglass cylinder in the center. It was probably ten feet in diameter, standing vertically from floor to ceiling, with a small door set into the far side. The tube was large enough to hold a medical gurney, which sat squarely in the center. It was loosely covered by a grimy bedsheet sheet. Pale pink splotches blossomed here and there, remnants of blood that had long ago soaked through the fabric. Thick straps hung from the ends of the gurney, straps of leather that was worn, but sturdy. Three large vents protruded down into the cylinder from above. A sizeable floor drain was set into the tile beneath it. The tile near the lip of the floor drain was stained a glossy pink.

The third and final room stretched the full remaining length of the lot and consisted of eight storage units, four on each side, with a narrow alley between them. The other units on the lot opened to the outside, but these eight were more secure, opening to the inside of the building. "For our most precious cargo," Roman smiled.

All throughout the building there were small metal desks with ancient computers and dot matrix printers, chopping out lines of text with their high-pitched, scratchy whines. Scuttling from room to room like cockroaches were four scientists in once-white jackets, their heads bent low, their voices quiet, moving around each other in patterns of choreographed chaos.

"This is extremely unorthodox," the scientist with the frizzy hair said, following quickly behind them and pushing her glasses up her nose in consternation. "We have a protocol."

"Which we'll return to momentarily," Roman said. The woman muttered with exasperation, but Roman simply waved her off. She stomped back to the front counter, where she grumpily began gathering jars of powders and vials of liquids and heaping them onto a cart.

"What is this place?" Patrick asked.

"This is where the new economy begins," Roman said proudly. "This is where we thrust humanity forward into its next evolution."

Patrick glanced doubtfully at the blood-stained gurney. "Is the evolution directed by Eli Roth?"

Roman gave him a strange look. "I don't get the reference," he said.

Ben would, Patrick thought.

"We're doing incredible things here," Roman continued, "incredible things! I know it doesn't look like much. That printer is from 1986! Wild, right? Old tech and new tech—and prehistoric tech!" he added, gesturing to the torches. "We've put it all together to achieve something you won't believe. And these people, they're the best. Most of them have been with my company for years, way before M-Day. The people outside are all new, the guns and everything," he said, waving his hand through the air dismissively. "But in here, the *sanctum sanctorum*, where the work of the gods is being done…these are some of the most brilliant minds that M-Day left behind, I guarantee you that."

Patrick frowned as he watched the men and women in old lab coats picking at the edges of the lab equipment, mumbling quietly to themselves, readying their instruments, though for what Patrick had no idea. "What's this test?" he asked.

"The latest in a series," Roman said excitedly, rubbing his hands together. "Maybe the last, maybe not, but man, we're getting close!"

"Close to what?"

Roman gripped Patrick's shoulder and smiled so hard, it looked like his lips might tear at the corners. "To a perfect *reversal*," he beamed.

Down the hall in the storage room, one of the scientists pulled a padlock from the second unit's door and rolled it up. He hissed out an order that Patrick couldn't quite make out; a man about Patrick's age emerged, blinking in the firelight. He was thin, like Patrick, but shorter, with dark, scruffy hair and almond-brown skin. His clothes were loose, and the hair on both jaws spiraled down to his chest. He shuffled uncertainly into the hall, goaded on by the scientist. A young girl leapt out of the storage unit, maybe six or seven years old, her hair tangled and long, and the same dark brown as the older man. She fell forward and threw her arms around his leg. The man gently pried her away, kissed the top of her head, and whispered something into her ear. He gestured back into the storage unit, but the girl didn't move. She stood there, her fingers curling into fists, her shoulders trembling. "*No!*" she shouted. "*Vuelves!*" A woman ran out from the storage unit and grabbed the girl around the waist, dragging her back into the shed. She murmured into her ear, stroking her hair and holding her tight. This only made the girl more frantic, more scared. She began to cry. "*Papá!*" she screamed. "*Papá! No me dejas! No me dejas!*"

The scientist shoved the woman and the girl backward into the unit and pulled the door down, slamming it onto the concrete.

The man walked forward bravely but sadly, his mouth twisting against a deep and bottomless pain. He lifted his chin and held his head high as he marched up the hall, toward the center room.

Patrick's heart was thumping against his chest. "What is this?" he demanded.

Roman was looking at the man with shining eyes. The tips of his ears were pink with excitement. "We're going to save them," he replied.

"Save who?"

Roman turned and smiled at Patrick. "Everyone."

The scientist half-led and half-shoved the thin man through the door and into the plexiglass cylinder. The man's entire body quivered as he stepped forward and lifted himself onto the gurney. A second scientist stepped through the doorway; together, the two men in lab coats set about securing the thin man's wrists and ankles with the thick leather straps.

"Stop this," Patrick said without thinking. His entire body flushed with blood. "What is this? Stop it."

"It's fine," Roman assured him. "Manuel is a volunteer. He and his family came to us asking for help, for food and shelter, and I'm glad we were able to give it. Value for value—remember? It was made very clear to Manuel before he stepped first foot on the property, he would meet all the needs in Maslow's hierarchy here—physical needs before anything else—and in return, he would provide the value of scientific assistance. See how calm he is." Roman added, nodding through the partition. "He's an honorable man, holding up his end of an honorable agreement." Roman looked like he might cry, as if the beauty of the frightened man's situation was pushing him toward the edge. "He is my Apollo 1."

Patrick's lips drew down into a tight frown. "The men aboard Apollo 1 burned to death."

"And we wouldn't have landed on the moon without them."

Patrick felt a hot prickling cover every inch of his skin. The air in the room suddenly felt close and overly warm. "What *is* this?" he demanded again. "What are you going to do to him?"

Roman exhaled far too calmly. "The duster repellant that you were so instrumental in helping me obtain is the key to a bright new world. It has the potential to unlock the door into a radical new epoch of peace and prosperity." He crooked his finger at Patrick. "Come on. I'll show you."

Roman crossed over to the mini-fridge. Patrick reluctantly followed, forcing himself to peel his eyes away from the man inside the cylinder. The scientists had stopped fussing with his bonds and were now hooking him up to a small, portable arsenal of machinery and monitors.

Roman pulled open the fridge and carefully removed a small vial of bright blue liquid. "This was my first visit to Dr. Philbin's lab, but it's not the first time I'd been introduced to her work. A woman came through the farm several months back, maybe a year or so ago. She needed supplies for a trip out west. She had an interesting story to tell about a makeshift laboratory in Asheville, and she offered a small bottle of liquid as payment."

"Zom-Be-Gone."

"It *is* a good name," Roman smiled. "But no. Not exactly. What she gave us was something of a minimum viable product. It didn't keep zombies away, but it did affect them. It was the start of something, you could see that. It made them confused. It took away their bite. That vial was the beginning of something big. We ran through the sample pretty quickly, but the promise was there. Our experiments with the early version were pretty conclusive: If Dr. Philbin managed to realize her vision, we could use that, paired with our work here, to achieve something extraordinary."

"So you've said." He glanced over his shoulder suspiciously at the man strapped to the gurney. The man's eyes were closed, but his chest was heaving with labored breath. "And that extraordinary thing would be what, exactly?"

"The reversal of the Monkey dust effects."

Patrick's brow furrowed. "Reversal…"

"Meaning we can turn dusters back into the people they were. The animals, too. We can reverse the effects of the dust and save not just the dusters themselves, but every one of the would-be victims they'd tear apart. We can essentially reset the world and start over, from scratch…building society back up without the threat of monsters."

"Sounds like a nice dream," Patrick grunted.

Roman grinned. "It's much more than a dream. We are *so* close," he promised. "Our trials have been going well. Earlier this afternoon, my scientists extracted the active ingredients from Philbin's serum and integrated them into this." He held up the bottle of blue liquid and showed Patrick the small, masking tape label with neat writing: #57. "At long last, this one may be the winner."

Patrick shook his head. "This is your 57th try at turning a duster back to a pre-duster? And you think you've gotten it right *this time?*"

"Correct and correct," Roman said.

"So you're going to use this on a duster to see if it works."

"You've got it."

"You've been experimenting on real dusters."

"Yes."

"On actual humans."

"On *dusters*," Roman clarified, a shadow crossing his brow.

"But that man," Patrick said, nodding at the cylinder, "is not a duster."

"Well, no," Roman admitted. "Not yet."

A chill rippled through Patrick's bones.

The scientists inside the cylinder finished their preparations and stepped out through the small door, closing it securely behind them. They nodded at Roman, then they went to one of the computers along the wall and started tapping at the ancient keyboard.

"Dusters are nearly impossible to control," Roman said. He walked up to the cylinder and stared softly, almost lovingly, at the man strapped into the gurney. "They make terrible test subjects. We lost a several good scientists in the early days, trying to get dusters into a contained space."

The color drained from Patrick's face. His knees felt weak. His head was spinning. "You're not going to…" he croaked. He had to grab the countertop to steady himself and keep himself on his feet.

"It's much simpler to restrain them *before* they become dusters," Roman said, placing a hand on the plexiglass tube. He glanced over at the frizzy-haired scientist emerging from her makeshift desk with a cannister in her hands. Roman nodded at her. She stepped up to a panel in the wall, opened it, placed the cannister inside, and removed the lid. She closed the panel door, locked it, and pressed a button on a small box mounted on the wall. A mechanism in the ceiling immediately whirred to life and wind began to whip through the cylinder. The man's clothes started to ripple in the swirling air. His chest rose faster and faster. His lips moved in a silent prayer. The vents in the ceiling began to hiss, and a yellow-green fog began to spill slowly into the tube.

"Dust goes in," Roman said. "Duster comes out."

Patrick felt the world shrink around him.

Clouds of dust tumbled down into the narrow space, thin at first and building as they billowed, becoming concentrated, almost viscous as they cascaded down over the restrained man. He coughed, choking as the thick fog entered his lungs. His fingers scrabbled against the leather of the straps, frustrated and ineffective. He screamed, a horrible, marrow-curdling sound of sheer terror and panic that sputtered into a wretched bark as the fog pushed down into him, so thick now that it cloaked the man—the gurney, the wires, the machines, everything in the tube, until the only thing Patrick could see was a swirling green mist.

"You can't…" he whispered, leaning against the desk. "You can't make a duster like this."

"You can if you know how the chemicals work," Roman assured him, his voice softly reverent as he watched Manuel's face disappear behind the curtain of green smoke. "You'd be surprised how far you can push the potency of the dust once you understand it—once you *know* it. And no one on earth knows it quite the way I do."

"And why is that?" Patrick asked, not sure he wanted to know.

Roman turned to Patrick with something like misplaced pride in his eyes, the firelight from the lanterns throwing shadows up over his face.

"Because I'm the one who designed it," he said.

62.

Patrick was falling through an infinite hole in space. The world was gone, gravity was gone; his hands on the cool concrete floor of the office building did nothing to stabilize him, and he was suddenly, irreparably unstuck from time and lost in the universe.

"You...designed it?" His voice was smothered, muted, as if he were hearing himself under water.

Roman stood at the cylinder, touching the glass, moored securely in the reality that Patrick had slipped off of. He stood straight and even while Patrick spilled and spun into the ether of chaos. "I did. Not alone, of course." He sighed as he watched the green fog ripple beyond the glass, doing its unseen work on the man imprisoned inside the tube. "I'm a venture capitalist, after all, not a chemist." Roman peeled his gaze away from the undulating smoke to lock eyes with Patrick; it snapped him back to their shared time and place. "You wouldn't believe the shit we get into."

Patrick blinked up at Roman as the man smiled. The shock and the confusion were so thick, they spilled into his eyes and clouded his vision. He strained against the encroaching darkness to focus on Roman's silhouette. "Why...why would you ever do *that?*"

"For the money, obviously." The answer was so bland, so blunt. "I know it sounds awful, but it's actually just business. Investment opportunities are presented to me, and I evaluate them. Usually there's too much on the downside, and I pass. Sometimes there's enough upside, and I go. Sometimes, it's a clean cash-and-equity deal; less often, it's a hands-on opportunity. I don't get many like that...and they're mostly apps and cosmetics and cheap Walmart disruptors that'll flare out in six months. But every once in a while, someone shows up with a Request for Proposal from a foreign nation for some *wild-ass shit* they need to keep off the domestic books, and bang—you're airlifting poppies from a farm in Arkansas to a hangar in Bolivia, or you're employing engineers to dig tunnels under the Mexican border, or you're pulling together a kick-ass team of lab rats to develop a next-gen chemical agent for the constitutional monarchy of Jamaica."

Patrick felt the ground firm up beneath him. Embers sparked to life in his gut; as the fire spread, it burned away the vertigo and confusion, forging his cells like iron into an impenetrable mass of plates that spread beneath his skin. "How could you do that?" he demanded, his fists trembling.

If Roman noticed the metallic rage rising within Patrick, he didn't show it. "The start-up was promising. Spun out of one of my cosmetic companies, actually. Believe it or not, cosmetics and chem-weaps have a pretty big overlap. I mean, the whole reason Monkey dust is chartreuse is because we started with a cosmetic foundation called Glowstick Green we rolled out for rave kids in the 90s. It turned out to be a killer base for the combustible compound."

Over Roman's shoulder, the green fog stopped falling into the cylinder. The mist began to melt away. Patrick could see the murky silhouette of the man inside writhing against the restraints.

"Billions of people," Patrick seethed. His whole body vibrated with anger. "Billions dead." *Two of mine.*

Roman shook his head slowly. "Boy, I could *not* believe they actually went through with it. I mean, in some ways, you have to hand it to them, you know? The absolute *balls* on those guys. I didn't think it would happen."

"You thought they ordered an extinction-level chemical powder so they could lock it in a drawer?" Patrick said through gritted teeth.

"You wouldn't believe how many countries do that—*did* that. I mean, all of them. I'm not exaggerating when I say, *all* of them. The ones that could afford it, anyway. This shit was always a deterrent; no one *actually* plans on destroying the world. Why would they? It's not in anyone's interest. But they want a bargaining chip so that *they* can't be destroyed—not without consequences. That's all any of this political subterfuge bullshit ever is. That's what we figured this was, too."

"But it wasn't." Watercolor images of Izzy and Annie washed through Patrick's vision.

"Boy, is *that* an understatement."

The last droplets of yellow-green mist evaporated from the tube, giving Patrick a clear view of the man inside. He was strapped to the gurney, thrashing and gnashing and spitting yellow flecks of froth from a mouth that snarled beneath eyes that were wild with confusion and fury.

"You made a thing that, if it doesn't reduce humans to puddles, does this instead," Patrick seethed, raising a shaking finger toward the see-through cylinder. "You *made* it to do this. After you created it to destroy humanity, you let *this* happen to whoever was left. You made something that massacred the majority of the planet and ravaged the rest. And you're still doing it."

"But now, I'm doing it so I can find a *cure*," Roman reminded him. "To make good on what's been done! The work we're doing here isn't to make more dusters. It's to find ways to *cure* them." He tossed the blue vial to the scientist with the frizzy hair, who cried out in surprise and nearly dropped it as she caught it. She scowled at him, and he grinned back. "Sorry."

The scientist picked up a hypodermic needle from a tray by the wall and sucked the serum out of the vial. Syringe in hand, she crossed over to the cylinder and cautiously opened the door. The man inside was thrashing against his restraints, snarling death from his lips. The scientist crept up carefully, checking the security of the leather straps that crossed the man's forehead. Then she shoved the needle into the corner of his eye— quickly, expertly. She pressed down on the plunger as the swirling blue fluid disappeared into the newly-transformed duster's bloodstream. Then the scientist removed the syringe and slipped out of the chamber, locking it behind her.

The room came alive with the sound of pens clicking as the men and women in white coats crowded around the cylinder and began jotting notes on the subject's reactions to the injection. At first, Patrick couldn't tell any discernible difference in the duster, despite the fact that the scientists were writing furiously and mumbling their observations to one other. But then the man stopped thrashing. His chest rose and fell quickly...*too* quickly. Spiderwebs of blue color streaked his arms as the serum filled his veins, stretching against his skin, throbbing and swelling as if they might burst.

The man's screams became strangled; the sounds he emitted dropped down to a low growl. Tears streamed from his eyes, yellow-green saline bled through with blue flecks. And then a horrible noise erupted, like the sound of a thick water balloon popping. Patrick watched in horror as the veins beneath the man's skin burst, some of them breaking through the skin, others disintegrating beneath the surface, soaking his body in a dark-blue tint. Then his eyes rolled up in his head and he went still. Blue and yellow pus oozed from every orifice in his face; bloody mucous dripped from his arms. Somewhere, a heart monitor pealed out an even, sustained squeal. He was gone.

Roman sighed sadly. "Well. It'll work one of these days." He nodded at the frizzy-haired scientist.

She picked up a walkie-talkie, clicked it to life, and said, "Clean-up on aisle 8."

Patrick's breath came through his nose ragged and hot. "You are a ghoul," he whispered. "You're the devil." He fought to control his words against the rasping impulse to scream, to shriek like a banshee, to bring down the walls of everything Roman had built with his furious volume. "You…" He couldn't find another name strong enough, bitter enough to define the black heart of Roman's depravity. "You broke the world."

Roman looked at Patrick with sympathy. "I know this is a lot all at once. Normally, I'd have spread it all out and given you a couple weeks to take it all in. But I need your help. I need you read into this, because you're smart, you're resourceful, and I need your help to figure out how to make this work." He stepped closer and placed a hand on Patrick's shoulder. His blue eyes were full of hope as he said, "I could really use a good engineer to help me cure them."

Patrick felt icy coldness under the weight of Roman's hand. "That man had a daughter," he said.

"That man was a volunteer."

"You just took away her father."

"He chose his path."

"That wasn't a *choice*. It was the only option you gave him if he wanted to feed his family."

"I think this has been a little much for you. Go back and rest, we'll talk tomorrow."

"He had a family," Patrick said through clenched teeth.

Roman tightened his grip on Patrick's shoulder. "I said, we'll pick this up later."

Patrick's vision had reached a white-hot clarity. Every crisp line of Roman's form was in sharp, scalding focus. Patrick bored into the deep black well inside Roman's pupils, the thick, oily emptiness behind his eyes. "*I* had a family. *I* had a daughter. She loved Ariel and Mad Libs and butterscotch pudding and riding her bike. Her organs turned to liquid and she died screaming and terrified and alone…because of what you made."

Roman rolled his eyes. "It was years ago, Patrick," he said. "You're going to have to get over that. The world is different now. We have to deal with what we have."

All sound stopped. The murmurs of the scientists, the hum of the machines, the thoughts inside Patrick's own head: it all went suddenly and perfectly silent. Roman lifted his hand and turned away. He was moving in slow motion, his body leaving a blurred trail of movement.

"Kill it with fire!" Ben said.

Patrick blinked. He was standing in the living room of 24C. Ben had leapt up onto a couch, pointing frantically at a cockroach that had scuttled beneath the coffee table.

"Patrick! Kill it! Kill it with fire!"

"It's not Frankenstein's monster," Patrick frowned. "I don't think fire even can kill a cockroach."

"We have to kill it!" Ben insisted. "It's disgusting and insidious and it'll eat our goddamn souls!"

"That's true; cockroaches do do that," Patrick agreed, rubbing his chin. The cockroach was crouched behind a table leg. Its antennae twitched.

"The only thing for it is death!"

"You know, I'm not sure killing it is the best thing," Patrick mused, looking thoughtfully at the insect. "If you've got a roach out here, then you've got a thousand roaches in the walls. That's just basic science. The death of one cockroach in the face of a cockroach horde is nothing."

"It'll send a message," Ben said confidently. "The other roaches will know we mean business, and they'll bug out."

"But consider this—"

"Did you even hear what I just said?" Ben demanded. "Bug out."

"Yes, I did hear your sad joke, but consider this. What if killing this one roach makes the other roaches angry? They might come for you. They might come for you while you sleep."

Ben gritted his teeth. "Then we'll kill them all," he decided.

"This feels like futility itself."

"You can't just let a cockroach stand!"

"But it's just one cockroach. There are a billion more cockroaches."

"But this is the cockroach we can handle! We may not be able to kill all the cockroaches in all the world, but by God, Patrick, we can kill this cockroach. And the world will be better for it."

Patrick frowned. "I'm just not sure the world cares too much about this one cockroach."

"I care about this cockroach, and I am a major part of our world!" Ben cried. "Kill it with fire!"

"I'm telling you, I don't think you can kill them with fire. Don't they say that cockroaches can survive an atomic bomb?"

"That can't possibly be true."

"I think it might be true. I don't think you can kill it with fire."

"Fine, I don't care, then maim it with fire!"

"I don't even have any fire!"

Ben looked at him with eyes like blocks of stone. "Patrick. Yes, you do."

Patrick felt heat on the back of his head. He turned and saw the camp lantern hanging on the wall of Roman's laboratory.

He looked back at Roman. He was still turning away, his lips curled into a snarl.

The sound was still muted in this world, in the now.

She died screaming and terrified and alone.

You're going to have to get over that.

Patrick reached up for the lantern. He felt the weight of the gas canister and the real glass housing. He felt the heat of the fire inside.

Then he swung the lantern with every milligram of fury in his body. It smashed into Roman's face so hard that the glass shattered, slicing into his cheek and puncturing his eye. The regulator on the propane tank popped off; the sudden burst of gas ignited instantly, exploding against Roman's skin, soaking it in gas and flame. His skin blistered and peeled as blood fizzled and popped across his face. Roman screamed.

Patrick heard nothing.

Roman fell to his knees, clutching at his face, burning his hands, his mouth open, twisted and grotesque.

Patrick said nothing.

Roman's legs kicked out as if his body were being hit with thousands of volts of electricity. The skin on his face turned black; his lips shriveled up and curled away. One of the scientists ran over and threw his white coat over Roman's face, smothering the fire. Pink and gray liquid soaked through the cotton.

Patrick watched all of this, and yet he didn't feel a thing. His nerves were dull. His mind was quiet. He could hear the sound of his thoughts, but they were muffled, suppressed—buried deep beneath layers of earth, with no hope of rising to the top. He looked up from the burned and bloody mass on the floor and saw men rushing in with weapons raised. *Security. Protection. Punishment. Clean-up.* They moved as if caught in a strobe light, their slow, jerky movements bringing them close…closer…closest. Patrick didn't move. He was a thing of clay, stationary. Pliable, but only from the outside. He tilted his head as the first security guard flashed into him, knocking him back, spinning him around. The guard raised a night stick and brought it smashing down into the back of Patrick's head. Patrick pitched forward, bent in half like a paper doll, his head cracking on the floor. His hips followed, and then his legs. He crumpled onto himself, his eyes still open, his mind still conscious, but only just barely. The world swam. His vision doubled. He stared across the floor and saw Roman's head, covered with the lab coat, as if he'd been painted there by Magritte, one single Lover, left to die. Burned, cold, and alone.

Hands grabbed Patrick beneath his arms and dragged him across the concrete floor. The volume knob slowly turned, and the silence gave way to frantic whispers, which became full-throated screams of panic as the world returned to normal speed and tore itself apart. People ran around, doors were thrown open, weapons flashed in the strange lights, and everyone, *everyone*, was screaming.

Patrick's captors kicked through the office doors and hauled him out into the lot. They dragged him across the rough cement, over to an open storage unit, hurling his scraped and bleeding body onto the concrete floor inside. A man dug his knee into Patrick's back, crushing the air out of his lungs. He wrenched Patrick's wrists together and locked them with a zip tie. The hard plastic sliced into his skin, and the ties quickly became slick with blood. The guards murmured to one another, their words obscured but their tones incredulous. The other guard reared back and kicked Patrick square in the ribs with his steel-toed boot. The incredible pain of it was the breaking point for Patrick's consciousness.

The light faded out behind his eyes as the guards walked out and pulled the door shut.

63.

"Well," Ben said. "That was unexpected."

He drummed his fingers against the metal bench that was bolted into the concrete. His shoes scuffed at the floor. Someone down the hall coughed up something wet. He glanced over at Patrick. "Any thoughts on the situation?"

Patrick frowned. "I'm honestly having a hard time remembering the details."

"Good. Use that line in court."

"I'm serious. It's all sort of…glary."

"Happy to sharpen it for you," Ben sighed. "You broke a bar chair over a guy's skull, and now we're in prison."

"We're not in prison, we're in jail," Patrick corrected him. "Big difference."

"Not a big difference to my parole officer," Ben insisted.

"You don't have a parole officer."

"I'm going to *now*, now that you've landed us in prison!" he cried.

"Not prison," Patrick said, shaking his head. "Jail. Big difference."

Ben stood up from the bench. He moved too quickly, and his whole body swayed as the blood sloshed around in his head. His left eye was bruised and swollen shut, and his lip was still dribbling blood. He caught himself against the wall; once his legs felt solid again, he shuffled over to the bars and gripped them with shaky hands. Flecks of dried blood dotted his knuckles. He wondered if maybe he'd vomit. "Can I get some ice?" he called out into the police station. There were a few officers at their desks, but no one bothered looking up. One of them may have said, *Sit down.* "I pay taxes, and you're all fired," he shouted grumpily. He plodded back over to the bench and lowered himself down. He missed the seat but didn't have the energy to push himself back up, so he just slid all the way to the floor and reclined until he was fully on his back.

"I'm not sure I *did* break a bar chair over that guy's head," Patrick mused, rubbing his chin. But it hurt to rub his chin, because his chin was badly bruised and likely fractured. He just liked the gravitas the act of chin-rubbing gave to his words. "It certainly doesn't sound like something I'd do."

"Good," Ben told him. "Say that in court, too. Give me a hundred bucks and I'll say the same thing."

Patrick shook his head. "Sorry, but I need my bucks. I need *all* my bucks. I'm having a baby soon."

"Wow…it hasn't altered your figure one bit," Ben said. He looked up at Patrick's puffy, purple face. "I take that back. You've clearly had some work done."

"Yes, apologies. Annie is having a baby soon, and I'm a co-financier of the project."

"There you go." Ben used his shoulder to wipe away the blood at his lip. "Seriously, though. What happened back there?"

Patrick sat up, leaned against the cinder block wall, and crossed his arms. He wasn't lying; he really couldn't remember the events of the last couple hours—not clearly, anyway. Some of that was due to the alcohol, of course. He and Ben had only meant to grab a quick beer at the L & L Tavern. But that quick beer turned into many beers, and then many beers turned into whiskey shots…and now that sunrise was only two hours away, Patrick was still pretty drunk. But it wasn't just the alcohol that had led to things getting out of hand. He'd gotten so mad at the dickhead at the bar, it conjured a deep, dark fury like nothing he'd ever experienced before. It made the world different, just for a few minutes. His vision had gone white, which made things look sharper and move slowly. Everything had gone quiet. Everything. "That guy just started wailing on you."

"He didn't *wail* on me," Ben protested.

"He smashed you in the head with a bottle, then he punched you so hard you literally flew across the room."

"It wasn't 'across the room,'" Ben muttered. "It was like two feet at most."

"I wanted him to stop," Patrick said.

Ben frowned. "Yeah. Don't get me wrong, I appreciate it and every-thing…but you've seen me get hit before. And I've never seen you engage in violence over it."

"I'm pretty anti-violence," Patrick agreed.

"So what the hell?"

Patrick leaned forward and put his forehead into his palms. "Benny Boy," he sighed. "That guy...he was a bad guy."

"No kidding," Ben snorted.

"No, I mean: he was a *bad guy*. Like, aside from picking a fight with you for no reason other than to have a punching bag——"

"I think I held my own, but go on."

"Aside from that, I was in the bathroom with him, next urinal over, and he was just bragging to—I don't even know, I guess me, or just...the world? There was no one else in there, but he was just saying loudly to the ceiling that his daughter was a bitch, and if she didn't shape up, he'd have to shape her up himself, the way he did with his whore wife."

Ben started. "What a dick."

"Then back at the bar, after you guys got into it and he knocked you down, he threw some cash on the table and told his buddies he had to get home, ''cause tomorrow's my kid's birthday - the big 0-5.'"

"The daughter he called a bitch is turning five?"

Patrick shrugged. "The whole thing...bragging about abuse, talking about his daughter that way, the way he hit you, the fact that she's *four years old*? I got so angry." He looked down at his hands. They weren't trembling at all now. "I lost it."

Ben shook his head. "Jesus."

"And I don't remember any of it."

"What?"

"The next thing I really remember is being thrown in the back of the police car. I have snippets," he said, tapping his temple, "but not much more than that."

They were quiet for a few minutes. The only sound was the nearby cops fumbling with their keyboards and slurping coffee from their mugs. None of them seemed too concerned about the two drunk guys in the holding cell, which Patrick guessed probably meant he hadn't killed the guy.

As if reading his mind, Ben said, "They were sitting him up when we got hauled out. There was a hell of a lot of blood, but head wounds tend to do that. Probably has one motherfucker of a concussion, but he seemed okay otherwise."

"Better him than his wife and daughter," Patrick said quietly.

"Ain't that the truth." Though they both knew that whatever happened, all Patrick had done was probably postpone the inevitable.

Ben blinked up at the fluorescent lights. "So are we going to talk about the blackout rage that apparently lives inside you?"

"I don't know what to say about it. That's never happened before."

"It sure happened tonight."

"I don't know." Patrick pressed his thumb into his palm and rubbed at some invisible stain. "It's like my brain couldn't process that much evil all at once."

"So this is what happens when The Great Engineer finds a problem he can't solve," Ben sighed. "He overloads."

But Patrick shook his head. "I'm fine with problems I can't solve. But bragging about hitting your wife and daughter? That's a problem I can't *fathom*."

"There is no solve."

"There is no solve," Patrick agreed. He pressed with more and more force, until his thumb shook. "All you can do is erase the disk and start again without it."

Ben gave him a sideways look. "Or you could ignore it."

"That would probably be healthier, yes," Patrick sighed.

"We can start by never going back to the L & L."

"Probably should avoid Lakeview altogether."

"Lots of d-bags in Lakeview," Ben nodded.

"Lots of d-bags in Lakeview," Patrick agreed.

"All right. So from now on, you keep your scary rage monster to yourself. We'll work on it. I'll help you."

Patrick turned his head and smiled at Ben. "Thanks."

"You're welcome. Thank *you* for avenging my defeat by breaking a chair over another guy's head."

"No sweat."

"And it's at least good to know you save your rage for the absolute worst monsters of the world."

"That's true."

Finally, one of the cops pushed back from his desk and sauntered over to the bars. "All right, you guys. One of you needs to call someone to pick you up."

Patrick's eyes widened. "We're free to go?"

"Your lucky day," the cop grunted. "You gave that guy a fractured skull. But it turns out, multiple witnesses saw him throw the first punch, and surprise surprise, he's got a warrant out for a DUI. So you can go. But someone's gotta come take you home. You smell like the fuckin' floor at Wrigley." He unlocked the cell and nodded toward the corner of the building. "Phone's over there."

Ben gestured toward the cell door. "Well. You're up."

Patrick sighed. "Yeah. Okay." He stood up carefully. His knees popped, and his back cracked. "How excited do you think Annie will be to get a phone call at three a.m. saying she needs to come pick up her drunk husband from the police station after a bar fight?"

"How far along is she?" Ben asked "Seven months?"

"Seven and a half."

"I actually think I'll catch my own ride home," Ben decided.

"Smart man." Patrick started dragging his feet toward the door.

"Hey," Ben said, and Patrick turned back. "You know your kid's going to need you to not be a rage monster."

"I do know that."

"So that's step one. Well, step two, I guess, after staying out of Lakeview. Be the person your family needs. As long as you've got them, you've got lots to be calm for."

Patrick smiled sadly as he watched the memory of Ben dissolve into the darkness of the storage unit. "It worked while I had them, Benny Boy," he whispered.

He leaned his head back against the wall and let the coolness of the metal melt away the hot flush that was suffocating his shoulders and his spine. His ribs ached and his lungs burned. His head felt muddled, like his brain was wrapped in a wet blanket, but it was beginning to clear, and reality was slowly settling back in.

He didn't know how long he had been there, alone in the storage unit with his hands bound behind his back. Minutes, maybe. Hours, probably. The world outside his rolltop door must be absolute chaos. People attending to Roman; people trying to get answers. The Red Caps being questioned. They were surely having discussions about what to do with him, or maybe they were waiting for Roman to receive enough medical treatment to be able to hiss his orders at them. He just hoped they weren't hurting the Red Caps, though he doubted they would. They were never really his, and Roman's crew knew it.

One way or the other, they'd be coming for him soon.

Patrick was no doctor, but he was pretty sure he'd done some serious damage to Roman's face. Permanent damage. The kind of damage that meant Patrick was never going to make it off this farm. The thought of enduring so much to get back to Fort Doom and almost making it tugged at something deep in his chest, something like a plug in a drain that, if it were pulled out, would send every ounce of his heart washing away into the dirt. The Red Caps had saved him, and he was grateful for that. But they'd also taken him away, and he tried not to feel anger, but all he'd worked for these last many months, all the pain and frustration, and the sudden soul-squeezing realization of what Roman had done, and how Patrick had championed his cause along the way…it was all so overwhelming, so unbelievably exhausting, and in the end he had nothing to show for it, and he couldn't even let Ben know that he'd been trying so hard to get back to him. "Sorry, Benny Boy," he said sadly to the dark world around him. "I got so close."

Then he remembered that Ben already thought he was dead, which made him feel a little better. At least he wasn't expected to return. Ben wouldn't be left waiting and wondering—and, ultimately, despairing. Patrick supposed that was some sort of mercy.

He sure would have liked to see him one more time, though.

Tears spilled down his cheeks. He couldn't do a thing to stop them. His wrists were caked with blood, and every slight movement threatened to reopen the wounds. So he sat there and cried, hating the feeling of tears that had nowhere go but down.

"Hang tight, Annie," he whispered.

The dark room glowed with her memory. The bend of her smile; the air in her laugh…the curve of her hip and the strange bluntness of her toes. Her love of The Stones, The Ramones, and The Smiths. The way she would dance in her socks and a sweater, like Carlton from *Fresh Prince of Bel-Air*. The way her mouth turned into a comma when she was working out a solution to some secret yet unserious problem. The way the morning light streamed in through their bedroom window and set her dark hair on fire. The way she fussed with his tie at rare formal events and always made it look worse. The way the air crackled every time she was angry, which was the same way it crackled whenever she laughed, which was the same way it crackled when they tumbled over each other, trying to stay quiet, the sheets twisting, the pillows sliding, their skin slick with sweat that setting off sparks and made the hair on their necks standing on end. The way she tied her hair up in a bandana when she went out to run errands on Sundays. The way she went barefoot. The way she watched baseball. The way she wore sweatpants and called them her "softclothes."

He tried not to think about her much, as a rule. As a new rule, here in this yellow-stained world. He missed her so much, his particles ached. They threatened to disband, to break and disperse, to disappear back into the cosmic fabric from which they'd come. He felt like he had to hold himself together, physically strain to hold the cells of himself together when he thought of Annie. So he couldn't let himself dwell on her too much now.

But God, he missed her.

And Izzy.

His love for Izzy was on another plane of reality.

He loved Annie with his whole heart, his whole spirit, his whole being, entirely. When she was pregnant, he sometimes wondered quietly when he was alone what would happen to the love he felt for his wife when he had to share it with this forthcoming miracle, this half-Pat new human who would consume him completely, he knew; the love for her was already squeezing through his pores, even though she still had three months in the womb. He worried that what he felt for Annie would be swapped out and replaced—that his capacity to love was finite and already full, and to make room he'd have to drain one away to become filled the other. But then Izzy was born. His conception of love buckled under the pressure, and somehow his feelings for Annie intensified and *grew*. Together, they loved their new little human bean so fully and completely and perfectly and hungrily that their capacities for love doubled and doubled again, and their feelings folded into each other. What they felt for Izzy was beyond description; there wasn't any point in trying to name it or define it. The only point was to hold it and share it together. If their love for each other was a yellow star, then what they felt for Izzy was an absolute supernova, exploding and collapsing without end.

Wherever they were now, he'd be there soon, too.

Patrick was shaken from his own mind by a rattling at the rolltop door. It lifted up a few feet from the ground and a dark figure slipped into the storage unit, closing the door from the inside.

Here we go, Patrick breathed.

The overhead light clicked on. He turned his face and squinted away from the glare, giving his eyes a few seconds to adjust before he peered back at the figure standing with him in the room. He blinked.

"Carla?"

She stood there, her hands balled into fists at her side, chewing at her bottom lip with her eyes wide. "Patrick," she said, her voice sick with fear. "What did you do?"

Patrick looked up, into her eyes. "Roman made the dust. He engineered the apocalypse."

Carla broke the stare. She looked down at her feet. "It's why they left," she said quietly. "The other women. It's why they set the boat on fire and ran. They knew it. We all knew it. Roman was a monster...he was *the* monster." Then she corrected herself. "He *is* the monster."

Patrick's bones began to sink beneath their own weight, growing heavy and dense, pulling his shoulders toward the floor. "Why didn't you tell me?" he asked.

Carla shook her head. "He's a monster, but he also built this place. This safe place. We have food and protection. We have *electricity*."

316

"And that's worth it to you."

"Yes." She didn't hesitate. "I'm weak and I want that, even though he's responsible for the death of billions. *Billions*," she said again, bewildered now, as if she'd never heard the number before…as if it was the first time she'd actually allowed herself to consider the true scope of what Roman's weapon had done. "I didn't want to lose this."

Patrick was even more stunned now. "Wow."

"And I now, I don't want to lose *you*. Or the Red Caps. And, I don't know…I didn't want *you* to go. Patrick. I've lost so many people, and the world is so fucking terrifying now, and you make me feel normal. I thought you'd leave. And Ella, Lucia, and I…we'd be alone. With him."

"With the monster who gives you electricity? Sounds rough." Patrick breathed heavily, taking in the warm, stale air of the storage locker. His lungs felt old and covered in dust, like relics pulled down from an attic.

"He keeps us safe," Carla repeated. It sounded so hollow. Patrick wasn't sure even she believed herself.

"Well, he told *me* to get over the death of my daughter. So I broke a lantern across the side of his face, and the whole thing exploded. Then I blacked out."

Carla blinked. "Holy shit."

Patrick's head bobbed. "It didn't even feel cathartic."

Carla wiped her eyes and took long strides across the room, kneeling down next to Patrick. "He's going to throw you into the cellar," she said urgently. "I have to get you out of here." She reached behind his back and fumbled for his wrists. She cursed under her breath as her fingers closed around the zip tie. "Shit. I don't have a knife."

Heavy footsteps thudded against concrete outside the unit. The overhead door rattled as someone gripped it from the other side.

"Goddammit," Carla spat.

She gripped Patrick under the arms and hauled him to his feet just as the door flew open. Two guards strode into the room, stopping short when they saw Carla standing with Patrick. "What the hell are you doing in here?" asked a guard holding a baseball bat.

Out of the corner of his eye, Patrick could see that Carla had forced her face into a mask of calm. "Figured I could be the one to walk him to the cellar," she said. "The son of a bitch made me think he was one of us." She turned and spat on Patrick's cheek. Patrick looked down. He looked away.

"Who told you he was going to the cellar?" asked the other guard, tapping the flat side of a hunting blade against his thigh.

"Am I wrong?" Carla asked, her voice as smooth as a steel rod.

The guards exchanged frowns. "Well…no…"

"Great. Then get out of my way so I can take him."

She shoved Patrick past the guards and out into the lot. Patrick drank in the fresh, cool air, letting it fill his lungs. Carla led him roughly toward the gate as the two guards followed uncertainly a few paces behind. "I'm sorry," she breathed, leaning her mouth in close to his ear as she pushed him away.

"It's okay," Patrick said quietly, low enough that the guards wouldn't hear. "Do everything you have to do. Okay?"

Carla didn't respond.

They made their way out of the storage lot. Carla directed him around the fence, cutting through the edge of the cornfield. As they rounded the corner, the Victorian farmhouse came into view. Someone had stabbed half a dozen tiki torches into the dry earth; their flames cast shifting shadows up at the house, giving it the illusion of a brooding, breathing creature made of planks and shingles and glass. A crowd had gathered outside, Roman's people mostly, but the Red Caps were there too, huddled together near the edge. Brett had his arms folded and his mouth turned down. Jimmy was wringing his hands, shifting uncomfortably from one foot to the other. The rest of the Red Caps looked totally at ease—Richie was smiling with rare self-satisfaction and Ted rubbed his injured fish leg with one hand while looking reproachfully at Patrick. Even Gary had come out for the occasion, standing there in the firelight, one sleeve dangling empty, a wicked grimace slashed into his face.

The whole group vibrated in a nervous hum, but as soon as they saw Patrick approaching, they quieted down, a blanket of silence smothering their whispers. The crowd parted on some unspoken cue and Roman stepped through them. Half of his mouth was curled down in rage and pain; the other half face was draped in white cotton rags, plastered in place by blood and viscous ooze in stains the color of cherry blossoms and pus. Roman's shirt was wet with dark stains where his face had melted onto his shoulder. He swayed as he stumbled, his entire body held upright by nothing but opioids and rage. He cracked his lips as if to speak, but the skin had sealed. Patrick could hear it tearing apart as Roman managed to let loose a guttural, agonized moan. He clapped his hands like a furious gorilla and pointed toward the Victorian house.

Carla pressed down on Patrick's hands and squeezed them tight, holding his wrists against the small of his back. "Good luck," she whispered. Her voice caught on the words. She was pushed aside by the other two guards who grabbed Patrick by the arms and dragged him toward the house.

Patrick gave no resistance as he was pulled across the lot.

He was so tired.

The guards hauled him up to the corner of the house, to a pair of storm doors set down into the earth.

"The charge is treason!" One of Roman's people stepped up from the crowd, her face bending wickedly in the torchlight. "The punishment for treason is death in the cellar."

No one said a word in response. The night was still. The only sound was the fluttering flames, crackling and spitting on their wicks.

It was Gary who broke the silence. "Throw him in!" he roared.

Roman's soldiers hooted and hollered, but no one was sure what to do. Ella stood at the back of the crowd with her arms crossed and her counsel quiet. Lucia shrank back and went to go find Carla, to huddle together until everything was over.

Roman shouldered his way forward, every movement punctuated by pain. He carefully broke through the crowd and gripped Patrick by the face, digging his fingertips into Patrick's cheeks and pressing against his jaw with the palm of his hand. His eye blazed in the firelight. "I should rip your face off," he gurgled between cracked and blistered lips. "An eye for an eye."

Patrick didn't respond.

Roman motioned to the guards. They stepped up to the cellar doors, reached down and pulled them open, revealing a deep, black rectangle of darkness. The steps leading into the cellar had been cut away; all that was left was a six-foot dead drop onto the hardpacked earthen floor below.

Roman released Patrick's face as the guards took their prisoner by the arms. They spun him around so that he faced the gaping maw in the ground.

Patrick's heart beat hard in his chest. He could feel the blood pumping, making mad vibrations in his skull. His hands were zip-tied behind his back, and the darkness below was near total.

The house is a decoy, Roman had said earlier.

So when people go inside the house. What happens next?

They don't come out.

Patrick shrank back from the edge of the hole. He bumped into Roman, who was leering over his shoulder, smelling smoky and sour. "You took my fucking eye," Roman hissed.

Sweat dripped down the back of Patrick's neck. "Well," he said, swallowing hard, trying to keep his voice even. "You're going to have to get over that," he said, echoing Roman's lack of humanity.

Roman punched him in the kidney as hard as he could and shoved him into the darkness.

64.

Patrick slammed into the packed-earth floor. Fire coursed through his veins, and his face exploded with pain where his bones collided with the ground. He struggled to roll over, looking up through the rectangular opening above.

Roman sneered down at him, his face swathed in stains and shadow. "Close it," he snapped. The two guards lifted the doors of the storm cellar and threw them down into place. The world above slammed shut, and Patrick was left to the darkness.

He let out a long, exhausted sigh. "Goddammit," he whispered.

The cellar was darker than the night. The only light that filtered into the room came from the top of a stairwell to Patrick's left, barely more than pale whispers of torchlight from outside passing in through the windows on the main floor. As his eyes adjusted, he could make out the dark silhouette of a railing and banister leading up the stairs, and a rectangle of gray space that was the open doorway.

What the hell was he doing down here?

The house is a decoy.

They don't come out.

Patrick struggled up to a seat, straining against the zip ties.

What was so dangerous about an empty house?

He dragged his legs around, trying to get to his knees. His feet knocked up against what sounded like a small pile of kindling. Was that it—was the cellar a firepit? He sniffed the air and didn't detect any gasoline or lighter fluid, nothing that might have fed a flame.

Then he heard it, from somewhere upstairs…not the floor directly above him, but maybe the one above that. It was a staccato pounding on the floorboards, uneven and rough. Footsteps, dragging on floorboards.

A pair of fast, clumsy feet...and then a second *thud-thump-thud-thump-thud*, and a third, and another, picking up speed, hitting the main floor and rounding the house. Getting closer and closer. Right overhead. Thumping to the doorway. *Stamp-clomp stamp-clomp stamp-clomp* down the basement stairs, two silhouettes, then another, then another, tumbling down into the cellar, snarling, slavering, hissing, growling. Hungry. The dusters that appeared were thin, starved, ravenous. And they smelled a meal.

"No..."

They hit the wall, blind in the dark and blind with hunger. They snarled and shoved, pushing off the cold stone and throwing themselves across the cellar as they reached him. The first duster bit down, its teeth snapping shut against Patrick's shoe. The leather held, but the force of the jaws crushed against his toes, a pressure he could feel in his bones. Patrick yelled and kicked downward with his free foot. It was like slamming a heel down into a block of concrete. Pain shot up his leg, but the duster opened its mouth to snap and freed his foot.

Patrick scooted away, but the second duster was on him, scrambling over the first and scratching at Patrick's pant legs. The fingers that gripped him were solid like iron. Patrick struggled against them, but the creature pulled him closer as a third duster sprinted around him and sank its teeth into his shoulder.

Patrick screamed.

Fire tore through his chest; he felt the warmth of fresh blood cascading down his arm. He could hear the sound of the duster chewing on his flesh but was too stunned to be sick about it. His brain turned itself off, shutting down his senses and unplugging to protect him from the agony of being eaten alive.

The last duster leapt into the pile and came down hard on Patrick's side. Something beneath Patrick shattered. *My hip,* Patrick thought dully. *Maybe my spine. What if I never walk again?* He realized what a ridiculous thought it was in the moment.

The dusters stopped suddenly, sniffing the air. *"HUUAAAARRRKK!"* one of the monsters shrieked.

It lurched up from the floor and threw itself backward. Then the other dusters screamed too, leaping away from Patrick as if he were burning them somehow. *"HUUUAARK!"* they screeched, scrambling away, hitting the steps. *"HUUUAARK! HUUUAAAAAAARRRK!"* They disappeared upstairs, thudding through the house to put as much distance as they could between themselves and the cellar.

Patrick lay on the floor, catching his breath, bound, bloody, and bewildered.

Whatever had driven them away, he was grateful for it.

65.

Richie shifted nervously on the balls of his feet, turning his hat over again and again in his hands. "Why do I have to tell him?" he whined.

"You drew the short straw," Gary said.

"I didn't draw *any* straw," Richie protested. "That asshole with the nail-bat just told me to do it or he'd bash my 'annoying fucking head in'."

"I mean in life," Gary sneered. "You drew the short straw at birth."

"Oh."

They looked down at Roman, asleep on his cot, his mouth twisted down into a distasteful grimace. He slept on the side that was whole, which meant all anyone could see of his face were the pink and yellow rags.

"He needs sleep," Richie frowned.

"He needs to know what happened."

Richie sighed. "Yeah," he agreed. He wiped his lips. "Shit."

He stepped up to the cot and touched Roman lightly on the shoulder. "Um…Roman?" He pushed down on his arm. "Roman," he urged again. Richie turned back toward Gary and shrugged. Gary waved his hands, gesturing *Let's get this over with*. Richie frowned. He turned back to Roman, grimacing as he reached past the bloody rag and shook Roman gently on the shoulder. "Oh man…I can feel heat coming off of his face! That's bad, right?"

"If the next words out of your mouth aren't absolutely vital, I will cut your head off," Roman mumbled without opening his eye.

Richie frowned. "Oh. Sorry. Um. Well. We may have a problem. Umm…he's gone."

Now Roman shifted and struggled to sit up, grunting through the pain. "He's gone."

"Yeah. Patrick is...gone." Richie said. "Maybe."

Roman took a deep breath. "Richie. The point."

Richie took a deep breath. "I wasn't there, but as I understand, your guards were on patrol just now, and they saw a window was open. In the house. I guess that's unusual."

"Dusters don't typically work locks," Gary grunted from the corner of the room.

"Right. That makes sense. So they did some recon or whatever...and the dusters are gone. And Patrick is gone."

Roman's jaw tightened. The dirty cloth bulged outward.

"They think he escaped through the window." Richie fidgeted with his hat. "Then the dusters got out."

Gary stepped in and Richie shrank back with visible relief. "Your guys swept the house and found the whole thing empty," Gary explained. "They found the zip tie in the basement, along with some pieces of glass. And this," he added, pulling a small rubber stopper from his pocket.

Roman took the stopper and held it close to his eye. "He had the serum..."

"Looks like it. Pulled the cork, scared the zombies, broke the glass, cut the zip tie."

Roman glowered. "Now he's gone."

"Yeah. But at least we know where he's going."

Roman looked at Richie. It was challenging to speak with so much opiate coursing through his system. Rage was doing its best to clear his head. "Get your friends. Take my weapons. Earn your keep."

Richie nodded and scooted out of the room. Roman turned back to Gary. "How? I counted."

"How'd he get a vial of repellant?" Gary asked. Roman nodded. Gary scoffed. "Yeah. I've got a good idea about that."

•

Carla lay awake, staring at the shadows sliding around beneath her unit door. Her lights were out; the torchlight from the camp's perimeter bathed the pitch-black air in a soft yellow-orange glow. She was lying on top of her sheets still fully dressed. She'd heard the commotion about thirty minutes prior: the guards were raising hell over at the house.

Patrick had escaped.

She sat alone in the darkness, waiting and hoping—waiting for Patrick to make his return, hoping against hope that he'd come; that he'd knock on her door, slip into her room, help her pack a rucksack, and take her with him. She'd go to Mobile, Alabama with him and the next place after that.

Wherever he went, she would go to.

It didn't really make sense that he'd come back; it was way too dangerous now, too big a risk. If he had any sense, he was halfway to the Alabama border. He shouldn't risk his freedom for her. But then again, they could be stronger together. They could fight against the darkness of the world. They could make light for themselves.

Couldn't they?

She was jolted from her thoughts by a light rap on the door.

"Patrick," she gasped as she leapt up from her bed, her heart pounding. She hurried across room, slipped back the lock, and quietly rolled up the door.

Her heart turned to ice.

It was Roman. "We need to talk."

Black-red splotches soaked the rags on his face. Silvery yellow pus dripped from the burnt corner of his mouth every time he moved his lips. Where his right eye should have been, now there was only darkness.

"Oh my God," she murmured.

"No. But just as hard to kill. Can I come in?" He shoved past her without waiting for a response.

"I'm—so glad you're alive," she said, her voice catching. She peered out into the storage lot. There was no sign of Patrick. *Of course not*, she thought.

"Let me get to the point," Roman said. He pulled a knife from behind his back and dug the point into her throat. "Tell me why you did it."

Carla froze. The sharp tip of the blade had already punctured her skin. She could feel a hot streak of blood rolling down her neck. She raised her hands slowly. "Roman, what are you doing?"

"I'm making you tell me why you gave him a bottle of zombie repellant that you didn't tell me you had." He reached up with his free hand and cupped the back of her neck. He pulled her forward a hair's breadth, forcing her neck deeper against the knife.

Carla gasped. "Roman! I—he—" Her eyes welled up with tears. "Please don't. I don't know…"

He leaned in and pressed his burnt, bloody flesh against her cheek. His skin cracked and flaked against her cheekbone; her skin grew warm where his ooze squelched against her pores. "Did you know *this* would happen?"

Carla swallowed down the bile that rose in her throat. "N—no," she gagged. "I just—didn't want him to die."

Roman pulled himself away. Pieces of his skin tore from his face and remained on her cheek, plastered with a smear of blood and white slime. He released the back of her neck and took a step back, pulling the knifepoint out of her skin. "Well," he said. "What am I going to do with you?"

Carla clapped a hand to her neck and heaved a string of sobs. She shrank back, shaking her head, wiping at the blood. "Nothing. I'll go. Okay? Now. Tonight. You won't see me again. I—" She was silenced by the view of a figure emerging from the shadows outside the door. He held one arm by his side. The other had been sawed away.

"I have some news," Gary said, speaking to Roman, though he was looking at Carla. There was something in his eyes…something dark and dangerous. Not anger. Hunger, maybe. Pleasure.

Vengeance.

"What?" Roman snapped.

"The lab's been cleared out. Looks like he slipped in after he escaped the house. The rest of the vials are gone."

Roman bared his teeth. "All of them?"

"All of them," Gary grunted. "And something else. He opened all the doors. Let your human guinea pigs run free."

Roman turned back to Carla. She looked up at him through her wet eyes, and what she saw there, hidden beneath a mask of bitterness and rage, was madness. True and absolute madness.

"Roman—" she started.

He swiped the knife across her throat. Her skin opened up like a seam, and thick flows of dark red blood spilled down her chest. Carla pressed her hands to her neck, pushing against the red flood. It was surprisingly warm against her cold, clammy skin. Her knees gave out and she slumped against the wall. The horror in her eyes gave way to dullness, and her body buckled onto the floor, her head cracking on the cement and meaning absolutely nothing.

"Send men to Mobile," Roman said, stepping over the body and out into the lot. "Three of yours, three of mine. I want them gone before sunrise."

"You got it. What about her?" Gary asked nodding down at Carla's body.

"Close the door," Roman growled. "Lock it. Let her fucking rot."

66.

It took Patrick four days to reach Mobile.

He probably could have walked it in half the time, if he'd had a goddamn map. But all he had was the sun—the sun, and a shoulder bag stuffed with the only things he could find in his frenzied tear through Roman's laboratory: a scalpel, a notebook, three Bic pens, and a few bags of stale chips from the year 2007.

And of course, the Zom-Be-Gone. That was the whole point.

But without a map, he had been relying on the sun for navigation, which worked reasonably well…except he wasn't quite sure how to adjust his Yankee understanding of the sun's arc to the Deep South angle. He made do the best he could, with a general inclination toward the "south" part of southeast, which was how, after two full days of walking, he'd ended up in Biloxi.

He thought it might have been Mobile.

"So *there's the ocean*!" he groused, gesturing at the water. "What did they do with Fort Doom?!" Thanks to the rusty navigation signs that were posted around the city, it took him almost an hour to realize he was still in Mississippi. "Well, this sucks," he decided.

The sun was descending, so Patrick turned his back to it and huffed off down Highway 90, climbing over cars, resting under overpasses, and thanking God for bridges that had managed to stay intact. His food was spare, and his only weapon was a scalpel. He had no idea where he was going, but he knew Roman's men would be following him. So he pushed on, despite his fatigue and his hunger; if he could just make it to the walls of Fort Doom, his friends would see him. His family would save him. Everything about the world would be right.

As the sun finally set on the fourth day, Patrick finally stumbled into sight of something familiar. His lips were dry and cracked; his legs wobbled with exhaustion while his head drooped on his shoulder. He could have nodded off at any second. But there at long last, against the darkening mist of the evening sky, still so far away, stood the towering ramparts of Fort Doom.

A sound left Patrick's chest—some buoyant, joyful, grateful sound that he didn't recognize and could hardly comprehend. It left his lungs like music through an organ pipe, melodic and sweet, sorrowful and heavy.

"Ben," he said softly. "I'm not dead."

The sight of Fort Doom's silhouette filled him like oxygen. His nerves fired, his blood coursed and his feet tingled as he picked up the pace. Then darkness fell, and the towers of Fort Doom were swallowed up by the mist. But he knew they were there—even if he couldn't see them, they were *there*. All he needed to do was cut a straight line through the darkness, which he could do, no problem. It was a pleasure to follow a guide star after months and months and four full days of wandering lost.

He pressed on, and soon the walls came into view through the darkness, through the dust. He could see the outlines of the blocks in the wall and had to stop, just for a second, for a moment, to let the overwhelming gratitude drench his body like a tidal wave. It pushed him back, pinned him down and battered him with unrelenting relief. He stopped and closed his eyes. He took a deep breath and smiled at the familiar smell of saltwater and firewood.

Then he opened his eyes just in time to see a tree branch swinging toward his face.

The branch hit Patrick with incredible force that knocked him off his feet and sent him flying onto his back. The wood was dry and brittle; it cracked in half after sending a shockwave of sound resounding like a gunshot through Mobile.

Patrick hit the ground like a sack of dirt. Blood flowed from his nose and his mouth. His left cheek began to swell immediately. He peered up through bleary eyes as three familiar forms stepped into view.

Brett. Ted. Richie.

Brett frowned. "You fucked up, man." He tossed the remainder of the tree branch into a ditch. Then he rolled Patrick over and pulled the backpack from his shoulders, opened it, and looked inside. "There they are—the missing vials." He tossed the bag to Ted.

"I think we're actually going to kill you now," Richie told Patrick, looking at the others. They nodded. Then he looked back at their former leader and smiled. "I didn't even know that I wanted that, but I'm kind of excited!"

Brett spun a finger in the air. "Do the thing, before he screams," he said.

"Oh, right." Ted pulled a handkerchief from his pocket and wrapped it around Patrick's head, stuffing it into his mouth and tying it off at the back of his neck. Patrick tried to struggle, but he was so tired. He beat his fists against Ted's arms, but even to Patrick, they felt like marshmallows bouncing off of wood.

"His wrists, too," Brett reminded them.

Richie produced a bungee cord from his back pocket, which he wound around Patrick's wrists.

Patrick strained against the bonds, screaming into the gag, crying tears of frustration. *Not like this,* he thought. *Not these three. Not so close.*

Not like this.

"Let's get him upstairs," Brett said. He reached down and hauled Patrick up into the air, threw Patrick's matchstick body over his shoulder.

They wound through the streets of Mobile until they came to a fire escape ladder that had been pulled down and prepped. Brett hauled himself up onto the first rung, carrying Patrick's weight and moving up the ladder easily as he ascended the side of the building. He climbing all six stories until they reached the roof. It had been hit by a Monkey bomb from above; there was a gaping hole near the center, and the edges were a tangled mess of rebar and jagged concrete.

Ted and Richie pulled themselves up over the ladder behind Brett, huffing and puffing and sweating—and mad. "Fuck...this plan," Richie gasped, collapsing on the roof in a heap.

"Shut up," Brett said as he dropped Patrick off his shoulder. Patrick fell to the roof like a cord of wood. "How's it looking?"

Ted reached into his bag and pulled out a pair of dusty binoculars he'd pulled from Roman's supply room. He held them to his eyes and focused in the direction of Fort Doom. "Looking good," he confirmed. "They're soaking it now."

Patrick squirmed to his knees, trying to peer through the darkness to see what was happening at the fort. He spat a string of frustrated curses, but they were muffled by the gag.

"That? Oh. It's gasoline," Brett explained. "Roman's guys are burning down the fort."

Patrick screamed and thrashed against the bungee cord. He fought his way to his feet and drove his shoulder into Richie's stomach. Richie wheezed and fell over as Patrick lunged at Ted next, but Brett stepped up behind him and cuffed him on the back of the head. It wasn't hard enough to knock him out, but hard enough to make the world spin.

"Calm down, or I'll throw you off the roof," he said.

Patrick fell back to his knees, helpless as tears ran down his face. His shoulders shook with his sobs.

Ted frowned. "It's all pretty messed up," he said uncomfortably. "Roman has this whole 'you burned my face, I'll burn all your friends alive' revenge thing in mind."

"I don't know what you thought was gonna happen," Brett said.

Patrick didn't know either. *I didn't think. I just broke.*

And now his friends and family were all going to die.

"Please," Patrick struggled to say through the gag. "Please don't let this happen."

"We can't understand you, dipshit," Richie said, climbing angrily to his feet. "Just shut up."

"Richie!" Brett said sharply.

Richie shrank back. "What?"

"Why don't you go down and keep an eye on the street."

"No way!" Richie whined. "I wanna be here for—"

"Richie. Get your ass down there or I'll—"

"Yeah, yeah, yeah," Richie said grumpily, "you'll throw me down there. I got it." He frowned at Patrick. He hocked up a glob of mucous and spat it onto Patrick's shoulder.

"Richie!"

"I'm going!" Richie slunk away and threw his leg over the ladder. He flipped Patrick off, as he climbed down.

"Has he always been like this?" Ted asked. "I don't remember him always being like this,"

"He's always been a whiny bitch," Brett said. "He's just louder about it lately." He walked over and lifted the wheezing Patrick to his knees. Patrick moaned into the handkerchief as Brett pointed his face in the direction of the fort. "You have to watch."

Patrick couldn't look away.

Orange flames roared life at the base of the wall. The light of the fire sliced through the darkness, through the fog, blazing a hole in the world so Patrick could see. The wooden gates of the fort were old—practically ancient for a country so young—and they went up like sticks of dry tinder.

It took only seconds for the fire to spread inside; one moment, it was a bonfire...then Patrick blinked, and it had become a wildfire. The grass behind the walls of Fort Doom was brittle and dry as straw, serving as kindling that caught fire with unthinkable speed.

Patrick watched as the entire fort became a lake of flames. Churning waves of fire billowed up the towers. The cabins looked as if they were built of flames, walls and roofs melding together into one massive inferno. Black smoke roiled upward, darkening the night even further. Something exploded inside and belched a fireball into the sky.

From somewhere amidst all the light and heat and smoke, there came screams…the screams of his friends, of Ben among them.

They screamed as the fire burned them alive.

Patrick threw up. The hot bile soaked the handkerchief and he gagged and threw up again, hacking and coughing, fighting for air. Brett reached down and cut the fabric from his head. It dropped away, stinking and wet, and Patrick puked onto the rough surface of the broken roof. His whole body convulsed, shaking and revolting. Deconstructing. "Not a sound," Brett warned him, flashing his knife. He needn't have bothered. Patrick's internal organs seemed to crushed in on themselves, squeezed with an anguish he had only known once before: the day when the Monkey bombs fell…the day he'd heard Annie's screams turn to dead static through the phone, when he'd felt Izzy's fear in his chest and his guts, the day he'd wanted to cut through his own skin and rip his insides out because that pain would have been less agonizing. He'd wanted to tear out his very heart and end it all, right then and there.

The world was spinning, but he tried to stand. The flames made him blind. The screams made him deaf. He collapsed to the roof, his whole being wracked with exhaustion, with guilt and regret. Eventually, the screams stopped.

That was so much worse.

All he was left with was the distant roar of fire.

There was only one thing left to do. Brett knelt down next to Patrick and held his knife close to his hip. "You don't have to be here for this," he warned Ted.

Ted chewed his lip and pulled at his hands. "Yeah, maybe I should go find Richie," he whispered, his voice heavy and sick. "He'll need help." He picked up the bag with the Zom-Be-Gone, turned and strode away from Patrick and Brett and the knife until he felt the hard iron of the ladder against his legs. He climbed over the edge and took two steps down, stopping before he went any further. "I actually always liked you," he said. He opened his mouth as if to say more, but nothing came. Then he disappeared down the ladder and out of sight.

And then, it was just Patrick and Brett and the knife and the darkness, all together on the roof. "Roman told us to kill you," Brett said. "He figures we'll do what he wants since it's our ticket to safety in his weird-ass cult.

And I figure he's right. We will do pretty much anything to stay ahead; you knew that about us from the get-go. You knew Bloom. You know what we are. You know what we do."

"You're gutless," Patrick murmured through the snot in his nose and the phlegm in this throat. "You're worms playing at being men."

"Well," Brett said. He spat out over the roof. "We can't all be the apocalypticon." He raised the knife and plunged it into Patrick's shoulder. Patrick screamed, so Brett pushed his free hand over Patrick's mouth and smothered the sound. Patrick writhed in agony as the three-inch blade pushed deep down, through muscle to bone.

"Sorry about this," Brett said, wrestling to keep Patrick still. "They'll want to see blood on the knife." He pulled the blade out of Patrick's shoulder. Patrick gasped from the rush of cool air on the wound, and the muscle-deep agony the knife left behind.

"Please just do it," Patrick whispered, his eyes red and raw with tears.

But Brett stood up. He stuck the bloody knife into the sheath at his hip. "You're better than most," he said, wiping his hands on his pants. "You saved our lives. And you helped people. I'm not gonna kill you. But I need them to think I did."

Patrick closed his eyes.

He was so tired.

"I'm telling everyone you're dead," Brett told him. "So. You're dead. Got it?"

Patrick exhaled a mournful, frustrated sigh.

It was good enough for Brett.

"His guys might come up here looking for a body, so..." He planted his boot on Patrick's shoulder. "Don't tell anyone, but I always liked you, too." Then he kicked Patrick through the hole in the roof.

The apocalypticon hit the floor without a sound.

67.

He had no idea how long he'd been unconscious. Hours, at least, though it could have been days. Or weeks.

His whole body hurt. He'd cracked some ribs when he'd landed. His hands were still bound by the bungee cord. Cloudy light washed in through the dirty windows, casting some version of daylight outside. Patrick worked gingerly to roll himself onto his back. His shoulder was still bleeding and he could barely move his left arm. His face was swollen and sore in the spots where he'd been hit by the tree branch. When tried to sit up, his sides and his chest all screamed in pain. He was out of breath by the time he was sat upright.

There was a length of sharp metal on the floor, a ceiling support that had crashed through years ago when the bomb hit. Patrick scooted over to it and used it to saw through his restraints, something he'd done for the second time in three days. It was no easy feat now that he could only move one arm without pain. Eventually, the bungee cord snapped and fell away from his wrists. He climbed to his feet, finding that parts of his body still worked as he picked through the rubble until he found a door.

It was locked. Of course it was. He thought about just lying back down and letting the world swallow him. But if he stayed in there, he'd die, from hunger or maybe from sepsis, and while he didn't feel especially motivated to keep himself alive, he knew he didn't want to die like that, so he found a broomstick and smashed out a window and climbed out of the warehouse, only cutting himself a little on the sharp remnants of glass.

The air was still thick with woodsmoke. Patrick vomited behind a dumpster.

The smoldering ruins of Fort Doom were just a few blocks away, but Patrick wasn't ready. First, he had to attend to his shoulder. He had no idea how clean Brett's knife had been; if he didn't take care of the wound, there was a good chance he'd end up like Gary—except this time, he'd be his own medical staff of one.

It took Patrick a long time to start a fire. He struggled with sparking a chuck of concrete against a steel rod until it became undeniably clear that it wasn't going to be enough. He poked through the warehouse and found a few unlabeled spray bottles that smelled like chemicals. He poured some of each onto a collection of old paper and tried to catch it on fire. Either the liquids weren't flammable or his sparks weren't hot enough, so he gave up. He went back into the warehouse and searched the whole building, eventually finding a blow torch buried under a pile of fallen shingles. The tank was about twenty percent full. After a quick cleaning and a few sparks, the flame caught and a jet of blue fire erupted from the torch.

"Helpful," he decided.

Then he found a pair of pliers on a shop table and heated the tips until they glowed. He grasped the pliers by their rubber grips and pressed the hot metal into the open wound on his shoulder.

He screamed in agony, but his shoulder stopped bleeding.

He took some time to catch his breath before continuing his exploration of the warehouse. He found an oily pair of overalls and tore them in half, wrapping the fabric tightly around his chest in hopes of it stabilizing his ribs. Then he grabbed the blow torch and climbed back out into the alley. The air still smelled like a campfire.

He took a deep breath and steadied his hands.

Then he walked out of the alley and started the short, slow walk to Fort Doom.

The world was lit by the green-diffuse sunlight, but even against that glare, the embers of the fort glowed angry and orange. The stone foundations poked through the earth like old teeth, but everything metal had collapsed, and everything made of wood had been turned to cinders. Patrick's whole body trembled as he stepped through what remained of the wall and crunched into the charred, smoking ruins. That was where the storage shed had been—over there, the garden where he'd once rigged up rainwater irrigation. Under the rubble in the middle, that was where he'd sat around the sandy firepit with James and Sarah and Other Annie and Ben, where they'd roasted tiny hot dogs they'd fished out of old cans, where they'd counted the stars and watched the comets and usually fell asleep in the open night air. And over there, the cabins where they all used to sleep. Now they were nothing but stone teeth and ash.

Patrick crossed the plain of embers, his sneaker soles warming under his feet. He picked up a smoking branch and dug through the piles of ashes. He would have thought he'd be sick when he found their remains, but when he turned up the first skull, he felt almost nothing. It didn't look anything like James at all.

The next bunk was Annie's. He found her, too, and Dylan, and everyone…except Sarah. He wondered where she'd gone, what had happened to her in the last year, but it didn't really matter. She was gone, however it happened; her bunk was empty, just ash and wood—no bones beneath the rubble. He wondered if she was still somewhere alive.

He saved Ben's bunk for last. Maybe he'd gone off, like Sarah. Maybe they'd gone together, scouting for food. Maybe. Maybe. As long as he didn't look, there was a chance still for Ben—a chance that one of the screams he'd heard in the night hadn't belonged to his best, his *only*, friend. But of course, that would have been a different ending to a much different story. And there in the last cabin he found Ben, reduced to an ash-covered skull, blackened and grinning about some quiet joke.

Patrick felt nothing now. He had no more tears to cry. He had no more sorrow to offer. This was the world now, ashen and ruined, broken so far past repair.

It didn't make sense to bury them or put up a marker—to say a few words or pay them respect with a moment of silence. Whatever he constructed would be destroyed again, dug up and defiled and made somehow worse by whoever happened along next. And nothing he could create would be enough to honor them anyway. So he simply shoved his hands into his pockets, turned his back on the open graveyard that Fort Doom was now, and left it behind without looking back.

He drifted away from the ashes like a wraith of bone and skin.

He tried to hear Ben's voice in his head. But he couldn't seem to conjure it up.

On his way out of Mobile, he stopped at a park and dug his hand into an old metal trash barrel by the swing set. He pulled up the shopping bag he'd stashed there on his way in. He looked inside and made sure they were still there: two old Pepsi bottles, the twenty-ounce size, now filled with a bright purple liquid.

He knew they'd come, he just thought he'd have more time. He may not have known it would be Brett and Richie and Ted, but he knew someone would be after him. He'd poured the Zom-Be-Gone into those two empty bottles and mixed up a batch of something passably purple by siphoning out some windshield wiper fluid from a car in the lot with two drops of his blood added in. Then he made the switch in the vials and stashed the real serum out here, just in case. It was the only thing that had gone right.

He swung the shopping bag at his side as he walked, out of the city and up into the hills. There was no destination this time, no more ideas or plans. No Ben to return to or to seek out, even. There was only him and the ruined world and the certainty of death, however and wherever and whenever it decided to come. He was a little surprised to learn when he bothered to think that he didn't really want to die—not exactly, anyway. He just didn't care to live, which was something altogether different. Sadder. Emptier. Numb. He was utterly, finally, and completely alone, without even the comfort of death to keep him cold.

When he searched himself—when he searched his heart—there was a simple and meaningless nothing.

The sun lowered behind the trees, and Patrick disappeared into the mountains like mist.

Epilogue – Three Years Later

"Hey. Mister."

A young girl looked down at the stranger snoring softly on a pile of pine needles. She nudged his ribs with his toes. "Wake up."

Patrick snorted himself awake and looked around, confused and drooling. "Wha—what? Go away." He rolled over and tried to fall back asleep, but the girl was pretty insistent. She kicked Patrick in the head. "Ow!"

"Mama says you're a witch, so you have to go."

"That's no way to treat witches," Patrick informed her. "I have half a mind to turn you into a pig."

The girl shrugged. "You can't, though," she said.

"You don't know that."

"You're not a witch. You just smell bad."

"That is a hurtful thing to say to someone who might be a witch." He sniffed under his arm. It smelled like onions and dead raccoons. "I smell fine," he lied. He picked up some of the pine needles and rubbed them in his beard.

"Mama says she heard about your drink that makes the zombies go away. She wants to buy some."

"It's not a drink."

"But she also said, 'Then make that witch go away. We don't want him scarin' the possums off our farm.'"

"I have so many thoughts about that," Patrick muttered irritably. "First of all, why do you even have an opossum farm—what is even the point? And it's only *three* opossums…that's not a farm. Your mother is insane. She's also a hypocrite. I have half a mind to not give her any magic potion at all."

"It's not magic," the girl pointed out. "It's science."

"Well, don't you just know everything," Patrick said sourly. "Lucky for you, I think even insane hypocrites should have a chance to run opossum farms without being eaten by drug addicts. So yes, she can have some of my *very dwindling supply* of Zom-Be-Gone. Do you have any idea how far I have to go to refill it?"

The girl held out a bundle wrapped in a dirty towel. "Here."

Patrick snatched the girl's bundle and opened it up. "What is this—foil...and a bent nail? This is garbage, kid—this is literal *garbage*."

"She thinks you might be able to trade it for a drink at Al's."

"Oh." Patrick brightened considerably. "I do like a drink. Is Al's a good place?"

The girl shrugged. "Three of my uncles went blind drinking the moonshine there."

"Why is your mother trying to kill me?" The girl began to answer, but Patrick cut her off, "I know, I know—because I'm a witch."

"You could get a drink from Kat instead. She's nice. She's got a whole de-still up there. I never known no one to get blind up there. It's a log cabin with a green-light train lantern out front. That's her place. Little further up the hill."

"'Up the hill,' like it's not a Blue Ridge goddamn Mountain," he grumbled. He looked at the bundle again, picking through the trash. There was no way he could pass any of that stuff off as having any sort of value. But he wasn't going to leave this girl to the dusters just because her mother was a real piece of work. He dumped the trash into his backpack and pulled out an old plastic bottle. He unscrewed the cap, dabbed the girl's towel around the inside of the rim. "Here. Give her this."

The girl frowned at the towel. "That's not very much," she pointed out.

"Trust me; it's plenty. It'll keep the zombies away for at least a year, guaranteed."

"Okay," she said dubiously as she rolled up the towel carefully and tucked it under her arm. "I guess she gets what she pays for."

"She's getting a lot more than that," Patrick sighed. "And *don't* suck it out of the towel and drink it!"

He zipped his backpack close, stood up, and brushed the pine needles off his pants. Then, thinking again, he picked up a handful of the needles and stuffed them into his pockets. "*Not* because I smell," he snapped.

It took him a few seconds to remember where he'd hidden his machete. He shook one bough of the pine tree; the machete fell out of the branches and hit the ground. He picked it up and pulled the backpack onto his shoulders. "Thanks for letting me sleep here, even though it's under a tree...outside...and I got very cold, because no one brought me a blanket."

"Welcome," she said. She watched as Patrick turned and hiked up the mountain, cursing and muttering as he slipped on the fir needles. "Hey," she called after him.

Patrick stopped and looked back. "Yeah?"

"You're the apocalypticon. Right?"

Patrick sighed. "No, kid. There is no apocalypticon."

The girl lifted her chin. "They tell stories about you. You done a lot of good for people. Saved 'em from bad guys. Helped 'em eat. I heard you left half a pig on the doorstep of some folks down the mountain so they could eat. My uncle Billy says you saved his high school girlfriend one time, when she got caught in barbed wire."

Patrick cast his eyes down. "Yeah, well," he said as he turned and started to walk again.

"You'd have given us this zombie juice even if we didn't give you nothin', wouldn't you?"

"Kid, I *did* give you that zombie juice after you gave me nothing."

"Okay," she shrugged. "Even if your not the apocalypticon, you're still a good person."

Patrick shook his head slowly. "Take care of yourself, kid. And your mom, too—take care of her, all right?"

Then turned back to the trees and pushed up into the mountain, swinging his machete to clear away the low-reaching branches. He didn't stop walking until the night closed in, the air turned chill, and he saw the twinkling green lamplight of the old log cabin.

He really hoped Kat, whoever she was, would let him have that drink.

ACKNOWLEDGEMENTS

It wouldn't be a Clayton Smith acknowledgement section without a huge thank you to Steven Luna. Luna, not only did you work all your incredible magic--and I do mean magic--on this manuscript, but you also take my stories, and my characters, to heart in a way that no one else possibly could. The love that you have for my worlds is something I don't know how to adequately express my gratitude for. And yeah, I can end that sentence with a preposition, because Merriam-Webster says so. I love you, brother, and I'm so grateful for your help. Thank you.

Thanks go also (syntax?) to my dear friend Patrick, who unwittingly served as a model for my main character, all those many years ago, and has only complained about it a little.

Patrick also gave me specific and mathematical advice for how to make someone crash through a window by swinging down from the roof of a building, and for that, if nothing else, I am in his debt.

Speaking of debts, Lisa Wilson figured out a pretty decent way to calculate the PSI of eating human flesh, and I needed that! Thank you, Lisa. And sorry about your browser history.

But the real hero of this story is my wife, Erin. We've been through a *whole* lot of life since I started this manuscript six years ago, and despite a pandemic, a couple major moves, launching--and then running, and then selling--a business, and the birth of two children, she has never stopped encouraging me to find time to write. Her selflessness and support have been invaluable. Thank you, panda. I love you.

ABOUT THE AUTHOR

photo by Emily Rose Studios

Clayton Smith is an award-winning writer who once erroneously referred to himself as "a national treasure." He is the author of several novels, short story collections, and plays, and his short fiction has been featured in national literary journals, including Canyon Voices and Write City Magazine.

He is also rather tall.

Find him online at www.StateOfClayton.com and on social media as @Claytonsaurus.